THE JERICHO ROSE

THE JERICHO ROSE

Olive Etchells

This first hardcover edition published in Great Britain 1996 by
SEVERN HOUSE PUBLISHERS LTD of
9–15 High Street, Sutton, Surrey SM1 1DF,
by arrangement with Warner Books
a Division of Little Brown and Co. (UK) Ltd.

British Library Cataloguing in Publication Data

Etchells, Olive
  Jericho Rose. – New ed
  I. Title
  823.914 [F]

  ISBN 0-7278-4874-7

Typeset by Palimpsest Book Production Limited,
Polmont, Stirlingshire, Scotland.
Printed and bound in Great Britain by
Hartnolls Ltd, Bodmin, Cornwall.

For my parents, remembered with love–
Elsie and Cecil Murray
of Ashton-under-Lyne, Lancashire.

They are a people kind and open-hearted . . . orderly and loyal. They are one of the most independent peoples on earth; they will bear no dictation, and will listen to no advice unless fully assured that it comes from a sincere heart. There is nothing finer on earth than a Lancashire man or a Lancashire woman.

Lord Shaftesbury
1862

Contents

The First Wagons

MATTHEW RAIKE WAS STEAMING. Wet clothes over a hot body gave off a visible haze that merged with the dampness around him. His night's sleep under the steps of a dockside warehouse had been broken by heavy rain, and he'd been soaked before he was fully awake.

He wasn't aware that he was steaming, and if he'd known he wouldn't have cared. He'd been wet before, and no doubt would be again; the same could be said for the men who worked beside him. It rained: if you were lucky you stayed dry but more often you got wet. If you had access to a fire or there was hot sunshine you could dry your clothes, and if not they dried on your back.

There was sun now, somewhere in that milky sky, but it hadn't yet risen above the buildings that shadowed the quay. It was a sombre scene, dull and muted like an old painting on the wall of a smoky parlour; the canal dark, almost black, with mist lying over the water in drifting grey bands. Narrow brown boats awaited their cargoes of raw cotton; the long-distance vessels that had brought it were already heading back to Liverpool, disappearing into the haze with a farewell blast on their whistles and a swirl of black water in their wake. The clothes of the dockers were sombre, too; dark moleskin trousers with grey flannel shirts and black waistcoats, and on their heads battered hats or small round caps that were faded with wear and weather. In all that busy scene the only splashes of colour were the fancy green waistcoat of the wharf manager, a rusty-pink shirt here and there,

and the bright red kerchief round Matthew Raike's
sweat-damp neck.

Conscious of the hostility around him he worked hard,
his long lean body adapting easily to the shared task of
moving the immense bales of cotton wool. The dockers
hadn't taken kindly to a new man in their midst, but the
wharfinger had hired him at once when he requested
a free passage on the first boat to Saltley rather than
payment in cash. The ganger bellowed, the men heaved
on the pulleys, and the boat creaked acceptance of a
capacity load. Matthew smiled with a touch of triumph
at anyone who forgot to avoid his eye. Had they really
believed they could frighten him off with sour looks and
hard words? He'd been reared on hard words, and sour
looks had come his way more often than smiles.

In any case he saw no need for hostility. He'd heard
enough to know there would be work enough for everyone now that the American Civil War was slowing down
and shipments were coming through again. And if the
mill-owners wanted their cotton at once, why shouldn't
he help to speed it on its way? He shrugged and turned
to the next bale.

Above him, his seamed face unsmiling, the boatman
stood watching. In his opinion these Manchester men
were rabble – wharf-rats was the term he used in his
mind – casual hands all of them, unskilled men hired
by the hour. He'd been given one of them as a helping
hand for the trip back to Saltley – that young 'un in the
red neckband who looked so pleased with himself.

The last bale on board, Matthew watched the grim-
faced old man check the ropes, hoping they were to set
off at once rather than wait for the other boats to be
loaded. He was lucky. The wharfinger signalled them to
slip the mooring. 'Right! Get under way! They're waiting
for this load up yonder.' He turned to Matthew. 'Now
lad, you stay with these bales right to the end – to the
mill. You'll help hoist them in, and when the last one's
on the mill floor you're done, and not before. Is that

clear? You're a fair worker, that I will say, and if ever you come here again I'll find you a few hours' work if I've got it.'

Matthew touched his hat. 'Thank 'ee kindly. I'm obliged.'

The man patted the pocket of his fancy waistcoat and drew out a timepiece. 'It's half-past-six!' he announced accusingly, and flicked a dismissive wrist at the boatman. 'Get off with you, and no shaffling!' He turned away, but swung back and laid a heavy hand on Matthew's arm. Shrewd little eyes glinted from under heavy brows, and what could have been concern softened the hard gaze for an instant. 'Have your wits about you while you're in Saltley, young fella,' he said abruptly, and then strutted away across the cobblestones.

There was no time to reply, or even to think about the mildly worded warning. The horses were waiting, held by a young lad, and the boatman was slinging their towing-chains to the quay. A moment later he took up two barge-poles and handed one to Matthew. 'Do what I tell thee, *when* I tell thee, and we'll be on the Saltley Cut in no time.'

Pushed off by the poles and then pulled by the horses, the narrow craft moved sluggishly towards the link canal. Matthew stood on the bales with his bundle beside him, and at that moment the sun cleared the rooftops and pale gold light spilled across the canal basin. His spirits rose. It was a good omen to be touched by the sun as he began the last stage of his journey.

He turned and surveyed the scene behind him, wondering how he could have thought it dull. The remnants of mist had cleared, and now colour leaped forward where there had been gloom. The sky was a pale, clear blue, and the sullen water glimmered with gold; the warehouses were revealed as a deep rose-red, and the bales beneath his feet had become golden-brown. It seemed to him that even the scent of the cotton had changed: on the quay it had seemed oily and faintly rotten, like wilting vegetables at the close of a busy market. But in the shifting air of the boat's passage it gave off a sweet, grassy scent, reminding him of new-cut hay in the fields around his home.

He pushed back his hat and wiped his forehead on his sleeve, then, pole in hand, awaited his orders from the grim old man at the tiller.

The boat moved along the sunlit canal, horses pulling patiently on their chains as they trod the familiar tow-path, and the boy who led them swishing idly at the grasses with his stick. On top of the cargo Matthew rearranged his limbs as his clothes dried out, his wide-brimmed hat tipped forward against the sun and his bundle between his feet. After the rough and tumble of the last ten days he found pleasure in their tranquil progress, and once through the series of locks there were no more orders to be obeyed.

They were passing through a village dominated by one of the big cotton mills that had so impressed him on his arrival in Manchester. It was a fine affair of red brick with white-tiled inserts and a tall, fancy chimney. Close by its walls were crammed terraced houses, like rows of stunted infants fathered by a well-fed giant. There was money up here in Lancashire, just as he'd been told. No matter what was said about hardship in the cotton towns the stamp of wealth lay all along this waterway. And the countryside was pretty, too, 'bonny' was what Peggy-oh Luke had called it in those endless tales of his home town. It was bonny, but oh it was flat to a man of Devon.

'Where be the hills, then?' he asked the boatman, hardly expecting an answer as he'd found him to be sparing with words. 'I say, where be the Pennines?'

Surprisingly, the man answered. 'Sithee!' he said, pointing ahead into the haze, 'them's the hills up yonder, beyond Saltley. Have you never been here afore?'

'No, never,' admitted Matthew. 'I'm from Plymouth, in Devon.'

'Oh aye?' A flicker of interest showed as the other's gaze swivelled in his direction. 'That'll be why tha talks so funny. Plymouth . . . I reckon they play a lot o' games down there?'

Matthew pushed back his hat. If anybody talked funny it was this old bag of bones at the tiller. And what did he mean? 'Games?' he repeated, mystified.

'Aye. Yond' chap playing bowls while he were waiting fort' Spaniards. Tha knows.'

'Oh. Yes.' Matthew allowed himself a small, superior smile. They were so confident, these Northerners, so know-it-all; but they didn't know everything, it seemed. ''Twas a long time ago, that game of bowls,' he pointed out mildly. 'Ordinary folk in Devon don't have time for games – they work hard, same as here.'

'Oh aye?' Something in the other's tone caused Matthew to look at him sharply. Was the old fellow having him on? The leathery face was suspiciously blank. Discomfited and somewhat put out, Matthew fell silent. If this was humour it was a variety not known to him. It was rare for him to be disgruntled, and his irritation soon passed. It was a beautiful morning; he was on his way to a new life, and for the moment he was quite content to sit and listen to the thud of the horses' hooves, and the creak of the boat as it cleaved the black water.

A convoy of coal barges passed them, heading for Manchester. So there was mining around Saltley – another snippet of information to add to the little he knew of the place. He was heading there because the long-ago ramblings of an old, one-legged sailor had found a response in a teen-aged boy's unsettled heart. Oh, he'd picked up hints about Saltley on the way here, of course, but not all of them had been encouraging, and so he'd dismissed them.

A group of road-layers at the other side of Manchester had nudged each other and sniggered when he told them where he was heading. 'Hey – you're all set to take on the army?' they asked him, grinning. 'You'll try your hand at leading the riots, lad?' Matthew had never liked admitting ignorance, so he'd laughed and pretended to know what they meant.

Before that he'd met a pieman at a country market in Cheshire; a kindly, tubby man with beautifully clean hands and wise, sad eyes that looked as if nothing could shock them ever again. 'Oh, I know Saltley,' he'd said. 'I had a stall on the market there. It's crowded, is Saltley. Have you got somewhere to stay?'

Matthew admitted that he knew nobody in the town, and the pieman shook his head admiringly. 'You're young,' he declared, 'that's what it is – the confidence of youth. Look, lad, if I were you I'd watch my money and my bundle in Saltley. If you've nowt of your own it's a big temptation to help yourself to somebody else's stuff, especially if you've a family to feed . . .'

Pondering these remarks Matthew knew he'd be a fool not to admit he was heading for a trouble-spot. Well, he wasn't a fool, but neither was he a stranger to trouble: he'd learned how to handle it in a hard and painful school. The Mizzen Mast was the worst trouble-spot in Plymouth, but he'd survived there for ten years. Oh yes, ten years with Fat Annie and the tribe in the room behind the stables had taught him a great deal about trouble. In that time he had grown from a timid eight-year-old who cried for his mother and was always hungry, to a thin, still-hungry lad of eighteen who could overcharge a tipsy customer with an innocent smile and use the money to feed his sisters and half-brothers; a lad who for years drank his step-mother's ale and then topped up the jug with water from the pump in the yard; who could sleep only on his stomach because in earlier years his back had so often been sore from a leathering. Then he grew too big to be leathered and Fat Annie too sodden with drink to raise the strap. And then . . .

Enough of that! He dragged his thoughts into the

present. He was twenty-two now, and Fat Annie a diseased, half-mad creature existing in a lonely shack because not even the workhouse would have her. It was four years since he had taken the younger ones away from the inn and left Fat Annie to rot; four years since he saw Maggie safely married, Liza settled as a dairy-maid and the two boys taken on as hands at the Ryders' home farm. He himself had been sacked by the head gardener at Ryder Hall, but he would have left in any case. He'd had no intention of spending his life as labourer to the under-gardener with the sole prospect of one day being made up to second gardener.

Four years. A lot had happened in those four years. He'd learned a lot, and in particular he'd learned that, to recall his time at the Mizzen Mast did him no good. It sent his mind into chaos and brought back the sick, helpless feeling that even had its own smell: fear and dirt and stale drink, and the spittle-wet sand that he'd swept from the floor more times than he could count. So, no more thoughts of Fat Annie. He closed the flimsy little door in his mind and for the thousandth time shrugged away his memories. There was another door there as well – a smaller, heavier door that was locked, bolted and barred against something that stayed imprisoned except in a totally unguarded moment or in his most sickening nightmares. That door remained tight-shut, and sometimes he almost forgot it was there.

Matthew stood up restlessly. What about now? What about Saltley? The green-waistcoated wharf-boss had said, 'Have your wits about you, young fella. . . .' He tipped his hat further over his eyes. If there was one thing he could lay claim to it was having his wits about him. Hadn't he travelled from Devon without it costing him a penny? By coach, by wagon, by the railroad and now by boat? Hadn't he worked his way here, just as he'd promised himself? He'd weeded gardens for a free ride and loaded baggage by the hundredweight; he'd looked after two little boys for an afternoon, and panicked when he thought their father had left them with him for good. He'd served at table wearing a borrowed shirt and apron, and the innkeeper had offered him his keep and a bed and three shillings a week to stay on permanently. He'd rescued two horses being driven to death by an unskilled carter and been given the fare for a fifty-mile stretch of railway by their grateful owner. He'd covered hundreds of miles in twelve days and arrived with more money in his belt than when he left Plymouth. He didn't need telling to keep his wits about him. Let the folk of Saltley keep their wits about *them* when Matthew Raike arrived!

The time for that was drawing nearer. The level fields had begun to dip and curve and the flow of the nearby river was more rapid. A forest of tall chimneys lay straight ahead and the sun-warmed breeze carried the first foul smell of a town. He was accustomed to the stink of the Plymouth slums and the cess-pits of Ryder Hall, but even so his nose twitched in protest. Then he shrugged. He'd been told that Saltley was crowded, hadn't he? Well then, where there were crowds there was filth – it was a law of nature.

The mills were along the edge of the canal now, boiler-houses open to the water, but no boiler-men could be seen, no workers in the mill-yards. Then the boat was sliding into a wharf that was like a village in itself, with market-stalls, open shops and a blacksmith's forge. Horse-drawn wagons were being loaded with goods from long narrow monkey-boats, and Matthew surveyed the scene keenly. He knew that the canal companies had long been in the hands of the railways, and the busy wharf reflected the thrusting self-confidence of its owners.

There was such noise and activity that the tranquil journey by boat seemed unreal even before the vessel came to a halt. Everyone seemed to be bellowing in the hard flat accents that seemed to him no better than the squawk of farmyard fowl. A shiny black railway train was picking up passengers only a dozen yards away, and with a blast on its whistle chuffed away across a newly-built viaduct. Horses neighed, gangers shouted, hammer clanged on anvil and Matthew saw that Saltley was busy, just as he'd been told.

There was little time to observe either the scene or the people because the cotton had to be transferred to two wagons that stood waiting with their horses in fancy harness decked with bells. Men and scrawny young boys swarmed over the great bales with a speed and agility that would have challenged the dockers of Manchester. When the last bale was loaded Matthew touched his hat in farewell to the old boatman and swung himself up beside the driver of the second wagon. With an amiable nod the man flicked his beribboned horses, and the carts rumbled across the cobblestones and out through the gates of the goods yard.

Matthew straightened his hat and couldn't help smiling. He'd done it. He was here in Saltley as he'd promised himself all those years ago. Here – and with a perfect excuse to get inside a cotton mill. The sun was shining and the great red mills seemed to lie back and bask in its warmth. It was quieter away from the wharf, and for the first time he noticed that smoke issued from few of the tall chimneys, even though it was not yet noon. He opened his mouth to question the man at his side, then closed it again. He had keen sight and good hearing – he would form his own conclusions.

The carts creaked up a dirt road past a church whose pale stone walls were streaked with black. From his perch Matthew could see beyond a tall hedge into the graveyard, where two sextons were hauling something from an open grave. He twisted round so as not to miss what it was, and saw them lift out a coffin, clotted with earth and falling apart at one end. The men were chatting as they stacked it to one side with several more, and one of them carefully tucked away a fleshless thigh-bone, as if to make his pile more tidy.

Matthew was sensitive to signs and portents and he turned hastily to face the road ahead. He saw from his companion's expression that he too had witnessed the incident, but seemed unperturbed, so he shrugged and raised a smile. He would have liked a more favourable introduction to Saltley, but maybe they did things differently up here. All at once it seemed dark. The sun still shone but now they were on a new-laid road between close-packed buildings, and he saw that the wagons were causing a stir among the townsfolk. They came to the doors of their houses and drifted from street-corner groups to stand at the roadside. A band of ragged children ran squealing along a boarded walkway above drying mud, and here and there a woman stood silently watching their progress.

Matthew observed them all and his stomach knotted in dismay. God in Heaven, what had he come to here? These folk were pitiful! Thin, sickly, undernourished – no, worse than that, they were starving, some of them. The children seemed all eyes and teeth, with limbs that were more crooked than any he'd seen at home, and feet that looked enormous at the ends of stick-like legs. It was all too true, then, what he'd heard about the cotton towns. There *was* hardship. There was *starvation*. He dragged his gaze from the scarecrow throng and looked again at the solid masonry of the mills that darkened their route. Where was the wealth he'd anticipated? Where was the prosperity? Would he ever find work?

'You've had it hard, hereabouts,' he said awkwardly.

'Aye, you could say that,' agreed the man at his side. He nodded at the onlookers. 'These here are the strong 'uns.'

'These?' repeated Matthew. 'These are *strong*?'

'Aye,' confirmed the other. 'The weak 'uns are all dead.' It was a flat statement, matter-of-fact and devoid of drama. Matthew could think of nothing to say in reply, so kept silent as they rumbled on past a deep ditch covered by a black mist of flies. He felt desperately in need of a drink of water, spring water for preference: clean, sparkling, spring water, though he doubted whether any was to be found in Saltley. This wasn't the 'bonny little place' of Peggy-oh Luke's nostalgic yarns, nor the prosperous town of his own imaginings. It was a hole. A hole in the very bowels of hell. He stared straight ahead and wondered why he'd been mad enough to come.

Then he heard the high note of a tin whistle, and a moment later the squeak of a fiddle. Somebody banged a cooking pot with a metal spoon and a strange, jaunty melody emerged. People came hurrying from side streets, from houses, from yards and dark cellars, and three teen-aged boys began to sing. He stood on the seat to look to the rear and saw a straggling procession forming behind them. Men, women and children walked, skipped, danced and hobbled; seemingly jerked out of their lethargy by the raucous little tune. Somebody twirled a length of rope and a young girl waved a piece of red flannel that might once have been a petticoat.

There were all ages following them, but his eyes fell on two little girls holding hands. Their heads bald-spotted with ringworm and their skin tinged yellow from some unknown ailment, they walked sedately in the midst of the throng, barefoot and beaming, and when one of them saw Matthew watching she waved to him. On a hot surge of indignation he blew them both a kiss. In the worst of their days at the Mizzen Mast his sisters had never looked like these two. 'Twasn't right – oh, 'twas wicked.

But what was all the excitement about, anyway? Surely not just for two cart-loads of cotton? Then, belatedly, Matthew thought back to the scenes at the canal basin in Manchester, to the urgency of the wharfinger, and at last he understood. 'Is this the first load of cotton to arrive in Saltley?' he asked. 'Is that what all this fuss be about?'

The wagoner flicked his horses affectionately with the whip, causing them to dip their heads and set the little bells tinkling. 'Aye, lad,' he said, stolidly concealing his surprise at Matthew's ignorance. 'That's why Billy and owd Jasper here have got their bells on – in celebration, like. This is the first load of proper cotton to come here in years. The folk have been waitin' and waitin', and they couldn't have waited much longer. That's why we're carryin' on a bit.'

Matthew's spirits soared. His luck still held. By an amazing chance he was on the first wagons to bring American cotton to Saltley – wagons that would set the people working again. Always ready to play to an audience, he lifted his hat and waved it in time to the beat of the spoon on the cooking-pot; as he did so two pairs of eyes observed him from the upstairs window of a pawn-shop.

Carried away by the crowd's good humour, Matthew looked up and waved his hat to the two young women at the open window above the three dingy gold balls. The plump dark one smiled back, but the red-head just stared, her eyes cool and faintly irritated. Unabashed, Matthew stood on the seat and bowed with a flourish, then resumed his hat-waving as the wagons rolled on towards the great double mills ahead. Behind them the crowd trailed more slowly. It was an uphill road, and climbing was hard on an empty stomach.

Joshua Schofield waited for his cotton at the gates of Jericho Mills, with his children by his side.

'Quiet!' he ordered, unwilling to have the next few minutes swamped by their talk. Sam was always babbling, especially when he was with Sarah. Joshua observed his daughter dubiously. Happen he should have left her at home, seeing she knew nothing of mill affairs; but she'd been a good girl these last twelve months, lending a hand with the schooling and helping her mother run the soup kitchen. Rachel herself wasn't here because it was her day for planning ahead in the kitchen – organising the rota of cooks and servers and washers-up – and she always said that a lack of planning resulted in chaos. He would have liked her here, at his side. She was a comfort to him, she was that, so tranquil and yet so capable. . . . Still, he'd insisted on the children being present, because he'd wanted to make an occasion out of the cotton coming back to Saltley. Not because the first load was for Jericho Mills – that was only to be expected – but because its arrival would mark a new beginning for his mills and for his family.

He flicked his finger-tips under the ends of his whiskers, as was his habit in moments of tension, then rocked back and forth on heels and toes to inspect the line-up of his offspring. He'd be a thankless devil if he wasn't proud of them, he told himself, because they were growing up to be even better-looking than they'd been as children. Still, he'd found out that what went on inside a head was more important than how it looked, and if at least one of them didn't equal their father in brains as well as their mother in looks then he'd be a disappointed man.

Did they realise, he wondered, did they realise how near he'd come to losing the mills? Did they? He doubted it. James might have guessed if he'd let slip a hint, but he'd never shared his worries with his sons, not even the eldest. Only Charlie at Mosley Street knew how things had been going, and even he didn't know everything. Of late he'd had uneasy moments about the future, almost as if he were losing confidence in his own ability. After all, what use was it having the sharpest mind in Saltley if he could be made almost bankrupt by a war across the seas in a country he'd never seen? It was bad enough having his business affected by manufacturers flooding the markets, or the greed of the Liverpool brokers, never mind a bitter, bloody war in America.

Joshua had always envisaged the future as a long upward road, broad and straight and well-surfaced by hard work; of late, through, he'd begun to see the way ahead as a lonely twisting track, darkened by tall hedges, pitted by pot-holes and haunted by knaves and vagabonds. Restlessly he fingered his whiskers again, and the feel of the coarse hairs brought to mind his image when he'd trimmed them that morning. Not only were there grey hairs a-plenty, there was white among the grey, and him not yet fifty-six. Impatiently he wriggled his shoulders. White hair or not, he was in his prime, and letting himself be plagued by doubts and fancies like an old granny.

He could hear Sam at it again, whispering to his sister, who hastily smothered a giggle. 'Samuel!' he said quietly, 'please be silent!' Anybody would think *he* was only seventeen rather than Ralph, he told himself edgily, because his youngest was so silent and self-effacing he sometimes forgot he was there. Forgot until he felt Ralph's eyes on him, as happened with increasing frequency these days. They were like Rachel's, blue as cornflowers, but in the boy's case as veiled and unrevealing as oh, he didn't know what. That was the trouble with Ralph: nobody knew what went on in that smooth blond head of his.

Now they could hear more clearly the rumble of wheels on cobblestones, and the wagons rounded a bend to climb the last stretch of road. It seemed to Joshua that the sun shone more brightly and the sky turned deeper blue. The tin-whistle tune and the beat of the spoon on the pot gained a kind of resonance as it echoed back from his mill walls, so that his eager mind likened it to the sound of trumpets backed by a drum-roll. 'Thank you,' he breathed silently. 'Thank you, God.' There was a swelling in his throat and an unfamiliar sting beneath his eyelids. What –? Was he going soft after all these years? For an unbelieving instant he thought he was going to weep. Sheer horror made him take in a great breath and swell out his chest. This was supposed to be a celebration, not a funeral.

With an effort he braced himself and thrust aside his weakness. He had always enjoyed a moment of drama, and now he motioned his eldest son to his side. 'James! Here, stand by me!' Then he leaned forward. 'Now listen to me, all of you. Mark this moment and mark it well. With work – hard work –

we'll see Jericho Mills re-born and Saltley back at work and better than ever!'

It wasn't much of a speech compared to what he often came up with, but that moment of weakness had robbed him of his customary flair for words. Realising it, he flung out an arm in a gesture that made up for his lack of eloquence, and four pairs of eyes focussed where his finger pointed. They couldn't see much to herald a re-birth in the massive red buildings behind them, nor to put smoke through the chimneys down the road. There were just two wagons pulled by bell-horses; two wagons loaded with huge, hessian-bound bales. On the second one stood a tall, gypsyish fellow with a red sweat-band round his neck, and he was waving his hat at the scarecrow throng behind him.

A reception party, no less. Matthew observed the group by the gates with interest and a touch of relief. They seemed well-fed enough compared to the wretches behind him. There was a broad, grey-haired man who had about him an air of authority, and three fair-haired younger men; one of them was holding the arm of a young lady with amazing silver-gold hair and a complexion that reminded him of the porcelain dolls owned by the Ryder children. The four young ones all had their eyes fixed on him, as if in obedience to a command, making him feel like a prize heifer at the market. He sat down hurriedly, quelling the urge to inspect them in their turn, and when the wagoner at his side doffed his hat to the grey-haired man with a deferential, 'Mr Schofield,' Matthew did likewise. Life had taught him that it was prudent to show respect to those better off than himself.

It was evident that Mr Schofield was in high good humour. He twirled his stick and walked in front of the wagons as they trundled into the yard, then signalled his men to drop the first bale. He watched them slash the hessian cover and then he stooped to dig out a handful of the contents, puckering his lips as he rubbed the

gritty cotton between fingers and thumb. 'James?' He
jerked his head at one of the young men, indicating
that he should examine it too; then waited, flicking his
finger-tips under his whiskers.

'It seems all right to me, Father,' said the young man
quietly.

Schofield nodded briskly. 'Good middling Orleans,'
he agreed. 'It'll do. Unload!'

Matthew jumped down and set to work with the
other men, wondering what Schofield would have done
if his eagerly awaited cotton hadn't been up to standard.
Judging by the set of his chin he would have refused it,
no matter how desperate his need.

Matthew missed little as the bales were heaved into
the ground floor of the mill, and at once opened up by
hand and the matted cotton stacked in high bays divided
by trellises. There was plenty of light from tall windows,
revealing the echoing room to be like the yard: bare,
clean-swept and meticulously neat. 'Over-swept and
under-used,' he told himself, remembering a phrase
common to the staff at Ryder Hall during his time there.
He would have liked to go through the two vast buildings,
but didn't yet see how he could accomplish it.

The young lady departed on the arm of her brother,
while Schofield and his son James talked to a warehouse-
man. The other young fellow, the quiet one, stood two
paces behind his father and brother, hands clasped at
waist level, smooth face expressionless. Was he a bit
lacking, wondered Matthew, noting the unwavering blue
gaze that the boy fixed on his father. The eyes were
beautiful enough to be the envy of many a woman, but
wasn't there a blankness there, an emptiness? Then, for
a second, they swivelled in his direction and he saw he
was wrong. The young man might be lacking in liveliness
and the expression that most folk wore on their faces, but
he was all right in the head. 'He's a deep one, that's all,'
Matthew decided as he turned to the next bale.

Followed by his son, Schofield strolled across and

spoke to the two wagoners. 'There's ale in the lodge when you've done,' he said affably, 'and for all drivers bringing in loads to-day. I don't make a practice of offering strong drink, as you know, but to-day's different – we're celebrating.' He turned and nodded benevolently at Matthew. 'You as well, young fella. Ale in the lodge.'

'Thank 'ee kindly,' said Matthew politely, 'but not for me. I'd prefer water.'

The mill-owner eyed him in amused surprise. 'Would you now? Signed the pledge, eh? Where are you from? Not round these parts, by the sound of you.'

Matthew removed his hat. 'No, Mr Schofield. I be from Devon.'

'Devon? What's brought you to Saltley, then?'

His luck was holding. Matthew swallowed a smile and said soberly, 'I be lookin' for work.'

Joshua Schofield gave him his full attention. 'You've come here – all the way from Devonshire – expecting to find work?' His lips thinned scornfully. 'Happen they haven't heard down there that we've been a bit short of work ourselves in the last year or two?'

'They've heard something of it, to be sure,' said Matthew defensively.

'Well, then?'

It was obvious that the older man thought him a fool, so he spoke up boldly. 'They say cotton pays good wages, and I knew a man once who came from here. He told me a lot about the place and I liked what I heard. So – I came.' Put into words like that he had to admit it sounded a bit rash.

But the mill-owner's interest was captured. 'This man you knew, who was he?'

Matthew would have liked to lay claim to a friend of some stature, but instead he had to admit, reluctantly, 'A sailor with a peg leg, called Luke Fawcett. He's dead now.'

Schofield stared at the floor and rocked back and forth

on his heels and toes. 'Red hair? Crooked teeth? A bit older than me?'

Matthew's jaw slackened in surprise, then he thought of Peggy-oh as he'd seen him the day he died – wispy white hair, half his teeth missing, his one leg stiff with rheumatics and looking all of seventy-five. 'He might once have had red hair, I suppose,' he said doubtfully, 'but he seemed a lot older than you, Mr Schofield. He told me he was the youngest of thirteen and that his father worked from home. Weavin', he said.'

Schofield smiled, and gave Matthew a congratulatory thump on the shoulder. 'That's Luke!' he said triumphantly. 'The Fawcetts lived near us out on the old Salt Road when I was a lad. His father ran a couple of hand-looms till the mills took all the work. Young Luke went off to sea when he was twelve or thirteen. They said he worked his way down the Mersey to Liverpool.' The shrewd blue eyes observed Matthew narrowly. 'Did he do well, then?'

Loyalty to his old friend made Matthew edit the tales he'd been told of Luke's years on board ship. 'Oh, yes, I think so. But he was paid off when he lost his leg, and so he came to live at the inn where I used to work. He said he wanted to stay near the sea.'

'Oh.' Schofield seemed to like the sound of that. 'He lived in some style, then?'

Matthew weighed his reply. This man seemed genuinely interested in Peggy-oh, had perhaps been his close friend in childhood. Was there any point in giving him the truth: that the old man had slept in a rat-infested stall in the stables, and existed on what he could buy with odd coins cadged from drunken customers? Schofield seemed a decent enough type for a man of business. Why disappoint him? 'It was a modest inn,' he said guardedly, 'but yes, I think he was content.'

'And he spoke to you of Saltley?'

'Often. He said it was the bonniest place on earth, and he'd travelled the world.'

Schofield looked past the still-lingering crowd to where
Saltley's tall chimneys were touched by the sun. 'It's still
bonny,' he said, nodding, 'but not everybody can see it.'
He turned back to Matthew. 'And it was because of Luke
that you left home and came here?'

'Yes. I wanted to make a new life for myself.' Matthew
decided to seize the opportunity, and said eagerly, 'Can
'ee give me a job, Mr Schofield? I'm strong and I'm
willin'. I'll take anythin' that pays me a wage.'

'That's what they all say,' the other answered heavily.
'What's your name?'

'Matthew Raike.'

The mill-owner took a little cloth-bound book from his
pocket and wrote in it with a lead pencil. 'Well, Raike,
it's like this: I have eighteen hands on maintenance and
twenty more started back this morning. That leaves over
twelve hundred laid off, twelve hundred and two, to be
exact. When they're all back at their jobs I might be
able to take you on, but not before.'

'Oh,' said Matthew blankly. 'I see.'

'Even when we were on full production we weren't
short of workers, you know. They come to Lancashire
from all over. Do you know we have nearly an eighth
of the total population of England and Wales? And in
only a thirty-third of the land? Now, I've got more cotton
arriving in the next week or two, and at a better price
than I've had to pay for this lot. With luck I'll be back in
full production soon. I've put your name in my book, and
the setter-on always checks with me each week. That's
as much as I can promise.'

'Thank'ee kindly, Mr Schofield.'

'Well, off you go and tell the lodge-keeper's wife to
give you your water, and that I say she can feed you as
well.' He shot Matthew a curious look. 'It was working
at the inn that put you off the ale, I suppose?'

They all thought that. In fact, he thought it himself,
most of the time. 'That's right,' he agreed, replacing his
hat as they parted. The mill-owner crossed the yard to

rejoin his son James, still shadowed by the quiet one, who had followed the exchange between them with scarcely a blink. Just then a stream of men, women and children came round the side of the building and headed for the gates. Matthew's dark eyes narrowed. There must have been close on a hundred of them. Schofield had said all his workers were laid off, so what had this lot been doing? Playing hoop-la?

Flanked by his sons, the mill-owner stood beneath the outline of a great brass trumpet emblazoned on the gate. It caught Matthew's eye. There was one on the other gate, as well. Was it Schofield's trade-mark, then? And why a trumpet? He eyed the broad, confident figure curiously. Schofield was nodding in response to murmured greetings from the slow-moving crowd. It seemed to Matthew that there was something unutterably weary in his expression as he watched them troop past, and to a lesser degree it was echoed in the face of the son, James. The quiet one remained impassive, the beautiful eyes flat as pebbles in still water.

At the door of the lodge Matthew paused and examined the departing crowd. Poor they undoubtedly were, and ill-nourished, but they were in far less desperate straits than some he'd seen that morning. A few of them eyed him curiously, and he stared right back. But *were* they workers? Two middle-aged men carried writing-slates and others held battered books. A young woman clasped an earthenware dish covered by a cloth, and for a moment their glances met: the sun-tanned man in his floppy old hat and red neck-band, and the young woman, scarcely more in size than a child, with a young-old face where flesh was too spare to give comeliness to the bones. Tired eyes observed him with a flicker of interest and then returned to the bowl she carried with such care.

Matthew picked up his bundle and went inside the lodge. There was much he didn't yet understand – about Saltley, about Jericho Mills, about the people going

out through the gates. Maybe the lodge-keeper's wife
would be willing to enlighten him. He rarely had trouble
persuading women to talk. More often the difficulty lay
in getting them to keep silent.

It was quiet on the hills above Saltley; so quiet he could
hear the hum of bees in the elders and the faint rhythmic
swish as distant farm-hands scythed meadow-grass. He
sat in the sun on a bank above a rutted track and stared
down at the town, which from that distance looked clean
and orderly with its blend of stone and red brick, and
its church-tower dwarfed by the vast, rectangular mills.
Beyond the town, shining blue with the sky's reflection,
he could see the river and the canal glinting purposefully
across the plain towards Manchester. He imagined that
the twin waterways were calling to him: 'You needn't
stay! See, look at us, we've left Saltley and we're heading
for the city!' And then, as if emphasising the message,
smoke plumed upwards as a railway engine took the
same direction.

Matthew was given to such fancies, and earlier in the
day he might have paid heed to them, but he was feeling
better now. The sick dismay that had knotted his innards
on arriving had eased a little as he walked the town. Oh,
it was awful – it was *terrible* – but then the dockside streets
of Plymouth were hardly the pavements of Paradise. He
had to admit too that there was something about the
people here that pleased him. Their hard flat speech
held echoes of old Peggy-oh, who had never quite lost
the inflection of his early days. Then their attitude: frank,
direct, aggressive, with a kind of dogged determination
brightened by flashes of humour. He had found them an
independent lot, more than ready to inform a stranger
that though they might be ground down by hardship they
were by no means beaten.

He had listened to the lodge-keeper's wife and to stall-
holders on the market; questioned gaunt men employed
by the parish on road-laying, and eavesdropped on two

drab whores in a part of the town known as Gallgate. He'd talked and he'd listened; he'd seen a lot too, and been in turn horrified, sick with pity, stunned by admiration and at one stage doubled up with laughter.

His mind was overflowing with impressions, so following his instincts he had left the crowds and sought a place where he could breathe good air and reflect on what he'd learned since he arrived. He tipped his hat over his eyes, put his bundle between his feet and his elbows on his knees, because long ago he'd found that he needed periods of peace and quiet in which to get his mind in order. When work at the Mizzen had exhausted his underfed frame, when Fat Annie had given vent to her resentment and frustration by ill-using him, when the younger ones were sick or hungry, he realised that a spell of quiet in which to marshal his thoughts could benefit him as much as a meal.

The loft above the stables included a small, boarded-off section known as 'the sleeper', once used to bed coachmen from long-distance runs. As the years passed and the Mizzen's reputation dwindled, coach companies by-passed the inn and the sleeper was left empty to the vermin. At the age of twelve Matthew claimed the space for himself; banishing the younger ones and exhibiting dead rats and mice to discourage visits from Fat Annie. He wondered now if in her softer moments she had sensed how he needed the privacy of that small space, because she rarely entered it; or perhaps the effort of getting her bulk up the ladder deterred her. Even her beatings took place down below, leaving him free to climb up there alone for the solace of lying face-down on the straw. There had been an aperture in the timber wall there. He covered it with sacking in winter, but in the summer he could look out and see the hills, the rounded green-gold hills outside the town; sometimes he would catch the fresh sea-scent above the stink of the streets.

Old Peggy-oh had been one of the few who were

welcome up there until the climb became too much for him. They would talk of the day's events, and the old man would assure him he'd be worse off at sea. Sometimes he dreamed up cunning ideas of how to combat Fat Annie, and he always knew which customers Matthew must hide from when the inn closed for the night. But best of all he told stories, marvellous stories. He had a gift for the telling of them, tales of his travels to far-off lands and the people he met there, about life on board ship and the little township of Saltley where he was born.

Matthew looked down at that town and thought of his years in the sleeper, and then in the lean-to behind the potting-shed at Ryder Hall. He could admit now that there were worse places. That afternoon he'd seen back-to-back dwellings where waste from the street channels ran back into ground-floor rooms; cellars surrounding black yards far below street level, where pallid babies wailed and were nursed by listless mothers; where older children sat on drying mud, clad only in old undershirts or bodices. Oh, yes, there were places far worse than the sleeper and the potting-shed lean-to. And he'd come all this way to find them. . . .

He considered his position. There was no need to remain in Saltley. He had no commitments in the town – no job, no home. There wasn't a soul who cared whether he stayed or departed, and because of his way of speech he would be taken on last rather than first by any local employer. He knew that Yorkshire lay at the other side of the Pennines, and that they dealt in home-produced wool over there, rather than stuff that must put to sea from blockaded ports. There should be plenty of work in Yorkshire.

Eyes slitted, he lay back on the grass. His dreams of a new life were what had sustained him through years of toil and misery. Perhaps he'd been mistaken in aiming for a cotton town, but his nature led him to rashness sometimes and it usually turned out well. He thought of the brains and the wealth behind the cotton industry, and decided that if it should flourish again there would be work enough for everybody – even a foreigner from the south.

That fellow Schofield, for instance – Joshua of the golden trumpet – if he was anything to go by then cotton-masters weren't so bad. He'd learned that the mill-owner was highly regarded for his actions during the time folk called the Cotton Famine. 'Twas true he had other sources of wealth besides his mills, but he'd still kept more than twelve hundred laid-off workers housed and fed; what was more he had provided schooling for those who wanted it.

It seemed to Matthew that if there was the stink of death and poverty in this town there was also the heady scent of future prosperity. He was already twenty-two, an age when some men were married with a family. Time was passing him by, and what had he to show? His worldly goods were in his bundle: a clean flannel shirt, a pair of fustian trousers, a bit of soap and a razor, two cotton squares that could be used as sweat-bands or nose-wipes, a pair of thick woollen stockings and the Bible that his mother gave him before she died. The contents of the Bible meant little to him, but she had written his name in it: Matthew Ezekiel Raike. He could remember quite clearly her writing it, propped up in the big double bed with the white sheets and the blue bedspread, with his father watching and then hustling him out of the room. . . . And of course there was his money. In the canvas belt beneath his shirt was twenty-two shillings and threepence, elevenpence more than when he left Plymouth.

If he could travel this distance and end up with a profit, surely he could exist in Saltley for a while? What if he set himself a limit of, say, six weeks, and if he wasn't earning by then he would move on elsewhere? He pursed his lips and thought about it. Yes. That was it!

The decision made, tension left him and his spirits soared. He rose to his feet, eyes alert. Down the hill was a stream where he could wash away the dirt and dried sweat, and beyond where the farm-hands laboured was a barn. He would wait until dusk and creep in there for a comfortable sleep. And then tomorrow? He smiled. Who could say what tomorrow might bring?

CHAPTER TWO

The Pawnshop

SUNLIGHT SHONE THROUGH HEAVY lace at the window above the three gold balls. It shone on dark, solid furniture, brightened the deep-hued carpet and plucked little rainbows from the prisms of the glass lustres on the sideboard. Many who visited the gloom of Abel Ridings's pawnshop would have been surprised to see the comfort of that upstairs room. A few, more cynical, would have expected no less, for Ridings was known to be a keen man of business. He was a hard man, it was said, though not unfair. It was even rumoured that on occasions he'd been generous, but nobody ever came forward with proof of that.

Saturday tea was finished and cleared away, and with Abel still busy in the shop Maria Ridings and her daughters were preparing for an evening stroll along the new pavements of Holden Street. Tizzie, the eldest, was waiting by the window. With her quick, decisive movements and nimble fingers she was always the first to be ready. Her mother, normally a rapid mover, became slow and stately in front of her bedroom looking-glass. Her second-best grey sateen must fall just so from her still-shapely hips; the gold brooch must lie flat on the good lace at her throat, and her blue straw bonnet must sit at a dignified angle on the luxuriant, grey-streaked hair. As for Mary, plump little Mary with her dimples and giggles and her frenzied searches for hair-pins and ribbons and gloves – she, of course, was always last.

Normally impatient, Tizzie was in pensive mood for once, gazing down at the three tarnished gold balls that

announced her father's business to all who passed by. She
had been nine years old when she protested about being
a pawnbroker's daughter, and received from her mother
a slap across the ear – a powerful, stinging blow quickly
followed by several more on her back and shoulders.

Her mother rarely struck either of them, but her plump
round face had been bright red with anger. 'Don't you
dare criticise your father's business! It's pawnbroking that
puts food on the table and keeps you two out of the mill,
remember that! Your father's in his own shop through
hard work and brains, and if you end up with half what
he's got up here – ' she tapped her head ' – you'll do!'

That had been ten years ago, but Tizzie remembered
it well. At the time she had sensed that her mother's
rage was directed at something deeper than her own
criticism of pawnbroking. It had been beyond her to
question or to reason what lay behind it. She couldn't
even have explained why the incident unnerved her, but
she never again found fault openly with their way of life.
Neither, though, did she lose her resentment at having
to live above a pawnshop; with its smell of used clothes
and camphor, its constant battle against fleas and lice,
its rows of coats hanging from ceiling rails, its brown
paper packages of cheap jewellery, and tickets, tickets,
tickets. There were tickets on everything, made out in
her father's neat, spiky hand.

Even worse was the dolly-shop in the cellar. A flight
of stone steps led down to it from the street, and a black
wooden doll was fastened over the door. The poorest of
the poor went down there to pawn their cooking-pots or
their blankets, or sometimes a stick or two of furniture.
They were dealt with by her father's assistant, Barney
Jellicoe, a quiet, intelligent creature who caused Tizzie
to cringe. Why, of all the men in Saltley, had her father
chosen a dwarf to work in the dolly-shop?

Being a pawnbroker's daughter had cost her something
over the years. They were above the common labouring
classes, and yet set apart from the very people her mother

sought to mix with. Coveted friendships never developed
because nobody wished to be linked to Abel Ridings.
People moved to one side when she and Mary entered
a shop, young men of the better families remained aloof
when introduced, and the members of their chapel,
Bethesda, kept a careful distance. Oh, it was true that
the Ridings were held in a kind of esteem by the poor of
the town, and in recent years the destitute among them
often approached her for coppers. She would have given,
willingly, just to be rid of them, but as she was rarely
allowed to carry money she ignored any who begged.
Their sunken faces and the smell of them turned her
stomach.

But Mary, with their mother's blessing, once a week
made cheese and onion pies or pans of mutton broth
to take round to the feeding centre. At first she had
delivered food direct to desperate families nearby, but
her mother had put a stop to that when she came home
in tears and couldn't sleep at night.

Tizzie viewed these efforts with approval because she
liked to think that someone cared for the needy, and in
any case she was fond of her sister. In fact the name Tizzie
had come from Mary's childish mangling of her given
name, Elizabeth. It was the desire to please her chubby
little sister that made her refuse to answer to anything
else as they grew older. Now, when she wondered if she
really wanted to be known as Tizzie for the rest of her
life, sheer obstinacy made her cling to the name; she
told herself that there were many Elizabeths, but very
few Tizzies.

A sudden breeze made the three brass balls squeak
on their metal bracket, and she eyed them balefully.
There must be more to life than she had here in the
pawnshop, helping her mother with the light housework
and her father with the accounts; sewing fine seams and
embroidering countless tablecloths. Why, earlier in the
week she had found herself envying the scuttling little
Irish girl who came in to do the washing and rough

cleaning; if Biddy was bored then at least she didn't have time to think about it. She, Tizzie, thought about it frequently. Boredom pervaded her life, whether she was attending functions like Bethesda's Summer Bazaar and the Ladies' Sewing Guild, or taking sedate little walks with Mary and turning a blind eye while her sister exercised her dimples at that great lump of a butcher.

Sometimes she glimpsed what life could be like, as a child in a dark hallway might peep through the door of a brightly-lit room. When her father brought home a copy of the *Manchester Guardian* she could read about what was going on in London or Paris or across the great oceans of the world. Not always understanding what lay behind the items of news, she ignored all mention of politics and avoided reading about the plight of the labouring classes, because she could see that for herself whenever she set foot out of doors. She absorbed like a sponge all references to money, whether it was fines imposed at the Petty Sessions, the price of tea and coffee, or a man disclaiming responsibility for debts incurred by his wife. She even told herself that she could understand the Stock Market figures, but if she tried to discuss them with her father he was apt to hedge, or make a sarcastic reply.

Tizzie would have liked to read works of fiction, because she fancied that from them she might learn more about men. Her parents discouraged the reading of novels, apart from the work of Mr Dickens, but if someone pawned a bundle of books she would sometimes extract one and sneak it up to their bedroom. That was how she came across Mr Thackeray's *Vanity Fair* in a bright yellow shilling edition, but just as she was warming to the exploits of Becky Sharp her mother pounced on it and bore it down to the shop with tuts and mutters and dark looks.

Sometimes Tizzie felt she was a captive in the comfortable rooms above the three brass balls; then a remark by a passing stranger or a paragraph in a penny news-sheet would set her mind striding along untried paths and her ears straining for accents other than those of her hometown. Why, they spoke differently only seven miles away in Manchester, a place that delighted her even though her father called it the city of the bankrupt. Sometimes he yielded to her pleas and took her with him when he visited a second-hand jewellers there; though he never said what went on in the poky back room in the shadow of the Cathedral, she worked out that he must be selling unredeemed items from the shop. Reason told her that in a town where starvation stalked the streets everything that was pawnable was already in his pigeon-holes and boxes, and unlikely to be redeemed. She wasn't allowed to see all his ledgers or have access to his iron safe; all the same she guessed that he had done well out of the destitution in Saltley, and that he had other financial involvements of which she knew nothing.

When she totalled the ledger or balanced his cash-box against the tickets he acknowledged her help with a satisfied grunt. She would have liked an admission that she was quick at figuring, she would have liked praise; but Father, quiet little Father with his puny frame and the withered arm that had prevented the mills claiming him in childhood, wasn't one for compliments. He treated her and Mary with resigned patience, and wasn't mean with money. They had clothes of good quality, and their bedroom was comfortable, with a fire when the weather demanded it. Mary, in fact, seemed fond of him, but he called forth no affection whatsoever in Tizzie.

Sometimes she watched him as he fingered his packets and boxes, and a kind of panic would seize her. She told herself that time was flying by, and she was just sitting there, rotting away. Everybody knew that marriage was the way of escape for a woman, but so far she hadn't even come near it. She needed a husband with money, of course, that was the first priority. The second was love. She didn't know a great deal about love, actually, but she and Mary knew how babies began. They talked

about it when they were side by side in bed. It had
wounded her pride to discover that Mary, who knew
less than she did about absolutely everything else, was
quite well-informed about what went on between men
and women, and infuriatingly vague about where she'd
learned it.

'Oh, I thought everybody knew,' she would say blithely.
Or, 'it must have been something Mrs MacReadie said –
you know, Mrs MacReadie who asked for the soup for
her little boys.' Tizzie could have throttled her.

'It's called sexual congress, Tizzie,' she said one night
as she fastened her night cap, 'and they do it in bed,
though Mrs Walker who collects relief tickets at the
centre says it's called "a bit of push and shove". Men
have this desire to possess a woman, you see, and I
can't see why women shouldn't want to possess men,
as well. I have the feeling that we're meant to enjoy it,
but nobody says much about that side of it – not to me,
anyway.'

They didn't say anything at all about it to Tizzie, but
she gave a reflective nod, as if in agreement. She liked
the sound of it, though it grated to listen to Mary holding
forth. She liked men. She liked the look of them – not her
father, of course, he was different – but men in general.
She liked their rough chins, their clothes and hairy wrists,
their strength and decisiveness, and the way they carried
money in their trouser pockets. She wanted a man of her
own, and frequently dropped hints about how long she
was having to wait for one.

Her mother was both brisk and dismissive whenever
Tizzie questioned her. 'There's time yet to meet your
life's partner, lady, and you barely twenty. When your
father says the time's right we're going to move to a
bigger shop nearer Manchester; then you'll be able to
pick and choose a husband.'

Well, the bit about Manchester was good, but the rest
of it was the same old story. A bigger pawnshop to attract
a wealthier type of customer, successful marriages for

her and Mary. . . . Didn't her parents see that she was capable of finding her own husband if she didn't have the dead weight of the pawnshop round her neck?

The door opened and Mary hurried in. 'Tizzie!' she hissed, 'will you suggest to Mother that we go along Peter Street? I don't want her to know it's my idea.'

Tizzie eyed her in irritation. Sometimes it was hard to remember she was eighteen. Her hair, newly-washed and very soft, was already escaping from its pins. Two of the tiny buttons down the front of her bodice were unfastened, and the smooth round cheeks were pink with suppressed excitement.

'Come here,' she said briskly. 'Let me fasten your hair properly or it will be down before we leave the house.'

Mary submitted with only half her attention on her hair. 'Will you put it in a twist, like you did before? And look, *will* you suggest Peter Street? You know you can make it sound right.'

Tizzie sighed. 'I suppose we've got to meet William Hartley accidentally on purpose again?'

'Yes, and there's no need to look like that about it. If Mother could just realise what he's like, gradually, sort of, she'd accept the idea of us getting married.'

'*Married!*'

'Ow! That hurt!' Mary clutched at her scalp.

'But you hardly know him!'

'I know him well enough. And I intend to marry him.' For once she sounded older than eighteen. There was a hardness there, a determination.

Tizzie stared, her jaw slack and her remarkable eyes very wide. 'Has he proposed to you?'

'Not yet. But he will. Mother is sure to object because she says when we choose a husband we have to improve our station in life.' They were still speaking in whispers, their faces almost touching.

'But I thought you told me that William's father is

quite prosperous,' said Tizzie abruptly. 'He's a master-butcher, isn't he? I think that's a more wholesome trade than pawnbroking.'

Mary rolled reproachful brown eyes. 'Anybody knows that, Tizz. I suppose it's not so wholesome in the slaughter-yard, though. I didn't like that very much.'

Tizzie was still staring. 'You've watched the slaughtering? In Bushell's yard?'

'Yes. *And* watched William and his brother loading sides of beef. You should see him, Tizzie, he's ever so strong.'

'I'm sure he is,' agreed Tizzie faintly, examining a mental picture of William Hartley, half-clad as the meat-carriers often were, straining his considerable muscles under a heavy carcass. She made herself speak reasonably. 'Look, Mary, if you really like William I think you should tell Mother. You're entitled to state your preference and if she objects you're entitled to know – '

'Ready, girls?' Mother had come down the stairs unnoticed. 'What's this? Secrets?'

They drew apart, Mary in confusion and Tizzie still stunned. What would Mother have to say if she knew that Mary had decided on her future husband? She observed her sister narrowly. It seemed she had underestimated her.

Maria was eyeing her daughters. They weren't beautiful, but they were fine-looking girls. Mary was like her as she'd been at that age, but better fed, and it showed. She wasn't particular enough about her appearance, though. 'Fasten those two buttons,' she commanded, 'and get your bonnet and gloves. Your colour's high again, so a walk will do you good. It's cooler now.' She turned to Tizzie and felt her customary bafflement when faced with her elder daughter. She looked elegant – that was the only word for her – and at least twenty-five. Tall, slender, her face too strong and bony for beauty but with its own undoubted appeal, the unruly red-gold hair stylishly subdued, and those alert, dark-lashed eyes, green as leaves in high summer, at that moment holding a measure of resentment. 'Very nice,' she conceded, 'and yes, you *can* borrow my silk wrap – don't bother to ask me! Come along, then.'

They went down to the shop to show themselves at the door of the back room. 'We're off then, Abel.' It was a ritual. Her father must see them before they went out. He never offered praise and rarely any comment, but Tizzie saw the pale eyes gleam as if with satisfaction at the sight of his womenfolk dressed for a Saturday evening stroll through the town. Then the other ritual, which Tizzie thought even more peculiar. Her father laid his good hand on her mother's wrist. Just for an instant. She never left the premises without this restrained little farewell, even when customers were present.

She told herself scornfully that it was probably as far as they ever went in displaying affection, because they were unlikely partners. Her mother was a fine figure still, the auburn lights in her hair fading, but with skin that remained clear and supple. Her father had wispy grey hair and moustache and a pale face that had no redeeming feature apart from the mouth – excellent even teeth behind shapely lips; it was the mouth of a young man set in an old, lined face. And it was an old, thin body inside the faded working suit, with his watch-chain sagging across his concave middle.

Her mother might have a lot to say about suitable marriages for them both, and about a better shop in Manchester, but Tizzie knew quite well who would have the last word. Mother, busy bustling strong-willed Mother, always gave way to her quiet, fleshless husband whenever there was a difference between them. What was more, she seemed quite content to do so.

After the novelty of treading the new flagstones of Holden Street it required little effort on Tizzie's part to steer their mother past the Old Cross and into Peter

Street. Maria, dressed in her good second-best, was not averse to leading her girls past the few shops of quality. Two paces behind, Mary squeezed Tizzie's arm in gratitude, and a moment later smothered an excited squeak as a soberly-dressed young man left two companions and approached them from a distance. Make way for the side of prime beef, Tizzie told herself, observing him keenly and with increasing surprise. Since her sister's revelations about marriage she had taken William Hartley's image into her mind and adjusted it so as to lessen the shock of Mary's announcement. Mentally setting him against the carcasses of Bushell's Yard, she had made of him a muscle-bound oaf, good-looking in a coarse kind of way but undoubtedly from the working classes; a red-faced inarticulate youngster, struggling to make a living.

Now, seeing him approaching in the flesh, she experienced one of the spurts of self-knowledge that came to her of late, recognising the mental adjustments she'd made and aware of her reasons for making them. Her lips twisted a little as he came nearer. This was no bumbling young oaf. He was bulky right enough, but he moved with assurance in his fine broadcloth and good leather boots, and in a town where so many were sickly and ill-nourished he made an impressive figure, glowing with health and well-being. Of course the Hartleys were well-known as a robust lot, six or seven of them and all well-made. Hadn't the grandparents come to Saltley from a life in farming up in the hills somewhere? He would have a strong enough bloodline to combat the heritage of her father's puny frame if he and Mary did marry and produce offspring.

'Tizzie!' Mary was still clutching her arm. 'Did you see? He was talking to the Schofields!'

Tizzie breathed loudly through her nose. Of course she'd seen! Who could miss the two oldest Schofield sons? Everybody in town knew them by sight, but apparently Bull-beef here was on speaking terms. And then he was facing them and raising his hat. 'Good evening, ladies.'

Maria was affable, but no more. 'Mr Hartley,' she acknowledged, nodding, and was moving on when Mary dropped her handkerchief, her prettiest one, edged with lace. Tizzie almost groaned. Was that the best she could manage?

It was enough. William bent to retrieve it while Maria turned to eye her daughter. She was looking up at William with a smiling self-possession that amazed her sister, who bestowed on him a smile of her own but in return received merely a pleasant nod before his gaze returned to Mary. All at once Tizzie became acutely aware of detail: her mother's eyes, suddenly alert, swivelling to watch the retreating Schofields, and the way she moved her head from side to side, a habit she had when contemplating something new or out of the ordinary; William, clean-scrubbed and brown-haired, his fingers still touching Mary's as the scrap of white linen slowly changed hands; and Mary herself, pink-cheeked and delighted, moistening her lower lip with the tip of a restless tongue.

In that instant Tizzie accepted that they would marry, no matter what obstacles lay in their path. Resentment struggled with affection and was subdued to a trouble-some ache that settled somewhere beneath her ribs. It was obvious they were besotted with each other. Face to face they shared the look of a starving man confronted by a tasty meal. A pity he hadn't got his own shop, of course; still, Mary had said that when prosperity returned to Saltley his father would set him up as he'd done with his older brother. Well, prosperity was in sight again, wasn't it? The cotton was coming back.

Oh, why on earth didn't they *speak*? Mary would stare at him all dewy-eyed for ever more if it was left to her. She, Tizzie, would move things along. She was good at making pleasant, natural-sounding observations, and so she said: 'I expect the Schofields are pleased to have the cotton coming through again, Mr Hartley?'

He turned to her and smiled with a hint of relief. Splendid teeth, she noticed; large and white and perfectly even. 'Aye, it's a relief to them all, I reckon, but we weren't discussing that just now. James helps with the business side at High Lee Farm, and he's getting to know a bit about the livestock. He was asking me to go up there to advise his agent on what prices to hold out for when he puts his beasts to market.'

Maria digested that, and her manner slightly warmer, said, 'What sort of place do they run up there, Mr Hartley?'

'Oh, a fine place, the best in these parts, Mrs Ridings. They used to sell direct to my father, and no doubt will again as soon as business picks up.'

Tizzie smiled to herself. He needed no more help. It had been pure chance that they saw him with the Schofields. They were the town's leading family, and Bull-beef was using his connection with them to show himself in a good light.

Her mother was nodding benignly. 'It must give your father satisfaction to see his sons coming up in the business,' she murmured politely. There was no question in her tone, but once again he was ready.

'Aye. He's teaching us everything he knows, but it's me who has charge of the buying and keeping the books. Mrs Ridings, would you allow me the pleasure of escorting you on your walk?'

Tizzie knew at once that he and Mary had rehearsed that sentence; it came out so smoothly, and they exchanged a congratulatory flicker of eyelids. But Maria wasn't to be bowled over. She smiled and with just the right amount of dignity, said, 'Perhaps just to the end of our street, then, Mr Hartley.'

They moved on as two separate couples: Maria and William in front and the sisters behind. Tizzie would have liked to see Mary side by side with Bull-beef while she followed with Mother, making favourable comments on him and assessing her reactions, but her sister was quite content to be left in the rear. 'She's finding out more about him,' she whispered, watching their conversation with wide-eyed intensity. 'Oh, Tizzie, I think it might come right for us in the end, in spite of everything.'

Tizzie gritted her teeth. 'I don't see the problem,' she said shortly. 'He isn't trying to marry into the peerage, for goodness sake, just the local pawnbrokers.'

'I know, but when I told Mother I liked the looks of him she said he was no more than a glorified farm-boy with a talent for the slaughter-yard, and that Father could buy and sell the Hartleys ten times over if he chose.'

'Could he indeed!' retorted Tizzie. 'If he's as well-off as all that why doesn't he get shut of the three gold balls and move to Manchester?'

But Mary wasn't really listening. Her eyes were on William's broad back. 'Doesn't he look wonderful in his Sunday-best, Tizzie?' she breathed.

Tizzie nodded and managed a smile. In front of them William took her mother's elbow because they were now at a junction of the streets and the going was far from even. The sisters lifted their skirts above the rutted walkway and silence fell between them, Mary gazing dreamily at William and Tizzie enveloped in growing fury. Not at Mary, who after all was just a little numskull, but at her parents, and herself. Why had she let her mother dismiss her hints and pleas about finding a husband? She was to blame for her wasting years of her life in that flea-ridden hole above the three gold balls, and her father must have backed her. But what was worse – far, far worse – was that she, Tizzie, had let them do it.

She shot a look at Mary's face, flushed and intent at her side. It was beyond belief that she'd let herself stay unattached until almost twenty; at eighteen Mary was half-way to the altar, and with a presentable man who was clearly besotted by her. She began to feel slightly

sick. Mary was chattering again, but the words were
lost on her. She had one urge, and an unexpected one
at that. It was to bestow on her sister a kiss of thanks.
She'd needed a shaking-up and Mary had given her one
with a vengeance. Things were going to change, and she
might as well start working out just how she was going
to change them.

'He shot off pretty quick, didn't he?' grinned Sam
Schofield. 'He has things on his mind besides the
butcher's shop by the looks of it. Three of them, all
round and made of brass.'

James laughed; the gentle, tolerant chuckle that could
make Sam's comments seem brash and insensitive. 'Abel
Ridings and his pawnshop, and his daughters. Yes, I
think William has an eye for the dark one. I saw them
deep in talk behind the market stalls the other day.'

Sam shot a curious glance over his shoulder. 'The tall
one's the more striking.'

'Perhaps, but the little one is pleasant enough.'

Sam's smile faded. His brother's tone revealed that
he wasn't really interested in any female other than
Esther Buckley. They were to marry in the autumn,
and Sam was on edge about it. In fact, the reason
he'd asked James out for a stroll was in order to have
a quiet word. The trouble was, Sam didn't like Esther.
Of all the family it seemed he was the only one who had
reservations about his brother's future wife. He didn't
like anything about her: the way she led his brother by
the nose, so very sweetly; her sinewy little hands, or
the non-existent bosom that was pushed and padded
into the semblance of curves; her eyes – they were
never still, but always watching, assessing, measuring.
He would admit she was pretty enough in a kittenish
sort of way, but when he thought of her unsheathing
her neat little claws on old Jimmy something seemed to
shrivel in his chest.

His own main concern was his sister Sarah. The bond

between them was deep and compelling and beyond definition; a thing of instinct and impulse and a twin-like linking of minds. They had been born a year apart to the exact day, and the family regarded them as twins in all but the year of their birth. He was concerned for his mother as well, but here his feelings were less clear. He knew she was a good mother; she cared about them all, monitoring their health and their food and their clothes just as she'd done since they were children. But in the last year or two she had spent so much time with the sick, the needy and the destitute that he doubted if she ever saw him as Sam, an individual with a mind of his own. As for his father . . . well, he had a regard for him, right enough, and a deep respect, come to that. But when it came to James – James was different. He was good – good inside – not just where people could see it and admire, but deep down inside, where it mattered. In spite of the two years' difference in their ages Sam had an odd compulsion to look after his older brother and guard his interests.

In their younger days he had sometimes resented James's sunny tranquillity. It had made his own childish whims and tantrums seem petulant, and Ralph's silent self-absorption almost sinister, but over the years he had come to realise his brother's worth. He was one on his own, was James, and far too good for Ephraim Buckley's daughter. He didn't relish it but he would have to have another go at him. 'When is Esther due back from her aunt's?' he asked.

'Friday. I'm going round to see her in the evening, and then – '

Sam interrupted him. 'James, I beg you not to take this amiss, but are you absolutely sure you're doing the right thing? Marrying her, I mean.'

James stopped in his tracks and swung towards his brother so that they stared into each other's eyes, concern facing resentment, blue to blue. 'Don't start that again, Sam. I know you don't like her, and I'm sorry about it,

but I can't see why you're so set against her. She's very
fond of you, and Ralph and Sarah. And as a matter of
fact, yes, I *am* sure I'm doing the right thing. She's –
she's very dear to me.'

Sam jerked his head sideways, indicating that they
should move on. People would think it funny, two
brothers talking face-to-face in the street as if they
were new-met friends. 'I accept that what appeals to
one fella doesn't necessarily appeal to another,' he said
doggedly, 'and I've taken account of that. You're right,
though, when you say I don't like her. To my mind
she doesn't ring true, and if you must know I don't
think she'll make you happy.' He stopped, as short of
breath as if he'd been running the streets for the last
half-hour. 'Look, I won't mention this again, but will
you give thought to what I say?'

'Spell it out,' said James ominously. 'Spell out for me
what you have against her.'

Sam hesitated, his mind whirling with visions of her
claw-like hands and bony chest. He could hardly quote
those as objections, and it would sound mad to talk
about her eyes. 'She's too fond of her own way,' he
muttered, 'and she watches everything like a hawk.'
Lord, it sounded so weak, and James was holding his
mouth in the way that meant he was upset.

'Rubbish!' he said now, 'utter rubbish! She's the
easiest person in the world. She falls in with my every
suggestion, and she's told me herself that she wants to
see everything we do at home so she'll know exactly
how I live and be able to have things as I like them
when we're married.'

Sam gnawed at his lip. He knew he wasn't wrong, he
just *knew* it, 'I'm sorry, James,' he said lamely. 'I – well
– I think a bit about you, you know, and I can't stomach
the thought of you being managed and manipulated.'

That had slipped out, and it was too much. When
James replied his lips were drawn back from his teeth
and for the first time in his life Sam heard in his brother's

voice the echo of their father. 'That will *do*, Sam! Listen
to me. I love Esther and she loves me. She's good,
she's kind, she's beautiful and – and she's virtuous. I
will marry her, and that's an end to it. The subject's
closed!' And James, quiet gentle James, whirled off up
Peter Street with the pale sheen of anger on his cheeks
and his coat-tails flapping.

Sam sighed wearily. A fine mess he'd made of that.
Well, let him get on with it, the fool. He'd learn the
hard way. It was a pity nobody else in the family
shared his doubts, because he could have done with
some backing. Even Sarah, usually so like him in her
reactions to people, seemed quite taken in by Esther.
He turned to go back home and then hesitated. James
was in love, and men in love weren't noted for listening
to anyone finding fault with the woman they'd chosen.
It felt really bad to be at odds with him. On impulse he
hurried after him and caught at his arm. 'I apologise,
James. I was misguided in trying to interfere. I don't
know her as you do.'

'No, you don't,' agreed James heavily. 'I'm sure you
mean well, Sam. You're mistaken, that's all.'

'Yes. Maybe I am.'

An uneasy truce between them, they crossed the dark
waters of East Brook to where the roads were unpaved
and deeply rutted. Ahead stood a tall gateway set in
a high stone wall, the entrance to Soar Hall, one of
Lord Soar's smaller properties; he had given it to the
town for use as 'a place of recreation'. Like many of
the townsfolk, the brothers liked to view the laying-out
of Saltley's first public park.

Few had ever set eyes on the Earl and his family. It was
said he had a huge place beyond High Holden, and some
sort of castle up in the Border country between England
and Scotland, not to mention a house on the moors in
Cornwall and another not far from the pottery towns.
Those who regarded a trip to Manchester as a great
adventure were awestruck that one man should own

houses all over the country. Others, more worldly-wise, pointed out that as he had all those houses it was an economy to give one of them away, and Sam was inclined to agree.

As they approached they saw the usual group of watchers at the gates; those who wandered the streets every day, and a few at leisure just for the weekend. As the brothers joined them there was a respectful murmur and a doffing of hats. Room was made for them at the front, but without undue fuss. Everybody knew there was no side to Joshua Schofield, nor his two older sons, for that matter. As to the youngest, Master Ralph, nobody knew much about him, but then he was hardly more than a lad.

Labourers were still hard at work inside the grounds, levelling a great sweep of gravel from which public walkways were being laid across the park. The grass was amazingly smooth and velvety, broken by banks of flowering shrubs whose tops caught the soft dark gold of the setting sun. It was a scene of deep peace and tranquillity; the workmen were silent, handling their rakes almost in unison, like men of the fields making hay.

One of the watchers spoke up. 'The new pleasure-boat arrived this afternoon, Mr James. It were on a long wagon pulled by six horses.' There was pride of ownership in his voice, and the others understood and shared in it too. It was their park now, their lake, their pleasure steamer.

James answered them with interest and civility. 'You saw it arrive, did you? That was a bit of luck. I've heard the *Chronicle*'s running a competition to find a name for the steamer – and there's a cash prize. You'll have to see what you can come up with, all of you.'

The man laughed self-consciously. 'Nay. Some of us aren't all that good with fancy words.'

'Oh, I don't think it will need to be fancy. Just a name that sounds right and sticks in the memory.

Catchy, you know – something that has a ring to it.'

The man fell to muttering with his companions, while Sam nudged his brother. 'If you're not careful they'll have you writing out their entries.'

'Well, I could do that,' said James thoughtfully. 'It would be a good thing if somebody without much learning could win; it would encourage all the others.'

'I was joking,' said Sam reprovingly. 'There'll be enough to do getting production under way again. I tell you what, I could have a word with Johnnie Stephens at the *Chronicle* and ask him to tell his man on the counter to fill in people's entry forms if they can't manage on their own. Would that help?'

James beamed. 'Of course it would. Thanks, Sam.'

It was there again, the closeness between them. 'Jimmy,' Sam muttered. 'About – about what I said just now. Will you forget it?'

'It's forgotten,' agreed James soberly. 'Look, I've noticed many a time how you can always come up with an idea, like about the *Chronicle*. Have you given any thought to the future of Jericho?'

'You mean as far as the family's concerned? Yes, I've thought about it now and again. Why?'

'Well, Father's set on having this family conference, you know. I think he's going to sound us all out on how we think the mills should be run. And the farm and the pit.'

'He's not going to hand over the reins, surely to God? As far as he's concerned we're barely out of the schoolroom!'

'No, nothing as dramatic as that, but I think he's after a different approach, a different way of running things. He wants us to take on more responsibility.'

'Well, well,' said Sam, somewhat stunned. 'Things are looking up.'

There was a stir of activity inside the gates. A cart, laden with planks of wood, was being drawn across the grass in the direction of the lake. 'That timber were cut a while back,' announced the same man as before. 'It's for the landing stage, where we'll all wait for a ride on the steamer.'

James heard him, but his attention had been caught by a man standing silently by the hinges of the right-hand gate. He was young and dark, wearing an old wide-awake hat and a red neck-band. 'That's the chap from the cotton-wagon,' he told Sam, 'the one Father was telling us about, who's come all the way from Devon.'

Sam nodded. 'I remember.' He eyed the man, who stood out in that company like a goldfinch in a gathering of sparrows. 'You haven't left Saltley, then?' he asked him with interest.

The man shook his head and smiled. 'No, Mr Schofield I'm still here, as you can see. I've given myself six weeks to find work, and there be five more still to go.'

Sam stared at him, relief mingling with approval. This one could look after himself.

CHAPTER THREE

New Beginnings

IT WAS ALMOST MIDNIGHT, but Matthew was still lying awake in the barn. He was hungry. After three weeks in Saltley it was clear that his savings wouldn't last if he was to eat, and the temptation was always with him. A cold pie . . . a plate of hash . . . a saucer of strawberries . . . a gill of milk.

Twice he'd joined the throng at one of the food centres. Watching from the gate of the yard he saw that those with relief tickets had to queue through a maze of stout railings until they reached the serving tables; anyone with money could go to a hatch in the wall. They gave him a great bowl of soup for a penny, but on his second visit he was questioned briskly as to where his relief was paid; when he admitted it was his own money he was asked to buy food elsewhere.

As yet he'd earned only coppers, and those by being quicker than the gaunt folk who waited for odd jobs in the centre of the town. He'd been paid for shifting the mess after a sale of cattle, and for helping to clear the dung-heap from the side of the Old Cross Inn when it blocked the path for all who wished to pass by. They were tasks that left him stinking and finally out of pocket because he needed to visit a bathhouse, and then, wearing his clean clothes, take the filthy ones across the West Brook to find Fanny Bright's laundry. That used up his earnings, but at least he was clean. And as he lay in the darkness he fingered his one extravagance, bought from a packman – a new neckcloth in dark blue dotted with little white stars. He hadn't been able to resist it, because it put him in mind of the night sky seen from the peep-hole of the sleeper all those years ago. The silence of the vast dark heavens and the remoteness of the glittering stars had always brought him comfort and tranquillity. Not so the moon, whose self-satisfied Fat Annie face had filled him with resentment as a boy and dimmed the radiance of the stars. He would lie on his stomach, neck twisted to watch the dark infinity above, but if the moon sailed there he felt thwarted.

There was no moon on his new neckcloth, and there must be no more spending on impulse until he was earning, and very little even then. By now he knew the whereabouts of every mill and workshop; he had visited outlying farms and tried for work at the local pits; approached gangs of road-workers and spoken to the man in charge at the new public park. The answer was always the same: 'We're settin' our own on first, lad.' And a few days ago, when he tried for a floor-cleaning job at the Salter's Arms, the landlord said quite kindly, 'I don't take gypsies on for indoor work, young fella.'

Sometimes, in spite of his resolve to hang on for six weeks, he was minded to go back to the Manchester docks or over the hills to Yorkshire, but his streak of obstinacy pulled at him to stay. Things would improve. One by one the mills were opening up, and those that had struggled along on inferior Indian cotton were preparing to change back to American as soon as deliveries improved and the price dropped.

He shifted in the straw, recognising a change in the weather. A draught whistled through the timber cladding at his side and he heard the first patter of raindrops. If the spell of fine weather was at an end it would hardly be worth his while to make the long climb up here, despite the welcome solitude of the barn. Besides, rain would finish his boots. They were already so far gone as to be past mending, and the old-clothes shops had yielded none to fit him. He would have no option but to lay out for new ones, because although he'd been brought low in the past he hadn't gone barefoot since he was thirteen.

Matthew stiffened as the barn door was unlatched. So far nobody had discovered him because he always slipped away at daybreak, and the farm dogs had merely sniffed at him and wagged their tails. Then he heard a woman's low whisper and the answering voice of a man. It was a couple, come here to be alone! He heard them climb the five steps to the raised platform where he lay concealed behind bundles of straw. The boards creaked under him as they took the weight of the new arrivals.

Tightness in his chest and a drumming in his ears told him that he was neglecting to breathe. What should he do? Stroll out from his hiding place, raise his hat and step over them? God above, he would have to stay where he was, next to grunting and wrestling and ugly postures that in the past had turned his stomach. He was eight years old when he first saw it, and his mother had been dead for exactly eight weeks. It was his birthday; he wakened late in the evening, crying for her, telling himself that he'd been one week without her for every year of his life. He heard sounds across the landing, and wet with his tears, went to see if his little sisters were awake. They were fast asleep, but light gleamed from beneath the door of his father's room, and there was the noise of movement within. He eased the latch noiselessly, as he used to do when he crept in to see his mother, and when he peeped through the crack he saw his father with the woman who came to help in the house. Her name was Mrs Shore, and she was here in his father's bedroom.

At first he thought she was attacking him, and he wanted to rush in and join her, because he didn't like his father; then he saw he was mistaken. They were both without clothes, locked together in a kind of frenzy, with Mrs Shore sitting astride his father in a position similar to that of the victor in a fight between two boys.

He watched them for a moment longer, amazed at the sight of her plump bare buttocks, then he saw that his

mother's blue bedspread had been kicked to the floor
as the two of them threshed on the bed. Fear caught at
him, followed by a sickness that was deep and painful,
wrenching at his innards. He crept back to his room
and vomited into his chamber-pot, then climbed into
bed, shivering and listening. A long time later he heard
footsteps go down the stairs and the back door being
unfastened.

Since then he had witnessed the sexual act many
times. Mrs Shore became Mrs Raike, and then the
Widow Raike, and in time the unofficial whore of
the Mizzen Mast, her bulk increasing with the years.
Matthew had watched her with her clients, had even
cleaned up her bed before the younger ones could see it,
and hidden away the leather thongs she kept for the two
sailors she referred to as her 'specials'. He had surprised
the inn's maids in the stables with traders and draymen,
and once he saw two vagrants locked in mindless union
beneath a Devon hedgerow in the moonlight. Now he
was to witness it yet again.

This time, however, there was no giggling, no drunken
horseplay. It was so silent he risked a peep between the
bales; by the glow of a lantern he saw the farmer's wife,
tall and slender with her hair unpinned and falling like a
dark cloud to her waist. She was kneeling upright, and a
man he didn't know was facing her with his head bent to
kiss her small breasts. It was a silent caress, gentle and
deliberate, but imbued with a passion that seemed all the
more intense for being devoid of any urgency; it was as if
they wished to savour each act before proceeding to the
next. When the man's mouth moved lower and he drew
her down to lie on a shawl, Matthew turned away and put
his hands over his ears. If there was to be grunting and
gasping he didn't want to hear it. It was their moment.
Let them have it to themselves.

He was well aware that they were committing adultery.
He had watched the place from the hillside and knew
the farmer to be stout and grey-haired, given to flashes

of temper and outbursts of cheerful singing. The man now making love to his wife was fair and sun-tanned; no youth, but well into his thirties or even older. More aroused than ever before on seeing a man and woman making love, Matthew lay there with his hands over his ears, and stayed that way until, much later, a rush of damp air announced the opening of the barn door.

It was almost dawn when the echo of a long-gone conversation came to him. Old Peggy-oh had found him white-faced and furious after Fat Annie had neglected to conceal one of her paid sessions from his sisters, and had put an arm round him. 'Try to remember it's not always ugly and lustful,' he'd said quietly. 'Folk say it's wonderful, and I well recall a little lass I would have wed if she'd have had me. It was a glimpse of heaven when we lay together, Matthew. God willing, it'll come to you one day.'

A steady drizzle was falling and the watchers at the gates of the new park drifted away until only Matthew was left. He couldn't have explained the compulsion that drew him there day after day, nor said why it pleased him to see the expanse of green and the massed banks of flowers and shrubs. It couldn't be that it brought back happy memories of his time at Ryder Hall because he hadn't been happy there – far from it. But as he watched the gardeners trimming the verges and staking top-heavy perennials he had to admit to missing the rich red earth of Devon, which was strange when he recalled that on his last day at Ryder he had scrubbed his hands savagely in the rain butt and vowed that he would never again lift a trowel.

The earth up here wasn't red, but black and peaty; in fact to the west of the town lay a great stretch of peat moss known as 'the Bog'. Matthew had been there in search of work, but found only a desolate morass where narrow paths straddled the black mire and solitary birds called from stunted hedgerows. Old men were there, cutting peat for fuel; someone had drained a section to grow vegetables, because it was fertile, like all the land hereabouts. Now he decided that the beauty of the park owed as much to the quality of the soil as to the skill of those who worked it.

His daily visits were giving him an insight into the change-over from private grounds to public park. He had walked the perimeter fence and stealthily climbed trees in order to see what was going on inside; from a wooded knoll he studied the long crescent of the lake and the fat little steamboat that was destined to provide rides for those who could afford them.

There was a sense of urgency inside the gates today. The foreman was bellowing more than usual and some of the gardeners had been taken from their tasks to help re-load a wagon of timber that had overturned on its way to the lake. Matthew watched in puzzlement. Could none of them see that it was unstable? Two smaller loads would in the end take less time and be far safer. As if in line with his reasoning the lengths of wood squeaked and shifted. The horses neighed in fear, and as a middle-aged workman ran to quieten them the timber shunted sideways. The man cursed and jumped clear, but another who was trying to fasten ropes across the top of the load slithered awkwardly to the ground. With a clatter the lengths of timber crashed down on top of him. As the last one landed all that could be seen was the sole of one wet boot beneath the piled and criss-crossed heap.

It was the boot that sent Matthew into action. It was full of holes, worse even than his own. He shinned up the tall gates and jumped down inside them to the gravel, then joined the others in freeing the man beneath the wood. He wasn't dead. The very nature of the weight – long, separate spars – had been in his favour.

The foreman seemed more upset at the delay than at the injury to one of his men. 'Clear the wagon and lie him flat,' he ordered irritably. Then he flipped a hand at the driver. 'Take him to the doctor. Over the brook – the big red house on the corner. Leave him there and come back right away. We're short-handed.'

A grey-haired man spoke up. 'Happen we should let his wife know, Mr Nuttall? He lives on Rope Street.'

The foreman sighed and nodded. 'One of you can go and find her later. Open the gates! You'll have to take it steady – he looks in a bad way. Right! Back to work all of you, there's no time to lose.' He remembered Matthew and turned on him. 'You know how to shift yourself, me lad.'

Matthew had scaled the gates with no thought other than to be of help, but he knew an opportunity when it stared him in the face. He touched his hat respectfully. 'I could see you were pushed for time, that's why I lent a hand. I'm a trained gardener and I'm used to handling timber. Can I replace him?'

The cart creaked away with the unconscious man lying flat among the wood-shavings, while the foreman sighed again and eyed Matthew narrowly. 'I'll take you on for the rest of the day,' he agreed reluctantly. 'If you're as good as you make out I'll keep you on. If not you finish at dusk. You'll get labouring rate until I see whether you can tell a daisy from a delphinium.' He flung his arms wide. 'Well, set to, all of you! His Lordship's due at three o'clock! Now, you, what's your name?'

'Matthew Raike.'

'Well, Raike, my name's Mr Nuttall, and I'm in charge here.'

'Yes, Mr Nuttall, I can see that,' answered Matthew politely.

It was seven o'clock on a Friday morning. From the bedroom of Meadowbank House Joshua Schofield looked out and was relieved to see a pale, cloudless sky. Bad weather in summer always dismayed him, and they'd had a fortnight of it. Damp was all right in the mill, but he liked to see the sun in his own back garden. He was in trousers and undershirt shaving himself, and as always talking through the lather; behind him Rachel was sitting up in bed sipping tea and listening, her calm intelligent gaze fixed on his reflection in the looking glass.

They both valued this time together each morning, with Joshua tossing off ideas and proposals as soon as his feet touched the floor. Schemes sprang from his mind like seeds sprouting in fertile earth, but Rachel knew that his keen business sense discarded most of them as not worth cultivating. Over the years he had come to value her opinion; they discussed most things together, so that now he could leave a sentence unfinished and know she would follow his meaning.

With a tap on the door Ellie the housemaid staggered in with a pitcher of hot water. 'Leave it, Ellie,' instructed Joshua. 'I'll pour it when I'm ready.' The girl bobbed her head and scuttled out with the distinctive rocking gait of the badly bowlegged, and Joshua sighed impatiently. 'That child looks petrified whenever I open my mouth.' He tapped his head. 'Is she all right up here?'

'She's bright enough considering she's one of only four left out of a family of sixteen. She's getting on well. Just give her time.'

'I'll give her time if she'll stop looking at me like a startled rabbit. And what about her legs? They're past getting right, I suppose?'

It was Rachel who sighed now. Did he ever miss anything? There were dozens of children with malformed limbs coming back to work in his mills, and he probably knew who they were and who were their parents; but even here, at this hour, and in the middle of talking about something else, he'd noticed that Ellie was bowlegged. Not that her legs were visible, because she was in her working skirt which was only inches from the floor, but he'd seen the sideways roll. 'They're bad,' she agreed, 'but she's still growing, so there's always the chance they'll straighten out a bit now she's better fed.' She was reluctant to discuss Ellie and her legs, because she

wasn't yet ready to face the day. This was their very own
quiet time, their talking time, when she liked to have her
husband to herself. Once outside this room she would be
gobbled up by the problems of all the Ellies of Saltley,
but here she was still Rachel Schofield who loved her
husband and children and could stay in bed for another
ten minutes if she chose.

Their room was at the rear and it gave the illusion
of being part of a country dwelling. No buildings or
mill-chimneys could be seen from the tall, lace-curtained
window; just trees in summer leaf at the end of the
garden, and beyond them plump meadows rich with
buttercups, crossed by the road that led out of the town.
Country-born and bred, Rachel loved that room with its
view of the fields. It gave her more than bodily rest after
a busy day, more even than the deep satisfaction of the
marriage bed; it refreshed her spirit to be free of the stink
of mean streets and the clamour of Jericho Mills, and it
rested her mind when she saw that little road winding
its way to the hills.

There was something on her mind now – something
that needed talking over with Joshua. She wasn't sure
how to broach it, because although they were at ease
with each other on any other subject this was a tricky one
– their youngest son. When it came to discussing Ralph
they could talk for an hour without saying anything of
significance; circling and skirting and coming out with
platitudes. Sometimes she wondered if they kept to
the surface to avoid uncovering their deepest fears,
and then she would pull herself up. What were their
deepest fears? She couldn't have put her finger on one.
He was obedient. He was healthy. He applied himself to
any task that was set him. He attended Albion Chapel
with the rest of them. What was she worrying about?

Rachel looked at Joshua's rear view, and for the
thousandth time acknowledged her good fortune in
having him. He was clever of course, everybody knew
that, and he had more than his share of energy; but he

was also an individualist with his own unusual ideas on
everything, including the handling of his children, and
by the greatest good fortune his views on that coincided
with her own. Current theories on disciplining the young
meant nothing to him. He had rarely raised a hand to
chastise any of them, and yet they leapt to do his
bidding. He saw them as separate people with their
own personalities, and whenever possible refrained from
imposing his will on them. That in itself was unusual in
Saltley, and she was thankful for it.

She stared absently at the movement of his shoulder
muscles under the soft undershirt. He was telling her
about the new lay-out in the cardroom at Jericho, but
her attention wasn't on what he was saying. With a start
she found the keen blue gaze holding hers through the
looking glass. 'What is it?' he asked, swinging round.
'What's on your mind?'

'Ralph,' she said simply.

'Again?'

'Yes, again. I can't help worrying about him, Joshua.
He's always been quiet, I know, and a bit wrapped up in
himself, but since he's turned seventeen he's been more
– well – haven't you noticed?'

'Noticed what? That he never takes his eyes off me?
That he keeps his face as blank as a cut of calico? That
he's taken to prowling the house at night and opening
doors without a sound? Aye, woman, not being blind,
I *have* noticed!'

'Joshua!'

'I'm sorry, love, but what do you take me for? One
talent I do lay claim to, and that's noticing what goes on
around me. It's what you might call one of my natural
advantages as a man of business, and it's stood me in
good stead over the years.'

'That's what I mean,' agreed Rachel, ignoring the
fact that she'd meant nothing of the kind. 'It's not only
that, though. I can't talk to him. He's closing up, and
I don't know what he thinks or feels. It's like having an

acquaintance in the house, a polite, handsome boy that
I don't know very well. I think he's deliberately shutting
us out.'

Joshua came and sat on the bed, pulling off her
nightcap and twirling her heavy plait in his fingers.
'Perhaps we're taking it too seriously, love. He's never
given us any trouble, after all. He's more sensible than
Sam, and every bit as conscientious as James, and we
know he's got a good head on his shoulders. It's a funny
age, seventeen – no longer a child and not quite a man.
We shouldn't expect an exact replica of the other three,
should we? Nor of us, come to that.'

They both stared at the window as if for inspiration,
joined in silence by a sense of unease about the boy.
He'd never been a carbon copy of the others, thought
Rachel, never. She couldn't recall him ever giving her a
kiss or a cuddle, even as a toddler. The others had clasped
her round the knees or caught at her skirt as soon as they
could walk, but not Ralph. Sam and Sarah's bed-time
prayers had been a high-spirited babble, and those of
James a long, earnest petition; but Ralph's had been a
calm, dutiful recital, with never an unnecessary word,
and afterwards never a proffered hug. She had accepted
years ago that this one of her children was different; not
as open as the others, and not as easy, but of late his
manner had become almost unnatural.

Joshua was absently unplaiting her hair and she
reached up for his hand. 'I know it sounds silly but I
keep feeling he despises us.' She waited for his robust
denial but to her dismay he said nothing. 'You think the
same!' she said bleakly.

'No, I don't. Not for a minute. What I do think is
that we're making too much of it all. In fact, I've been
wondering if he feels a bit inadequate and left out, being
the youngest. He has a different nature from the rest
of us, a different temperament. I think he needs more
to occupy his mind, and tomorrow night we'll see what
we can do about it. When I was his age I was working

a sixteen-hour day and learning accounts in my spare time, while yond' mon just shoves his head in his books and then walks the town, with folk bowing and scraping to him. It's not enough.'

'But you wanted him to have a year without responsibility.'

'I know I did, but I might have been wrong. If he has any ability it can be put to the test, and he'll have no option but to speak if he's giving orders to somebody. I've made up my mind that they're all going to play a proper part in everything – the mills, the farm, the mine, and all the other pies I have a finger in. Leave him to me, love. I'll sort him out.'

He could still banish her worries, if only temporarily. She pulled his head down and kissed him, getting a smudge of lather on her chin. With a chuckle he wiped it away and said, 'Don't give me ideas. It's time I was off down the road.' He finished dressing, and then said, 'About this family get-together tomorrow night. I want to make it a new beginning, for all of us and for Jericho. Let's make it a bit of a do, shall we? Esther should be here as she'll soon be one of the family, and I'd thought of asking Charlie. What do you think?'

She accepted Charlie Barnes because he'd been Joshua's friend for more than forty years and knew almost as much as he did about the mills, but to have him here with the family? She wanted no outsider witnessing Ralph being 'sorted out'. 'Let's have just the family, Joshua,' she said gently. 'You can discuss things with Charlie beforehand, and afterwards as well, if you like.'

'Aye, maybe you're right. You'll fix something special, then?'

'Yes,' she said, smiling. 'Down you go, or Hannah will be coming up here with your breakfast, thinking you're still in bed.'

That tickled him, and he left the room in high good humour.

*   *   *

'He likes William, Tizzie, I know he does. But what about Mother? She hardly says a word.' Mary pulled on her nightgown and began to brush her hair without removing the pins. 'Oh, what am I doing?' She snatched them out and in her haste knocked the pin-box on the floor. Scrabbling on hands and knees she looked up at her sister. 'What do you think, Tizzie? As – as a detached observer, what do you think?'

Tizzie was sitting up in bed, making a pretence of reading. 'As a detached observer,' she said drily, 'I think Father approves of William, but for once Mother is opposing him.'

Mary leapt on the bed and clutched her sister's hands. 'She asked him in, though. Don't forget that.'

Tizzie sighed. She seemed to be spending every minute of every day discussing William, and she had more important things to think about. Twice he had accompanied them on their Saturday evening walk, and the third time, this evening, Mother had asked him in for a bit of supper. Hadn't Mary noticed that Father had been wearing a good suit instead of the usual black trousers and linen jacket? And what about the dainty jellied pies from Bellmans and the home-made sponge cake with strawberry jam, and the best china that had been washed during the afternoon and then left out instead of being put back in the cabinet? Was she really so busy goggling at Bull-beef that such things escaped her?

'Mother had planned to ask him in,' she said wearily. 'She's not blind. She knows quite well how you both feel, and she intends bringing things to a head so they'll have an answer ready if William proposes.'

'You mean "when",' corrected Mary quickly. 'When he proposes.'

'All right. When.'

'But it's just guess-work, Tizz. You don't *know*, do you?'

Tizzie managed a tight little smile. 'I think you'll find

I'm right. Come on, I'll brush your hair for you.' She knew she was right because last Tuesday when Mary was out at the food centre she'd overheard her parents talking in the back room of the shop. Restless and idle, she had gone down to ask if she could help with the books, and must have missed the start of the conversation. It was the tone of her mother's voice that had halted her outside the door. 'You what?' she had heard her say sharply, 'but I thought we said we'd wait until we move to Manchester. You know I want them to have a chance with Manchester men, rather than those round here. And surely we should see Tizzie settled first?'

Then her father's voice, firm but very gentle, so that Tizzie wondered if he was grasping her mother's wrist in that familiar, idiotic gesture. 'Look, Maria, I've told you before that we can't move to a new shop till things pick up. Manchester is still on its beam-ends, and I can't move yet.'

'But a butcher!' Mother's brisk, sensible tones were reduced to a disappointed wail. 'I've always seen professional men for them, Abel. A lawyer, perhaps, or an architect, or an engineer on the railroad.'

'Listen to me. We aren't the only ones with daughters to marry off. They're fine girls, both of them, but let's keep our feet on the ground.'

'He hasn't even got his own shop yet, and when he does our Mary will end up scrubbing it out and sprinkling sawdust from a bucket!'

'She could do worse. Have you forgotten sorting rags in Miller's shed, ready for the shoddy-man? Old Hartley is well thought of in the town, and remember this: people have to eat. Haven't we learned they'll pawn their trinkets, their bedding, even the clothes off their backs in order to feed themselves? And when they've got ready money what do they buy? Meat! That's what they crave, meat. Now look, this town will be on the way up again once the mills are back in production. If that lad gets a shop in a good position he can't fail to do well unless he's either lazy or a complete fool. From what I hear he's not lazy, so just bring him to me and I'll soon weigh up whether he's a fool. It'll be time enough then to talk about letting him marry our Mary.'

'But you won't encourage her, Abel? She's got eyes for nobody else, and I don't want her encouraged.'

'No, I won't,' replied her father; and then, amazingly, 'but I know exactly how she feels. Have you forgotten, Maria?'

There was a long pause, and Tizzie stepped back so that if the door should open she could pretend she'd just come down the stairs. When at last her mother replied she hardly recognised the voice. It was flat and very quiet, with an odd edge to it. 'I haven't forgotten anything, Abel, anything at all. You should know that by now.'

When the door opened Tizzie was halfway down the stairs. 'Come with me, my girl,' cried her mother, rushing upstairs and bundling Tizzie in front of her. 'There's mending needs doing this morning.'

Tizzie said nothing to Mary about what she'd heard, because she liked the feeling of power that came from keeping it to herself, and in any case she was sick of hearing William's name. There was another reason for keeping silent, something she couldn't have explained. It was to do with that sense of groping towards a meaning that escaped her, of there being something between her parents that was out of sight, glimpsed and then submerged beneath the commonplace words and thoughts of every day. One moment her mind pounced on this nebulous thing and then when it gained shape and form it was swept away out of sight. Once, long ago, before the first drains were laid, she and Mary had seen a chequered pot-towel swirling along the Town Ditch after falling in one of the soughs on Peter Street. They saw it, and then it was gone, making her wonder if she had really seen the flash of red and green on creamy cotton. From time to time that image came back to her, of something submerged that should be clearly visible, and always, in her mind, she linked it with her parents. Beyond that she couldn't go. Hers was a mind that grasped facts and figures, that liked things clear-cut and definite.

As for the bit about her mother sorting rags for the shoddy-man. . . . That was new. Her parents said little about the early days of their marriage, beyond a hint or two that they had worked hard; but sorting rags! Tizzie wrinkled her nose in distaste. Old rags had the same smell as the destitute folk who begged for coppers near the market, and those who gathered by the tally bridge. It was amazing that Mother, clean, brisk Mother, had sorted them in Miller's shed. Tizzie had heard of that place, it was down by the canal at the bottom of Gallgate – a haunt of the destitute and those too weak to walk the streets.

She pondered on what she'd overheard, but soon her mind went back to her own problems. How could she have been so slack as to let Mary beat her to it? Oh, she could find excuses: she'd been brought up to obey her parents; she'd been waiting until they moved nearer Manchester; there was a shortage of suitable young men in Saltley – at least a shortage of those who were willing to be linked to the pawnshop. Yes, she could find excuses, but excuses wouldn't get her married and away from the three gold balls.

'Tizzie, Tizzie! You aren't listening!' Mary was sitting in front of her on the bed, hair neatly plaited but her nightgown still unbuttoned. 'I've been telling you about the empty shop near the market-place. You didn't hear a word I said, did you?'

'Sorry. My mind was elsewhere,' she said unrepentantly. How could she reorganise her future if she had to listen to every doting word about Bull-beef? It looked as if she would have to confine her thinking and planning to the hours of night. Later, with Mary fast asleep at her side, she reviewed what she had accomplished in the last few weeks. Not much, she had to admit. She hadn't shown by look or deed that she was stunned by the way things were going with Mary and William. She hadn't said a word about being determined to find herself a man within the month. Her mother would have thought her forward, and in any case she didn't want to be fobbed off with just anything in trousers. But she had met a man who fitted her requirements – perhaps even surpassed them. It had been at the Subscribers' Rally for the new Infirmary. They had gone to the Town Hall in a hired carriage, because of the rain, with Father making one of his rare public appearances as he intended to subscribe to the Fund. There had been a good turn-out of townspeople, all anxious to see and be seen, but it was no local man who had taken Tizzie's eye. Edward Mayfield was an architect with the firm commissioned to design and build the new Infirmary. He was up on the platform with Lord Soar's son Francis, who they said was a Viscount but who was called Lord Alsing; the fat little Mayor of Saltley, Eli Walton, was also there.

Tizzie saw at once that Mr Mayfield was quite unlike the men of Saltley. Next to the platform were ranked the business families: the Schofields, the Boultons, the Dobbs and the Fairbrothers. Most of their menfolk were well set-up, and all of them well-dressed, but to Tizzie they looked cloddish and lacking in style next to the young architect. She thought young Lord Alsing could have done with a brush-down to remove dog-hairs and the odd hay-seed, and his clothes were no more than country tweeds, straining across his plump form. By comparison Edward Mayfield looked as if he had just left his London tailor. He was wearing a lightweight coat and waistcoat in pale fawn; dull cream linen and a bronze silk necktie; shoes of soft brown leather. . . .

Tizzie sat between Mary and her father and was able to stare at him without losing the modesty that her mother prized so highly. He was very slender, with a long, narrow face that was tanned to a pale, even gold. His hair was light brown and wavy, worn longer than was customary in Saltley; and this, combined with the sun-tan, gave him a slightly theatrical air. Tizzie wriggled restlessly in her seat. Was it just the set of his brows that gave him an air of surprise? Or was it that he couldn't quite believe what he was seeing in this grim town where the most impressive architecture was that of the great mills, where the majority of the population were under-fed and wore rags that were often sodden from the rain?

Tizzie was even more intrigued when he spoke, inviting all subscribers to examine a model of the buildings. His speech was so different. It was, it was cultured. She sat up straighter. How fortunate that she was wearing her new blue-green poplin. It showed off her hair, and emphasised what she saw as her main asset, the creamy, unfreckled skin so unusual in a red-head. As he spoke his expression was candid and interested, and she saw that his eyes were almost perfect ovals; but what was their colour? She couldn't see from where she was sitting, but as he surveyed his audience they lingered for a moment on her. And quite deliberately, he smiled. It was just a little quirk of the lips, but she saw it, and felt a distinct thud in the centre of her chest. She just managed to stop herself clapping a hand to it, and thought: so that's why women in paintings are always clutching their bosoms. Perhaps the heart really is the centre of feeling. . . .

Then the speeches were over, and everyone was making their way to the ante-room where the model was on view. 'Tizzie! Did you see him?' Mary was chewing her lips with excitement and her hand was hot as she clutched her sister's arm.

Tizzie's mind was still on Edward Mayfield. 'I certainly did,' she replied. 'Quite a change from the locals.'

She realised her mistake when Mary stared at her blankly. 'I meant did you see William,' she said reproachfully. 'Who are you talking about?' Then the brown eyes widened. 'You mean the architect, don't you?' she hissed. 'Tizz-wizz, do you like him?'

Mother was within earshot, and so was Father, dressed in his best and looking less insignificant than usual. 'How can I like him when I haven't even met him?' she whispered. 'But yes, he does look interesting.'

Mary stared over her sister's shoulder and clutched at her arm again. 'Tizzie! Here's William!'

Tizzie gritted her teeth. 'I'm just about to examine those sketches,' she said shortly, greeting William with the briefest of nods. 'I'll leave you two to yourselves.' She saw that her parents had moved to the table where pledge cards were being filled in, but Edward Mayfield was nowhere in sight. Surely he should be making himself available to answer questions about the new building?

She moved along the display boards, waiting for him to put in an appearance. She was determined to seize this chance to meet the kind of man who interested her, and if possible to do it without her mother breathing down her neck. She concealed an expectant little smile. This close-packed throng, the grand room with its tall windows and chandeliers, the air of excitement around her. . . . She couldn't have chosen a better setting for the start of a new chapter in her life.

Then her attention was caught by a chart showing several sets of figures. It proved to be lists of estimates for the cost of every aspect of the new Infirmary – drains, buildings, fittings, equipment. . . . She studied it carefully. It came to just less than fifteen thousand pounds. She moistened her lips. Very impressive. A man working on a commission of that size must be earning a considerable fee.

A voice spoke in her ear. 'I'll be glad to explain any part of our financial estimates.'

She turned slowly, savouring the moment. 'Mr Mayfield,' she said with a small smile. 'I've been studying your estimates. Saltley isn't exactly thriving, so do you expect to obtain the full amount from donations?'

She saw that the eyes were hazel; a light golden-brown, flecked with green. They were observing her with keen interest and some surprise. 'Most ladies are interested in the appearance of the Infirmary rather than its cost,' he said slowly.

It was a reasonable enough remark for him to make, but in spite of her lack of experience with men Tizzie read into it what was undoubtedly there. A prelude to flirtation. She opened her beautiful eyes very wide, and blinked her lashes slowly. 'But I'm not most ladies, Mr Mayfield. I'm me. Elizabeth Ridings, better known as Tizzie.'

He pursed his lips into a soundless whistle. 'Miss Ridings – ' he acknowledged, sketching a small bow. A man touched his shoulder and murmured, 'When you're ready, Edward,' but he shrugged him away and continued without pause, '– better known as Tizzie. In answer to your query, yes, we do hope to raise the full amount from public subscriptions. In spite of Saltley having fallen on lean times things are about to improve, so they tell me. Those concerned with such matters are anxious to keep pace with other towns of similar size throughout the country. Do you know of anyone wishing to make a donation?'

'My father is making his pledge at this very moment,' she said calmly. The man hovering at the side of them coughed and shuffled his feet. Tizzie could have kicked his legs from under him, but managed to remain pleasant. 'Don't let me detain you, Mr Mayfield,' she said smoothly. 'I'm sure you have a great deal to attend to this evening.'

'Not sufficient to prevent me furthering our acquaintance, I hope,' he said, and with another inclination of the narrow head, allowed himself to be led away in the direction of his model building.

Tizzie thumped her pillow restlessly and stared at the glimmer of fading light between the heavy curtains. Her parents had acted as if she was a fallen woman when she suggested that they linger until Edward Mayfield

was free of his questioners, and had hustled her and
Mary into their wraps and outside without allowing so
much as a blink in his direction. She hadn't been unduly
upset at the time. Her mind was so full of how easy it
was to meet a man and keep her wits about her, that it
was only later she wondered how her mother imagined
she would get to know these mythical men of better class
if she didn't let her speak to any of them. The feeling of
let-down came later, as the endless days dragged past.
She'd been certain he would contact her. Anyone could
have told him who she was and where she lived.

Now, a week after their meeting, she was forced to
ask herself the same old question. Had the fact that she
was the pawnbroker's daughter put an end to something
that had barely begun?

CHAPTER FOUR

Martha

A GALE WAS BLOWING, wild and unseasonal. It had started in the night, making the hut groan and sway with each blast of the wind.

Matthew shifted on his bed of sacks. He was supposed to guard the place – that was why he was here – but he wasn't sure if he could guard against the roof blowing off. He chuckled at the thought of Know-all Nuttall's face should he arrive to find his labourer's hut floating in the lake. There wouldn't be much to laugh at if such a thing did happen, because Nuttall was a nasty one, and close-fisted with it. They all said he couldn't have been meaner if he was paying them out of his own pocket. Matthew was getting paid the labourer's rate of ten and six a week; yet Nuttall used him on heavy carpentry on the landing stages and as an extra gardener on the flower beds and roses, both jobs at a higher wage.

He was guarding the hut because first of all a rip-saw had gone missing and then six cleats. They'd expected Nuttall to go down with a stroke, because the blood had surged to his cheeks and forehead and his eyes had bulged in disbelief. For a moment he was unable to speak, and then he'd ordered them up in front of him one by one, cross-examining them and making them turn out their pockets. 'If I wanted to help meself I'd take summat from what's left of the kitchen garden to fill me belly,' Billy Warhurst told Matthew wearily, 'not steal a bloody great saw and half a dozen stays.'

It became clear that somebody had forced the lock

of the shed during the night. A pair of trousers had disappeared, along with three knives and a spoon and a piece of fruit cake from Nuttall's tin. He was livid with rage, but the men weren't surprised. What did he expect in Saltley? It seemed a bit daft stealing a rip-saw, but if you knew somebody who was after one and would ask no questions it could bring a fair sum. . . .

Nuttall addressed them all as they clustered in the hut for their half-hour break at noon. 'Right. I'm willing to accept that none of you are implicated,' he bellowed briskly. 'I reckon it was some unprincipled scum who got in during the night. So I've decided that what's needed here is a night-watchman to sleep in this hut, do the rounds of the glasshouses and potting-sheds, and keep an eye on things in general.'

'You mean you're taking somebody else on, Mr Nuttall?' asked one of the men.

'No I am not! But I'm willing to let one of you sleep here, rent free, in return for guarding the tools and keeping an eye open.' As he spoke the rain drummed on the roof and then pinged into a bucket placed in a corner to catch leaks. There was a smell of damp sacking and wet earth. The men coughed and shuffled their feet, but nobody spoke.

Nuttall waved a hand at a rusty stove set on a slab in one corner. 'I'm told this here stove worked well enough when a forester lived here some years back. There's a few off-cuts of wood to spare, so it could be lit for an hour now and again.'

One or two of the men looked thoughtful at that. Clothes could be dried off round a stove. A can of water could be heated on top of a stove, or maybe a frying-pan. . . . Matthew spoke up before any of them were tempted further. 'I'm willing, Mr Nuttall. I'll guard the place.'

The foreman eyed him with his hostile, watery stare. 'Raike? Aye, you'll do. You're a fair size if it should come to a dust-up, and you're a single man, aren't you?

Bear in mind, though, when I say night-watchman I mean
night-*watchman*. What about your things?'

'I bring my bundle with me every day, Mr Nuttall.
It's by the door here.'

'Right. You can start tonight. I'll tell you your duties
later. Now I'm making no charge for this accommoda-
tion, Raike.'

One of the men gasped and coughed loudly into
his fist, but Nuttall ignored him. He was waiting for
thanks. He was expecting it. And Matthew was willing
to oblige him. He'd spent a night at Billy Warhurst's
house, sharing the one bedroom with four sickly children
and an aged mother, and sleeping on clean straw on
the floor. Next morning, breakfast was watery porridge
made from Indian meal; then Billy, highly embarrassed
and prompted by his wife, asked him for tuppence for
his board and lodging. Matthew hadn't been paid his
first week's wages then and was down to his last few
coppers. He looked at the children, sitting side by side
on the floor, with the baby in a wooden box in front of
them. They were all silent except for the wheeze of their
breathing, and embarrassed in his turn that he couldn't
make it more, he handed over the two pennies. Later
that day Billy invited him back again, but he made the
excuse of having booked lodgings elsewhere. Earlier this
week, after a day of torrential rain, he'd laid out another
threepence for a bed in a lodging house. It had been
good to have a roof over his head, but the smell of wet
clothes and sweaty bodies had outweighed the comfort of
the mattress, especially when he found it came complete
with bed-bugs.

Oh yes, he would keep an eye on the tool-shed, and
he didn't mind saying thank you for it. He'd learned long
ago that words were cheap, and with such as Nuttall you
didn't have to mean them. 'Thank'ee kindly, Mr Nuttall.
I'm obliged,' he said politely.

So here he was, installed as night-watchman, and it
wasn't turning out too bad. He did his rounds last thing

by the light of a lantern, and then settled down among the sacks. If the morning was fine he was wakened by the clamour of the dawn chorus, and almost before it was light he would be having a wash in the sparkling little stream that fed the lake. Then he would put on a dry shirt and socks and the strong boots he'd bought with his first wage, and sometimes, if the stove had stayed in, he had hot water for a shave; that was a luxury he'd never enjoyed at Ryder Hall. He'd been given a key to a door in the wall, and could come and go as he wished. Most mornings he went out to the baker's and bought a buttered muffin, and he planned to buy a pan so he could cook himself bacon or a piece of belly pork for his breakfast. Already he had an enamel plate and a mug, and Jonas Carter had given him a knife and a spoon. Oh, to be sure, things could have been worse. . . .

The wind was rising to a scream, and beyond it he could just make out the note of the half-past five blower from Greenbank Mill down by the brook. Here in the park they started later on Saturdays, at half-past six instead of six o'clock, so he had an hour before Nuttall began his daily bellowing. On impulse he decided to go out and buy a good breakfast. He had a few coppers left, and he would get his wages later in the day. Ten minutes saw him washed and dressed. Another ten and he had done the rounds of greenhouses and potting sheds and stacked timber, finding no signs of a break-in; the only damage from the gale to be a cold-frame broken when the branch of a tree had come down on it during the night. Head lowered against the wind, he skirted the grove of birches and went out through the wall to make for the centre of Saltley.

Once outside the park it was worse than he expected, and when he reached the pavements the shriek of the wind was far louder than the clatter of clogs. Mills were slowly opening up, and each week they were taking on spinners, winders, weavers and the like. It was only his fancy, of course, but when someone left a terraced house to head for the nearest mill it seemed as if the great red building held the very essence of safety and prosperity. It would take more than a gale to bring down one of those places, he thought. He'd heard something of cotton from his workmates, and he knew that wages for skilled operatives made those at Soar Park seem like hand-outs from the relief. After all, that was why he'd come to Saltley, to join the best-paid workers in England.

The road climbed a little, and when he reached an exposed section the blast nearly knocked him off his feet. Away to his left he heard a crash and a frightened shout, and guessed that slates were being ripped from the roofs. Guilt nagged that he'd left the park. What if damage was being done there at this very moment? It was hunger that forced him to go on. He would buy a muffin with crispy bacon and a piece of fried bread, and return at once, eating as he went. In front of him he could see a child battling against the blast, her small clogs seeming barely to touch the ground when the wind buffeted her and whipped her striped skirt round her ankles. She forged on doggedly, a basket of some sort clasped in front of her and a light shawl wrapped tightly round her head. It looked as if she was making for Jericho Mills, whereas most of the others were turning off towards the gates of Boulton's.

All at once there came a gust of wind so powerful it made a bang like a clap of thunder. The child's skirt billowed out. She was lifted up off her feet and blown basket and all against the wall of Boulton's weaving shed. Matthew heard the smack of the impact and she fell face down on the earth. Two women started towards her, then seeing Matthew's approach struggled on their way, arms around each other for safe anchor.

The child didn't move when he reached her, so he tried to raise her up. She was surprisingly heavy, and he bent lower to slip his arms beneath her. It seemed quiet now he was down on his haunches out of the wind, and he spoke against her ear. 'It's all right! Don't be frightened.

The wind took 'ee, that's all.' She made no response. He bent lower, not sure if she was conscious or not. He was so close that the smell of her came to him, faint and fleeting, and then it was blown away. It was a clean smell – soap and starched cotton, and a hint of lavender. He shifted his grip to turn her over, grasping the narrow ribcage; and his hands encountered the unmistakable swell of breasts. This was no child! He'd better prop her against the wall and get a woman to see to her.

He rolled her over on to her back, and at once she struggled to sit up. 'I'll be late!' she gasped, and then looked into his face, only inches away. She stared at him, dazed, and rubbed her shoulder.

No, she was no child. She was a young woman whose age could have been – what? Somewhere between sixteen and thirty? Fine brown hair showed beneath the head-shawl, and she had a small, bony face with skin like smooth parchment. It was an ordinary face, with grey-blue eyes and a straight nose; a plain, prim little face but with a mouth that was full and soft, giving a child-like cast to its old-young setting. Her forehead was bleeding where it had struck the wall. She put up a hand to it, staring at the blood on her fingers, and he saw that she wore no wedding ring. A chord of memory sounded in his mind. Did he know her? Had he seen her somewhere? 'The wind blew 'ee across the road,' he said simply.

The girl, or woman, searched a pocket in her heavy apron and found a calico rag. She pressed it against her head and scrambled to her feet. She was very small, inches below his shoulder; for some reason she seemed to be staring intently at his neckband. 'I'll be late,' she said again, and picked up her basket. 'Thank you for – for seeing to me.'

He grabbed her arm in warning. 'We don't want 'ee blowing away again. Do 'ee feel fit for work?'

She looked at him as if she didn't know what he could mean. 'I've only banged my head,' she said. 'I'm all right, Mr – '

'Raike. Matthew Raike,'

'I'm Martha Spencer.' She hesitated, then spoke in a rapid gabble. 'I have to go, but thank you again. Look, I know this woman coming up – she runs the looms next to mine. I'll hang on to her.'

Almost as if she were being pursued, she rushed and grabbed the arm of a well-built woman coming towards them, and with a quirk of the lips and an awkward little nod to Matthew, trudged off up the road. He watched as they bent forward against the wind. She was a strange little thing. And where was it he'd seen her before? He couldn't remember, but he'd better move, or he wouldn't have time to get himself some breakfast.

The stall-holders were lighting their lamps beneath a sky streaked with the last remnants of bronze. Few signs of the storm remained, apart from a pile of broken spars where stalls had been blown away and smashed. Saturday night was busy, because people had just been paid and were buying in for the coming week. Women were examining the produce, keen to get good value, while in the shadows nearby stood those on relief payments, waiting for traders to sell off stuff cheaply, rather than have it left on their hands.

Matthew walked along feeling well-pleased and well-fed: a tasty breakfast first thing, a mug of milk and a tea-cake at mid-day, and just now a dish of hot black peas and a pint-pot of tea from Dolly Redfern's hut. It had been a good day. Even Know-all Nuttall had been reasonable for once, and quite unperturbed about the broken glass in the cold-frame. 'An Act of God, Raike,' he said grandly, lifting a hand palm upwards. 'We can't prevent damage by tempest, and we've got off light compared to some parts of Saltley. Remember this though, the work of the Almighty is one thing, but somebody stealing from the Borough – and from me – is another. Keep your eyes open at all times.'

'Yes, Mr Nuttall,' agreed Matthew dutifully, adding

under his breath, 'as long as I can close 'em now an' again for a sleep.'

So with the prospect of a day at leisure on the morrow, his spirits were soaring. The crowd around him was noisy, shouting to each other and laughing. He tried not to look at the silent watchers grouped at the corner of Rope Street. There wouldn't be much laughter over there, nor in the black depths of Gallgate stretching behind them.

He was at the baker's buying a loaf and wondering whether to treat himself to a quarter of butter, when a small female figure at the next stall caught his attention. She was wearing a starched cotton bonnet and had a bandage round her forehead. It was the little Spencer girl, buying a dozen of flour. She looked worn out. Exhaustion showed in the way she moved her arms to pay the grocer. He recognised the economy of movement; remembering a time when to extend an arm an inch more than necessary called for energy that he dared not squander. Martha Spencer was in that state now. She wasn't up to carrying the flour.

Up to it or not, she dragged the small sack off the stall and hoisted it to her shoulder, then picked up her basket of shopping and turned away. Quickly he paid for his loaf, and their eyes met beneath the warm glow of the lamps. He touched his hat. 'Evenin', Miss Spencer.'

A dull flush flooded the pale cheeks. 'Mr Raike,' she said, moving her head only a fraction because of the weight at her neck.

Matthew pushed all his purchases into the string bag holding his frying pan, and without more ado lifted the sack of flour from her shoulder and slung it on his own. 'I'll just help 'ee with this,' he said easily.

She stared at him unblinking, and he wondered if it was anger that flared in her eyes and was gone. 'This is twice today you've come to help,' she said quietly. He noticed that she mouthed some of her words as if speaking to a deaf man, and he couldn't see why. 'I know it's too much to carry this home as well as all me other stuff,' she said hurriedly, 'but I wanted to save meself another journey.'

'Have 'ee far to go, then?'

'Ledden Street. Near where you saw me this morning.'

It was a fair step. Too far for her to carry such a load, however wiry she was. 'I'll just see 'ee back home, then,' he said. And because he was in good spirits and had money in his pocket, he smiled down at her. 'Would 'ee care for a cup o' tea at Dolly Redfern's?'

She stared back up at him with the same fixed expression. It was very intent, as if he spoke in a foreign language. Then to his deep dismay he detected the glint of tears. She blinked, looked away, and pulled in the corners of her pretty mouth. 'Not just now, thank you, Mr Raike. I have to get back.'

Together they crossed the street, and he felt a tightness build up in his chest as they approached the silent group at the corner of Rope Street. Children were there, and a woman holding a baby in her shawl. At her side were two little girls; one of them in canvas shoes and the other barefoot, holding hands as they leaned wearily against the wall. It was their bald-spotted heads that told him who they were – the two little maids who had followed the cotton-wagon the day he arrived in Saltley! They had smiled then, he remembered, and waved to him. And he had blown them a kiss. . . .

Martha Spencer was at his side, looking straight ahead and by now carrying only her purse and a cabbage. 'Would 'ee walk on a pace or two?' he asked her. 'I've just seen somebody I know.'

He saw doubt and disappointment in her eyes. They swivelled from side to side, seeing if assistance was to hand should she need it. He sighed. Did she take him for a ruffian about to run off with her shopping? 'Wait here,' he said shortly, and plonked her basket at her feet and next to it the sack of flour.

He left her standing guard over her purchases, and retraced his steps. The little girls watched him, eyes wide, and moved closer together when he squatted in front of them. 'Do 'ee remember me?' he asked gently.

The bigger one nodded. She might once have been pretty, he thought. 'You're the man on the cart,' she whispered.

'That's right. What are you both doing here?'

'We're with me mam,' she said, looking up at the woman with the baby, 'waiting till they start selling stuff cheap.'

'And when's that?'

'Ten o'clock.'

Matthew reckoned it couldn't be more than half-past eight. He stood up to speak to their mother. Dark-eyed and hollow-cheeked, she was watching him warily. 'They're wi' me,' she said warningly.

'I know. It be a long wait till ten,' he said awkwardly. 'Here, take this and get them a meal. Yourself and the baby as well.' There was a stir behind her as the others saw money about to change hands, so Matthew quelled them with a look.

'Have they axed you for summat?' asked the woman suspiciously, nodding at her girls.

'No. No, I just recognised them from my first day in Saltley.' He slid a shilling into her hand, and shuffled uncomfortably when she said chokingly, 'God bless you, whoever you are.' Her thin fingers tightened round the coin, but he couldn't leave until he had watched her to the brightness of the stalls and safe from any who might covet the shilling. Then he rejoined Martha. 'Somebody I recognised,' he said carelessly. 'Just as I recognised you this mornin', except I couldn't quite recall where I'd seen you.'

'At Jericho Mills,' she said promptly, and seeing his blank look, went further. 'Schofield's, the day the cotton arrived. You were standing by the lodge when I passed by with the dinner people.'

He could hardly say he didn't remember her. It would be insulting, and in any case not true, because he had known he'd seen her before. 'Of course. That's it!' he said cheerfully, and saw the tired shoulders straighten. He concealed a smile. Even this plain little soul liked to think she could mark a man's memory.

She was silent as they walked, except to make her only reference to him giving away money. 'You're in work, then.' It wasn't a question, but a statement, with no hint of curiosity.

Equally brief, he answered, 'Yes, of a kind,' and then smiled to himself for the second time, knowing he would have been ready to say far more if he'd been earning two pounds instead of ten-and-six. For an instant his mind lingered on what he could have done with the shilling he'd just given away on impulse; then he thought of the little girls, and their beaming smiles behind the cotton wagon. They had given him his first real welcome to Saltley. . . . Ah, let the mother have the shillin' and good luck to her! She needed it more than he did.

Ledden Street proved to be an improvement on some he'd seen. A dirt road of red-brick cottages, with neat sandstone arches above the doors and a line of scoured flagstones outside each house. Not downright ugly, like some, and there was no open drain down the street.

Seeing him assessing the terrace, Martha gave the twitch of her lips that he suspected might be a smile. 'Schofield's houses,' she said with a touch of pride. 'Most of his are nearer Jericho, but he has a couple of blocks down here, as well. Thanks again, Mr Raike. P'raps – p'raps you'd like to come in for a cup of tea?'

He didn't want her thinking he was after free food and drink, and in any case he could see she wasn't too keen on him accepting; he felt a strong desire to set foot in a Lancashire home, though, almost as if old Peggy-oh was at his elbow, urging him on. After all, Martha Spencer's house could only be an improvement on the Warhursts'.

'Well, just for a minute, then,' he said guardedly, 'and thank'ee kindly.'

He had known she was clean from when he was close to her that morning, but even so it came as a shock to walk straight in from the dirt road to the smell of soap and the faint scent of flowers. Inside was a very small woman backed by pillows in a long cane chair and sitting next to her a gaunt old man with only one arm. When he put down Martha's purchases and removed his hat they both stared at him as if he was a visitor from another world. His string bag containing the frying pan made a metallic thud as it hit the table, and there in the centre of the scrubbed boards was a little blue jar. That explained the scent of flowers – it contained sprays of fragrant bedstraw and a few bright moon daisies.

He glanced at Martha, confused by his own surprise. Why shouldn't she pick flowers to put on the table? There would be little enough of beauty around her. . . . And why had he a tightness in his chest? And why – But she was speaking now, with the same odd, unblinking stare in her eyes.

'Mother, this is Matthew Raike, who helped me when I was blown off me feet this mornin'. He's just carried me things home.' She turned to Matthew. 'This is me mother. She's an invalid. And this is me Uncle Jack.'

Mrs Spencer was eyeing him closely. She had the same pale skin and neat features as her daughter, but the eyes were darker and sunk amid black shadows. She wore a lace cap on her head and a grey woollen dress, and over her legs was a faded red blanket. She nodded to a wooden stool by the table. 'Sit you down, lad. We've been waiting for our Martha comin' in so we could have a brew. I expect you could do with a cup?'

'Yes, thank'ee Missis, but I mustn't stay.'

'Why, have you somebody waitin'?'

'Uh – no – but I don't want to take up your time.'

'Well, a sup of tea won't take all night, will it? Jack here's ready for his tea.'

The old man nodded. 'I'm ready for my tea,' he repeated obligingly.

Was he one of those in their second childhood? Matthew wondered. The old fellow's hand plucked aimlessly at the buttons of his shirt, and his head wobbled on the scrawny neck. There was a flash of interest in his eyes, though, and when he spoke it was sensible enough. 'Are you in work, lad?'

'Yes. I was lucky to be set on at Soar Park.'

The wavering gaze steadied. 'What, labourin'?'

'Yes,' admitted Matthew, 'and a bit of gardenin' and carpentry when it's called for.'

'I heard tell a young fella was killed there a week or two back.'

'Yes. I saw it happen, though he didn't die until next day. His name was Dancer. A load of timber fell on him.' He cleared his throat. 'I was given his job, as it happens.'

'Norman Nuttall took you on?'

'Yes. He was left short-handed when John Dancer had the accident.'

Uncle Jack chuckled, and it wasn't a pleasant sound. 'I've no doubt you're enjoying working for Nuttall?'

If there was one thing Matthew had learned in his search for work it was caution. This old chap might well be a friend of Nuttall. 'It's a job,' he said quietly, 'an' it pays a wage. I was lucky to get it because I'm not from these parts.'

The old man nodded. 'We're wary of outsiders,' he agreed. 'We've had to take on that many in the past. Boat-loads of Irish, farm-hands from the south, cart-loads of paupers. Aye, they used to bring 'em in over the Pennines in carts – child paupers, and the cotton-masters had to take one imbecile to every twenty as were normal. Them as survived are full-grown now, and fighting for work like the rest of us. We've had us fill of outsiders in times gone by, lad, that's why we don't welcome strangers.'

'I can understand it,' said Matthew. 'I'm not complainin'.'

'It's no good complainin',' barked the old man suddenly. 'The next shift's waitin' to go down. If you don't like workin' wet take your money and clear off, and make room for them as aren't frightened of a bit of water.'

Martha turned round from the fireplace. 'Uncle Jack was a miner,' she said quietly. 'That's how he lost his arm. His mind comes and goes, like.'

Matthew smiled reassuringly. If she didn't sit down soon she'd drop in her tracks, by the looks of her. When she poured the tea and had given her mother and uncle theirs he jumped up so she could have the stool, because there was no other seat in the room; Mrs Spencer waved him back again. 'She can perch on here,' she said, patting the end of her chair. 'We've come down a bit, but we don't have visitors standing in this house, do we, Martha?'

'No, Mam. Not unless we have more than one at a time.' It was a joke, of sorts, and because she looked too far gone for humour Matthew laughed, just to please her. From being a young-old woman of uncertain age, she seemed in the company of these two to be like a girl still in her teens. He took in the details of the room whenever he felt he was free of their eyes. Whitewashed walls and a flagged floor, well-scoured; a black grate with an oven to one side and a small fire that had boiled the kettle for their tea; a curtain let in the inner wall, concealing what was probably a bed, perhaps for the mother. Apart from the two chairs, the stool and the table, there was only a small chest of drawers against a wall, Over it there was a picture in a gilded frame, showing a man in an old-fashioned uniform bidding farewell to a young woman beneath an apple-tree laden with blossom. He was impressed. It was a fine painting, and he wondered where it had come from; perhaps it was of sentimental value to the Spencers, as it hadn't been pawned. He finished his tea and got to his feet, reluctant to leave but anxious not to outstay his welcome.

'I'll be on my way, then,' he said, picking up his hat and his purchases. 'Thanks for the tea.'

'And thanks for helpin' our Martha, Mr Raike,' said Mrs Spencer, wagging her head so hard that her little lace cap fell askew. 'You're welcome to come again if ever you're passing.' Uncle Jack stared vacantly into his cup, and said nothing.

Matthew didn't want to go. 'Twas a fact, he didn't want to go. All at once he felt a tugging sensation behind his ribs. He must be hard up for company, that he should wish to linger with a worn-out little creature like Martha, an invalid woman with a brisk tongue, and an old, one-armed man who was a bit weak in the head.

Martha said good-night at the door, giving him a twitch of the soft lips and looking more exhausted than ever. He held out his hand in farewell. 'Good-night, then, Miss Spencer.' She laid her small hard hand in his, and he shook it, as if they were two men of business sealing a bargain; then he set off for Soar Park. The prospect of his cosy bed among the sacks and being wakened at daybreak by the blackbird's song held none of its usual appeal. Was it the clean house that had unsettled him, and the smell of soap and the flowers in the little blue jar?

Matthew unlocked the gate in the wall, and thought of his plans for next morning. He was going to make a little cupboard to hold his belongings. He would have to hide it from Nuttall, of course, because he would use odd bits of wood that he'd hoarded during the past week. If it was fine maybe he would take a walk through Saltley in the afternoon, to see folk out in their Sunday-best.

It was starting to rain by the time he reached the hut.

CHAPTER FIVE

The Jericho Rose

AT MEADOWBANK HOUSE THE dining table had been cleared and left bare but for a bowl of red roses in the centre and a pencil and paper at each place, for all the world as if a business meeting was about to begin. That was how Joshua wanted it. He had also wanted 'a bit of a do' and so Rachel had provided one – a splendid cold supper that had taken hours to prepare.

There was beef cut wafer-thin with young beetroot, a ham roasted in honey, jellied chicken pie, a vast green salad, home-made pickles and relishes and the little crusty plaits of bread that Rachel could bake to perfection. Then there were shortcakes topped with strawberries and thick cream, Alice's special iced sponge cakes, port-wine trifle and a variety of cheeses. The table looked lovely, and Joshua, called in to inspect it, had brought seven red roses and laid one beside each plate. When they sat down Esther enquired as to their significance; he chuckled, patted her cheek, helped himself to pie and said, 'Wait till we have our little discussion, my dear, and then you'll find out. . . .'

He had even provided champagne, a rarity in that Methodist household, chilling it on ice sent over from Joe Chadwick's ice-house. He was in such good humour that Rachel made a pretence of enjoying it to please him even more, telling herself it was an over-rated drink if ever she'd tasted one, and warning Alice on the quiet to make plenty of good coffee.

Now the younger ones murmured together restlessly, stimulated by the unaccustomed champagne, edgy about their futures, and confused as to what they were supposed to be celebrating. Joshua, always one for a spot of mystery and excitement, revealed nothing; he paced the room in silence, waiting for Rachel to come back from sending out the food. It was family routine that after a good meal anything that remained when the servants had eaten was despatched at once to the needy, a process laid down years before by Joshua. He had been carving a saddle of lamb at the time, and waved the knife in support of his idea.

'Things are bad in Saltley and I believe they'll get much worse,' he announced baldly. 'Now, we eat well here because I have the means to buy, and we get stuff sent down from High Lee. My stomach craves good food and so does my brain – it seizes up when I'm famished – but your mother and me can't rest easy if we all feed our faces while folk go hungry less than half a mile away. I'm told by those who should know that the war in America will be over and done with in another six months, so until we're back to normal we'll do our best for those who need most help. Eat your fill, all of you – you'll never see food come back a second time to this table!'

What began as a six-month conscience-easer had been established practice for two-and-a-half years. Food at Meadowbank remained plentiful, but gradually meals became plainer except on special occasions. Alice and Hannah loaded baskets each day under Rachel's supervision, and the food was sent where she decreed. The family didn't question it; nor did Esther, though Joshua knew she could have seen few acts of charity at home, as her father was known to be a close one with the purse-strings.

Apparently deep in thought as he walked back and forth, Joshua was observing his offspring closely. He'd been right, it seemed, to have a private word with each of them beforehand. They seemed a bit on edge, and that was what he wanted. He'd given them champagne to lower their guard and loosen their tongues, though he'd had to watch what they put away as he didn't want them muddled with drink when it came to a sorting-out.

He noted the faint flush on Ralph's normally pale cheeks, the constant nervous shrug of Esther's narrow shoulders. And James? – well, James looked as if he'd lost a guinea and found a sixpence, sitting there patting Esther's hand as if his mind was miles away. Sam and Sarah were muttering together as always, but for once without that ridiculous giggling. Maybe tonight Sam would be serious, and show he could talk sense. As for Sarah, once or twice of late she'd given him a look, had that one. Not pert or rebellious, like Eli Walton's two little madams, but cool – that was it – cool and somehow assessing, as if she was taking his measure. Still, she was almost grown-up, with friends who were already married. Was that what ailed her? Had she got her eye on some young fella? If so Rachel could have no idea of it or she would have told him, but it might be no bad thing for Sarah to take an interest in somebody besides her brother. Lord, but she was a picture sitting there in her new pink dress with her hair gleaming under the gaslight – uncannily like her mother at the same age.

Obediently his memory brought forth a well-loved image – Rachel as he'd first seen her, in a blue cotton bonnet and a gingham dress, carrying a milk-pail across the yard at High Lee Farm. That had been thirty years ago, with him twenty-five to her eighteen; at first he'd taken her for the dairy-maid rather than the only child of a prosperous farmer. He'd fallen in love with her before she so much as set eyes on him standing at the gate. It had always pleased him that he'd wanted to marry her before he knew she wasn't just a skivvy in the dairy.

Joshua eyed Sarah as he turned on his heel in front of the sideboard, and had to admit that she lacked what her mother had had, even at eighteen; a strength that had shown itself in the line of her mouth and the set of her head; an inner strength that had appealed to him just as much as the smooth sun-kissed skin and the amazing silver-gold hair and the shape of her. Sarah had inherited the looks, but did she have her mother's character – or her father's, come to that? Joshua pulled in the corners of his mouth, knowing the answer. She'd had it too easy, he told himself for the thousandth time, and so had her brothers. How could he expect them to be fighters when they'd never had to battle for anything because it had been handed to them on a plate?

'That's done,' said Rachel gently, coming in and giving him the warm little glance that she kept for him alone. 'Alice will bring the coffee in later.'

He waited until they were all back in their places, enjoying the uncertainty and anticipation on their faces. Just in time he stopped himself rising to his feet to address them. He'd warned himself beforehand to keep it informal, but it was hard to make an announcement other than on his feet.

'Well, you all know why we're here,' he said. 'It's to decide on a new way of running the family businesses. I've kept things pretty close and in my own hands these last few years. James here has known more than any of you – him and Charlie – but there's a lot I kept up here,' he tapped his head. 'I've given the matter some thought, and I believe I've been wrong there. Yes, wrong! There's no need to look goggle-eyed at that, Sam. It's a poor man as can't admit a mistake, and a rare man who never makes one. However, before we get down to talking things through I want to tell you about one of my final decisions.'

Sam shifted back in his chair, eyes alert. Surely he wasn't going to take a back seat, and him only in his fifties? Uncertainty gripped him and brought an empty, sinking feeling to his stomach. None of them knew enough to take over; between them they didn't know a tenth of what his father knew about cotton, or mining, or farming for that matter. His eye let on Esther's and he groaned inwardly at the intent glitter he saw there. Why didn't she lick her lips and have done with it?

But Joshua was still going on. 'I'll tell you in a minute how we've weathered the last few years financially, but first I want to show you my little idea, I hope the last decision I will make alone. It's my tribute to the people of Lancashire.' He picked up a folded cloth from beside his chair; clasping it to his chest, he went on, 'You all know how they've earned the admiration of the entire country for the way they've conducted themselves during the cotton famine? And a couple of years back Lord Shaftesbury paid them a fine tribute in words – you're aware of what he said. Well, as Schofields' salute to their fortitude I've come up with this!'

With a flourish he unrolled the bulky cloth across the table in front of them and they all stared down. It was a newly-stitched version of the flag from the mill-tower at Jericho – the golden trumpet that sounded the name of Joshua Schofield throughout Lancashire and the world of cotton – the symbol that was recognised by illiterate labourers and wealthy cotton brokers alike. It was a long, slim, biblical sort of trumpet on a backgound of cool grey-blue, but now there was a red rose superimposed over the long tube of the instrument

In spite of his resolves Joshua was on his feet. 'The red rose of Lancaster,' he said with satisfaction, 'the Jericho Rose. Well, what do you think of it?' The shrewd blue eyes were assessing their first unguarded reactions. From Sam, there was what looked like unwilling admiration; from James, a slow nod of the head as if to say, 'Yes, it's another bright idea.' Sarah, all at once his little girl again instead of that distant young woman, was beaming in generous approval, bless her; while Esther looked puzzled and a bit disappointed. Surely in a business family she'd learned the importance of a distinctive trading symbol? And what about Ralph of the unrevealing features? Joshua drew in his breath. There was scorn in those usually blank eyes; aye, and

contempt. Rachel was right. He *did* despise them all!
For a moment Joshua was at a loss. Did the lad think
his father was some bungling amateur? Didn't he know
that the trumpet trademark was instantly recognised by
shippers the world over?

Joshua glanced at Rachel and lost the thread of
what he'd planned to say next. She'd seen it too;
that flash of impatient disgust on the fair, clean-cut
features of their youngest son. Belatedly his natural
belligerence surfaced. 'You don't approve, Ralph?' he
asked shortly.

Ralph smiled his rare and quite beautiful smile. 'On the
contrary, Papa, it's very impressive. I did wonder though,
just for a second, whether it was worth demeaning your
own instantly recognisable symbol for the sake of mere
sentiment, that's all.'

Sam leaned forward at that. His face was the only one
of the four set in his father's rough-hewn mould, and now
it was red with indignation. 'I hardly think Father built
up his business on sentiment, Ralph! I don't believe the
rose detracts from the trumpet, either. It shouts out loud
Lancashire, and Cotton, and Schofield, and I for one
think it's good. It wouldn't surprise me to see a white
rose blossom before long on Wadsworth's worsted over
in Bradford, or on the Priestley Brothers' flagpole in
Huddersfield.'

Well, well! Joshua watched the two of them with
interest. There were times when young Sam showed a
likeness to himself at the same age. And Ralph? Well,
Master Ralph had reverted to the blank-eyed stare, with
only the tucked-in corners of his mouth betraying any
reaction to his brother's outburst.

Joshua sat down. 'Approve of it or not, it's going
ahead,' he said with satisfaction. 'I've given orders for
the new mark to be stamped on all bales bought for me
in America, before it's shipped across. I'm having nobody
profiteering out of Schofield's, trucking and trading in
raw cotton, re-shipping and buying back and all the other

tricks they get up to. Brokers, merchants; I tell you, if
I had the time I'd sort that lot out – I wouldn't part.
But I won't dwell on it. Let's get down to what we're
here for.'

Looking round at their expectant faces, he said, 'Now
you all know what I want: to find out which aspect of
Schofields appeals to you most. The British sales and
import/export in Manchester, and without that the mills
couldn't exist, don't forget; or Low Lee mine, without
which we'd have to buy in coal to run the mill engines
and lose a sizable income from selling it locally. Or High
Lee Farm and all the land and property up there. It's the
farm that's helped to feed us in the last few years, and
the workers too, come to that; though the villages are
Lord Soar's, we own the land bordering his, and houses
here, there and everywhere. And then, of course, there's
Jericho Mills.' Without realising it he stroked the fabric
of the embroidered flag that still covered the table in
front of him. Rachel quelled the urge to lean across and
give him a kiss, and contented herself with folding the
flag and laying it carefully to one side.

'I want to bring you all in and give you responsibilities.
Forget about the allowances you're getting – they'll finish
as of the end of the month. You'll get good pay if you
earn it, and a share in the profits. But first you must tell
me what appeals. Just as – ' he lowered the piercing blue
gaze for an instant – 'just as you must tell me if you want
no part of it. Oh yes, I've given it some thought and I'm
not taking anything for granted. If you leave the firm
I'll support you for your first year, and after that you're
on your own. So let's not mess about. We're all family
here. Let's have an open discussion.'

There was silence for a full half minute, then Ralph
leaned forward, hands clasped neatly in front of him. 'But
I thought you were going to tell us about the finances,
Father. "How we've weathered the storm financially"
was how you put it.'

'Oh, so I did. I'm getting ahead of myself.' They were

all waiting, so he jumped to his feet again, informality forgotten. 'In plain words, another three months without cotton would have finished me. I'd have lost the mills, the Manchester holdings, the mine and maybe even this house. Not High Lee, mind. That was your mother's inheritance and I kept it safe. And I wouldn't have let myself be declared bankrupt; no, I couldn't have that, dragging other folk down with me; I didn't fancy a spell in a debtor's prison, either. I would have sold up and withdrawn from business in a proper manner, with my debts paid and my conscience clear; the day for that was fast approaching, I can tell you.' Then he shrugged his shoulders with the hint of a swagger. 'But it hasn't arrived. The cotton's come through again, and we'll soon be in full production.'

There was complete silence round the table. Joshua glanced at Rachel and for the second time in five minutes they joined in assessing the reactions of the young ones.

James looked stunned and acutely uncomfortable, while at his side Esther had lost colour. Lips tight, she sat bolt upright and dabbed at her mouth with a tiny handkerchief. Sam leaned back in his chair and eyed his father soberly, his expression guarded. Sarah's cheeks were deep pink, her eyes bright with tears. And Ralph . . . oh, this was the way to bring a reaction from the silent one, thought Joshua. A table-top conference, a glass or two of champagne, a bit of an eye-opener about money, and that blank, beautiful face was filled with an anger he couldn't conceal. Well, if he had something to say they were all ready to listen. Joshua shuffled the papers in front of him. 'Any comment?' he asked quietly.

Sarah gave a loud sniffle, and Sam leapt from his chair to her side. 'You should have told us, Papa,' she said tearfully. 'This – this dress! It's new, and it cost a lot. I could have done without it, or made my own. And w-w-what if we'd lost Meadowbank?'

Tears rolled down her cheeks and glistened in the gaslight.

Sam bent over her, his handkerchief ready, while Rachel hurried round the table. 'We haven't lost the house, love,' she said, holding Sarah close. 'And you haven't had all that many new dresses this year, now have you?'

Joshua watched his daughter. She might not have her mother's strength of character, but her heart was in the right place. Her first thought had been how she might have helped him. And what of the others? Sam there was bending over his sister, but for some reason watching Esther, and not looking too pleased at what he was seeing, either. James was saying nothing, but for once Ralph was in the mood to talk.

'You're not serious, Father?' he asked, his upper lip lifting from his excellent teeth.

'Well, I'm certainly not joking,' said Joshua shortly.

'But – but you're the leading manufacturer in Saltley!'

'Of course I am. There's nobody to touch me this side of Oldham. But it can't have escaped your notice that more than half the mills in Saltley have shut down their engines for good?'

'I know that,' said Ralph tightly. 'I know it quite well, but they were smaller concerns than Schofield's. I simply cannot believe that you've almost been ruined, and I'm sure the others feel the same.'

'Leading manufacturer or not, I couldn't have prevented it affecting me,' said Joshua, striving for patience. 'And as I've told you before, there's more behind the Cotton Famine than the Civil War. Cotton is money – big money, and – '

'I know all about that,' Ralph interrupted. 'In 1860 the turnover on cotton was six million more than the gross national product.'

Beneath his irritation Joshua felt a twinge of pride at Ralph knowing that. The lad showed signs at times, and at others was just a numby-head. 'What I was going to

say, Ralph, is that where there's money, there's greed.
Gladstone was right when he said the manufacturers
aren't without blame in this little lot. When there was
a glut of cotton they over-produced – me as well – but
I did see the light sooner than some of 'em. I never ran
my mills right round the clock. The more we cut prices
the more we sold, and the more we sold, the more money
we made. By 1860 a pound of flannel cost about three
shillings, a pound of linen two and fourpence, and a
pound of calico a shilling. We all thought we had the
world in a bant, but in spite of that some of us were
warning as long ago as '57 against relying over-much on
American cotton.'

He eyed his sons curiously. Surely they knew all this?
They'd listened to him over the dinner table for long
enough. But they were hanging on his every word. 'When
cotton became scarce and speculation pushed the price
up there were manufacturers in this town – men you
all know – who had stocks of cotton that would have
lasted their workers for weeks. What did they do? They
sold their own cotton at a vast profit and sent it out at
dead of night, with the wheels of the wagons muffled.
That's something else Gladstone got to know of. What
I'm saying is that the seeds of trouble were there before
ever Fort Sumpter was fired on. But when the blockade
took hold we were in real trouble, deep trouble.'

'You didn't adapt your machines to take Indian surat
though, did you, Father?' It was Ralph again.

'Take the shorrocks? No, I did not. To begin with,
West End of Jericho is geared up to take medium
staple, and East End for medium and long; shorrocks
is short, coarse rubbish, and would have ruined my new
machines. You won't find an operative in Lancashire
who has a good word for it. At its best it breaks if you
so much as look at it, and it cuts their hands to ribbons.
And when the demand for it went up the Indians sent
us the sweepings of the cotton bazaars. No, the only
folk who've done well out of the shorrocks are the

roller-makers. No offence, Esther, love. Your father supplied a demand, that's all. Anyway, we can discuss all this later. Right now I want to – '

'But Papa – '

Joshua stared at his youngest. They'd spent years worrying because he never opened his mouth, but just put the wind up him about money and there was no silencing him. 'Go on,' he said tolerantly, 'I'm listening.'

'You've almost been ruined, yet in the last few years you must have spent a fortune on the workers – hot dinners, soup kitchens, classes for reading and writing, letting them live rent-free and the rest of it! And they've been getting relief all the time.'

They all stared at him in amazement, while Joshua took a long, deep breath. 'Yes,' he said evenly, 'they got relief, most of 'em, like half a million more in the rest of Lancashire. But the Board of Guardians aren't known for their generosity, and even if they were they're not in charge of a bottomless purse. As an employer I've sat in on the Guardians, and seen them take just half a minute to decide if a man's entitled, and there's no appeal if they decide against him. If he protests about the amount they allow him, they say, "Take it, or we'll give you the House!" So, not wanting the Workhouse, he takes it.

'And don't forget it's not all in cash. Part of it's in kind – food tickets and clothes and such – and what cash they got would have been owing to me for rent if I hadn't let them off it. The riots in March last year were all about relief, and you might recall that armed Hussars set about folk who were only intent on feeding their families. So just watch what you say to me about relief.'

Joshua eyed his youngest keenly. 'I recall you tackling me about this a year or two back, Ralph; in case you've forgotten what I said then, I'll repeat a few things that must *never* be forgotten again, by you or by your brothers.

'Jericho workers are the best in Saltley – it's an accepted fact in the town. Long before the American war I had a waiting list of folk who wanted a job at Jericho. And for why? Because I pay a bit more than Eli Walton, and don't make them spend it at a tommy-shop? Because my weaving-sheds are more up-to-date than Johnny Fairbrother's at Greenbank? Because my cottages don't run with vermin? Aye, those are some of the reasons. Another is that in my mills they're treated like human beings, and they seem to like that. I can't think why, unless it's because they *are* human beings, the same as all of us round this table.'

Sam shifted uneasily at the sarcasm, and watched curiously for Ralph's reaction, but Joshua forged on regardless. 'They must be treated fair – common human-ity demands it, lad. I've said this before, and I'll say it just once more. The men, women and children in Jericho Mills are *our bread and butter*. Treat them fair and they work well. Treat them harsh and they'll be unwilling and filled with resentment.'

Ralph sat facing his father, his hands still clasped, his expression unreadable. Rachel tried to catch Joshua's eye, but there was no stopping him. 'Feed 'em in a famine and they'll live to work for you again. Ignore them and they'll starve. Good God, lad, where's your brains? You walk the town often enough – haven't you seen the graveyards overflowing? The living skeletons on the tally bridge and the women at the top of Rope Street, waiting for scraps from the market? Well, to the best of my knowledge there's none of them from Jericho.

'I'm not a walking charity, mind, and I don't get up and prate at Albion, nor thump the Bible at every turn. I demand a day's work, and hard work at that, and if they don't like it they can take their pay and clear off. But I'll look after them, Ralph, if it takes my last penny. Because I know what it's like to be one of 'em. I started in the mills when I was seven, don't forget; believe me, it's no picnic!'

James, always the peacemaker, spoke up. 'I'm sure none of us would dream of criticising you for looking after the workers, Father. It's a bit of a shock, that's all, to find you in such a bad way financially. We'll all have to buckle to and help from now on.'

Joshua was unappeased. 'Oh, aye? Who's first with their offer, then?'

Once again it was Ralph. 'As I seem to be lacking in concern for the workers, perhaps I should keep clear of them and volunteer for Manchester. It's what I've been wanting, anyway. I study the markets, I know something of overseas trade – I've been an observer at the Exchange. That's what I would like, Papa. To go to Mosley Street.'

'Would you, now?' Joshua pretended to be considering that, while his mind leapt with relief at the success of his scheme. Who would have expected Ralph to hog the floor? They needn't have worried – he wasn't backward at coming forward when there was cause. 'Thanks, Ralph. Let's see what the others want and then you and me'll have a chat in the morning. James, you and Esther have talked it over, I expect?'

'Yes, indeed we have. But we didn't know about the financial situation, so maybe we should – '

'Never mind that. Your settlement's taken care of. In fact, a marriage settlement for all of you is safe and sound in a special account. Come on, out with it.'

James wriggled in his chair, but said doggedly, 'I've never been keen on the cotton, Father. You must have seen over the years that I have no natural ability in the mill. I detest the heat and the clatter and the dust. So when Esther and I get married we would like to move up to High Lee. You told me yourself that since Benjy Riddlesworth died there's nobody with real knowledge up there, and I'd like to do my best with it.'

Joshua gaped at them both. 'Leave Saltley? For High Lee? I'm sorry, Esther love, no disrespect, but I don't see you as a farmer's wife.'

'No, and nor do I,' said Esther, smiling gently. 'James wants to be more of a gentleman farmer, a sort of agent-manager. Like Mr Riddlesworth, but with the added authority of being the son of the owner.'

'So you don't want the farmhouse?'

'No. As you've so kindly set aside a sum for us, and my father has been more than generous, we have a mind to buy High Lee Court, and live there, away from the actual farm.'

Joshua flicked at his whiskers. He'd wanted a sorting out and he was damn well getting one! 'Right! James and Esther have stated their preference, and we'll come back to it later. Sam, what about you?'

'The mills,' said Sam flatly. 'And when I know the business from the docks to the cut-lookers' table you can give me lessons on the mine.'

Joshua let out a heavy sigh. He needn't have listened to the sour little inner voice that had warned him they would want no part in it. Of them all, Sam was probably the nearest to him in outlook, so perhaps it would work out well if he was the one at Jericho, providing he could cut out the skylarking. At that very minute he was nudging his sister. 'Just as well we don't all want the same, isn't it?' he said, and roared with laughter.

Joshua frowned. Couldn't he be serious even now, when his future was being decided? 'Well,' he said briskly, 'it looks as if we're getting somewhere.' He turned to Rachel. 'What about that coffee, love? I've got a pile of facts and figures here on how production's picking up.'

'And what about me, Papa?' Tears forgotten, Sarah was staring at him accusingly, lips jutting, hands clutching the edge of the table.

'What? How do you mean, love?'

'What about me? Aren't you going to ask what I want to do?'

That look was in her eyes again; cool, challenging, and defiant. He grappled with a sense of loss. What had happened to his little Sarah, always so willing, so eager to help, so biddable? 'I've told you before what a Godsend you've been to your mother and me,' he said reproachfully, 'helping with the schooling and the food centre. Now things are picking up a bit surely you can help your mother at home, and go visiting with her and suchlike?'

'No, Papa. That isn't what I want at all.'

He stared at her, baffled. 'Well, what *do* you want, then?'

'To be a probationer at Miss Nightingale's Training School.'

Joshua sat down and looked round helplessly at the door. Where was Rachel? He was sure she couldn't have heard of it or she would have told him. 'Sam, do you know about this?'

'Yes, I do, and I think it's an excellent idea.'

'But the Nightingale School is in London! Your sister can't go and live in London!'

'Why not? The young ladies are carefully supervised, and it's well known that Miss Nightingale herself has laid down the rules of behaviour.'

Joshua eyed them both. They were in accord on this, as on everything. 'I do read the newspapers,' he reminded them drily, 'and if I was pressed I'd admit to admiring the woman, because unlike some who've been born to privilege, she gets things done. I'm well aware that ideas on nursing are changing, but folk round here still see it as an occupation for – for women of low morals.'

'That's out of date, now, Papa,' said Sarah pityingly. 'I think it's a challenge. I like looking after people when they're ill.'

He recalled her busy in the bedroom when Rachel was laid up with a bad chest. 'You were good when your mother was poorly last winter,' he admitted, 'and I know you helped with Alice when she scalded her foot. But it's one thing to trot upstairs in this house with bowls of broth and egg custards on little trays, and quite another to cart off amputated limbs in buckets, or clean up the mess in a public ward after vomiting and diarrhoea.'

He'd wanted to shake her with mention of such things, but she smiled with amazing self-possession. 'I would be trained in all kinds of nursing, Papa, however unpleasant. Please, will you give it some thought?'

'Your mother knows nothing of it yet, young lady. Let's just say we'll look into it. I suppose you've enquired whether there's a school at the Royal Infirmary in Manchester?'

She exchanged a quick glance with Sam. 'No, we haven't. Not yet.'

Joshua shuffled his papers and stifled a sigh. The most obvious moves never seemed to occur to other people, not even his own children. 'Well, we'll find out about that,' he said, 'and then next year there'll be the new Infirmary opening here in Saltley. That'll be on the doorstep, won't it?'

'Yes, but if I'd already done my training I could be in at the start, and help to set it up.'

Joshua pulled at his whiskers, fast relinquishing images of his lovely daughter going out visiting with her mother, attending grand functions and meeting some bright, well-educated young businessman who would make her a good husband. While he recoiled at the thought of her in the unbecoming garb of a Nightingale nurse, he experienced a spurt of pure joy at her initiative, because he could see it was her own idea, and not Sam's. In his mind's eye he had pictured her, comely and content, in a fine house with a devoted husband and three or four young children at her knee. But like a shadow that suddenly dwarfs the substance, he saw her now calm and authoritative, unassailable; ordering the care of the sick in vast hospital wards, and speaking on equal terms with physicians and surgeons. Times are changing, he told himself heavily. Stick to the old ways and you'll stagnate, my lad.

'Leave it for now, and I'll talk to your mother,' he

promised. 'And the rest of you, when we've had that coffee you can concentrate your minds on a few facts and figures.'

With perfect timing Rachel returned, followed by Alice pushing a wheeled trolley. Joshua smiled at the sight of his wife. She was in for a surprise, all right.

'Martha Spencer?' The cut-looker eyed her up and down and rubbed a bony hand round the back of his neck. 'We never saw much of you in here in the old days. What's up? Lost the knack or summat?'

Martha shook her head and stared miserably at the cut of fine shirting from her No 2 loom, the flaw in it plainly visible in the light from the great window. 'No, Mr Lingard, I'll never lose the knack of weavin'. What I have lost, though, is a lot of sleep. I'd been up with me mother the night before, otherwise I'd never have let a float through. I'm very sorry.'

Harry Lingard folded his lips. He could count on the fingers of one hand the times he'd had to send for this one. Not like some of 'em who let faulty work through until they ended up with their name in his bad book. When that happened it pulled 'em up sharp, because one more time and they were given the sack, or in the case of women with dependants, removed from their looms and put on work at lower pay.

Unfortunately this little scrawn wasn't one to appeal to him – he liked them big. Not that he ever made suggestions to a weaver in so many words; but a thoughtful glance to where the book lay open on his desk, a doubtful shake of his head, and if there was nobody about it wasn't unknown for some of then to edge nearer, all worried like, and make it easy for him to fondle them.

He saw no risk in that, because he knew they would keep silent. The weavers were strong-minded women, and wouldn't hesitate to condemn one of their number who let it be known that Harry Lingard had handled her in the cut-room. Such moments brightened the day for him, especially when Lily Bracewell had to be sent for. . . . Ee, the times he'd examined her stuff twice over in the hope of spotting a float. . . . But the Spencer woman was waiting. He compared her small form to the big-bosomed Lily, and flipped a dismissive hand. 'You can't let troubles at home affect your work at Jericho.' he said shortly. 'That'll be sixpence you're stopped. And mother or no mother, don't let it happen again.'

'No, Mr Lingard. Thank you, Mr Lingard.'

She hurried back across the yard to the weaving sheds, her clogs clattering on the cobblestones. In the distance she could see Joshua Schofield and Mr Sam, deep in conversation as they headed in the direction of the engine house. Above them reared the mill tower with its flagpole, where the deep red rose on the golden trumpet gleamed bright against a grey, wind-whipped sky. Everybody was talking about the new flag, but Martha found she could spare it no more than a brief upward glance. She'd been back on full time for less than three weeks, and already she'd let a float down and had to be sent for. And it had cost her sixpence off her wages.

That was bad enough, but something much deeper was gnawing at her scanty self-esteem. It was well known among the weavers that Harry Lingard was too free with his hands. Those who experienced it either laughed or fumed or wept, according to their natures, but not one of them ever complained about him. As head cut-looker his position was such that no woman would challenge him. Martha knew she should count herself lucky that he hadn't tried anything with her, but all she felt was the old, bitter weight of resentment and inadequacy. She was twenty-six years old, yet no man, not even Harry Lingard, had ever looked at her as she'd seen men look at other women.

Why had she grown up to be little more in size than a child, and plain at that? Why? Was it as her mother had said, that she'd been short of nourishment when she was carrying her? Her sister Bella had been born during a spell of full employment, and she was of normal size. Normal size spelled attractiveness, apparently, because she had married a burly, good-natured coalman from Rochdale, and lived in a house with three bedrooms. She had three sturdy children, as well.

Martha hurried on, her bony face pale except for two pink patches high on her cheeks. It hadn't been true what she'd told Harry Lingard about her mother. Well, it was true that she'd lost sleep because of her, but then she always did. That hadn't been the reason for her faulty work, though. It had been because she'd been thinking of Matthew Raike, a man who looked like a gypsy and talked in a strange, sing-song, soft-toned way. A man who didn't even work in the mill, but was a mere labourer in Lord Soar's new park.

She'd had a funny feeling when she first saw him outside the mill lodge as she carried home that bowl of broth for her mother and Uncle Jack. It had been as if she already knew him, and had been waiting for him to come to Saltley. Then of all people it had been him who picked her up when the wind took her. Dazed as she was, she'd known them to be a man's hands on her, and they'd been his. Then she'd seen him again, at the market stall, when he'd asked her to have a cup of tea with him. She'd been ready to drop from weariness, and had known she must look a fright; to confirm it she glimpsed pity in those dark eyes rather than the expression she craved when a man looked at her. But at least her mother had been civil when he took her home, and Uncle Jack had made sense for most of the time. That had been nearly a fortnight ago, so why hadn't she forgotten all about him?

Back in the weaving shed the noise hit her with its customary violence: it was deafening, overpowering, yet at the same time safe and familiar. Even the smell gave her a kind of comfort – hot metal, machine oil and human sweat. When she first started work at Fairbrother's mill as a reacher-in, the smell had often ruined her appetite before she ran home for her breakfast at eight o'clock; but in those days workers relieved themselves next to their place of work, and the smell of urine and excrement from the buckets had turned her young stomach. Mr Schofield, though, had built his Jericho mills with necessaries installed on every floor, and the days of unspeakable smells in the mill were long gone.

The minder relinquished her looms with a brisk nod and a wave, leaving Martha scurrying round making sure everything was in order. From across the walkway Jessie Lane asked how much she'd been stopped from her wages, using the exaggerated mouthing and miming that enabled the weavers to communicate in spite of the noise. Martha held up six fingers, and Jessie rolled her eyes and shook her head in sympathy. She was kind and motherly, and much too tactful to ask about Harry Lingard's wandering hands. Grateful to be spared questions, Martha bestowed on her friend her rare smile, shrugging her shoulders in a pretence of bravado.

Then it was time for the afternoon's clearing up. Down on her knees she began to gather up the fluff that lay inches deep beneath her looms. She did it warily, knowing there might be a sticky black globule among the fluff. The head overlooker chewed tobacco, and could spit accurately between the racing looms, missing the rolls of fine cotton cloth by less than an inch. In the hot moist atmosphere his gobbets stayed wet all day long, and so Martha performed the routine task more slowly than any other.

Martha's heart sank when she reached home. Uncle Jack wasn't there, and her mother looked none too pleased about it. 'Yes, he's gone!' she snapped. 'Don't ask me where! He said – ' the pale little face was tight with irritation '– he said he wanted some peace. Peace! I told him he'd find no peace clutterin' the streets up when the mills come out, but he went off without even makin' me a drink.'

'All right, Mother. I'll put the kettle on now and we'll have a cup of tea before I go and find him. Then I'll get us all somethin' to eat.'

Mrs Spencer pulled at the blanket over her legs, and sighed. 'It'll be the cold mutton, I suppose?'

'You suppose right,' said Martha shortly. 'There's pickles and bread and butter to go with it, and that's more than we had a few weeks back.'

'Don't get on your high horse with me, lady! I've had a day of it, I have that, what with our Jack and me leg.'

Martha filled the kettle and rammed it on the embers of the fire. She could have done with a day lying in a chair herself, and would have thought rheumatism and Uncle Jack a small price to pay for it.

'Have you seen any more of Matthew Raike?'

The question was so unexpected she felt the blood rush to her cheeks, and turned hurriedly away. 'No. Why?'

'Because you've been a nowty little madam since the night you brought him home, that's why.'

'I didn't bring him,' said Martha, 'he brought me. And if I'm nowty maybe it's because I'm back in the weaving shed as well as looking after the two of you and this house. Has that occurred to you?'

'Aye,' said her mother quietly, 'a lot of things occur to me in the length of a day.'

There was something in her tone that made Martha look at her carefully. Her mother was often sharp and always touchy, but today there was something more. She watched the blue-veined hands picking tensely at the blanket. Was it the same old thing? Again? 'Mother, I've told you times without number that I'll always look after you. Now haven't I?'

'Aye, you have. But what if you get wed? A husband might have summat to say about me and your uncle.'

Ah, now they were getting down to it. A husband was suddenly in the picture, and all because of Matthew

Raike. Martha laughed – a hard, bitter sound. 'A husband? Oh aye, they're queuing up for the job, aren't they? I don't think you need to worry about that, Mam. Men aren't interested in me. I'm too small and too plain.'

Her mother bridled. 'I was exactly like you when I married your father, and I was your age, as well.'

Martha had heard that before, of course, but all at once it held a new significance. She crushed the stunted flower of hope beneath the heel of her hurt and resentment, and managed a dismissive shrug. 'Well, you must have had more about you than me, that's all.'

'You're thin, admitted,' pronounced her mother, 'but there's many a one in Saltley who's thinner. And I'll grant you're small, but you have a proper woman's shape. A few more weeks of feeding up and you'll have flesh enough on your bones to please many a man.'

Martha held the teapot to her chest like a battle-shield. What was this? Kind words? Encouragement? 'Are you feeling poorly again?' she asked uneasily.

'No more than usual. I've been doing some thinkin', though, this last week or two. Your father and me, we didn't have much, but we were what you might call suited. He had somethin' about him, you know, he had that. When he died I wished I could go and join him, but you and our Bella were only little and I had to buckle to. Stop gawpin', girl, and listen! I might not feel like sayin' this ever again. What I've been thinkin' is this: I mustn't stand in your way if ever you want to get wed.'

A tightness took hold of Martha's throat, and she felt the sting of tears. Hurriedly she blinked and swallowed. Her mother couldn't abide weeping. 'What's brought this on?' she asked abruptly. 'You've always said it was my bounden duty to put you first.'

A familiar spark lit her mother's eyes, heralding aggression. 'Honour thy father and thy mother – it's one of the commandments,' she said sharply. 'So it *is* your duty, and you shouldn't need me to tell you!' She plucked at the blanket again. 'You ask what's brought it on? Well, you can tell me I'm wrong if you like, but when that young fella was here I could see you fancied him. And ever since that night I've kept thinkin' about your father and me. . . .'

Martha stared at her, shrinking inwardly. She hadn't let *him* see anything, had she? 'He's – different,' she admitted. 'He's different; he's kind, and – yes – I did like him. Just a bit. But he's only a labourer at Soar Park, you know.'

'Labourers in parks have done better than cotton spinners in the last year or two,' Mrs Spencer pointed out, 'so just listen to me. You've admitted that men aren't falling over themselves to get you, so you'll have to give 'em a bit of encouragement, that's all. And you can stop looking as if there's a smell under your nose; there's many a raving beauty had to scheme to get the man she wanted, and that's a fact. Now, arrange it so you bump into him, accidental like, and ask him round for a bite of supper. Say your mother would like to see him – or no, say Uncle Jack was asking after him. We can offer him a bit more than last time he was here, and a comfortable chair as well, now we've got it back from Ridings.'

Martha liked to have things clear in her mind. First things first. 'Are you saying you'd agree to me gettin' married, Mother?'

'Yes. I am.'

Martha felt her legs go slack and the knees weaken as if they might fail her. Half an hour ago she'd come through the mill gates and seen her future stretch before her – years of hard grind on the looms at Jericho, and the weight of her mother's tongue and Uncle Jack's broken mind at home. Now all at once she'd been given hope of something else and from her mother, of all people.

She sat down and poured their tea. Pictures from the past edged into her mind. . . . Her mother, white with exhaustion after a twelve-hour day at the mangle and dolly-tub doing other people's washing; or counting out precious coppers for her and Bella to go on the Wakes, or feeding her gruel by the light of a candle when she was poorly. That was her real mother, she thought with sudden compassion, not this peevish invalid, old before her time.

'If ever I get married, Mam, you an' Uncle Jack will stay with me,' she said quietly. 'I promised you I'd always look after you.'

Mrs Spencer eased herself back in her chair, the cup and saucer clutched between her hands. 'I know you did,' she agreed soberly. 'You're a good girl.' For a moment they drank their tea together, and Martha savoured the unique bond that can join a mother and daughter: deep, comforting, unfathomable. And then it was gone. 'Come on, look sharp!' said her mother impatiently. 'Drink up and go and find your Uncle Jack. I want me tea!'

CHAPTER SIX

Open to the Public

SOAR PARK WAS OPEN to the public at last – all the public, as specified by young Lord Alsing on behalf of his father. It was Saturday, so those who walked the immaculate paths came from two extremes of society – the affluent and the unemployed. The rest of Saltley – mill-workers, shopkeepers, craftsmen, servants – were of necessity at their work.

It was all very impressive: the great stretches of grass were close-cut and velvety, the flower-beds bright with colour, the lake glittered in the sunshine; the fat little pleasure steamer, newly named *Daisybelle*, was adorned with bunting. The competition to name it had been won by one of the mayor's daughters, who must have discovered the unlikely fact that one of Lady Soar's many names was Daisy. That, and the implied compliment of the 'belle', had eliminated all other entries.

Maria Ridings, plump and stately, was there with her daughter Tizzie, who was burning with suppressed excitement. It had taken him twenty-six days, but Edward Mayfield had at last made contact. The relief of it made her feel a little lightheaded. Two days earlier her father had shut up shop for the day and come upstairs for his customary late supper. The sisters were sewing, Tizzie bored and Mary dreamy, while Maria prepared a plate of cold morsels to tempt her husband's poor appetite. He came in and stood by the sideboard, his watch-chain sagging across his sunken middle and his sparse hair flattened against his skull. 'I've had a visitor in the shop,' he announced drily. 'That young man who designed the infirmary.'

Tizzie jabbed her needle into the fine linen on her lap. Not before time, she told herself triumphantly. Now she knew what it felt like to have a man doing as she expected, and she liked it – very much. She wiggled one foot impatiently. If her shrivelled father and his appalling shop hadn't put him off there was hope of something happening.

Maria was all attention. 'Mayfield,' she said briskly, 'his name is Edward Mayfield. He didn't come to pawn, then?'

'No.' Abel's colourless gaze rested on Tizzie. 'He said he met my daughter, Miss Tizzie, at the Town Hall Rally. He was so impressed by her grasp of financial matters and her interest in the infirmary that he would like permission to put her name before the fund-raising committee as a possible member.'

Maria's jaw dropped in silent amazement, but Mary let out a squeal. 'Ooh, Tizzie! Did you know he was coming here?'

'No, of course I didn't. I only spoke to the man for a couple of minutes. We did talk about money, though, and where it's all coming from. What did you tell him, Father?'

'That we would discuss it and let him know,' said Abel. 'And then he asked if we would all take afternoon tea with him on Saturday in the new tea-rooms at the opening of the park. I said you would both go with your mother, but that I would have to stay here with my business.'

Tizzie eyed her father thoughtfully. He'd handled that quite well. There were times when he behaved like a normal man, and one of some stature, at that.

'I can't go,' said Mary flatly. 'You said I could walk through the park with William, just the two of us. He's taken time off from the shop, specially.'

'I'd forgotten,' admitted Abel. 'All right, Tizzie, you and your mother can go and have tea with Mr Mayfield.

I'll send him a note to confirm it. That's if you're interested in his suggestion?'

'She's interested,' said Maria. 'Aren't you, love?'

'I'd like to hear what he has to say, yes,' agreed Tizzie with composure, deciding there and then to concentrate her mind on ways of raising money. Once on that committee she would make her presence felt.

Now they were on their way to meet him, with the music of the band getting louder as they approached the tea-room. Tizzie's sharp eyes noticed a wooden hut set deep among a grove of trees. A workman was there, lifting timber from a small handcart, and as he straightened up with a bundle of spars on his shoulder, his eyes met Tizzie's through a network of leaves. She remembered him at once, as she remembered any interesting male – it was the man from the cotton wagon, the one who had waved his hat to her and Mary as he passed beneath their window. Maybe he remembered her, because he touched the floppy felt hat and gave the ghost of a bow. Tizzie raised her eyebrows and followed her mother. For a labourer he wasn't without a certain attraction.

Seconds later he was obliterated from her mind. Edward was waiting for them, wearing silver-grey with a lavender-blue necktie and looking like a peacock among blackbirds compared to the Saltley men. He came forward, smiling. 'Mrs Ridings? A pleasure, Ma'am, ah – and Miss Tizzie. . . .' He bent over her hand. 'I've reserved a table for us. Shall we go in?'

Tizzie observed him carefully as they settled in their seats and he ordered tea. He was even better looking in daylight than under the chandeliers of the Town Hall, but in the polite small-talk of the first few minutes he was projecting his amazing charm solely at her mother. She felt let down. Where was the fizzing in her veins, the ache in her chest, the tightness in the pit of her stomach? Had she imagined them, built them up in her memory when they'd never existed?

She brought her mind back to the conversation, and cringed. When her mother first encountered William Hartley she had been dignified, aloof, somewhat condescending; but faced now with Edward's confident elegance and upper class accent she was fulsome, almost fawning, and so determined to be genteel she was tripping herself up every time she opened her mouth. Typical, thought Tizzie. This is the first presentable man I have ever, *ever* met. He hasn't – so far – been put off by my father or the shop, but he'll certainly be nauseated by my mother.

'Oh, this is lovely, Mr Mayfield, so select,' Maria was saying, casting an eye at the occupants of the other tables. 'And is it true that the authorities have catered for the labouring classes by making an eating house from his lordship's old stables?'

'Yes, Ma'am. I was able to advise on the conversion. Saltley is fortunate in having Lord Soar as a benefactor.' The bright eyes in their singular oval sockets were fixed earnestly on Maria, but Tizzie's senses were at such a pitch she could see quite clearly that her mother was being assessed. She wasn't given to flashes of inspiration, but all at once she knew that Edward was a calculating man. This didn't detract from his appeal one bit. A man who knew what was or was not to his own advantage was far more interesting than some pliant ninny. Thoughtfully she bit into a tiny egg sandwich, and listened to her mother. How odd that until this moment she had always considered her father to be the main obstacle in landing an interesting man.

Maria was on her favourite topic of Saltley's shortcomings, and relating her ambition of moving to Manchester when prosperity returned to the city. Tizzie decided to interrupt as soon as she could get a word in, and take the conversation her way. She looked at Edward under her lashes, and to her amazement saw his left eyelid droop and rise again. It was so quick her mother missed it, but Tizzie allowed herself a small, delighted smile. He had winked at her. It confirmed what up to now she had only hoped for. This meeting and its declared purpose was just a contrivance to get to know her better.

Enough was enough. She interrupted, scorning her mother's falsely refined tones, and speaking slowly and clearly in the tongue of Saltley. 'Am I right in thinking that the new infirmary would not have been contemplated if Lord Soar had not given land for the purpose, Mr Mayfield?'

'Only in part, Miss Tizzie. Most boroughs of any size are building their own hospitals now, and it would have come to Saltley in time, gift or no gift.'

'And do all these other boroughs raise funds for their hospitals?'

Maria sat back and stared at her daughter, pride battling with astonishment. Tizzie didn't need help in making conversation with this impressive young man; she was more than capable of speaking for herself, and her not yet twenty.

Maria would never have admitted it, but in her heart she knew that her own confidence evaporated when dealing with her social superiors. Confront her with a beggar, a labourer, a woman waving a pawn ticket, and she was never lost for words; but put her in front of somebody with a better background and she was frightened of making herself look ridiculous. Her days of toiling out on the Bog and in Miller's shed were long gone, but deep inside her the echo of them still sounded.

Here was her daughter, though, talking as an equal to this fine architect – and who was to say what might come of it? What was more, she was his equal in appearance. The green and white striped dress that she'd demanded to wear showed off her neat waist and narrow rib-cage; her remarkable eyes lifted the strong features to near-beauty, and her abundant red-gold hair, firmly-anchored, looked as if it was so full of life it would crackle if you happened to touch it. Then all at once a tide of deep pink surged into Tizzie's cheeks, and Maria leaned forward. What was this? She never blushed. It wasn't the talk that had caused her to colour up – it had been of fund-raising and the committee and the hospital – innocent as the day. Then Tizzie calmly asked for more tea, and the blush faded without comment.

Every second was pure enjoyment. Tizzie would never have believed that a man could flirt with her right under her mother's nose, while talking about a new infirmary. It had startled her when he touched her knee under the tablecloth, but she was sure her mother had noticed nothing amiss. As they talked she was able to study his face, only inches away, and she found it exciting. The narrow red lips and the even, very white teeth; the hazel eyes, so light they were almost golden; the hands, slender and well-manicured, with longer nails than she'd seen on any Saltley man. She needn't have worried, she was feeling the fizz, the ache and the tightness of their first meeting – and more besides.

'What do you think of Saltley?' she asked curiously.

'A typical manufacturing town, Miss Tizzie, though I can't say the same for some of the inhabitants. And it's very different from my native county, of course.'

'Which is?'

'Hampshire. Yes, I'm a country boy, believe it or not, the youngest of six sons, so I have to earn my living. I studied architecture in London, and now I travel the country, supervising my firm's various commissions, and enjoying myself at the same time.'

Tizzie was consumed by envy. What a way to live! And how many women did he meet? Dozens? Hundreds? A phrase she had picked up from a borrowed book dropped into her mind. 'Love 'em and leave 'em.' Was that what he did? Not with her, it wasn't. Not if she could help it!

'It's good to be at leisure and feeling the sun after working like a dog at Jericho.' Sam was walking with his sister along one of the woodland paths in the park, their first outing together for more than a fortnight.

'You're enjoying it, Sammy.' It was a statement, not a question, and Sam grinned and patted her hand on his arm. Nobody else called him Sammy – not his parents, his brothers, his friends, or the various daughters of Saltley's manufacturing families. He told them he didn't like it, and to call him Sam or Samuel. Sarah, though, was different; Sammy had been her first word, when as a flaxen-haired toddler she and her brother were already inseparable; even now they preferred each other's company to anyone else's. Their parents encouraged them both to mix with members of the opposite sex, and from time to time, good-humouredly, they complied; then they laughed together about the shortcomings of the young men and women who sought them out so eagerly.

Sam knew quite well that their extreme fondness for each other could give rise to unpleasant speculation. He was no wide-eyed innocent. He knew of the dark under-life of Saltley, mixing as he did with robust country-folk up at High Lee; most instructive of all, he walked the streets of Manchester when he visited the Jericho establishment. The city appealed to him; its vitality echoed his own, and he savoured its links with Liverpool and the world that lay across the seas. His gift for mixing with all classes – a quality bestowed by his father – meant that all aspects of city life were laid open to him.

Wherever he went he looked, he learned, he remembered; and he evaluated his own personal needs. His body needed fulfilment, but not enough to drive him to the couch of some grubby whore, or to one of the anonymous houses where he'd been told that half-a-crown would buy him a twelve-year-old virgin.

Too fastidious for the low life, he had then turned to the high; but in spite of his brisk self-confidence, he left the ornate luncheon clubs and daytime gaming-houses without availing himself of the services of the 'ladies' who waited there. He wanted what they offered, right enough, but he knew, he just *knew*, that there could be more between a man and woman than what went on in those plush-draped little rooms. Like a child who looks forward to his birthday or Christmas, watching all that goes on and waiting with scant patience, Sam watched women very closely indeed. But he waited.

And because he watched and waited and examined his own reactions, he knew that his love for Sarah was natural and normal. He loved her as a sister, not as a woman. He loved her innocent mind and her gentle spirit and her laughter; not her body. What was more, he was positive she felt the same way about him. Of late, she had spoken somewhat wistfully of the kind of man she would marry. 'Sammy,' she would say sometimes, 'I do want to marry a man I can admire. Somebody I can look up to, who will be a good father to my children – you know, like Papa.'

Such was the closeness between them that he had even been able to tell her, tactfully and without graphic detail, of the physical union that resulted in children. She had smiled tolerantly and squeezed his hand. 'It's all right, Sammy, I know a bit about it. Mama is a farmer's daughter, don't forget, and the girls I know talk about things other than fashion and embroidery and their favourite hymns.'

Sam had laughed, relieved. She might be angelically pretty, but her feet were firmly on the ground. Then she said, 'I think in view of all the fair-haired men in the family, I'll marry somebody with black hair, all curly, and side-whiskers. That will make a change from you and James and Ralph. What sort of woman will you choose? A tall Amazonian blonde, or a cuddly little brunette?'

He had laughed again at that, but answered her honestly, because long ago they had vowed always to be honest with each other. 'I want a woman to love me as Mother loves Father,' he said soberly. 'I've watched all the other couples of their age – the parents of our friends, those they invite for meals, all those at chapel – and none of them have that – that bond. They really love each other, Sarah.'

'I know they do, but I think it's a bit unusual,' she said half enviously. 'Do you think we'll ever have that kind of marriage?'

'We'll be lucky if we do. But one thing I can tell you quite definitely. If your husband isn't good to you I'll kill him.'

She giggled in delight. 'I know! And if your wife doesn't make you happy, I'll – I'll ask her to dinner in my fine house and poison her roast beef.'

They fell silent as they walked the sun-dappled path. It was quiet there; the crowds were either on the main walk with its spectacular flower-beds, or over by the lake. As if he'd spoken out loud in the silence, Sarah answered his thoughts. 'Esther isn't all that bad, Sammy, so stop worrying about her. She's really nice when we chat together on our own, and I know she thinks the world of James – why, she hangs on his every word. She's affectionate with him now, so surely she'll love him to death when they're married? And what's more she isn't objecting to going up to High Lee.'

'Of course she's isn't objecting! Because up there she can play at being lady of the manor! Look, would you say I'm a fanciful sort of chap? One who has wild ideas and lets his imagination run riot?'

Sarah considered what her brother had said. 'No, but I'd say you're given to strong likes and dislikes, and you can be obstinate to a degree. Sammy,' she stopped and tugged at his arm, 'look at me, Sammy.'

Obediently he stopped and faced her. They were quite alone in the shade of the trees; he saw that the deep blue eyes were huge and intent, the silky cheeks pink, and the white teeth catching at her soft lower lip. 'Well,' he said lightly, 'I'm looking, funny face.'

'You won't be like this – like you are about Esther –

when I want to get married, will you? Please say you won't.'

He stared at her, then tucked her arm through his and turned her back to face ahead. 'Listen love, I know I'm in a minority of one about Esther. It may be that marriage to Jimmy will bring out the good in her, if there is any, but I'm well aware that my objections have in some measure spoiled his engagement for him. So I can tell you now, unless I know for a fact that the chap you choose is a rotter, I won't spoil it for you.'

'Promise?' she asked doubtfully.

Sam nodded, 'I promise. If ever I'm less than pleasant to the man, just casually mention this place – ' he looked around him at the whispering trees '– this little dell in Soar Park, and I'll mend my ways. In any case, he'll probably be above reproach, a professor of anatomy or an eminent surgeon, if you get your wish and become a nurse.'

'If!' She repeated the word despondently. 'Since Papa found out that they haven't got their training school under way at Manchester Royal he acts as if it's inevitable that I must wait until it opens.'

'Well, if the Nightingale School itself has a waiting-list it seems as if you haven't much option.'

'Oh, there are always options,' said Sarah obstinately. 'For instance, I believe there should be a little sick-bay at Jericho, for those injured in the mill, or for women nearing their confinements, and to keep an eye on the children. I could see to cuts and bruises, and send the more serious cases to the doctor, and maybe help the expectant mothers.'

Sam stared at her. 'You don't see yourself as a midwife, surely?'

'No, but I'm capable of forming an opinion as to whether women are fit to keep working until they're in labour.'

Sam's bright gaze met his sister's darker blue. 'It's my belief they should give up work before the last hours,' he said slowly, 'and I think Father agrees. But he says you can't force them to stop if they can stand the pace and their work doesn't suffer.'

'You could persuade them, though, by paying them a small sum to stay at home and then keeping their jobs open, or maybe allowing only part-time work after they reach seven months.'

'Quite the little reformer,' he teased. 'Let's get you installed in your sick-bay before we start on the radical stuff, shall we?'

Once in the sunlight she turned and looked at the dark trees behind them. 'I'll remember the promise you made me in that little dell, Sammy,' she said, and reached up to kiss his cheek. Then she shivered, there on the sunlit path. 'How odd, I've gone cold,' she said uneasily. 'What do they say it's a sign of? Somebody walking over my grave?'

'Raike! Warhurst! Right, that's the lot of you, then.' Norman Nuttall finished handing out the men's wages and locked his cash-box with a flourish. He was in rare good humour, dressed in his best after sitting near the platform at the official opening, having shared the first ride in the *Daisybelle* with the mayor and corporation of Saltley, and the son of Lord Soar himself.

It was six o'clock in the evening, and outside the tool-shed the people of Saltley were still thronging their new park, but inside in the gloom the men shuffled uneasily. Nuttall had warned them that he was finishing them all except for two who could stay on as general handymen for the park authority; they were waiting to hear who had been chosen. Every man in the hut was desperate for such regular employment. Jonas Carter had turned up that morning in a clean shirt and with his ancient boots oiled and polished in a last attempt to impress Nuttall; Billy Warhurst was gripping his old felt hat and wringing it like a woman with a mop-rag.

Matthew stood at the back near the door. It was clear

that the foreman was enjoying his last moments of power over them, deliberately delaying the announcement of who was to be kept on. His own tenancy of the shed was at an end, of course; Nuttall had told him that days ago. 'Even if you're kept on, and it's a big "if", we can't have you sleeping in here after next week, Raike.' As he spoke he had prodded with his stick at the bed of sacks in the corner. 'Hey!' he said curiously, feeling something hard and square under the coarse hessian. 'What's this, then?'

It was Matthew's little cupboard, the one he'd made to hold his plate and mug, his knife and spoon and frying pan. He'd fitted a shelf in the middle, and on that stood half a loaf wrapped in a piece of calico and a knob of dripping on a blue saucer. 'It's a cupboard I made for my belongings, Mr Nuttall. Out of those off-cuts you said I could have for the stove.'

Nuttall nudged the cupboard with the toe of his boot. 'What, them bits from the benches on the landing stage? You must have done some sanding down, then – it's as smooth as silk.'

'Yes, but it was my own sand-paper,' Matthew pointed out, 'and I bought the screws myself, and the brass knob. I did use the borough's saw, though, and the borough's screwdriver.' Sarcasm edged his words, causing Billy Warhurst to whirl round, eyes wide.

But because he didn't expect sarcasm, Nuttall didn't recognise it. 'You've not made a bad job of it, Raike,' he conceded. 'If I'd known you were as good as this I'd have got you doing a cupboard for Mrs Nuttall. Bigger than this, of course, and better quality. Have you been trained in carpentry?'

'I was taught a bit about it by a man who'd worked in the carpenter's shop on board ship.'

Nuttall swivelled his watery gaze from the cupboard to Matthew. 'Well, this is no ship, Raike. Get it out of here by Saturday night at the latest. This shed is to be used for maintenance tools only. It'll be locked at all times, and the park-keepers'll be responsible for it.'

Saturday night had come, and they were all waiting. 'What about you, Mr Nuttall?' asked one of the men. 'Will you be staying on at the park?'

'No. I'm employed by the borough. I was only on loan to the park authority. My next task is to supervise the laying of land drains on the edge of Saltley Bog.'

'Have you got men for that?' persisted the same questioner.

Nuttall threw out his chest and shook his head. 'Not yet, but I've had instructions to hire men from Ryeworth. There's many a one there has had no work for years, and the Guardians are concerned about the cost of them.' He smiled. 'About all of you, though. With the exception of Jordan, here, whose mouth is too big for a labourer, I'll give any of you a note of reference if you put in for a job.'

Big Joey Jordan pulled a face behind Nuttall's back, but Billy Warhurst could wait no longer. 'Who're the two who can stay on, Mr Nuttall?'

'Oh, didn't I tell you? Carter and Raike. On my recommendation, so mind you both behave. A month's trial. You start at six on Monday and ask for Mr Broadhurst, who's in charge of maintenance. He'll tell you your pay and your duties. The rest of you be on your way, and take your bits and pieces with you. I want this shed emptied in five minutes, and no rubbish left. Is that clear?'

For once there was no obedient chorus of 'Yes, Mr Nuttall,' so he strutted out and slammed the door, leaving the men silent and despairing, except for Matthew and Jonas Carter, who could hardly believe their good fortune. Jonas slipped out quickly, reluctant to discuss it, and a man called after him bitterly, 'It were worth spendin' a couple of hours on your boots, then, Jonas!'

Matthew felt he must offer them all a word as they left, and it was an uncomfortable five minutes. The last to leave was Billy, who put out a hand. 'All the best,' he said heavily. 'It's been grand working with you, lad.'

Matthew thought of the pale-faced Warhurst children with their coughs; of the sickly baby in the box on the hearth; of the wife who grabbed at coppers from her husband's workmates. He would have done the same in her place, and more besides, given the chance. He took one of the half-crowns from his wage and pressed it into the other's palm. 'Just a liddle bit to help 'ee, Billy,' he said awkwardly, lapsing into broad Devon in his distress. 'I'll let 'ee know if a job do turn up.'

For a moment the other seemed lost for words, then he straightened his shoulders and managed a shrug. 'Thanks, lad. And don't upset yoursel'. We'll manage.' With a nod he walked out and weaved away through the trees.

Matthew put his belongings in two of the sacks from his bed. Last weekend he'd spotted a place under the new railway arches, and with luck nobody else would have claimed it. He made for the main gate, his spirits rising in spite of his dismay about Billy. He had never expected Know-all Nuttall to put him forward for permanent work. The man must have the hide of an ox not to see how he detested him. Sobering, he thought of the day he left Ryder Hall, vowing never again to pick up a gardening trowel. Since working for Nuttall he'd picked one up more than once, and used it. As a park handyman he would likely have to use one again – but only until he was taken on in a cotton mill.

A small figure in a weaver's apron and striped skirt was coming towards him, and with a rush of pleasure he recognised Martha Spencer. She looked livelier than the last time they met, but the wisps of cotton fluff clinging to her hair showed she'd come straight from the looms. He put down his sacks in order to touch his hat. 'Miss Martha! Welcome to the park!'

Martha's cheeks were faintly pink, and she stared up at him in that odd way of hers, as if he spoke a foreign tongue. 'I thought I'd just walk through on my way home and have a look round,' she said quietly. 'It's – it's very beautiful. Almost like fairyland.'

He laughed. 'Fairyland? Oh, fairyland is all rainbows and roses, dewdrops and daisies, didn't you know? Better'n Soar Park, any day.'

She didn't smile, but looked at his bundles uncertainly. 'You're not leaving Saltley, are you?'

'No, I've been given a permanent job here at the park. I'm just moving out of the tool shed where I've been sleeping for the last few weeks.' He looked down at her, and felt a faint pressure on his ribs, as if old Peggy-oh was by his side, nudging him. He tipped his hat forward against the sinking sun, and heard himself say, 'You don't want a lodger at Ledden Street, do you?'

The slight colour ebbed from her cheeks and she stared at him, saucer-eyed and as pale as death. 'What do you mean?'

He tried to laugh it off. 'Don't fret yourself, 'twas only a joke. I'm on my way now to find myself a bed.' He touched his hat again, and closed his mind determinedly to the memory of a little blue jar of flowers and the smell of soap and starched cotton.

'Just a minute,' she said stiffly. 'We – we might.'

'Might what?'

'We might think about takin' a lodger. We – that is, me mother – had been wonderin' whether to put another bed in me Uncle Jack's room. I don't suppose you'd want that? Sharin', I mean?'

'I might,' said Matthew slowly. 'Oh, to be sure, I might at that.'

CHAPTER SEVEN

Settling In

MATTHEW COULD RECALL NOTHING like it since he slept
in his own room before his mother died. There was a real
bed, with a deep flock mattress on a wire mesh frame,
and there were sheets and blankets and a knobbly cotton
bedspread. There was a tiny iron fireplace, and next to
it an alcove with a rail for hanging clothes, screened by
a curtain. A chest of drawers stood beneath a framed
picture of a grand house surrounded by rolling green
fields. Most impressive of all, there was a wooden
washstand with a marble top that held a big jug and
bowl, decorated with garlands of flowers.

So this was Martha's room. He knew he should feel
guilty to be taking it from her, but he didn't, he felt
glad, triumphant, almost. It was only nine weeks since
he had left the potting-shed lean-to at Ryder, and here
he was with a room of his own and the means to pay for
it. A room containing an actual bed and a washstand; a
room with curtains at the window and pale floor-boards
that knew a scrubbing-brush, and with a shiningly clean
chamber-pot under the bed.

He paced back and forth, and gazed out of the window
at the mill chimneys spearing the skyline. There was an
unfamiliar sensation in his chest, as if a poultice had been
laid on an open sore. It was a soothing feeling, like when
his mother used to give him blackcurrant tea and put a hot
bottle to his feet in bed when he had a chill. He couldn't
have explained it in speech, but he recognised that some
deep-seated craving was being satisfied by taking over
Martha's room. He pushed away the thought of her on

a makeshift bed downstairs. If you took a lodger you
had to lose something – space, privacy, a bed – and
in return you got money. He had a feeling that Martha
liked money; her mother certainly did.

Things had moved rapidly since his impulsive question
in the park. The strained exchange between them had
ended with Martha saying abruptly, 'You can come
back with me now, if you want, and I'll see what me
mother says.'

Hardly had they walked out through the gates than he
was beset by doubts. He could count on the fingers of one
hand the times in his life when he'd shared his sleeping
quarters; he'd been fortunate in that, if in nothing else.
He'd had his own room before his mother died and Fat
Annie took her place. A year later, his father dead too,
had come the time of being crammed into the stable loft
at the Mizzen with the tribe, until at last he'd laid claim
to the sleeper. Years after that he was given the potting-
shed lean-to at Ryder; once up here in Lancashire he had
known the tranquillity of that hillside barn, followed by
the haven of the tool shed. The long sequence of solitary
nights with their mental renewal had been broken only
by his visit to Billy Warhurst's and to the bug-infested
lodging house.

Basket on arm, Martha was stepping out briskly at
his side, when in spite of himself his doubts surfaced
and his step slowed. She turned to him at once, her
face expressionless. 'You've changed your mind.'

'No, let's just say I'm having a few doubts,' he said
quietly. ''Tis true I'm a man who likes company, but
ever since I was twelve I've had my sleepin' quarters to
myself. Perhaps I'm being foolish to consider sharing,
even with a nice old chap like your uncle.'

Martha faced him and gazed at a spot past his left
elbow. 'His room *is* small,' she said, half to herself,
'because it's over the back kitchen. I suppose the front
bedroom would be better for you . . .'

'But what about you and your mother?'

'Oh, she sleeps in the house-place – she can't manage the stairs. I have the front bedroom to meself since me sister got married seven or eight years back, though sometimes I'm in and out of bed all night long. I'm always wonderin' whether I'd be better with a makeshift in the back kitchen, to save runnin' up and down the stairs.'

He stared at her doubtfully. 'Come on,' she said, 'let's go and see what she says. There'll be nothin' lost by talkin' it over.'

Martha had asked him to wait outside for a minute, so he put down his sacks and leaned against the fence that edged a row of little gardens opposite the terrace. There was a tiny plot facing each house, and he saw that in theirs the Spencers had a few neat rows of vegetables and a great clump of comfrey. Did Martha look after it, then, or did the uncle manage it with his one arm? Matthew eyed the black peaty soil, and reflected that he might be willing to pick up a trowel, after all, for a plot such as this.

At last the door opened and Martha came out. He saw that her pleated bonnet had gone, as had the tenacious wisps of cotton fluff from her hair. She was small to be sure, he told himself – she was tiny – but she'd filled out a bit since the day they first met; as she came towards him it was clear she had the shape of a woman, rather than a young-old child. One thing she didn't have, though, was the look. Since his mid teens women in all walks of life had looked at him in a certain way. He was accustomed to it, and he knew how to make use of it: there were times when it had got him a meal or a mug of milk. He had learned how to turn the look away from himself by distracting a woman, and he knew how to kill it stone dead if she had anything about her that put him in mind of Fat Annie.

Martha Spencer had no such look. He was positive she didn't know how to give a man the eye of awareness and invitation. He could relax with her. No guarding his words in case he was misunderstood, no putting up the 'keep off' signs.

'She says come in and have a chat.' There was a breathless quality to her speech, causing him to wonder what had been said about him; she was mouthing her words more clearly than ever, and even performing actions to suit them.

Following her over the step he was greeted by a smell of cooking that made his mouth run with saliva. At once he felt ravenous with hunger, but he removed his hat and greeted the mother and uncle politely. 'Evenin', Mrs Spencer, Mr Ogden.' He couldn't help adding, 'Somethin' smells good.'

Mrs Spencer was in the same chair as before. 'Mr Raike,' she said, almost smiling, 'you like your food, then? Tater pie always smells good. It's a favourite in Saltley because you can leave it cookin' while you're at work, and then finish it off quick when you get in. With Martha back on full time we have it once a week, on Saturdays. Sit you down, we don't charge.'

He pulled out a straight-backed chair, one of two that he was sure hadn't been there on his previous visit. Mrs Spencer watched him intently, but the old man nodded benignly and plucked at the buttons on his shirt. Martha, pale of face but calm of manner, stood silently behind her mother's chair.

'Well, our Martha tells me you're after a bed. Many's the time we've talked of having a lodger, but with no cotton in the town there's been nobody with the money to pay. No good'll come of rushing things, though, so how will it be if you have a meal with us first. See what you'd be getting, like, if you should pay for board as well as a room; you must bear in mind it's been cooked for three, though, not four. No obligations on either side, and no decisions until we know a bit more about each other.'

Matthew swallowed a smile. He was as good as in, and with only two vital questions to settle: which room he was to have and how much he would pay. Well, he might be free with hand-outs to Billy Warhurst and others like him, but he wasn't going to be free with the Spencers, because they seemed to want for nothing. But he must move with caution. 'I take it kindly, Missis. I'll be glad to have a meal with you and put your mind at rest about my character.'

The little woman gave the same twitch of the lips that he'd seen on her daughter. 'Well, that's all right, then. Come on, Martha, set to! We're all famished!'

Martha put on a big calico apron and bustled between the back kitchen and the fireplace, stoking more coal under the oven and putting a round of pastry on top of a brown earthenware dish that sizzled and steamed on the shelf. Her movements were rapid but precise, and Matthew wondered how so small a woman managed to run the massive machinery of her looms. Perhaps she was raised up on a boarded walkway between them.

While they waited Mrs Spencer interrogated him. She used no finesse, no concealment of what she was after; just asked countless bald questions about his job, his background and his way of life.

'I'll have to know if you're a drinking man, Mr Raike?'

'Never touch it, Missis. Never. Ever.'

'Well, now! And you're still at Soar Park, under Norman Nuttall?'

'Not under Nuttall. He works for the borough, so with the park laid out he's off on another job. Only two of his gang are being kept on, me and another chap. I start on Monday under a Mr Broadhurst, and I don't even know what I'll be paid. I'm hoping for more than I've been getting under Nuttall.'

The old man snorted. 'It'll hardly be less, lad. Nuttall's a boss's man, and well-known for keeping wage bills down.'

A glimmer of warmth lit Mrs Spencer's neat features for an instant. 'You've done well to be kept on, Mr Raike. Have you had experience on public parks?'

'No, but for four years I was employed on the gardens of Ryder Hall, a grand house outside Plymouth.'

'Well now, and what was your job there?' The questions continued unabated and Matthew answered good-humouredly. Let the old girl find out all she wanted. He had nothing to hide. They sat round the table, Mrs Spencer swathed in her blanket on one of the high-backed chairs, and Martha perched on the stool once she'd served up the savoury pie and its rich, flaky crust.

It was so delicious Matthew had to force himself not to gobble. What was more the table was covered by a white cloth; in the middle of it was the little blue jar, this time containing two or three short sprays of honeysuckle. He couldn't remember when he last sat at such a table, or when he last ate such food. There was a sudden silence, and he realised that he'd missed one of Mrs Spencer's questions. 'I'm sorry,' he said hastily, 'what was that again?'

'I say have you any brothers and sisters back in Devon?'

'Three,' he said without thinking. 'Three sisters and two half-brothers.'

'Three sisters,' repeated Martha, with interest. 'What are their names?'

He realised his mistake. He'd made it once before, and been caught up in a web of misunderstanding. 'No, 'taint so,' he said awkwardly, 'that was a slip o' the tongue. I only have two sisters now. Maggie and Liza. The other one – ' he swallowed, and took a sip of water from his mug, '– the other one – uh – she died. I sometimes forget she's gone.'

'I can understand that,' said Mrs Spencer unexpectedly, 'I can an' all. It was the same with me when me husband was killed. Every time I heard the latch I would turn and expect to see him in the doorway in his working clothes, all black from the boilers, with his eyes shinin' and his teeth gleamin' in his dirty face.'

Matthew turned to her with gratitude. She understood.
She had a heart after all, this woman, though he doubted
if it would ever rule her head. Then she put out a thin dry
hand and patted his, and he felt Martha staring at them
both. A moment later the talk moved to other things, and
they all had sago pudding followed by a cup of tea.

'That was a fine meal, Miss Martha,' he said with a
smile. 'It's a wonder they aren't lining up in the street
to lodge at this house.'

'Well, if our Martha's willing to tackle the extra work
we can take you on,' said Mrs Spencer. 'It'll cost you
seven and six a week, and all found. No, don't answer.
Let Martha show you your bedroom, and then stay up
there while you think about it. And shall we say a
fortnight's trial? Take it or not – it's up to you, and
no hard feelings if you refuse.'

Martha led him through the back kitchen, but he'd
decided to accept before he set foot on the stairs, before
he saw the room. 'You'll have to excuse the state of it,'
she said edgily, 'I know it's dusty, but I only have time
to give it a good do on Sunday mornings. It's a comfy
bed, and I'd see that you had hot water of a morning for
your wash and shave. I – I'll leave you to think it over.'
She had slipped out, then, and closed the door behind
her. So here he was, in this big square room with its
proper furniture, and the picture on the wall. . . .

Seven and six. It wasn't cheap, but even if Mr
Broadhurst paid him only the same as Nuttall he would
be left with three shillings to save or to spend as he chose.
He'd had little more than that left each week in the hut,
after buying ready-cooked food or what he could manage
in his frying pan, and he'd slept on a bed of old sacks.
For the first time since he left Devon he savoured to
the full the freedom of no longer having to help out
with his sisters and the boys. He was twenty-two, nearly
twenty-three, and at last he could spend his earnings on
whatever he liked.

Gazing out at the mill chimneys marching to the

horizon he thought of the man who had been like a father to him, better by far than his own. 'I'm still in Saltley, Peggy-oh,' he said silently, 'and I think I'm here to stay.'

Joshua was in high good humour. It was Tuesday, the day he visited his business rooms in Manchester; though he liked to drop in unannounced now and again this was his official day, when they expected him. The books would be made up to the minute, and samples of the latest consignment of raw cotton ready for inspection. Not that he was likely to find fault with it – no, he would tell anybody that Charlie Barnes could spot good cotton a mile off. And with production under way again his best fine shirtings were coming through from Jericho for export. He would enjoy seeing the heavy rolls packed and stamped with his new trademark, ready for shipping across the seas. Visits to Mosley Street were getting to be just like old times.

Today was even better, because he'd got Sam at his side; a fine figure the lad cut in his smart grey coat and waistcoat and new tall hat, and the dazzling linen that was Rachel's pride and joy. Although never a dandy, Joshua liked good clothes and recognised the value of being well turned out for business. It was a relief to know that his sons needed no hints from him on how to dress for the city. He couldn't help smiling when the thought came to him that perhaps the three of them discussed how they could smarten up their father. . . .

They stepped out along Deansgate, and Joshua flapped a hand at the speeding carriages and jostling crowds. 'It doesn't look like the city of the bankrupt this morning, does it? Perhaps *The Times* wasn't as premature as we thought in saying that "the Cotton Famine is now a matter of history", eh? Things are picking up a bit in Saltley, but they're standing still compared to here. We'll see whether all this hurly-burly's justified when we call in at the Exchange.' He eyed a small child as she held

out a grimy hand, and without breaking his stride laid
a copper on her palm. 'And we'll see less of her sort
in another couple of months,' he added briskly, 'or my
name's not Schofield.'

They turned into Market Street, and he shot a sideways
look at his son, feeling again the odd surge of excitement
that rose in him increasingly of late. Because Sam, the
fast-talking joker of the family, was showing signs;
he'd said it to Rachel more than once: their son was
showing signs of business ability, and revealing a keen
intelligence. What was more he seemed to know by
instinct how to talk to the workers.

Joshua wriggled his shoulders, annoyed with himself.
He should have had that family conference long since.
There was Sam here absorbing facts and figures like a
sponge. There was James, off up to High Lee at six
every morning, and taking to country life like a duck to
water. There was Ralph – young master angel-face – who
according to Charlie was amazingly quick on the uptake,
and a positive wizard on the state of the markets.

Not usually one to indulge in pointless regrets, Joshua
walked on, deep in thought. Why had he let his sons mess
about when he could have given them the motivation
to work, to make something of themselves? All right,
he'd been busy keeping his business from bankruptcy,
but even so he should have shared his worries with
them instead of cushioning them against the realities
of life, and letting them believe it was milk and roses
all the way.

'Ne'then, Joshua,' called a stout elderly man, followed
by a clerk loaded with ledgers. 'How's business?'

'Middling, middling,' replied Joshua, waving his stick.
'You'll have met my son, Samuel? How's things in
Rochdale, Arthur?'

'Picking up,' said the other with a grin. 'Will you be
at the Exchange?'

'Oh aye. We want to see whether Manchester's as
busy as it looks.'

He fell silent again as they walked on, and Sam eyed the energetic figure at his side with wary respect. He was finding that close contact with his father stimulated him. It buoyed him up, putting him in mind of the effects of the champagne they'd drunk on the night that had heralded this new way of life. He told himself that if it was possible to grow up in three weeks flat, then that was what he had done. When he looked back at his former self he could hardly recognise that aimless young buffoon. What a layabout! What a puerile young fool he had been. Although he felt he should be grateful for the change in his life, he had to admit to a gnawing resentment that his father hadn't made it happen sooner.

They were taking a short cut through a maze of back streets, each wrapped in his thoughts, and he looked up absently to where a hoist clanked as bales of cotton were lifted to the upper floor of a warehouse. His father seemed pleased with the results of his 'sorting-out', so why had he left it so long?

As if his son had asked the question out loud Joshua said quietly, 'Aye, I was wrong, there. I should have done it sooner.'

Sam's reply was equally low. 'If we'd known how bad things were, we could have tried to help.' They faced each other in the dark chasm formed by tall buildings. An uncanny transfer of thought had been there for a moment; a linking of minds, of impulses, of hearts. They didn't speak of it, but awareness was there in a bright meeting of eyes.

'Look Sam, maybe you'll understand a bit better when you have children of your own. It becomes second nature to protect your young, to cushion them from harm. I was so busy staying solvent, so determined to look after you all and guard what would one day be yours, that I didn't see you were getting to be young men. I think that's why I left it so long.'

Sam's festering resentment disappeared like mud swirled away by summer rain, and he grasped his father's hand. 'It's all right,' he said simply, 'don't castigate yourself. Any earlier and I wouldn't have been ready. And Papa – ' he reverted to the childhood name without noticing, 'I want you to know that – uh – I'm proud to be working with you and learning the business.' He grinned, half-embarrassed. 'And keep on tossing your facts and figures at me – I like it.'

Joshua swallowed audibly and then threw back his shoulders. 'Thanks, lad. I'm glad I've got you as my right-hand man.' Taking his son by the arm, he turned him towards Mosley Street. 'While we're on the serious stuff, I'd value your opinion – your confidential view, shall we say – on how your brother's settling in. Charlie gives me glowing reports on his brain-power, but doesn't say whether he seems happy at his work. I thought you might learn Ralph's side of it when you talk together. If you do I'd be grateful if you'd pass it on.' He paused, aware that his words could be taken as a request for Sam to tell tales on his young brother. 'He's only seventeen, you know, and your mother and me – well – we don't find it all that easy to talk to him ourselves.'

'Neither do the rest of us,' Sam assured him bluntly. 'Ralph isn't one of life's communicators, Father.'

'No, I know. I've fancied he's been a bit easier, though, these last few weeks.'

'Oh, yes. Definitely. Don't worry, I'll let you know my impressions.'

Then they reached the imposing entrance to the Jericho building. Sam had always thought the elegant script of the *J.J. Schofield and Sons* on the windows somewhat restrained for his father, but the great golden trumpet over the doors and the enamelled red rose on top of it showed the touch of flamboyance that had helped to establish an international business.

Charlie Barnes was waiting, tall, gaunt and wispy-haired, dressed in sober style and with his long sagging features unusually hardened by the set of his mouth. 'Joshua,' he said with a nod, 'and Sam, nice to see you.'

Joshua shot him a keen look and marched through the office. 'How do, Charlie.'

Greetings over, they left the elderly clerk studying a manifest and went through to Charlie's room. There, open and waiting on the chest-high desk were the ledgers, the order book, the bills of lading, the shipper's invoices. Joshua gave them a glance. 'Where's Ralph?' he asked.

'In the sample room,' said Charlie quietly. 'He's had a few ideas on altering the lay-out there, so he's got the men on it.'

'Has he now?' Joshua pulled at his whiskers. 'And you don't agree, I take it?'

Charlie's spaniel-like eyes flickered doubtfully to Sam, and Joshua said impatiently, 'It's all right, Sam's my right-hand man. Anything you say to me can be said to him as well.'

'If you insist. It's not that I don't agree with Ralph. I daresay the sample room could do with brightening-up, though we hardly need to tempt folk to buy. We'll have our work cut out to supply what's already ordered. But that's not – ' He fell silent.

'Come on,' said Joshua testily, 'that's not what?'

'That's not what's bothering me. Look Joshua, if I could just have a word on our own, like. No offence, Sam.'

'None taken,' Sam assured him. 'Shall I wander off for a bit, Father?'

'Aye, go on then. Be back in five minutes, though.' From the doorway Joshua watched his son's broad back disappear in the warren of passages, then he turned and closed the door behind him. 'Sit down, Charlie, and spit it out.'

Charlie pulled at his high collar as if it was suddenly too tight. 'Well, I expect he's talked it over with you at home, Joshua.'

'Talked what over? You must have realised over the years that Ralph's no talker.'

Charlie stared at him. 'I know he's never been as noisy as Sam, nor as easy as James, but not a talker? I keep telling you he's bright – quick on the uptake, full of ideas.'

'But he's quiet with it, wouldn't you say?'

'No, I wouldn't. He talks a lot. About the changes we need to make, about the lay-out up on the floors, about how much goes through the city banks and whether the Exchange is rising or falling. He's very – well – he's very bright, Joshua. Very alert.' Charlie paced back and forth, flattening his hair first with one hand and then the other.

Joshua eyed his old friend, deliberately silencing the misgivings that jangled like an out-of-flunter spinning-mule in his chest. 'Sit you down, man, and take it easy. It's me, Joshua, not the Spanish Inquisition. That's better.' Charlie sank into his chair and he perched on the edge of the table facing him. 'Now – he's bright, he's full of ideas and he talks a lot. What else?'

Charlie crossed his long, bony legs. 'Well, he's settling in, you know. Finding his feet, and that. He's young, and you remember what we were like at his age – impatient, weren't we?'

'Yes, I remember. I remember how you worked like a dog, first of all with me and then for me. I remember you've never played me false in forty-four years. I remember I've always trusted your judgement, and always trusted you. Out with it, man.'

'Very well, then. He was fine for the first fortnight. Taking it all in, asking questions – intelligent questions – very searching. Then last week he said he'd got the business side sorted out; his next task would be to re-organise the sample room and then the floors – and that in future I was to call him Mr Schofield and not Ralph. Well, Joshua, I'm afraid I said I was on first-name terms with his father, and as I'd seen him with a bare backside when he was two days old, I'd carry on calling him Ralph.'

So it was just a touch of self-importance, bad enough but no tragedy. Joshua managed a laugh. 'Good for you! What did he say to that?'

Charlie looked away and gnawed at his bottom lip. 'Nothing at the time, his face just went blank, like it does sometimes. Then yesterday he came up to me, quiet like, and said to make the most of my last few weeks with Schofield's, because he was going to see to it that I was replaced.'

Joshua fumbled for the edge of the table beneath his thighs, and gripped it hard. For a moment he felt as if he might fall to the floor. 'He said *what*? Repeat it. Can you repeat word for word what he said?'

The other man's tone was heavy and sing-song, like a child who has learned a lesson by rote. 'He said: "my father has placed me here to assume responsibility for this office, this warehouse, and the imports and exports. You, Barnes, are out of date and therefore expendable. Make the most of the next few weeks, because I intend to have you replaced."'

Joshua felt as if a very hard fist had smacked him in the chest. From anybody else he would have dismissed it as a joke, a mistake, a misunderstanding. But not from Charlie. His eyes had always been revealing, and the sadness in them told its own tale. Rage filled him. 'The arrogant young bugger!' he roared. 'And I'd been telling myself I'd made all the right moves. There's Sam doing well at Jericho, and James getting to know what's what at High Lee; I put the quietest one here, at the heart of Schofield's, where the life-blood of Jericho flows. I put him in the hands of my best friend, my most experienced man. . . .'

'Steady, Joshua. I thought it was funny you hadn't told me he was in charge.'

'Bloody hell! He hasn't warmed the seat yet, never mind in charge! He's seventeen, surely to God you didn't think I'd give him authority over you?'

'I didn't want to think it, but he was pretty convincing.'

Charlie squirmed in his seat. 'Look, you don't have to bother Rachel with this, do you?'

'What? There's no secrets between Rachel and me, Charlie.'

'But it would worry her, her youngest son getting the wrong idea, and with her not being well – '

'Well? Of course she's well!' Joshua was almost dancing with impatience to be off. 'What do you mean?'

'You said last week she was under the weather.'

'She was, but it was only a cold. She's all right now. Wait here – I've got to speak to yond' mon.'

He found Ralph with his brother in the sample room, watching as two warehousemen moved a set of polished shelving. Sam glanced warily at his father, but Ralph gave him a composed, 'Good morning.'

From force of habit Joshua greeted the workmen, then said quietly, 'I'd like a word with you, Ralph – in private. You as well, Sam. Is there anybody up on the floors?'

Ralph's eyes were like two unruffled pools, he thought, two *empty* pools, deep blue and very tranquil. Joshua frowned as they made for the stairs. There was no point in coming the innocent. The first floor was empty, apart from fifty or so bales near the doors of the hoist. 'This'll do,' he said briskly. 'Now, Ralph, what's this I hear from Charlie?' He was certain that surprise flashed across the perfect features, and as quickly vanished.

'Why? What has he been telling you?'

'That you've threatened to have him replaced.'

'Me? Threatened –?' Ralph looked him straight in the eye, puzzled and slightly indignant. 'He's mistaken, Papa. I said no such thing.'

'But Charlie assures me you did say it. He quoted you, word for word.' Joshua was watching his son very closely indeed. He was flesh of his own flesh, so he wouldn't knowingly deceive him.

Ralph shrugged. 'Barnes is lying.'

'*Mister* Barnes to you, Ralph! Or Uncle Charlie, which is what you all called him through childhood.

Look, lad, Charlie hasn't lied to me in forty-four years.'

Ralph's upper lip lifted slightly to reveal his perfect teeth. 'There's always a first time, Papa. Has he told you he doesn't want me here? Now that *would* be the truth. He made it obvious on my first day.'

'Then surely it's odd that he's given me glowing reports of your progress?' Sam shifted his feet uncomfortably, and Joshua put out a restraining hand. 'You stay where you are,' he said shortly. 'We said there'd be no secrets now you're all in the business. This is your brother, don't forget, calling my best and oldest friend a liar.'

There was silence in the big, half-empty room. All that could be heard was the distant sound of carriage wheels and horses, and the clatter of a winch in the street outside. Joshua rocked back and forth on his heels and toes. Above Ralph's golden head he could see specks of cotton dust in a beam of sunlight from a window. His mind was racing. If he didn't handle this right his plans for his sons were jeopardised almost before they'd begun. 'Maybe it's a misunderstanding,' he said at last, 'and maybe you're right about Charlie not wanting you. I'll look into it further. For now, perhaps you'd give me your ideas on what you're here for, how you understood what we said that Sunday morning in my study.'

'You suggested, and I agreed, that I was to come here to learn this end of the business, so that when I know it inside out I'll be capable of running this office and warehouse, and of handling the imports and exports without the services of an agent.'

'That's it, more or less,' Joshua agreed peaceably, 'but we didn't mention a time span, did we? How long do you envisage it will take you to learn everything "inside out"?'

'Several months, I suppose.'

'Months? Years, more like. I've been at it since I was seven, nearly fifty years, and I don't flatter myself I know

it all even now. But we'll have to discuss that later. Before
we go down let me be clear on what passed between you
and Charlie. He insists you said it, so I ask you once more
– did you threaten to have him replaced?'

'Certainly not, Father.'

Even as he took the weight of that denial Joshua
noted the abandoning of 'Papa'. Was it Ralph's way of
announcing that he considered himself a man? 'Right,' he
said sombrely, and stared at the floor. 'I'll have another
word with Charlie.' He looked upwards suddenly from
beneath his brows and glimpsed Ralph's unguarded
expression. His stomach knotted in dismay. Triumph!
Master Ralph thought he'd won!

'And in the meantime,' he continued, with no change
of tone, 'you will take the next train home. Don't
speak of this matter to your mother or your sister,
but keep yourself available to see me in my study at
seven o'clock.'

Ralph's composure vanished, and the flesh around his
nose went pale and waxy. 'You're not taking that old
fool's word over mine?'

Careful, Joshua warned himself, he's only seventeen.
'The next train, if you please,' he said quietly. 'Let's call
it a temporary suspension until this is cleared up. Seven
o'clock in my study.'

With a flap of his coat-tails Ralph whirled from the
room. Joshua walked heavily to the hoist and unbarred
the door. A cool breeze blew in and brought the smells
of the city, and he sat down on a bale and breathed
noisily through his nose. 'Come here, Sam,' he said over
his shoulder, and patted the bale next to him. 'Tell me,
how do you read that little lot?'

'I don't believe Ralph,' said Sam bluntly.

'I see. Why not?'

'For one thing, just now in the sample room one of
the men called him Mr Schofield, not Mr Ralph. I said
to him on the quiet that as far as I knew there was
only one Mr Schofield; he said that if he was to have

authority here at Mosley Street he would insist on being
addressed properly.' Sam sat down next to his father and
stared at his feet. 'It should have been funny coming
from a seventeen-year-old, or maybe a bit pathetic, but
somehow it was neither.'

No, thought Joshua, it would have been unnerving,
like someone speaking a foreign tongue and expecting to
be understood. 'He said something of the sort to Charlie,'
he admitted wearily. All at once anger gripped him and
he jumped to his feet. 'Damn me, I've got no time for this
kind of thing. I'm trying to get Jericho back on its feet,
never mind worrying about me-laddo's vanity. Fasten
these doors, Sam, and then come down and we'll look
at the books. No – with Ralph gone you'd better check
what those two fellas are up to in the sample room.'

Charlie was waiting, pacing the floor. 'He denies it,
and I've sent him home,' said Joshua briskly. 'We're
going into it this evening. Now, we'd better see what's
been invoiced for this week, and as for the Exchange,
we need to buy every decent bale we can get our hands
on, don't we? Ah, here's Sam. I've been telling him
how business to the value of a million takes place there
at one o'clock on Tuesdays, all by word of mouth and
handshakes. Come on, both of you, let's start on these
books or we'll never even see the place, let alone do
business.' He shot a look at his friend's set face. 'Put
it out of your mind for now, Charlie. We'll discuss it
when we get back.'

Sam thought that friends of forty-four years' standing
should be able to talk to each other in private, and
cudgelled his brains for an excuse to leave them in peace.
'Don't forget that Henry Fairbrother has asked me round
to Whitworth Street to see their alterations, Father.'

'Has he now? It's the first I've heard of it. All right,
Charlie and me'll discuss things on our own, then, when
we get back.' Joshua took off his coat and marched across
to the desk as if he was ready to take an axe to it.

*   *   *

'Of course Charlie wants him there.' They were in bed, discussing the day's events, and Joshua was feeling better now he had Rachel's familiar softness at his side. 'Or he did until Ralph started giving himself airs. Don't forget it was Charlie who suggested he had his own room, when I'd have been content to see him with a table and chair in a corner. And he fixed him a beauty, the one with the panelling and the good fireplace and the view across Piccadilly. I must admit I did wonder if he'd have preferred working with James or Sam, but he gave no hint of it.'

'But why did Ralph say it was obvious on his first day that Charlie didn't want him?'

'As far as I can make out he didn't do enough bowing and scraping when he arrived, nor showed him round the Exchange like a prize heifer at the market.' He pulled her closer. 'He might be quiet, love, but he's got a high opinion of himself. I just don't know who he takes after.'

Rachel would have laughed if she'd been less worried. 'His father isn't exactly a modest violet,' she pointed out, and gave his neck a little kiss.

'No, maybe I'm not, but I didn't think I knew it all at seventeen. I buckled to and learned the hard way – trial, error and experience.'

'But does he truly believe that Charlie's not up to the job?'

'Oh, he believes it,' said Joshua grimly. 'He hasn't been there five minutes but he thinks he knows more than a man who's devoted his life to the business. I've tried to make him see it's a long hard slog, getting to know cotton; but he seems to think if he can tell the difference between long and short staple, and recognise good middling uplands, then he's well away. He believes it's all finance, you see, the state of the markets and whether you can buy low and sell high. There's no doubt he has a distinct flair for it.'

For a moment Rachel allowed herself to bask in

maternal pride. Perhaps this most difficult of her children would make a name for himself as a financier? A cotton merchant like those in the great mansions of Liverpool? Thoughtfully she twirled a few of the hairs on Joshua's chest. 'I still don't see how he and Charlie can work together after this. Surely there'll be too much resentment on either side?'

'Well, like I said, once he accepted that I'd rather lose his services than Charlie's, he changed his tune. He's agreed to apologise to Charlie and to keep his opinions to himself in future. And as I'm not quite a fool, I've arranged for him to spend less time at Mosley Street. He can visit the Exchange when he likes and learn more about his precious stocks and shares. He'll spend two days a week here in Saltley – Fridays at the mine and Saturdays at Jericho – and I'll see he won't be sitting on his backside in the offices all the time. He's got to learn that the wealth they play about with on the markets comes from human sweat. Don't worry, love. I'll sort him out.'

Rachel tried to relax. Joshua would guide him through the next few years, mould him, instil into him his own humane principles and scrupulous honesty – and with luck his own love of hard work.

As always, they went to sleep in each other's arms, and it was in the early hours that she awoke and eased herself gently to the edge of the bed, where it was cooler. Joshua's words echoed disagreeably in her head: 'Once he'd accepted that I'd rather lose his services than Charlie's . . .'

Rachel thought of Charlie Barnes, with his long, ungainly frame and lined, dog-like face. He was a good man, she'd always known that. In the early days when Joshua was building up his business Charlie had never been away from the house, and often she wearied of hearing his name on her husband's lips. Charlie says, Charlie thinks, Charlie believes. . . . Yet he'd proved time and again that he was a true and loyal friend to them both. It was just that for some reason she was never completely at ease with him. There was something about the intensity of that spaniel gaze that unsettled her. And if she wasn't at ease with Charlie, was it so very surprising that her son wasn't, either?

Mary was wearing a new dress. It was pink, with tiny velvet bows down the bodice and a pointed lace collar. She was bubbling with happiness, and having more trouble than usual with her hair. 'Help me, Tizzie, there's an angel. I want to look just right because all the family will be there – aunts, uncles and cousins, as well as his parents and brothers.'

Tizzie seized the brush and the pot of hair-pins, and told herself that if she heard one more word about the Hartleys' musical evening she would flatten her sister without a qualm. In the meantime she contented herself with a few ferocious jabs of the pins.

'Ooh, careful! When we're married I'll be able to keep it tidy more easily under my cap, though of course I shall wear one of the small, pretty ones except when I'm cleaning or washing. William says I mustn't have my hair cut, not even an inch. He says he wants to run his hands through it, because he knows it will feel like soft, warm silk.'

Tizzie sighed wearily. What a load of drivel. She blanked out a sudden mental image of Mary and William in the intimacy of their bedroom, substituting the far more enlivening one of herself and Edward in the same situation. Not that she could see him coming out with that sort of stuff; she didn't think he was a sentimental man. He would be more one who knew what he wanted, and would plan and scheme to get it. After all, he'd planned and schemed to get her, hadn't he? Oh yes, things were moving between them, but not quickly enough for her, so she planned to hurry them up as soon as the chance presented itself.

First of all, though, there were things she needed to know.

Really, it would go against the grain to ask Mary exactly what she and William got up to if they found themselves alone together, but she needed information. One day, she vowed – and soon – she would know everything about what went on in private between men and women, and then Mary could come to *her* with questions.

'Are you listening, Tizzie? I said I was asking Mother earlier on whether I could put another row of lace on my new shimmies, and – Tizzie, listen! – and she went all funny and stiff-faced, and said, "Stop babbling, girl. I've just told you that your father's not so well, and all you can do is talk about your underwear", and then she marched out of the room. Have you noticed anything wrong with him?'

Tizzie shrugged. 'No. But then, he always looks so ghastly you could hardly tell the difference if he was dying, could you? Just a minute, though, he said something about asking Barney Jellicoe to come up from the cellar now and again to help on the counter. That could have meant he was feeling in need of a break. As long as he didn't want me down there I didn't pay much attention.'

'But I thought you liked helping?'

'I do. On the books, though, not in that flea-ridden hole. If I was a man I could do the books and the cash and have access to the safe and go to Manchester on my own to conduct business. Whereas when I went with him yesterday he said I was never, ever, to venture along Long Millgate on my own.'

Mary was twitching at her best petticoats. 'What made him say that?'

'Two women came towards us, well-dressed but a bit loud and painted-up. They sniggered at Father and one of them touched my sleeve and whispered, "Want a job, love?". Then they passed on, giggling. Father was livid.

He practically ran me along the street to the jewellers, and then could hardly breathe when we got there. He made us both look ridiculous, and all because of those two women.'

Mary was putting on her best bonnet over the smooth heavy loops of her hair, and she watched Tizzie curiously through the looking-glass. 'But they'd be prostitutes. No wonder he was angry.'

Tizzie was so intrigued she forgot to conceal her ignorance. 'Women of the streets, you mean? And they asked if I wanted a job.' She examined the idea. 'But they weren't like those gargoyle creatures we saw in Gallgate that day, the ones with the sores who kept scratching themselves. Mary, what exactly are prostitutes?'

Her sister whirled round, her surprise tinged with scorn. 'Tizzie, you must know! They're women of easy virtue. They sell their bodies, let men use them for money – whatever the going rate is according to the district where they work, and whether they're pretty or not. Everybody knows there's dozens of them in Saltley, and hundreds in Manchester – whole houses full of them, so they say.'

Tizzie ground her teeth so hard she could hear the grating noise inside her head. How did her giggly little sister come by her knowledge, when she, Tizzie, knew absolutely nothing? She watched Mary dash to the window to look for William's aunt and uncle who were to call for her on their way to the Hartleys'. Her mind raced. Guile was called for. 'You're so well-informed,' she murmured admiringly, 'so well-up on matters we aren't supposed to discuss. I expect it's because you get out and about and mix with more people than I do. Mother isn't likely to tell me anything, is she, so perhaps you could put me right on the things I'm so ignorant about.'

Blithely ignoring the careful plea, Mary bounced around in front of the window. 'They're here!' she cried. 'Do I look all right, Tizzie?' She patted her

bonnet and then pursed her lips and stood immobile,
like a doll.

Tizzie couldn't help smiling. However irritating, Mary
could always win a smile from her in the end. 'You look
lovely,' she said sincerely. 'I hope William knows how
lucky he is.'

In a whirl of pink dress and white petticoats Mary
dashed down to the sitting room to say goodbye to
her mother, while Tizzie watched the street outside.
A moment later a man in good unfashionable clothes
handed Mary up into a smart trap. His plump little wife
patted her hand, and she was chattering happily as they
headed away in the direction of the Hartleys'.

Evidently the aunt and uncle approved of Mary.
Everybody approved of Mary. She herself did, with
reservations. There was something appealing about her
sister, something open and very lovable. And in the last
few weeks their mother had warmed towards William.
He had been to supper three times, and once to Sunday
dinner; perhaps most important of all he had talked with
Father in the privacy of his dusty little counting room
behind the shop.

'He's telling Father about his plans for the future,
and I'm sure he'll be impressed,' confided Mary while
the men were closeted together. 'Mother's still a bit
disapproving, but she knows by now that she'd be a
fool to oppose us getting married.'

Tizzie had grave doubts as to whether her mother
would view herself as a fool, when it was obvious she
considered Mary to be one. But Father had spoken, and
as always the shrivelled little man had won the day. She
knew it was only a matter of weeks before a date was
set for the wedding. This would all have driven her mad
with envy and frustration if it hadn't been for Edward
Mayfield.

It seemed very quiet with Mary gone, but two floors
below she could hear the three gold balls creaking and
swaying in the breeze. Listening to the hated sound, she

gave a small, triumphant smile. The pawnshop hadn't put him off, after all. It would be forty-eight hours before she saw him again, and the time lay ahead of her like a desert confronting a thirsty traveller.

Sitting back in the bedside chair, she felt reluctant to face another evening doing nothing of significance. Everything seemed flat and boring after the challenge of that first committee meeting. Edward had called for her in a hired cab, and returned her the same way, as agreed with her mother that day in the park. Brief journeys, both of them, with scant opportunity for talk; yet by the end of the evening they were on first-name terms; he had kissed her fingertips and the inside of her wrist; and laid a hand against the small of her back. She told herself she could feel the heat of his palm through the waist-gathers of her dress and petticoat.

She had arrived home stimulated and well-pleased with herself, but on reflection unsatisfied, and she wasn't sure why. The meeting had been at the home of Eli Walton, master of Bluebell Mill and mayor of Saltley. Tizzie missed very little as they were shown in; a dozen or so men and women were assembled, well-known figures in the town, and she saw at once that Edward was warmly regarded. He introduced her with a small flourish, as a conjuror might bring a nosegay from up his sleeve. 'Miss Tizzie Ridings, here at my request because of her keen interest in raising funds for our purpose.'

Awareness of her background showed on some of the faces, but not all. An elderly man came forward with a pleasant word and led her to a place at the big table, and there was a general murmur of greeting. Tizzie seated herself with composure, seeing two things very clearly: one, she was being accepted so readily because of the man who had brought her; and two, the acceptance would be permanent only if she made herself indispensable.

Then Edward took his place with easy self-assurance; she watched with her intent emerald gaze, telling herself that he could unlock the door to the kind of life she wanted. She would *not* let him go, and that was that.

Then someone else arrived to a flurry of attention and a chorus of 'Good evening, your lordship,' and 'Glad to have you with us, Sir.' Plump, amiable and untidy, young Lord Alsing was offered the best chair, 'Don't swoon,' Tizzie warned herself crossly. 'He might be nobility, but he's an oaf compared to Edward.'

Slender and erect, she sat there with her hair glinting in the gas-light, and listened as Eli Walton held forth in sonorous mayoral tones. Each successive phrase increased her confidence. 'His lordship here for this first official meeting . . . future fund-raising for beds and equipment . . . volunteers to organise whatever we decide on. . . .'

Tizzie was in her element. This was what she could do – she knew it. In her notebook she had details of a dozen fund-raising schemes, with full costings and estimates of possible profits. It had taken her almost a week to prepare, badgering caterers and the owners of halls and meeting-houses. She had revelled in it, finding that tradespeople forgot her youth when she talked business, and that sometimes the name Ridings brought forth reluctant respect rather than disdain. She hoped Edward would give her the opening to enlarge on her ideas.

Viewed from five days later, it wasn't so very surprising that she'd been elected assistant secretary. Nobody else had volunteered to play second fiddle to the formidable Eleanor Boulton, but at the time she had almost leapt at the chance; when nobody was looking Edward had lowered an eyelid in a conspiratorial wink.

As for her mother, it had taken only a mention of who was on the committee, only a passing reference to Francis Soar, to obtain her permission to attend meetings as often as she liked, and be taken to and from them by Edward. She couldn't help wondering if that had been his aim all along.

She smiled as she recalled the surprising thrill of his nearness, and had no doubt she could speed things up between them. Maybe, yes maybe, she would leave it a bit longer before asking Mary about the things that puzzled her. Closer acquaintance with Edward might teach her what she wanted to know.

CHAPTER EIGHT

Beneath the Surface

'IT'S NOT FAIR!' cried Mary, running up the stairs behind Tizzie. 'It took weeks for her to let me walk out alone with William, but she lets you go out with Edward right away.'

Tizzie's mind was on other things, but with an effort she dragged it to the present moment. She hadn't told Mary that she was to be allowed out alone with Edward. 'I suppose it's because we're fund-raising for a good cause,' she said mildly, 'rather than courting.'

'Because you're mixing with money, more like! My William is every bit as good as your fine architect!'

'Of course he is,' agreed Tizzie absently. 'Don't upset yourself, love.' She untied her bonnet and balanced it upside down on the knob of the bedpost.

Mary eyed her closely, and then gave her a shamefaced kiss. She was never bad-tempered for more than a minute. 'Sorry, Tizz. I'm a meanie to be annoyed as soon as you come in, but Mother's only just told me. I was furious with her, not you.' She hitched up her skirts and climbed on the bed to sit cross-legged. 'Do you really like him? He's ever so elegant, isn't he? Has he held your hand yet?'

Tizzie smiled faintly. 'Oh, yes.'

'Has he – has he tried to kiss you?'

Tizzie smiled again. 'Tried, and succeeded.'

Mary gave an excited wriggle. 'Heavens! What would Mother say?'

What indeed? Tizzie climbed up next to her sister and stared at their joint reflections in the mirror. It was easier that way than confronting the eager, pink-cheeked face at close range. Go warily, she warned herself. 'I've been meaning to ask you,' she said carefully, 'because you're better-informed than I am about so many things. It's a bit private and personal, I know, but what sort of liberties does William take when you're on your own together?'

'None,' said Mary blankly. 'Why? What sort does Edward take?'

'I'm not sure what are liberties and what aren't,' admitted Tizzie. 'But – you know – would he touch your bosom, for instance?'

Mary blushed, and swallowed guiltily. 'Well, yes, just once, when we kissed, his hand did brush against my bosom.'

Now they were getting down to it, thought Tizzie. 'Your bare skin, do you mean?'

Mary was outraged. 'Certainly not! How could you think it?'

Tizzie felt a surge of triumph. Bull-beef wasn't like Edward, then. They sat and stared at their reflected faces until Mary said awkwardly, 'Look, Tizz, let's talk for a minute, shall we? I'm sure Edward's a gentleman, but he's kissed you the first time you were alone together. Has he done anything else?'

Tizzie hesitated, and at last said flatly, 'Yes. He unfastened the buttons of my dress and the drawstring of my shimmy, and fondled my breasts. He bit them as well, but not hard.' It pleased her to see Mary's mouth fall open at least an inch, making her look plain and a trifle vacant. 'But what I was most unsure about was when he put his hand up my skirts.'

Mary whirled round, her dark eyes immense. 'Up your skirts?' she repeated hoarsely. 'Oh, Tizzie! Where were you when he did it?'

'Oh, there was nobody around. We were down Back Lane, in the trees behind the reservoir. He urged me to lift my skirts and lower my drawers, and then he touched me – you know, here, in the private place. Only for a moment, of course, because I stopped him almost at once.' She recalled Edward's bad humour at that point, and her own amazement that her body seemed to be in charge, rather than her mind.

Mary remained unnervingly silent, but Tizzie's brilliant green gaze held hers defiantly. 'I liked it,' she said, 'but I did wonder if perhaps he thought me forward.'

'Forward?' hissed her sister. '*Forward*? Tizzie, how could you? And how could Edward?' Tears gathered in her eyes, and she grabbed Tizzie by the upper arms. 'How could you not know? How could you let him take you behind Boulton's reservoir like that, a man you hardly know? How could you?'

'I like him, and I was curious. That's how.'

'Listen to me. This is important. We are virgins, you and me. We're unmarried, and no man has intimate knowledge of us, sexual knowledge, that is – intercourse. Don't you see, he treated you like a trollop, a loose woman. You asked me the other day about prostitutes. Well, that's how they behave. He – he didn't show you *his* private part, did he? Tizzie – he didn't touch you with it?'

'With what?'

'His – his member. You know, down here.'

Tizzie wasn't sure whether she was pleased or sorry to have to deny it. 'No, of course he didn't. Is that what it is, though, this intercourse or whatever you call it?'

'No, there's more to it than that. I should have told you when I found out properly from Mrs Kenny. It's when a man inserts his member into your private part. It's what can give you a child, even if it's the very first time. That's why you have to be married. If you were single and expecting a baby you'd be a fallen woman. You remember Annie Dewsnap who was sent to the asylum? Well, I heard she was put away because of that.' Weighed down with guilt, Mary rocked back and forth with her hands tight around her knees. 'I should have told you at once, but I was worried you might think me lacking in modesty for having talked about it.'

Tizzie was stunned, yet filled with relief that she hadn't let Edward do anything further. She felt quite sick at the thought of having a baby. Didn't women sometimes die in childbirth? And wasn't it absolute agony? Babies wakened at all hours and screamed to be fed, and dirtied their undergarments all the time. She wasn't sure she wanted one when she was married, let alone before.

She was mortified at Mary's remark about prostitutes. It explained Edward's surprised little smile when she went down Back Lane so readily with him; his haste and urgency, as if he expected her to change her mind at any moment. Still, he must have taken her for a woman of some experience rather than an innocent. Oh, why did the most enjoyable activities always carry some kind of penalty?

Looking at her sister's tear-streaked face, Tizzie knew that once again she was in her debt. On impulse she gave her a hug. 'It looks as if I have some serious thinking to do before the next time I see Edward,' she said soberly.

They discussed it no further, but prepared for bed and then slept cuddled together as if they were still children. Tizzie wakened before dawn, her mind eager and alert, analysing the events of the evening. She felt Mary's warm breath on her shoulder, and with rare tenderness sought and held her sister's hand.

Another spur to serious thinking came the next day when she was helping her mother in the kitchen, peeling potatoes with barely concealed boredom. 'Perhaps you could bring Edward in for a bite to eat after your meeting tomorrow,' suggested her mother. 'Your father wants another look at him.'

Tizzie didn't like the sound of that. Her mother had embarrassed her in the park tea-room, and it might be even worse with her father. 'He's just one of the committee,' she said briskly, 'not a suitor.'

'Not yet,' agreed her mother weightily, 'but we thought

it would be polite, like, to ask him in when he's walked you home. I know he's used to grand houses, but you've nothing to be ashamed of here.'

Nothing except the smell of camphor and flea-powder, thought Tizzie wearily, and shot a glance into the next room. It was shiningly clean and better-furnished than many a home in Saltley, she was sure; but compared to the Waltons' it was a poor sort of place. 'Can't we leave it for another week or two, until I know him better?' she asked edgily.

They exchanged looks, and Maria hid a relieved smile. Those eyes announced Tizzie's intentions, right enough. She smoothed her white sleeve-guards. 'Look in the oven and see how the stew's coming on,' she instructed, 'and Tizzie – you do know how, that is, I hope . . .' This was going to be difficult, but Abel had insisted. 'You do know how to behave when you're alone with Edward?'

Bending over the oven, Tizzie let out a scornful sigh. 'If I do, it's not because of what you've told me, Mother!'

Dull colour rose in her mother's cheeks. 'Up to now I've told you as much as you need to know, madam,' she said sharply. 'But your father insists you must be spoken to. . . .'

'What? Like you spoke to Mary?'

Her mother glared at her. 'That was different. We made clear to William that we expected him to – to respect Mary. But Edward's a gentleman, from a different background, and though we'd expect him to be above reproach, we know nothing about him.'

Tizzie relaxed. It *was* different. They didn't feel they could lecture Edward, and for that she was thankful. As for her father – what did that dried-up little husk know about how men and women should behave? The most he ever managed was to clasp her mother's wrist. She shrugged, but reluctant respect hovered at the edge of her mind. He had realised, goodness knew how, that

she might need guidance; and according to her mother
he had insisted she was given it. He'd surprised her once
or twice just lately. Was there more to him than she'd
ever guessed?

'All right,' she said impatiently. 'How should I
behave?'

Maria tugged at her cuffs again. 'You must never allow
him to kiss you or touch you anywhere but on your hand.
And you must never, ever, allow him to disarrange your
clothes.'

'And what would happen if I did?'

'You would lose your good name, lady, and more
besides. Some men would take advantage of any girl
they found themselves alone with. Just remember what
I say, that's all.'

'I'll remember, Mother. And don't worry.' Then,
because at times he did come close to being half-way
acceptable as a parent, she asked, 'Is Father any
better?'

'It's taken you long enough to ask,' retorted her
mother. 'I don't think he's well, but he won't see
a doctor, so all I can do is persuade him to take
things easy.'

Well, if the silly man wouldn't take medical advice, she
certainly wasn't going to waste time worrying about him,
thought Tizzie, losing interest. She had more pressing
things on her mind.

She knew she wasn't imagining an increased warmth
from the committee. When she arrived Eli Walton had
said, 'Ah, here's Tizzie – she'll put us straight on the
profit margins.' Mrs Boulton had slapped the chair next
to her and commanded, 'Sit here, my dear, in case I need
a bit of quick figuring.' Clear-headed, quick and efficient,
Tizzie couldn't help but see that she would soon fulfil her
ambition of making herself indispensable.

They were planning four fund-raising schemes, and
three of them were hers: a Clothes Fair in the main hall

of Bethesda Sunday School – that was for the labouring classes; a Variety Concert at the Little Palace Theatre – that was for anybody who could afford a ticket. The most ambitious was an Autumn Ball at the Town Hall, aimed at the moneyed classes.

Tizzie could have smiled at the way these top business people were so impressed when she came up with an estimate of profit within minutes of somebody's off-the-cuff suggestion. For years she had waited in vain to hear her father praise her ability with figures, and it boosted her self-esteem that the master of Bluebell Mill should lean across the table and say things like: 'Give us that break-down again, Tizzie. Aye, that's it – good girl!'

From time to time in the next hour she caught Edward's gaze on her, and tried to fathom his expression. Was it surprise? No, more like pride. She recalled the way he had introduced her a fortnight ago. Perhaps he felt like a conjuror performing his most skilful trick. Or maybe he was just impatient for their walk home? It had been all decorum and small talk on their way to the meeting, because then it had been daylight. Going home would be different; and in more ways than one.

At last they were finished. Mrs Boulton closed her notebook and said, 'If you're free on Friday afternoon, Tizzie, perhaps you'd come round to our house to help me write up the minutes? And we have to send letters to the variety artists, and confirm the date of the ball with the orchestra.' It was as Tizzie had anticipated: assistant secretary was a high-flown title for unpaid drudge, but it didn't matter. Already she had access to two of the best houses in Saltley and was on good terms with the mayor and his wife. As she had planned, she was making her presence felt.

They left with an air of pleasant propriety, the assistant secretary and the committee member who would see her safe home. Their footsteps echoed on the flagstones and they walked well apart. 'Well', said Edward, 'how do you like helping the dynamic Mrs Boulton?'

Tizzie smiled. 'She's not so clever. I can handle her.'

He laughed. 'I believe you can, at that. You're good, you know. One or two of them have thanked me for persuading you to help.' Once out of sight of the house he took her arm. Boulton's mill loomed ahead of them and Tizzie tried to ignore the thudding in her chest. 'I haven't been able to stop thinking about you since the last time,' he whispered. 'You're so very beautiful, Tizzie.'

Then the dark void of Back Lane gaped at their side, with the mill reservoir glimmering faintly in the starlight. Remembering her plan, Tizzie turned to look deliberately up and down the street. There was nobody about, so she let him lead her into the overgrown lane. At once his arm went round her waist and he hurried her along, then whirled her to face him and pushed back her bonnet to kiss her.

Something in her stance checked him. 'Come on!' he said eagerly.

She ducked her head and avoided his mouth. 'Let's talk for a minute.'

His smile shone briefly. 'We can talk anywhere, at any time Tizzie, but we're alone now. I want to kiss you and hold you.'

'That's what I want to talk about,' she said firmly. 'I've been thinking very hard since the last time we were here, and I've come to the conclusion that you treated me like a trollop.'

He gave a short angry laugh, like a bark. 'You weren't exactly averse to it, as I recall.'

'No, I wasn't,' she admitted. 'I liked it.'

'So I gathered. What's the problem, then?'

'We're just acquaintances, so far, and that kind of intimacy isn't proper between acquaintances.'

He tightened his hold and gave her a little shake. 'You've been telling somebody about it, haven't you?'

So he didn't want anyone else to know. Mary was

right – it *was* shameful. 'My mother warned me in general terms,' she told him, 'but my sister knows all about it.'

'Hey!' he said uneasily. 'It was just between us. Our little secret. It will spoil it if anyone else knows.'

'You mean I mustn't tell anyone at all?' She tried to sound very innocent. 'Mrs Boulton or Mrs Walton, for instance?'

'What? Of course you mustn't! What is this?'

His words gave her a surprising little pain, as if a blunt knife was prising her ribs apart. Did he know how he was revealing himself? Did he care? 'Come on, Tizzie,' he said impatiently. 'A kiss, at least.'

'All right,' she said. 'A kiss, and maybe more, but when I say "stop", you stop. If you don't, or if you try to force me, I'll tell everybody that you attacked me without warning.'

As he stared at her she could see the whites of his eyes and the pale blur of his face. Then he laughed, and the sound of it sent the blood racing to her head. 'Quite the little schemer, eh?' he said softly, and slid his hands lower down her back. He was still laughing when his open mouth found hers.

The ten-thirty train sped from Saltley to Manchester, with Rachel and her daughter sitting side by side with their backs to the engine. They rarely travelled without one of their menfolk, so the guard had been solicitous in seeing them into their seats.

Sarah was glowing with pleasure and excitement. Her father had made an appointment for her to visit the Royal Infirmary for advice on how to set up the new sick-bay at Jericho. Anxious to appear mature and responsible, she was wearing a pale grey dress and bonnet and a short poplin cape in darker grey. The night before she had removed a flutter of pink ribbons from the bonnet. 'I don't want to look like a woman of leisure, Mama,' she said earnestly as she stripped them away.

At her side Rachel stared out at the lush fields bordering Saltley Bog and told herself she should be feeling on top of the world. A more leisurely life beckoned now that the food centre and school at Jericho were closing down. She would rediscover the pleasures of visiting friends, doing fine needlework and making Joshua's favourite dishes, – the ones that had been too fiddly to tackle in the last few years; and she would have time for her own children again. Sarah, eager to devote herself to nursing the workers; James, loving every minute he spent at High Lee, and supervising work on his fine house ready for when he and Esther moved in after the wedding; and Sam, surprising everybody but herself by his interest and application at the mill.

As for Ralph, things were easier with him, or so it appeared. Joshua reported that all was in order at Mosley Street, with Ralph seeing less of Charlie under the new arrangement, and apparently enjoying his days at the mine and at Jericho.

Other mothers spoke of their children's late teens as the most difficult years, and Rachel had concluded that this must be the reason she always felt at a disadvantage with her youngest. Sometimes, plagued by guilt, she would question whether she loved him as she did the others. Was she at fault for not showing more affection? Did he feel deprived of true love from his mother? Then a blast from those empty eyes would chill her, and the lack of feeling between them would eat into her soul like frost into soft foliage.

That was why she'd agreed to Sarah visiting the Infirmary alone, leaving her free to call on Charlie Barnes. She wasn't easy in her mind about it because she hadn't told Joshua – she wasn't sure why. She wasn't even sure why she wanted to see Charlie herself, when Joshua knew him so much better than she did. She only knew that it felt right, so it must be instinct, and when she followed her instinct things usually turned out for the best.

Sarah pulled at her arm when they reached the line of cabs outside Victoria Station. 'We're early, so can't we walk, Mama?'

Rachel agreed with a smile. She liked Manchester. She liked the grand new buildings that were displacing the mills in the city centre. She liked the hurrying crowds and the well-dressed women, and Joshua had told her there were less of the destitute about than for a long time. Once, a couple of years ago, she had come across a whole family singing hymns near St Ann's church. Clean, but gaunt and ill-clad, they sang in choir-taught harmony, with the youngest holding out a box for coppers. Rachel thought she recognised the eldest girl, and on enquiring found they were from Saltley; they had walked the eight miles to Manchester that morning, as they couldn't face begging in their home town. That had been another family to receive baskets of food from Meadowbank House, and more names to be written in Joshua's book of prospective employees.

But today it was bright and sunny, with the first scent of autumn on the air. Her spirits rose as they headed towards Piccadilly, and she reflected on the happy chance of Sarah's appointment falling on a Friday, when Ralph was away from the office. Once at the great pillared portico of the Infirmary she gave Sarah a quick farewell kiss. 'Come across the road when you've finished here, love. If I'm not in the downstairs office I'll be with Uncle Charlie, and Mr Wagstaff will send somebody to find me.'

She smiled when she saw the new red rose on Joshua's trumpet over the entrance. He came up with so many ideas, and this was one of his best. The clerk nearly fell off his chair when she walked in. 'Mrs Schofield, what a pleasure, ma'am! Please take a seat. What can we do for you?'

Rachel smiled. 'Good morning, Mr Wagstaff. Miss Sarah has an appointment close by, and I just thought I'd call in and have a word with Mr Barnes. Is he in?'

John Wagstaff stared at her dotingly. He had admired Mrs Schofield since the days when he carried rolls of Joshua's cotton to Manchester on his two-horse dray back in the forties; he was a Dutchman if she wasn't as lovely now as the day he first saw her. 'He's on the floors, somewhere, seeing to the stamping of the rolls, and such. I'll send the lad up for him.'

'No, I'll go and find him myself. The exercise will do me good. Please, Mr Wagstaff, there's no need to bring him down, really there isn't.'

She didn't put on airs, he thought, which was more than could be said for her son. Master Ralph didn't get his ways from his mother and father, and that was a fact.

Rachel went up three flights without finding Charlie or anyone else, and knew that the next floor was the last one for goods, because Charlie had his own suite of rooms on the very top floor. It was years since she'd been up there. Nowadays he took them to dine at some hotel or other whenever he invited them both to a meal. Then she heard his voice against the rattle of the hoist. He was in his waistcoat and shirtsleeves with three workmen; the metal hoisting arm was swung out through the tall arched doors, and the men were winching hessian-wrapped rolls of cotton cloth down to the alley.

Rachel waited until one of them should turn and see her. It always gave her a thrill to see the end-product of her husband's ventures, whether it was the shiny coal sacked up for domestic use, the good meat and produce that came down from High Lee, or this fine shirting destined for overseas and stamped with the trumpet and rose.

Stencil and ink-pad in hand, Charlie turned to the next stack of rolls and saw her standing in the shadows in her cream-coloured dress. 'Rachel!' He couldn't have looked more amazed if an angel had descended.

'Good-morning, Charlie.' She nodded pleasantly to the men and moved nearer the opening to look down to the alley.

'Come away!' Charlie said sharply. 'And mind your dress on the wheel behind you!'

She knew he was flustered at her sudden appearance or he would never have spoken to her like that. Obediently she stepped back from the rope and the wheel, catching the smell of the grease that covered its broad hub. It was tallow – reesty fat, as her mother used to call it – a smell she detested. In the last few years she'd been in homes where such stuff had to be used for both cooking and lighting, and even a hint of it could turn her stomach. She began to feel queasy, but didn't know if it was because of the smell or Charlie's attitude. Why was he so stunned to see her? Was it to do with Ralph?

'I'm afraid I'm disturbing you all,' she said in apology. 'I had a spare half hour, Charlie, so I thought I'd call in to see you and have a word. That's if you can spare the time?'

'Uh – of course I can. Just give me a minute, will you?' He glanced at her dress. 'I'm afraid it's a bit grubby in here. I know, you can wait in comfort, up in my rooms. We'll have coffee or tea, or maybe you'd like a glass of Madeira?' He led her up a wooden staircase, and still flustered, threw open a door. 'Please, Rachel, take a seat and make yourself at home. I'll be with you in five minutes.'

He was so on edge she was embarrassed. 'I'm really sorry to interrupt you like this.'

The dog-like eyes held hers with the intensity that often unnerved her. 'Please,' he said quietly, 'don't apologise for coming, Rachel.' Then he smiled. 'And don't look at the dust – my cleaner doesn't come today.'

He hurried back down the stairs, and she looked around her with interest. She was in the main room with its three circular windows. It was well-furnished: bookcases in rich mahogany, sofas and chairs in soft dark leather edged with brass studs; to cover all three windows there was one vast velvet curtain in a soft red that picked out a deeper red in the patterned carpet.

It was a man's room: orderly, unfussy, well-used and maybe well-loved.

Feeling an intruder in this private domain, she perched on a chair by the end window and studied the view that he must see daily: sky and rooftops above the bustle of Piccadilly, the line of new buildings facing the Infirmary; and the end of Watts' magnificent warehouse on Portland Street. This was probably his favourite chair, she thought idly, and this little table would be for his book or his glass of wine. Its polished surface held a little picture, a miniature in a delicate gold frame. Curiously she looked at it. It was her! A miniature of her! Puzzled, she picked it up. It must have been done years ago, and she certainly hadn't posed for it. But she once had a dress like that: palest pink, with a low-cut bodice; Joshua had bought it for her to wear at a party they'd given to celebrate his purchase of the land for the mills. It was an amazing likeness, if somewhat flattering. The painter had given her an expression that was thoughtful, tender almost, as she imagined she must sometimes appear when she looked at Joshua.

Putting it back on the table exactly as she found it she looked round to see if there were other pictures of the family. Yes, there was Charlie's sketch of Sam and Sarah sitting on top of a five-barred gate at High Lee; she remembered seeing that years ago. And on a lovely old desk in the corner stood a studio photograph of the six of them; Sarah's hair was dressed in ringlets over each ear, and the boys were looking very young and well-scrubbed. She knew about that, as well. They'd given it to Charlie four or five years ago.

Still feeling puzzled, she looked at the miniature again. Surely it was a very expensive frame? It looked like gold, and the delicate scrollwork – was it what they called filigree? And were those real pearls? And what were the little blue jewels that matched the pictured eyes so exactly? Could he have had it painted as a present for Joshua? Perhaps she shouldn't mention it. Then she heard him on the stairs, and jumped up to stand at the window. 'I'm just looking at your view, Charlie,' she smiled, 'and you have a real gift for creating a beautiful room.'

He laughed awkwardly, and moved restlessly around. 'It suits me. It's warm and comfortable, and it couldn't be much closer to the job, could it? Please sit down, Rachel. What can I offer you to drink?'

She agreed to a cup of tea, and he went to the kitchen to make it himself. Her eyes returned to the miniature, but it was no longer there. He must have moved it when she wasn't looking. How very odd. In spite of her looks Rachel was a modest woman, but a disturbing idea jumped into her mind and wouldn't be moved. Did he harbour a fondness for her? A special regard? More than might be expected for the wife of his best friend? Was this why so often she'd been uncomfortable in his presence? Half-forgotten incidents came back to her, puzzling at the time, and then dismissed: years ago, when he snapped at Joshua for helping Sarah across a muddy path and then neglecting to do the same for her; the baskets of glorious flowers he sent when the children were born; the occasions when he'd moved at speed to offer her her wrap, or to warn her if it was unusually cold out of doors; the exquisite little notes of thanks after one of her special meals. Always he contrived to see her on her birthday, bringing some small gift that had been chosen with care, but often, she suspected, with scant regard to cost.

Rachel stared unseeingly out of the window, and knew it to be true. Thirty years. . . . It was more than mere fondness or high regard – he must believe he loved her. Oh Charlie! Charlie Barnes! She felt a crushing weight of responsibility, tinged with guilt. Was this why he had never married? There had been women in his younger days, a procession of them, because he was a rising man of business with a certain ungainly charm. Always, though, he had avoided marriage. 'Another of Charlie's lady-friends has had her marching orders,' Joshua would report in exasperation. 'I've warned him he'll live and die a bachelor, at this rate.'

But in all that time he had never, ever breathed a wrong word to her, never so much as touched her fingertip unbidden; which made his loyalty to Joshua shine across those thirty years like purest gold. And if that was a measure of his regard for the father, surely he would never lie about the son? All at once she felt again the sickness that had bedevilled her by the doors of the hoist, and she shivered as she sat hunched forward in her chair.

'Rachel, Rachel! Are you all right?' Charlie hurried in with a tea-tray, and hovered anxiously in front of her.

She sat up straight. 'I'm fine. Just a momentary nausea, that's all.' She accepted the cup of tea, dismissing her half-formed intention of challenging him about Ralph, or at the very most, offering an oblique apology. Instinct took over again. 'Charlie, I've thought of little else just lately but the situation between you and Ralph.'

He grunted in distress and waved a silencing hand. 'No,' she insisted, 'please hear me out. I've come to say, to – to tell you, how very sorry I am that you, our dearest and oldest friend, should suffer because of our son. Ralph isn't easy – we know that, Joshua and me. You must know it too, now you're in close contact with him. . . .' She wavered to a halt, then found her voice and went on doggedly.

'Joshua doesn't know I'm here, Charlie, and I'm not sure why I didn't tell him. I just felt I must come, and now I'm here I want to say something that he might find too difficult.' She wiggled her fingers in a delaying fashion while she marshalled her thoughts. 'I have a feeling that if anything else happened with Ralph, you might minimise it or even keep silent about it so as not to distress us.' She bit her lip and turned even paler. What kind of mother was she, seeking to reassure a friend rather than back her own son? 'I – I just had this feeling about it. Am I right, Charlie?'

Charlie was still gripping his untouched tea, and now the cup rattled on the saucer. He put it down and clasped his bony hands, while the colour edged up from his jawline. 'Yes, you are,' he said quietly. 'After the bust-up I vowed I wouldn't come between a son and his parents ever again. My regard for – for both of you is too high for that.'

'What would you do, then?'

He avoided her eyes. 'Leave Schofields, probably. I've had many an offer. Or I might start up on my own as an agent, or move to Liverpool.'

'No!' she said urgently. 'Don't leave Joshua! He needs you!'

Charlie gave a small, tight smile. 'He has three fine sons, a lovely daughter, and you. I think he could manage very well without me.'

Rachel moistened her lips, feeling the need to recompense him for those thirty years without a wife and family of his own, and at the same time ease the weight of this strange, new-born guilt. 'Please don't think of doing any such thing. We're not blind, we don't think our children are perfect. You must be quite open with us about Ralph. Joshua could keep him at Jericho for a year or so, until he grows up and gets some sense. Will you promise me that, Charlie? Promise me not to leave Joshua?'

'I promise,' he agreed slowly. Their eyes met, and she thought she read puzzlement in his, or was it awareness? Was he aware that she'd guessed his secret? She reminded herself that he'd always been perceptive; it was she and Joshua who'd been blind. All at once she knew she must leave. It would be catastrophic to jolt him into some kind of admission or revelation. 'I think it's time I went to find Sarah,' she said gently. 'But I must say this. I might not have shown it as I ought, but over the years I've always known you were a true and loyal friend, and I've respected you for it. Will you remember that?'

He gave that tight little smile again, and nodded. 'I'll remember it.'

Under John Wagstaff's warm regard he saw her out, and when she turned a moment later he was standing beneath the trumpet and the rose, watching her.

CHAPTER NINE

Three Shillings More

IT WAS TWENTY TO six on a Monday morning, and Matthew was on his way to work, A light drizzle was falling, and he told himself he could smell the approach of autumn. Inescapably, that brought to mind winter, and he almost shuddered. He had hated every winter for the last fourteen years. At the Mizzen it had meant steaming horses and wet straw, with the yard a sea of mud or ice; a constant battle to keep the young ones warmly clothed and bedded, and his peep-hole in the sleeper nailed over with sacking. Then at Ryder, the lean-to had been so cold his billy-can of water was often frozen solid when he awoke in the morning. Winter had few good memories, but if he stayed on at Ledden Street the one that was fast approaching might well be the best he'd known since his mother had died.

Jonas Carter was hurrying past Greenbank Mill and, as they always walked the last half-mile together, he waited for him. A small, wiry man with prematurely grey hair and a bony, long-jawed face, there wasn't much to Jonas beyond an amazing capacity for hard work: not much size, not much talk, not much laughter, but apparently plenty of what was needed to father a child, because his total to date was nine, with seven of them surviving. Sometimes he let slip a remark that revealed his wife as a shrew, but between themselves the men said she wasn't so shrewish as to refuse him his rights.

'Matthew, lad,' was his greeting. 'A damp one this mornin'.'

Matthew nodded. 'There be a smell of autumn, Jonas.'

They walked along in companionable silence, well aware of their good fortune in being employed by the park authority. They were on thirteen and sixpence a week, three shillings more than under Nuttall, though it was still a fourteen-hour day. 'I been thinkin' of the winter,' said Matthew quietly, 'and whether Mr Broadhurst will be able to keep us on.'

He would if he could, they knew that, because Daniel Broadhurst was no Norman Nuttall. He had a feeling for his men, and a way of giving an encouraging word. On Friday he had said, 'We're well into September now, lads, and as the days draw in your hours'll be shorter; but I thought you'd like to know I've managed to keep your pay the same, at least till the end of October. I'm pleased with the way you've all worked over the last month, and so is Mr Vessey and his committee. If you keep hard at it I'm hoping they'll let me keep you on through the winter, to help the gardeners in the greenhouses, or to work in the big house when the weather's at its worst. Do your best for me, lads, and I'll do my best for you.'

They all muttered in agreement. There were six of them; 'handymen-labourers' was their title, and such was their respect for the foreman they gave him the title 'Mister' behind his back as well as to his face. By contrast, the head park-keeper must be addressed as 'Sir', but they referred to him derisively as 'Messy Vessey', a gibe at his tendency to spray spittle when he spoke.

Now the two men made for the former stables. An old tack room had been set aside for the labourers' use, where they each had their own hook on the wall and a bench to sit on while they ate their packed meal. Mr Broadhurst was waiting with his list, and allocated jobs with his usual speed. Cheerfully Matthew collected shears and a sack to cover his shoulders against the drizzle. For the first time in his life he was working in a happy atmosphere, and the prospect of a job in the mill had become something to aim for in the future, rather than urgent necessity. He whistled between his teeth as he snipped at what seemed like miles of lawn edges, while the drizzle turned to rain. At least he could dry off properly now he was at the Spencers'. Life as a lodger was turning out better than he could have dared hope after that disastrous first night.

It began well enough, when he handed over his first week's money in advance, and then offered to go with Martha to the market to help carry her purchases. Clogs clacking, she walked well apart from him, saying little but with two spots of colour high on her cheeks; he knew she was self-conscious at being seen round the market with a man.

On their return her mother demanded tea for them all, and then Matthew waited while Martha moved her belongings out of his room and put clean sheets on the bed. Such was the novelty of having a woman seeing to his needs that he longed to go and watch her, but he could tell she expected him to stay downstairs. When he was allowed up he found the room even cleaner than before, with the sheet turned down over the knobbly coverlet. Martha hovered in the doorway. 'I wondered – I wondered if you'd mind if I leave my dress and bonnet up here behind the curtain, and a few things in this bottom drawer? Do you think you could forget they're there, sort of?'

He laughed. 'I have my bundle to unpack, but what's inside it won't take much room, I can tell you.'

She had nodded, still tense. 'I do the wash every Monday night, and put it in soak before I go out in the morning, so if you'll leave your dirty clothes on top of the boiler tomorrow night. . . .'

Once alone, he undid his bundle, laying his soap and razor on the washstand and his change of clothes in the top drawer. A sudden tightness in his chest made him take in a deep breath and give himself a reprimand. 'Twas a lovely room, sure enough, but he was payin' for

it, wasn't he? He unwrapped his bible, and from force
of long habit studied his name on the fly-leaf. Matthew
Ezekiel Raike, in his mother's own hand. He laid it
centrally on top of the drawers, and held his candle
aloft to get the full effect.

He was still smiling as he climbed into bed, expecting
sleep to claim him as rapidly as always; but he lay
wide-eyed and restless, his mind whirling with images
from the past and scraps of the evening's talk. The bed
was too comfortable, he thought, and too warm. He
could hear the old man snoring and muttering in the
next room, and once he heard Mrs Spencer call out
and Martha's quiet reply. It was all so very different
from what he'd been used to.

At last his tired body conquered his active mind, and
he drifted into welcome oblivion. Hoarse screaming
wakened him, and he shot upright to find himself
bathed in sweat. His mouth was agape, and he knew
that the screams were his own. He couldn't move, and
the fire roared and crackled and glared. There was the
high, terrified squeal of horses, and then Fat Annie was
cursing and tugging at him. . . .

The door of his room flew open and Martha stood
there holding a lighted candle. The relief of it caused
him to sob aloud, and then shame made him ram a
fist against his teeth to force himself to silence. She
peered fearfully round the room as if expecting to find
an intruder; he saw that her hair was in a long plait that
was tangled up in a shawl thrown over her nightgown.
'What is it?' she asked sharply. 'You've woke me mam
and me Uncle Jack, and the neighbours as well, for all
I know. What's the matter?'

Matthew would have liked to sink for ever beneath
the bedclothes. 'A nightmare,' he said limply. 'I'm sorry,
'twas a nightmare, a bad one.'

She stared at him, and then moved her gaze away
from his damp bare chest to the brass knob of the bed
behind him. 'Do you often have them?'

'No. This is the first for five or six weeks. Sometimes I go months without one.'

'Is this why you didn't want to share a room?'

He could hardly explain that he shut his mind to the nightmares and pretended they didn't happen, and that sometimes he even convinced himself he didn't know their cause. "Tis one of the reasons, to be sure,' he agreed. 'I be truly sorry I woke 'en. Will 'ee tell your mother that?'

She nodded. 'Do you know what brings them on?'

'Yes, I think I do. Maybe I'll tell you about it one day.' And maybe I won't, he added silently.

Dubiously she pursed up her mouth, then shielded the candle flame with her palm and left the room. A moment later she came back again and put a cup of water and a slice of bread and dripping on top of his little cupboard. 'I thought these might help you to sleep,' she said quietly, and hurried out.

Mrs Spencer was up and dressed when he went downstairs at seven the next morning, and in typical fashion lost no time in tackling him. 'Our Martha tells me you can go months at a time between these dos,' she said, nodding her head and at once re-fastening her cap. 'So we'll see how long you manage before the next one. Me and our Jack aren't used to that kind of noise, you know, specially at two on a Sunday morning. We thought you were being slaughtered.' She waved aside his apology, and like Martha asked no questions as to what his nightmare had been about. 'We'll say no more about it for now – there's none of us can rule our dreams. Come on, Martha's done you a rasher of flitch, and she'll tidy your room while you eat it. See, Jack, he's all right now – it were a nightmare, like I said. Jack! Do you hear me?'

The old man nodded dreamily. 'I'm in good time for the early shift, aren't I, Annie? I'll not have to work in the wet?'

Mrs Spencer rolled her eyes. 'Aye, you're in plenty

of time,' she said heavily. 'You and this young fella are a good pair, you aren't part; one awake all night and the other half-asleep all day!'

Now, a month later, the shame of that moment when Martha found him sobbing had faded beneath the routine of everyday life. The knocker-up came at a quarter to five, and he would jump out of bed to tap on the window in response, and then give Martha a few minutes of privacy for her morning wash before he went down for his hot water. It was one of the highlights of his day, to wash and shave in his room, using a proper towel and a real looking-glass. Breakfast was usually porridge and a slice of bread, or on Wednesdays a boiled egg. Then it was off to work with his snap of bread and dripping, a brew of tea in a twist of paper, and his billy-can in which to boil water. He left before the clatter of clogs reached its peak, because once he was out of the house Martha had to help her mother get dressed before hurrying off to Jericho for the five-to-six blower.

It was an orderly, organised life, and he wondered why a man of his temperament should find it so satisfying. Sometimes he felt almost like a son of the house, with Martha a solemn older sister and Mrs Spencer an overbearing mother who could be charmed into spoiling him now and again. As for Uncle Jack. . . . 'He's a lot better since you come here,' Mrs Spencer declared. 'He doesn't live in the past as much, and he has more sense, like. You've give him something to think about besides himself.'

Sometimes in the quiet hour before bed the old man could be led into tales of his youth, when he and Annie had helped their father and uncle on the handlooms in their weaver's cottages up beyond Holdwell. Matthew liked those evenings. Mrs Spencer would sit wrapped in her blanket, busy with a bit of sewing, and Martha would be ironing or cooking for the next day; always quiet, always in the background, eyes observing all that went on. Sometimes he would turn to find her watching him, and she would give him a twitch of the lips and then look quickly away. Uncle Jack sometimes repeated himself, but he could tell a tale, looking back over the years with only an occasional prompting.

'We were our own masters, then,' he would say. 'My father and his brother kept a couple of cows and a pig or two and some hens, and we all used to work together, the little 'uns and the grown-ups, combin' and cardin', spinnin' and weavin'. Folk in them parts did a bit of bleachin' and dyein' an' all, and when the factor called for the cloth we'd all have a bit of a do.

'It were power that put paid to the handlooms – we couldn't compete and make a livin'. Maybe you'll have heard that many a one in Lancashire rose up and smashed the power looms; but by then we knew we were beaten, and me and Annie were in the mill. She settled in well, but like many another I couldn't stomach it, not after working in a quiet little room overlooking the fields and hills, and being able to take a walk in the fresh air when I needed a break.' He stared at the fireplace. 'In them days we were fined for lookin' out of the mill window, because the machines never rested and we hadn't to take our eyes off 'em. And the childer . . . I've seen 'em that young they had to be carried to their work; they'd be fast asleep on their mothers' backs when they got there, and cryin' when they were put down. I vowed I'd never let a child of mine set foot in a mill.

'In the end I left and went on the canals for a bit, and then got married and had the childer.' He shifted in his chair and smiled gently at his memories. 'Bright little lads they were, three of 'em; but their sister were a poor little thing, always ailing. Four childer take some feedin' though, and that's how I come to go down the mine.'

'And are they grown up now?' asked Matthew.

Uncle Jack shook his head. 'Nay, lad, they died of the cholera, and so did their mother. Five of 'em gone inside a week. I couldn't grieve for me little lass – she had no sort of life, anyway – but losing me wife and the

boys nearly finished me. Our Annie here helped me
through. In the end I come to see they were all better
off where they were – in the cholera burial ground, with
their spirits roaming free in a better place than Saltley.
At the time I were on the wet shift in Shuttleworth's pit,
and I wouldn't have wanted that for me little lads.'

Matthew didn't know what to say to that, so he
hastened to other topics. 'Was it there you lost your
arm?'

'No, that were at Joe Chadwick's. It were a runaway
bogey that did it. The fella next to me were killed,
but I just lost me arm. Chadwick paid all the medical
expenses, and give me a pension.'

'Three shillin' a week,' said Mrs Spencer with satisfaction, 'and free coal for life. That three shillin's been
a Godsend these last few years, I can tell you, and
we've never been cold, or had to eat cold food.' Her
tone implied that it was worth losing an arm for such
benefits, and Matthew concealed a smile. A moment
later Uncle Jack lapsed into garbled muttering, and they
all prepared for bed.

Up in his room, Matthew looked with pride at the
latest additions: another picture, this time of a knight
in armour kissing the hand of his lady. Items kept
appearing week by week, and though neither Martha
nor her mother said as much, he guessed they'd been
redeemed from the pawn. He kept thinking about Uncle
Jack's recollections, and what struck him was not the
difference between life in Lancashire and Devon, but
its similarity. Perhaps poverty and hardship had much in
common wherever they occurred. He wondered whether
it was the same with wealth.

Bent double, the brim of his hat trickling with rain,
Matthew snipped away at the wet grass, his mind dwelling
on Martha as it often did these days. She worked
amazingly hard considering she rarely got a good night's
sleep. Her bed in the back kitchen was screened by an
old blanket pegged to a clothes line across the room;

once, seeing her white with exhaustion on a Saturday night, he asked if she was comfortable on her makeshift bed. She gave him that odd, uncomprehending look. 'By the time I get there I could sleep on the floor, if I had to,' she said quietly. 'There's no need to worry about me, Matthew.'

He told himself he didn't worry, not at all. He paid his lodging money, and that was that; but he took care to bring in the coal and to be on hand when she filled the hot-water boiler next to the fire. And always he went to the market with her on Saturday nights, because that was when she was at her lowest. He didn't like to see her worn out; he was uneasily conscious too that if she dropped in her tracks her mother and Uncle Jack would head rapidly for the workhouse. He would then have to find another place. Further exploration of Saltley's streets and alleys had shown him that he could do far worse than Ledden Street. He didn't want to leave, though a couple of nights ago he had found himself considering it.

Looking back, he wasn't sure how it had come about, but instead of Uncle Jack telling his tales, the talk had turned to his own early days. 'Everybody called her Fat Annie,' he found himself saying in answer to their questions, 'but I don't like to talk about her, or even think about her if I can help it. Her was a – she wasn't the sort of woman who'd be welcome at this house.'

Martha was ladling hot water from the boiler, and she paused with the lading-can in both hands, her face warm with fireglow. 'She can't have been all that bad,' she pointed out, 'or she wouldn't have kept four stepchildren as well as her own, after only a year of marriage. I've heard of cases like that where the stepchildren have been sent to the orphanage.'

Astounded, Matthew stared at her. What did she know about it? Over the years other people had made that very point, and he'd always refused to consider it. 'She *was* that bad,' he insisted. 'She only kept us so we could

work to keep her in idleness and drink. For ten years
I slaved at that inn, and was beaten for it more times
than I could ever have counted. And the young ones
slaved in their turn, but at least they were spared the
beatings.'

The two women exchanged a look. 'Don't get in a
state,' said Mrs Spencer hurriedly. 'Tell us – er – tell
us about your little sister – the one who died.'

He felt his cheeks go cold and knew he'd lost colour.
'Her name was Dorcas,' he said quietly, 'and she was
two years old when my mother died. The three of us,
we looked after her; in time she was able to help in
the inn, like the others. When she was nine there was a
fire in the stables. Everybody got out and all the horses
were saved, but Dorcas had gone to sleep in the hay,
and they – we couldn't get to her in time. She burned
to death.'

The three of them were hanging on his words, and
all at once he couldn't bear to see them waiting to
hear more of what he so rarely told. How could they
ever know what it was like, sitting in their warm, tidy
little house with clean ironing on the line and a white
cloth on the table ready for morning? What did they
know of the stables, and his sisters huddled under old
horse-blankets, with Fat Annie threshing about in the
end stall with her latest sailor?

Without a word he snatched up his hat and stalked
from the house, slamming the door with such force
the latch rattled and pinged and the frame shook. His
footsteps echoed along the flagstones, and across the dirt
street the tiny gardens looked black in the twilight. He
swung round the corner and walked rapidly up the slope.
Could he live with people who had no understanding
of what he and the young ones had suffered? People
who thought Dorcas a subject for light conversation?
He would be better off sleeping under the stars than
having to answer questions from that old harridan . . .

Hat jammed down over his brow, he walked on,

letting his feet take him where they willed. It was a battered street sign that told him he was crossing Gallgate, the lower end of the thoroughfare that gave the whole area its name. Hot and irritable, he stopped to get his bearings, and felt a tug at the back of his trousers. 'Mister,' said a small voice that was vaguely familiar.

A child was standing behind him. He peered at her and saw she was one of the two sisters who had followed the cotton wagon. Her face was still dirty and her feet still bare, but the ringworm was better – her scalp was covered all over with hair, brown and wavy, but very short.

She was regarding him warily. 'What's wrong, Mister?' she asked.

'Wrong? Why, nothing at all. Why should 'ee think it?'

The child squirmed inside her rags. 'You're angry,' she whispered hoarsely.

Put-out that his feelings were visible to this pathetic little soul, Matthew tipped back his hat and squatted in front of her. She stared at him solemnly with big grey eyes that put him in mind of mist high on the Devon moors. 'I bain't angry,' he said gently. 'I be pleased to see a friend. Where's your liddle sister?'

'She's got the fever. She's in bed.'

'Oh,' he said, dismayed, 'and what about the baby, and your mother?'

'Me mam's at home, looking after our Ruthie, but me brother – the baby – he's dead, Mister.'

Matthew swallowed. 'I'm sorry to hear that.' He fingered the outline of the coins in his pocket, knowing he had a shilling, a sixpence and six pennies. 'Hold out your hand,' he commanded.

She edged away. 'Me mam won't let me beg.'

'Then I'll come home with you and give it her myself.'

'No,' said the child bluntly. 'You mustn't.'

'Why ever not?'

'Because me mam would tell me off.'

'Now why would she do that?'

'Because you'd smell the bugs,' she said simply, 'and she doesn't like people knowing we've got bugs.'

'Oh,' he said for the second time. 'Where is it, then, your house?'

'Miller's Yard. It isn't a house, though, it's – it's a cellar. Me mam says we'll move as soon as she gets work.'

'Listen, this isn't begging. Just tell her you met me by accident. Give her this shilling and these three pennies. Right? And these three are for you – just for you – to spend on what you like. Off you go, straight home now.'

She clutched his arm and laid her shorn head against his sleeve, then scuttled away on stick-like legs into the warren of streets that was Gallgate, leaving Matthew wondering why he had thought he knew all there was to know about childhood misery. He walked on, knowing he was nearing the spot where he saw Martha blown off her feet by the gale. Yes, there was the wall of the weaving shed where she'd cut her head. The street was deserted but for a young lady and gentleman coming on foot from the big houses away up the hill. They were well-dressed, and he wondered why they should be in this part of Saltley.

The young lady looked up and down the road, then allowed herself to be hustled into the dark lane at the side of the mill reservoir. A glimpse of red hair glinted under her bonnet in the light of the lamp, and Matthew's eyes widened. It was the Ridings girl from the pawnshop, the one he'd seen in the park with her mother. What would Mrs Ridings say to her daughter slipping down a dark lane with an elegant young man? Come to that, what was the elegant young man thinking of? Matthew shrugged. No doubt he was thinking what they all thought. Why was it that such furtive little sessions seemed to appeal to men more than the marriage bed? Pondering the question, he headed back to Ledden Street.

He lifted the latch and walked in. Uncle Jack nodded amiably and asked, 'Had a busy day, lad?' as if he'd just come from work. The two women were motionless, like statues, but he would have had to be blind not to see the relief on their faces. Mrs Spencer wagged her head and opened her mouth, but Martha held up a hand. 'Mother, let me,' she said firmly. 'Matthew, we're that sorry. Me mam said the first thing that come into her head when you got upset about your stepmother. It wasn't that she wanted to – to delve into your sister's death. We respect your grievin', and we should have seen you can't bear to speak of it. But you see here in Saltley we're used to losing children. Me mam's first two died before me and our Bella were born, and Uncle Jack's told you about his four. They've lost children from nearly every family in Saltley. It doesn't mean we care any the less, but we get used to it, sort of.' She glanced at her mother. 'Please accept our sympathy about Dorcas, and we're sorry we mentioned it.' She held out her small, hard hand, and when he took it she squeezed his, hard, and colour flooded her pale face.

He knew he couldn't even attempt to explain his thoughts and feelings when he left the house, so he just said simply, 'I'm sorry too. I can't talk about it, and I shouldn' 'a' tried.' He attempted a smile. 'You're not plannin' to throw me out, then?'

'No,' said Mrs Spencer, looking as if she'd kept silent for long enough. 'We don't want you to leave us. But if I'm allowed to speak I must just say one thing. It's a mistake to bottle it all up. If it hurts, you must let it all come out, or it'll fester inside you for the rest of your days.'

Looking from mother to daughter he saw deep concern in the two pairs of eyes. Something eased inside him, like a wet rope loosening as it dries in the sun. He stored the advice away in his mind, to be examined later, and thought about the single sixpence that was left in his pocket. 'The black-pea fella's up at the corner,' he said. 'I'll treat you all to some, if you like.'

Basin in hand, he joined those waiting while the man ladled hot savoury peas from the iron pan on his trolley. Behind his aproned figure the lamps of Saltley twinkled and blinked, and for a second Matthew fancied he saw a small, dark-haired girl skipping away across the cobblestones towards the lights. Ignoring the chatter around him he stared sombrely into the distance. Whether he spoke of her or kept silent, he would never forget his little sister.

It was late evening, almost closing time at the park, and Matthew was raking the gravel paths of the rose garden. The second blooming was almost over, and he lingered near a bush that still held a few fine specimens. The sweet heavy scent came to him on a drift of cool air, and he was filled with a strange, restless yearning that bewildered him.

What did he want or need that he didn't have already? He was content at his work and his lodgings, and he felt at home in Saltley's grim streets. He was at ease with the hard squawk of the local speech, and knew it was because he felt a real kinship with the people. Something about them appealed to him – he'd known it since his first day. When the lamp was lit at Ledden Street, with Mrs Spencer sewing and Martha busy in the back kitchen, he told himself that old Peggy-oh had been right in recommending his home town.

He was moving backwards with his rake, reflecting on his life in Saltley, when he caught sight of a young couple walking a deserted path beyond the rhododendrons. Surprised to see members of the public in the park so late, he started forward to warn them against being locked in for the night. Then he halted. They had an air of purpose that he recognised. Yes, it was the pawnbroker's daughter and her young man. Leaning on his rake he watched them, as arms around each other's waists, they made for the enclosing trees of the dell. He caught the girl's expression and was surprised. He had thought her to be confident, high-handed, maybe even arrogant; but in that fleeting second he saw something else in her handsome, bony face – uncertainty, a desire to please, as if she really cared for her dandified young man. It was evident they knew their way around the park, and needed no warnings from him. He didn't know how such young women were expected to behave, but surely she should be more careful of her reputation?

As he went on raking he told himself that Martha would never put herself in such a position. In his mind's eye he saw her in her clean pinafore kneading dough at the scrubbed table, and later knocking the bottom of the loaves to see if they were cooked, her small face intent as she listened. Impulsively he took his knife and cut a single perfect red rose, trimmed it of thorns, and laid it on top of his head under his hat. A moment later he headed for the tack room and joined the others as they packed up for the night.

Daniel Broadhurst was there, surveying them good-humouredly. 'We've got work over at the lake tomorrow, lads, so let's hope for a fine day. Mrs Broadhurst has made us a fruit cake, so we'll share it out when you have your snap.'

Matthew smiled and touched his hat, deeply conscious of the stolen rose that lay cool on the thickness of his hair. If it should be discovered not even Mr Broadhurst would be able to save him from the sack. It was an unshakeable rule in the park that if any man stole a plant, a bloom, or even a leaf, he was dismissed instantly.

He joined Jonah for the walk home, and wondered what Martha would think of the rose.

Clogs clacking, she was out searching the streets for Uncle Jack. 'He's been gone since half past one,' her mother had cried as she came in from Jericho. 'Walked out without a word and I haven't had a cup of tea all afternoon.'

Here we go again, thought Martha wearily, ramming the kettle deep into the dying coals. 'All right, Mam, keep your hair on. I'll make you a drink and see to the fire, then I'll go and find him. Was he himself, or what?'

'No. He was back fifty years or more, when we were childer. We had our bread and drippin' at one o'clock and he just wandered out.'

Martha seethed with impatience. There was mutton stew prepared, one of Matthew's favourites, and she'd wanted their meal over and done with so she could have everything nice for him to eat on his own when he came in. She put the stew near the hob and then headed for the tally bridge over the East Brook. It was a regular meeting place of the unemployed, and sometimes the old man went there to chat with out-of-work miners.

Uncle Jack wasn't there, nor was he on the stone benches at the market cross or among those who gathered next to the Salter's Arms. Her spirits plummeted. Once it had taken her three hours to find him; tired of waiting, her mother had tried to put a dish of pig's trotters to heat up in the oven, and had dropped it. When they got home their meal had been all over the floor, the dish broken and her mother beside herself with hunger and frustration.

She hurried on, taking herself grimly to task. She needed bringing down to earth, because it couldn't last. The pure joy of having Matthew under the same roof just couldn't last – she knew it. Life wasn't as kind as that – not to her anyway. Since he came to Ledden Street the housework had become pleasure instead of drudgery, and her mother's sharp tongue something to be dismissed with a smile.

Not that he sought her company. After dinner on Sundays he went out to the tiny garden and the vegetables, or went walking in the hills above the town, never asking her to join him. But who could blame him for that? She wasn't bonny, she was under-sized; she had little conversation; she was often tired. He would only see her as his landlady's daughter.

And another thing – he was restless. One day he would move on, and she would be left with her mother and Uncle Jack, and a life centred on the weaving shed, the dolly-tub and the oven. When he marched out of the house the other night it had taken all her will-power not to run after him and beg him not to leave them. Instead she had turned on her mother angrily for questioning him about his little sister, but at least he had come back. Though he might talk to her mother and Uncle Jack more than to her, he brought in the coal and helped her with the shopping. Once he even carried wet washing out to the line, something she had never seen a man do in her life. And last Sunday – her step slowed dreamily – she had hurried through her tasks in order to have time to put on her good dress before they sat down to their dinner; he had pulled out her chair and saw her seated, as if she was a grand lady.

She was so strung-up she had taken to wakening in the early hours, picturing the impossible, such as what it would be like to feel his arms around her, and – and other things. Last night a full moon had shone through the kitchen window as she lay on her hard little bed. People said moonlight was for lovers, and seeing it, she dreamed her ridiculous dreams. This morning she mentioned the moon when she gave him his porridge, but with a set look on his face he said abruptly, 'I bain't fond o' the moon. Give me the stars, not that silly fat face.'

Martha had taken it as a snub, and it had spoiled the day for her. She had been so upset she let down a float, which meant that Harry Lingard would be sending for her again and docking her pay. Oh yes, she needed bringing back to earth. . . .

She walked on through the hamlet of Ryeworth, past

a new mill that was being built there, and reached the Swampings, the road that led to Saltley Bog. Once she had found Uncle Jack down there, sitting by the side of a ditch talking to a drunken old man. Should she carry on searching or go back home to see if he'd turned up? A small boy was coming towards her, eating a crust of bread. She caught at his ragged shirt and he backed away, hands guarding his food. 'Have you seen an old man with one arm?' she asked. 'White hair, he has, and only one arm.'

The boy nodded and without a word pointed to a black hut at the side of the track. Martha approached warily and pushed open the door. He was there, sitting on an old wooden box, playing cards with three other men. 'Hello, lass,' he said affably. 'How is it you're not at work?'

'Work's finished for the day, long since,' she said shortly. 'I've come to find you and take you home for your tea.'

'Well now, I thought I were feelin' peckish,' he said mildly. 'See you again, lads.' Without more ado he allowed Martha to lead him outside.

They were back before Matthew, so she bustled about to have everything ready for when he came in. She was in the back kitchen mashing potatoes when she heard the latch go. As usual he came through with his billy-can, and she wondered why he was still wearing his hat. It was very quiet. Out in the street the clatter of clogs had ceased, and for once her mother was silent in the next room.

Matthew leaned against the middle door and gave his easy, captivating smile. 'Don't 'ee rush, Martha. We can wait a liddle while.' Her heart thumped just once, then regained its accustomed beat. He wasn't annoyed with her, after all. Something else must have made him speak sharp about the moon.

When she put down the heavy pan, he held out an arm to prevent her picking up anything else. With one hand he removed his hat, and with the other plucked a deep red rose from its bed among his hair. With a little flourish he held it out to her. 'With my compliments,' he said.

Staring at him, and then at the rose, Martha felt her cheeks burn and then turn very cold. It was the first time any man had given her a flower, the first time any man had given her anything. She took the rose and lifted it to smell its scent. It felt warm, from his head. 'Thank you,' she whispered, and smiled.

Intrigued, he looked down at her. This wasn't her customary twitch of the lips. It was a full, wide, joyous smile that stretched her pretty mouth and put a shine in those serious grey-blue eyes. She was almost pretty. On impulse he leaned forward and kissed her. It was brief and sweet, entirely innocent and very tender. Her lips were warm and soft and he felt them tremble before he lifted his.

Speechless, she stared at him and touched her lower lip with her forefinger, while between them the rose breathed out its fragrance. She looked quickly at the middle door, and he sensed that she shrank from being questioned. He took an empty jam jar from the shelf behind him and handed it to her. 'Why not keep it in the kitchen here, next to your bed?' he suggested quietly.

Her colour high, she filled the jar with water and stood the rose in it, placed it next to her candlestick on top of the mangle. With a conspiratorial flicker of her eyelids, she pulled the blanket screen along the clothes line to hide the flower from view.

Then she wriggled her shoulders. 'Right,' she said briskly, hurrying back to the slop-stone. 'Do you want to wash your hands before I put out the mutton?'

CHAPTER TEN

Ultimatums

TIZZIE WAS ON EDGE. She was going to see Mrs Eleanor Boulton, but her mind was on Edward. Things were changing between them, and her plans were in danger. He still obeyed her ruling about the final intimacy, but it seemed to her they did everything else that could possibly be attempted clothed and out of doors. It was a dangerous road, but she trod it with relish and used only one guide – what Mary had told her about conceiving a child.

She never spoke of it, because she knew how her sister would react; but one night when they were both in bed Mary asked how things were going with Edward, and she reassured her. 'We understand each other now. He knows I won't permit such intimacies before marriage.'

Mary had seemed relieved, but she was very quiet, and Tizzie knew she was lying awake at her side into the small hours. Then after the next committee meeting she asked again. 'I know it looks as if I'm prying, Tizzie, but I can't help worrying whether he's quite – quite honourable.'

Honourable, thought Tizzie scornfully, what was honourable? Safety and boredom and correct behaviour, so she wanted none of it. But her sister was a love, and she dredged up another lie to set her mind at rest. 'Don't worry. He knows how I feel, and he's promised that nothing will happen again until we marry.'

'Has he actually asked you?' squeaked Mary. 'Are you going to get engaged?'

'He hasn't asked yet,' admitted Tizzie, 'but he will.'

Mary clutched the counterpane in excitement. 'Won't it be lovely when we're both married, Tizz? What about his family, though? Is he going to take you to see them? I picture them as frightfully grand, don't you?'

'That's all in the future,' said Tizzie firmly. 'We're both on the same committee, he walks me to and from the meetings, and that's all there is to it.'

All there was to it, she thought. Mary would be staggered if she knew the half of it, let alone all. It had been obvious from the start that Edward was experienced with women, and at first she pretended there had been other men in her life. She was mortified when he roared with laughter. 'Don't give me that, Tizzie! You'd never even been kissed until you met me. Come on, admit it.'

She had shrugged, swallowing her annoyance. 'All right, I admit it. And now you admit that you took advantage of an innocent young girl.'

He laughed again. 'Innocent? You might be inexperienced, but innocent you are not, Elizabeth Ridings. You're different, though, do you know that? As for "girl" – you're no girl, you're a woman, the most exciting woman I've ever met.'

That was sweet music to her ears. Looking back on the boring, frustrating years of her teens she had the odd conviction they'd been lived by somebody else, a submissive nonentity who knew nothing at all about men. And she had come to know a great deal about one man, in particular the enormous importance to him of sexual intimacy.

In the early days she had thought that the restraints she imposed would bind him to her until they married, but now she saw a real possibility that he might tire of her and look elsewhere. That would be catastrophic, but it was a risk she must take in order to protect her virginity; she warned herself daily that she must not have a child before marriage. The trouble was that exercising will-power for both of them was more of a strain than she had expected. . . .

He had taught her things that amazed her, finding her an eager pupil; sometimes she called to mind her resolve that one day she would tell Mary things *she* didn't know. At last, finding she was adamant about remaining a virgin, Edward had shown her how to satisfy him without the full sexual act. This had become the pattern of their lovemaking, and he was more content. It left her restless and unfulfilled, but with a feeling of power, until she realised that a more content Edward was less likely to contemplate marriage than an eager, unsatisfied one.

What put her on edge now was the subtle shift in supremacy between them. She no longer had the upper hand. He was still passionate, still gratifyingly impressed by her intelligence and financial acumen, but no nearer seeing her as a wife. While she – she could hardly believe it of herself – was like some dim-witted village maiden trembling at his smile and aching for his touch. She couldn't seem to help it. Even to herself she hesitated to use the expression, but she thought she must be in love with him. One mistake she hadn't made, though, was to let him see it. Her shrewd common sense urged her to foster the 'difference' he prized so highly, but she was so desperate she dropped broad hints about marriage.

'My darling Tizzie,' he had said the previous night, 'if I've told you once I've told you a hundred times, I cannot consider marriage just yet. My superiors say I must remain single until I finish this spell of travelling around the country, and I have two more years still to do. Even if that were not the case, there is my family to think of.'

'Ah yes,' she said silkily, 'your family. Have you told them yet about me?'

'No, because they see Caroline as my ideal mate. Our families are friends, she's only seventeen and thinks she's in love with me. I've told you before, they believe it's a suitable match.'

Tizzie's eyes glinted. 'You've also told me she's fat, stupid and ugly.'

He laughed. 'Three adjectives which could never in a million years be applied to you, my sweet. The fact remains, her family have a certain position in the county – not terribly wealthy, but well-connected.'

It couldn't be clearer. The pawnshop wasn't well-connected with anyone except those in need of ready money. For years Tizzie had fumed about that very aspect of her life, but at the first hint of his disdain she felt a surprising surge of loyalty to the three brass balls that had blighted her life. 'I am not ashamed of my background,' she said belligerently. 'My father is an excellent man of business.'

'Of course he is,' Edward soothed. 'It's just that my parents may not take kindly to the idea of a pawnbroker's daughter. I must have time to prepare the way for you.' Then he lost patience. 'Oh, come on, Tizzie, help me unfasten your buttons.'

Now, her committee notes in a neat folder, her mind still occupied with Edward, she walked up the hill to the Boultons' house. It was almost a mansion, set in a vast shrubby garden. Inside it was opulent and well-appointed, but to Tizzie's eyes ugly and far too dark. In the boring hours at home she sometimes planned its redecoration and that of the Waltons' house, as practice for when she and Edward had a home of their own. The middle-aged maid opened the door with her usual resentful stare, and Tizzie handed over her bonnet and wrap without a word. Silly old bag – if she didn't like being a maid why didn't she do something more interesting?

'Tizzie, my dear!' Tall, stately, large-featured, Eleanor Boulton sailed out of her sitting room to take her by the arm. 'Come along, we have letters to write,' she said briskly, then over her shoulder to the maid, 'Tea at three-thirty sharp, Robinson.'

She liked to dictate from a high-backed chair in the

window, while Tizzie took down quick drafts of the
letters and then copied them out in her strong, graceful
script; sometimes she made adjustments to the text which
Mrs Boulton never seemed to notice when she signed
them. Once settled with her tea-cup and a slice of cake
Mrs Boulton leaned forward purposefully. 'I want a word
with you, Tizzie, in confidence of course.'

Well, of course. What was it now? Her private
correspondence? Her household accounts? Outwardly
submissive, Tizzie sat with her eyes fixed dutifully on
the well-preserved face opposite.

Mrs Boulton finished her tea, put down the cup, and
said bluntly, 'There's talk in Saltley about you and
Edward Mayfield. People know you are my assistant,
and I find it unacceptable to be connected in any way
with loose behaviour or, even worse, scandal. I must
make that point before I go on, Tizzie.'

Tizzie gaped at her, then gathered her wits and
hurriedly closed her open mouth. She felt her tongue
moving around, as if searching for speech, while the
older woman continued remorselessly. 'Mrs Walton has
heard things as well, but we haven't mentioned it to the
rest of the committee – so far.' She waved a hand at
the tea-tray. 'Another cup, if you please. Now let me
be quite clear about this: is there an engagement in the
offing, or an understanding?'

'Not exactly,' admitted Tizzie carefully, 'although we
do have a – a regard for each other.' She poured
another cup of tea, relieved to be able to look at
something other than the older woman's cold grey
gaze. 'He walks me to and from committee meetings,
that's all.'

Mrs Boulton shook her large, well-tended head. 'All?
I think not. Do you see each other apart from committee
evenings?'

'No. He is too busy on affairs of business, and at
weekends he is often away from Saltley.'

'I see. Does he visit the – your home?'

'No, but my mother has invited him to supper next week, for the first time.'

Mrs Boulton regarded her intently, heavy lids half-covering steely eyes. 'I'm told he has rooms in a private house up near the site of the infirmary. Do you visit him there?'

'No, of course not, Mrs Boulton.' It was incredibly difficult to keep her tone quiet and respectful.

'I must tell you that you have been seen together, more than once, in places and situations that have led to talk. What do you say to that?'

A hard little voice in Tizzie's head gave ready answer: 'I say you've made sure you got your letters written before tackling me.' Such words were unutterable, of course, and she contented herself with asking, 'Would you tell me exactly what you've heard, Mrs Boulton?'

The other woman sighed. 'I'm not your mother, but I can't believe she knows anything of this. In the last day or two I've been of a mind to call and have a word with her.'

The idea of Mrs Boulton calling at the pawnshop about anything at all, let alone this, was horrific. Tizzie kept silent in case there was worse to come.

'I've heard from several sources that you and Edward don't go straight home after our meetings,' Mrs Boulton went on. 'You've been seen leaving Soar Park through a gap in the railings – yes, Miss – the railings! You've been seen entering the lane behind the reservoir of my husband's mill; I have even, myself, seen Edward touch your knee beneath Mrs Walton's table, and you showed no objection. It won't do, Tizzie. Such behaviour belongs to the labouring classes. Your good name is at stake. Can't you see it?'

'What about Edward's name?' asked Tizzie abruptly. 'Have you spoken to him, as well?'

'He's a man,' said Mrs Boulton irritably. 'Surely you know it's different for men? Also, he isn't connected with me, except indirectly through the committee. You are my assistant. You visit this house, you write my letters, you speak to tradespeople on my behalf. I don't want to lose your services, but if you don't alter your ways I'll have you removed from the committee.'

Beneath the weight of her humiliation Tizzie's mind raced. Mary had been right and she had been wrong. More than wrong, she'd been a fool. It was extremely painful to admit it. 'Perhaps we've both been thoughtless and lacking in consideration for other people,' she said reluctantly. 'We do have an understanding, but it can't be made public just yet.'

Mrs Boulton was plainly unconvinced. 'He's a striking young man,' she conceded, 'but he's from down south, and it's well known they're more lax in their morals than we are. Remember this, though, when the infirmary's finished he'll move on, and you'll be left with a ruined reputation. You may be known in your own town as a fast young woman, or perhaps even worse – do you follow me? You have intelligence, you have energy, and you're a good-looking girl. You could go far. Take my advice and protect your reputation. Now, can I assure Mrs Walton that you'll give thought to what I say, and then act on it?'

'Yes. Thank you, Mrs Boulton.'

'I won't need to mention it again?'

'No, definitely not, Mrs Boulton.'

'Good. Let's get on, then. First, instructions to the Town Hall staff; second, confirmation to the caterers, and let me see a copy of our letter to the orchestra.'

Tizzie had walked home from the Boultons' by the longest route, in order to be free of interruptions while she decided how to react to Mrs Boulton's ultimatum.

Never one for lengthy cogitation, she had sorted out her thoughts in ten minutes of brisk walking, accepting that with his experience Edward must have known all along that he was risking her reputation. By the standards of the respectable, chapel-going classes of Saltley his behaviour was shameful, but by hers it merely added the welcome spice of danger to their love. Hadn't she always recognised his ruthless streak, his self-interest? He had gone all-out to get what he wanted, and what he wanted was her. The satisfaction of that pushed aside all her doubts. She wanted no well-behaved ninny, and apparently, neither did he.

But if his family were to accept her, she would need a spotless reputation to outweigh her pawnshop background, rather than the disgrace of being thrown off the committee; and she must also be on visiting terms with Saltley's top families. Therefore, no more lovemaking in the thickets of Soar Park. No more grappling in the moist darkness of Back Lane. Not even any more walking home together. There must be nothing, *nothing* that could give rise to more talk. Mrs Eleanor Boulton might not be as clever as she thought herself to be, but she had power; Tizzie knew she would discard her without a qualm if she gave her cause.

That decided, the next move was to inform Edward. He was coming to supper next Tuesday. She would arrange it so that they discussed finance together, and under cover of it tell him of her decision. She stepped out more slowly – no, she couldn't wait four whole days.

The next afternoon found her and Mary in their second-best dresses and best wraps, heading past Soar Park towards the site of the new infirmary. Mary had been only too pleased to act as companion. 'Of course I don't mind, Tizz. I owe it to you, after all – you were ever so good at helping me to see William before Mother accepted him.'

'Edward may not even be there,' Tizzie reminded her, 'but as I'm occupied with raising money to equip the place I thought it was high time I saw how it's progressing.'

At the sight of the vast stone building she felt a surge of pride that Edward should be in charge of it all. Two floors were already erected, and the third was half-finished. There he was, talking to a workman,

immaculate as ever in black business coat and tall hat,
with a sheaf of papers in his hand. When he spotted
them both he at once made his way between newly-cut
blocks of stone and a stack of timber, removing his hat
with a flourish. 'Miss Tizzie, and I believe this must be
Miss Mary. What a delightful surprise!'

The force of his attraction surprised Tizzie afresh every
time they met, and she glanced at Mary to see if she
felt it, too. No, if anything her sister looked glum and
slightly uncomfortable. Tizzie was familiar with every
expression on that plump, innocent face, and knew at
once that she was thinking of how he had behaved in Back
Lane. 'Perhaps I might have the pleasure of showing you
round?' he said, and they agreed at once.

He led the way across the busy site, and she tried to
observe his tall, graceful form with eyes as critical as
Mary's, but all she could feel was a longing for his touch.
When he turned she pretended to stumble, and at once
he was by her side, his hand on her upper arm; only the
two of them knew that his knuckles were pressed tight
against the side of her breast.

Edward showed them over the two half-completed
floors to the sound of chisels and hammers and saws,
while workmen touched their caps at his approach. It
was all highly gratifying, and in spite of what was on
her mind Tizzie couldn't resist asking what flooring was
to be used, and who was responsible for deciding which
estimates to accept.

When they returned to the half-finished entrance
hall, Mary, with admirable self-possesion, asked to be
excused in order to examine a series of small rooms
near the door.

Edward watched her rear view appraisingly. 'Well
done, Mary,' he said in amusement, and turning to
Tizzie, 'and now, my sweet, there's something on your
mind, I take it.'

She made no pretence. 'I was with Mrs Boulton
yesterday. She says we're causing talk in the town –

we've been seen in Back Lane and coming out of the park. She's threatened to have me thrown off the committee. Mrs Walton knows as well.'

His red lips lifted in irritation, baring his very white teeth. 'The interfering old nanny-goat! Do the rest of them know?'

'Not so far. She says I'll lose my good name if we're not careful.'

'That's why we've *been* careful, my love, but apparently not careful enough. I'll have to think of something, and let you know on Tuesday.'

'What about Manchester?' she said urgently.

'Manchester?' His eyes avoided hers. 'What do you mean?'

'I – I just wondered if we could meet in Manchester one afternoon, or something?'

He relaxed. 'Oh. It's an idea, though I can't often get away from here. We'll just have to try and find somewhere else.'

Tizzie felt that odd little pain between her ribs again. 'No,' she said quietly. 'I've already told my mother that you think it more fitting for me to use a cab, now the evenings are closing in. She's pleased you're so considerate of my reputation.'

'Is – she – really?' He drawled the words, and she didn't know whether he was annoyed or pleased. 'Look, I have to go,' he said, 'but I'll have thought of something before Tuesday. Ah, here she is,' he said loudly as Mary came into sight. 'It's been a pleasure, ladies. Just the thing to brighten my working day.'

Sarah was happy in her fine new sick-bay at Jericho Mills. Never one to do things by halves, her father had provided a square, bright room opening off the main staircase in the tower of the east mill, and equipped it down to the last bandage. Then, with his flair for suiting the worker to the job, he had presented her with a gaunt, intelligent sixteen-year-old called Polly as an assistant.

'Don't argue, it's all arranged,' he said, a week before they opened. 'If we're providing medical care for the workers then it must be from setting-on the engines to switching 'em off, and those sort of hours might be a bit too much for you. That means you need an assistant with sense, to keep an eye on things when you're not there.

'This young lass is only sixteen, but she's been a ward-maid at the Royal for three years, so she's no stranger to injuries and such. Her family lived in Ancoats; but first her father died, then her mother, so she's brought her brothers and sisters to Saltley to live with their granny. You'll know her – Bessie Lomas, one of the winders – she says you taught her to read and write at the school.'

On her first morning he climbed the stairs with her at six o'clock, Polly a silent shadow behind them. Sam was nowhere to be seen, having told her on the quiet that he thought their father might like to have her to himself for the first few minutes.

'Well, love,' he said, 'you've worked hard to get all this stuff as you want it – the rest is up to you. Young Polly has her head screwed on the right way. She's used to taking orders and she'll expect you to give them. The errand lad for this floor – he's the youngest of the Booths, by the way – knows he's to stop whatever he's doing if you want him to take a message or run for the doctor.'

Sarah beamed at him. He was so good at thinking ahead, at planning. Look at the way he had chosen Polly: someone with experience, but younger than her, so she wouldn't feel awkward telling her what to do. She was so pleased at the way he had calmly arranged for her to be an observer for a week at the casual injuries department at the Royal, and fixed up for the Booth boy to run errands. She could never admit it, even to Sam, but she was nervous about being in charge of the sick-bay. Yet without fuss, without apparent effort, Papa had wiped her worries away, just as he used to wipe her

tears after a childhood tumble. She loved him so. How
would she ever be able to leave him and Sam when she
got married?

'I want detailed reports kept of everyone attended
to,' he reminded her. 'If I can quote figures proving
that production hasn't suffered through having a nurse
on duty, it might persuade other mill-owners in Saltley
to do the same. You'd like that, wouldn't you?'

Eyes sparkling, she was putting on a big white apron.
'Of course I would, Papa!' She pinned a severe starched
cap on her bright hair, and cheeks pink, twirled round in
front of him. 'First patient, please,' she said, laughing.

Joshua's shrewd blue eyes softened as he watched her.
His little girl, his beautiful little Sarah. . . . He swallowed
and said abruptly, 'I'm proud of you, love, I am that.
And I'm glad you prodded me into taking this step. I'd
have got round to it one day, I expect, but not yet, no
– not just yet.'

Serious now, she took hold of his hand. 'Thank you,
Papa. For all this – and, you know, for Polly and
everything.'

He dropped a kiss on her cheek. 'Don't forget, your
mother insists you go home for your dinner and a bit
of a break. I'll pop in later to see how you're getting
on.' At the door he turned to Polly with his own special
blend of authority and friendliness. 'I've heard excellent
reports on your work, Polly, and if you're as good as
your granny you'll do! Now, can I rely on you to help
my daughter in every way you can?'

She dipped the knee. 'Yes, Mr Schofield.'

He flicked at the ends of his whiskers. 'There's another
thing. If at any time for any reason whatsoever you're
worried about Miss Sarah, or concerned for her safety,
I want you to send young Booth for me or Mr Sam
without a second's delay. If we're both out of the mill,
then send him for Mr Whitehead in the spinning room
– I've spoken to him about it. Will you remember that,
Polly?'

Huge eyes in hollow sockets stared at him from the long plain face. 'You can rely on me, Mr Schofield.'

'I thought I could.' He smiled at her, blew Sarah a kiss and marched out, leaving his daughter touched by his concern.

Now, almost a fortnight later, the sick-bay was working well. With more than a thousand of the workforce back on full-time there were minor injuries and illnesses to deal with several times a day. The doctor had been called on only four occasions: a man badly scalded by a fractured steam pipe; a labourer with a broken leg; a young weaver haemorrhaging in a difficult premature labour; and a twelve-year-old piecer from the spinning room who collapsed and was diagnosed as severely malnourished.

When things were quiet Sarah either sat by the window embroidering initials on the bed-linen that was to be her wedding gift to James and Esther, or gave Polly her daily writing lesson. Sometimes Sam dropped in for a cup of tea or coffee and a chat, and when he or her father arrived Polly relinquished her role as guardian and disappeared to fetch water, or to go and empty buckets.

Sarah was working on a pillow-case when Ralph strolled in. Like her mother, she suffered pangs of guilt about the lack of communication between them. 'Ralph! How lovely! This is Polly, my helper.'

Polly dipped the knee, but Ralph gave her a blank look that sent her hurrying out with the water-bucket. He crossed to the window and stared out at the fields. 'Where are all your patients, then?' he asked idly.

Sarah was wary. Sam had told her of Ralph's objections to the sick-bay. 'Those who needed dressings have been already,' she said defensively. 'We're waiting for accidents or emergencies now. Details of all those who've been seen so far are in the record book.'

He nodded towards the door. 'What's that ridiculous drawing?'

'The lamp?' She laughed. 'It was on the door when we arrived on the second morning. We don't know who did it, but I think it's meant to be a compliment to me, and a thank-you to Papa.' She wrinkled her nose in exasperation. 'It's supposed to be Miss Nightingale's lamp. Surely you see that?'

Ralph leaned against the edge of the scrubbed table. 'Not being retarded, yes, I do see it. I also see that it defaces mill property.'

'Papa doesn't seem to mind.'

'He doesn't seem to mind what he spends on all this, either.' He flipped a hand at the neat, white-washed room.

Sarah bit her lip. 'He's done it partly for me and partly for the operatives. They're so pleased about it one of them must have come in specially early to do the drawing of the lamp. And look, a labourer brought me these flowers from the hedgerow this morning. I've been dressing his septic finger, and now it's getting better.'

The beautiful, empty gaze travelled round the room, revealing nothing, missing nothing. She tried to dismiss the unease that always overcame her when he was close at hand. 'How are the markets?' she asked, feigning interest. 'Sam says you're becoming quite the expert.'

A glimmer of warmth softened the perfect features. 'I like the Exchange,' he admitted, 'but not as much as Liverpool. That's where the money is, Sarah.'

She knew little about the marketing of raw cotton, apart from what she'd heard from their father. 'Hasn't there been an awful lot of profiteering in Liverpool, because of the war?' she asked doubtfully. 'Papa says half of them don't want peace in case they lose money when cotton becomes plentiful again.'

As was his disconcerting habit, Ralph didn't bother to reply, either from boredom or because he disagreed. He studied the record book, and jotted down two or three of the names.

'Are you looking forward to the Autumn Ball?' she asked, to fill the silence.

'No,' he said.

'But – you're going, aren't you?'

'Probably not.'

'I thought we were all going, as a family.'

He looked at her, then. 'I've been invited to a birthday party in Liverpool, a friend of mine who works on the Exchange will be twenty-one.'

'Does Mama know?'

Ralph almost smiled. 'I've warned her I might accept,' he said coolly, and strolled from the room.

Irritated and unsettled, Sarah stared after him. He might have mastered the rudiments of conversation, but he was no easier to deal with than when he never spoke more than two words at a time. She thought of the ball and the new dress she was having, uncomfortably aware that she would enjoy it all the more if Ralph wasn't there.

All at once the door crashed back and one of the spinners rushed in. 'Miss Sarah – get ready! A lad's hurt bad – real bad!'

Two more men followed him, carrying between them a boy of about twelve, who was crying out in agony, a thin, high, wailing sound that spurred Sarah into rapid action. 'Send Tommy for the doctor – tell him to run,' she told Polly calmly, and to the men, 'His back? Lie him here, face down, but don't go, I'll want you.'

The flesh of the boy's shoulders was shredded, lacerated beyond belief. An icy calm gripped her, and she held the small dirty hand firmly. 'We're going to help you,' she said in his ear. 'The doctor's coming, and he'll give you something to stop it hurting. Go on, cry out if you want.'

Still clasping his hand, she turned to the men who stood awkwardly by the door. 'This was caused by machinery, surely? What happened?'

'He were caught undert' spindles,' muttered one
of them.

'But did you see it?'

They shook their heads and avoided her eyes. 'No,
we were busy, like.'

'What's his name, then, and his job?'

'Johnny Barnes, Miss Sarah. He's a little piecer under
Zebbie Sutcliffe. Can we go, Miss?'

She flapped a hand at them. 'Yes, but I might want
you later. We'll do our best for him.' Polly came back
and together they cleaned the surrounds of the wound,
while the child moaned in agony and his blood soaked
into the draw sheet.

The doctor arrived, and took one angry look. 'My
God, I never thought to see this at Jericho. The
Bluebell, yes, or Boulton's, but not your father's mill,
young lady.' He dosed Johnny with laudanum, and began
to ease the strips of flesh back across the shoulder
blades.

'Shut the door, Polly,' ordered Sarah. The clatter of
machines would cover the boy's screams, but folk on
the stairs and landings couldn't fail to hear him. It was
the worst ten minutes of her life.

Once or twice the doctor shot her a look, then
grunted in satisfaction, telling himself the girl must
have something of her father in her. 'If you want to
ask him anything, you'd better do it now,' he warned.
'He'll be out like a snuffed candle in a minute.'

'Johnny, what happened? You can tell me, and I
promise you won't get into trouble. Tell me, then I
can be sure it won't happen again.'

The child mumbled into the sheet below his face.
'Mr Sutcliffe makes me clean undert' spindles,' he said
faintly.

'Yes? That's all right, isn't it? You have to clean the
fluff up, I expect?'

'Yes, but sometimes I have to do it while they're
switched on. Don't let on I've told you, Miss. Me mam

– she needs me wages!' The boy's eyelids drooped, and the doctor carried on with his task.

But Sarah had whirled out of the room and was racing up the stairs. Afterwards, many a spinner related with relish how she burst into the room, demanding to see the overlooker, Joe Whitehead, and causing men clad only in calico loin-cloths to cower bashfully behind their machines. 'Send for my father!' she cried, cheeks flaming. 'I'm sure he knows nothing of this, Mr Whitehead. I won't leave this room until he arrives. I want the man responsible suspending immediately.'

Joshua arrived almost at once, calm and authoritative, his lips tightening ominously at the sight of his daughter standing feet apart on the oily floor, surrounded by half-clad men and boys treading back and forth to the constant rattle of the mules.

'Switch off, Joe,' he ordered shortly, and the machinery whined to a stop. 'Now, let's have it one at a time. First, Sarah, what are the boy's injuries?' He listened to her description of the boy's back. 'I see – it's evident he could have been maimed for life, if not killed.' He turned next to the overlooker. 'Joe, did you know of this?'

'No, I didn't, Josh – er – Mr Schofield. It's gone on in the past, of course, but they all know it's never been allowed here since Jericho first opened. If it happens now it's out of my view or when I've left the room for a minute.'

'Right.' The vivid eyes surveyed the silent workers and returned to the overlooker. 'I'm sorry about this, Joe, but I must have it straight. Hands up all those who can vouch for what Mr Whitehead has just told me.'

All hands were raised at once. 'Thank you,' said Joshua calmly, concealing his relief. He scanned the men, and unerringly picked out the spinner, Zebby Sutcliffe. 'Come here, Sutcliffe.' A tall thin man with a lined, sagging face stepped forward. 'The boy says you made him crawl under moving machinery to clear the fluff, and that you've done it more than once. Is it true?'

'Aye,' admitted Sutcliffe, glowering resentfully. 'But Mr Schofield, the fluff were holdin' me up, and givin' me piecers a bad time.'

'You're sacked,' said Joshua briefly. 'Collect your pay at the office on your way out.'

'But I've got seven childer, Mr Schofield, an' only me eldest lad in work.'

'Then I hope he doesn't have to risk life and limb to earn his boss a few extra coppers,' said Joshua grimly. 'No arguing, Sutcliffe. On your way.' He watched impassively as the man gathered his garments from the hooks, then scribbled in his notebook and tore out the page. 'Give them this at the office,' he said, and then turned to Joe Whitehead. 'Promote who you think fit to take his place, Joe, and get switched on again.'

Then he turned to his daughter. 'Come with me, Sarah, if you please.' At the top of the stairs he flicked at his whiskers and tapped his foot on the floor. 'You'd better get back to your patient, hadn't you? When the doctor's finished and the boy's comfortable come down to my office.'

Johnny was face down on the couch in a drugged sleep when she went down to her father's office. He never asked her to go there; if he wished to speak to her he called at the sick-bay on his way through the mill or waited until they got home. 'Shut the door,' he said quietly when she arrived. He didn't pull forward a chair, but left her standing in front of his desk. 'Now, Sarah, first of all let me tell you, and not for the first time, that I'm very pleased with the way you're running the sick-bay. You're orderly, capable and calm, and you don't talk down to the operatives. They think the world of you.

'But I was hard put to it just now not to give you the length of my tongue in front of everybody on the floor. What on earth were you thinking of to rush up there demanding this, that and the other? Your job is to treat the sick and injured, and if you come across injustice or ill-treatment to report it through the proper channels. You do not take matters into your own hands, and you do not interrupt the men at their work. It causes loss of concentration, which can be dangerous when they're working with machinery. Not only that – they're all half-clad because of the heat, most of them would be overfaced at having a young lady barging in, and the boss's daughter at that. It simply isn't acceptable to have a young, single girl in a room full of semi-naked men. Now, what have you to say?'

'That boy's back was ripped to shreds, Papa! He'd been screaming in agony, and yet the men who carried him down wouldn't incriminate one of their workmates. Do you expect me to stand there and say to myself, "Now, I must report this through the proper channels, but only when I've finished what I'm doing at the moment."? I acted on impulse, Papa.'

The shrewd gaze was lowered, as if to conceal some emotion, she didn't know what. 'Listen to me, Miss,' he said shortly. 'There are more than twelve hundred people employed in these mills. If they all acted on impulse there would be complete chaos. The only way to keep the place running effectively is to have rules and regulations that are followed without question, as a matter of course. Do you see what I'm getting at?'

'Yes, I do,' she said contritely. 'I'm sorry I've upset you, Papa.'

He nodded. 'Very well. Now, I know I've told you this many a time, but if today's affair was to happen all over again, what would you do?'

Sarah flashed him a mutinous look and tapped her foot defiantly; then she gave a shamefaced wriggle. 'I'd write out a preliminary report, and send Tommy to ask Mr Shuttleworth, the floor manager, to call in at the sick-bay at his convenience. I would ask Mr Shuttleworth to discuss the matter with Mr Whitehead, and I would tell you or Sam about it as soon as I saw you.'

'So you knew all the time what was correct, Sarah?'

'Yes, I suppose I did, Papa.'

'All right. Just see that you remember it in future.'

'That man – Zebbie Sutcliffe – what will his family do?'

'Go hungry, I expect,' said her father shortly.

'Will he get another job?'

'Not at Jericho. He's a good spinner, so somebody with less scruples than me might take him on.' Joshua looked at his daughter's face, pale now that the flush of anger had faded. 'You can't have it both ways, Sarah. He disobeyed a strict rule, so he was given the sack. If his family suffer that's unfortunate, but I can't sack a man and then run round and give his family baskets of food. He's left my employ. That's an end of it. Now, you'd better get back to your patient, hadn't you?'

She hesitated. 'Papa, I know you'll tell Mama and Sam about this, and maybe James, but does Ralph have to know?'

'Why shouldn't he? It's obvious you're not ashamed of what you did.'

'He interferes in the sick-bay, and tries to find fault. He – he disapproves. He says it costs a lot.'

Her father drummed his fingers on the top of his desk. 'Does he now? All right, I won't tell him, but if I'm any judge it'll soon be the talk of Jericho, so I expect he'll hear it from somebody.'

'I don't see how,' said Sarah. 'Nobody speaks to him willingly!'

Her father sat in his big leather chair, and at her words he looked smaller, somehow, and then she heard him sigh. But he waved a hand in brisk dismissal. 'Off you go, Miss. And remember. . . .'

They were all round the table for Sunday dinner at Meadowbank House. Joshua was carving the roast beef and Rachel dishing out potatoes and vegetables. She liked Sundays, with the family dressed in their best and serving themselves, so that at the same time Alice and the others could have their own Sunday dinner in the kitchen. Charlie was there, and in the last few weeks she had found to her surprise that she was more at ease with him now than in all her married life. It was as if the knowledge of his devotion had at last explained his odd, intent gaze, and made it acceptable to her. In fact, she was amazed that she had never realised it before, and that Joshua, always observant, had remained in ignorance all these years.

Charlie was sitting there, all knobbly wrists and bony neck in his smart grey worsted, laughing at something Sam had just said, and she felt a surge of deep affection for him. What a husband and father he would have made. . . . Next to him was James, tanned and looking very fit, and Esther helpfully jumping up and down to refill the gravy boat and fetch more horseradish sauce. Even Ralph was being pleasant, making an occasional remark to his brothers, and seeing that Charlie had everything he required. She was sure he was improving – perhaps they needn't have been so worried about him, after all. She sighed with contentment as the meal progressed. This was what she loved: her family all at table together eating good wholesome food, at ease with themselves and each other, as if the years of the cotton famine had never been.

Joshua spooned cream over his apple tart, and looked across at Charlie. 'So we can't persuade you to come to the bun-fight at the Town Hall next week, then?'

'It's a *ball*, Papa,' protested Sarah. 'They say it will be the finest ball ever given in Saltley.'

'See what you'll be missing, Charlie? Ralph won't be there either; he's off to Liverpool for the weekend, but the rest of us are turning up in force.'

Charlie smiled. 'If you're all going you won't miss me. I'm not one for balls, nor for parties – you know that; but even if I was I'd arranged this trip to the theatre with John Wagstaff and his wife many a week back. And another thing – I'd rather sleep at Mosley Street until we get the night watchman on duty.'

Joshua answered Rachel's question before she asked it. 'Nothing to get alarmed about, love. Goods have been going missing in the warehouses this last week or two, on Mosley Street and Whitworth Street in particular. Charlie thinks it might be as well to put a man on watch, so he can sleep in peace at nights, especially when we have a valuable consignment ready for shipping out. That's all.'

'And when does this man start?' she asked.

'Monday night,' said Charlie easily. 'It's all arranged.'

Sarah was looking pensive. 'I would have liked you to see my new dress, Uncle Charlie. Mama is having one, as well – hers is blue, and mine's a sort of glittery yellow.'

An image of herself in a new pink dress all those years ago leapt into Rachel's mind. She dismissed it instantly. 'We're all having something new,' she said lightly. 'The boys have outgrown their evening suits – especially Ralph, who's shot up two or three inches in the last year.'

'I tell you what Sarah, I'll be at Jericho on Friday,' said Charlie. 'Perhaps you could show me your dress when we've both finished at the mill?'

'Of course I could. I like to have a full trying-on beforehand, and so does Mama. We'll give you a fashion show!'

Rachel couldn't have silenced her, so she smiled quite calmly and nodded in agreement. 'Come to your tea when you've finished at the mill, Charlie, like you always do.'

'Only if the fashion show's on,' he said, winking at Sarah.

'No pictures for the illustrated papers,' warned Joshua. 'No drawings or sketches allowed.'

She almost missed it – a tremor of guilty surprise on Charlie's face. Then, recognising that his old friend was joking, he laughed like everyone else, and relaxed in his chair again. Rachel gave him a calm, friendly smile as she went out for the coffee, but once outside the room she paused. Her intuition had taken another leap, and now she knew that Charlie himself had painted the little miniature.

The last train to Saltley was ready to leave Victoria when Edward Mayfield leapt aboard and nodded permission to the guard to wave his flag. He was in good spirits after spending the evening with friends: three of them, as it happened, named respectively Lottie, Bernice and Angelique. He knew them well, and had seen a Friday evening in their company as an urgent necessity on two counts: he hadn't been alone with Tizzie for ten days, and he was about to spend the entire weekend in that hub of the universe, Saltley.

He settled in a corner seat opposite a respectable couple in their forties, and from force of habit discreetly assessed the wife. She was well-preserved, well-corseted, well-upholstered, but with what he at once recognised as a restless, unsatisfied eye. A few hours earlier he might have accepted the challenge of awakening her interest, for such diversions could enliven even the shortest journey. His expensive session with the girls, however, had left him with scant enthusiasm for a silent flirtation right under the husband's nose.

Studying his reflection in the carriage window he thought of the events that had prevented him being alone with Tizzie, and was somewhat stunned to realise how much he had missed their frenzied grappling among the trees. She was quite a girl. Yet even if she didn't have the three brass balls round her neck he wasn't sure if he could let himself in for that accent. What was more his old man and dear Mama were hardly likely to fall on her neck in welcome.

Edward was having to think very hard about Tizzie,

though, because Tuesday evening had been an eye-opener. She'd been edgy as a cat when he arrived, and her mother so busy being genteel she was at best a comic turn and at worst a pain in the backside. Sister Mary had been out with her bucket-of-blood butcher-boy, for which he was thankful. He was used to interest and approval from women, and her shocked accusing stare had unsettled him, to say the least. As for the father, there was evidently more to him than the withered arm and puny physique. Edward saw him as a man of ability and considerable means. Take that room, for example. It had been a shock to find it as well-appointed and furnished as his own home in Hampshire. As for the food on the table – it was the best free meal he'd been offered since leaving his previous commission in Blackburn. The way the Ridings women dressed was another thing. Edward was something of an expert on women's clothes, and though the other two might lack Tizzie's style, none of the three wore inexpensive stuff – far from it.

Yes, it had been an odd, informative evening. He himself had carried it socially, of course, with his unending supply of pleasantries and small talk. At the same time he gave a convincing impression of an earnest young suitor at present unable to declare himself. It had been laughable to see the mother lapping it up, but he would have to watch his step with old Abel. There had been something in the shrewd, weary glance that warned him not to overplay the part.

Then after that delicious supper he and Tizzie had settled at the cleared dining-table on the pretext of studying the proposals for equipping the infirmary, papers he had borrowed for the sole purpose of getting her next to him at the table. Once there, it was childishly simple to fondle her thigh under the red plush cloth, to touch hands across their papers, and to write each other notes as they discussed committee affairs. Unfortunately the only suggestion he'd been able to think of for being alone together was pretty weak. He scribbled: *My Darling Tizzie – I ache to hold you close. Can we both escape from the ball for a while? If we leave at different times I can see you for ten minutes behind the stables in Gatefield Lane. Any good?*

Her reply, prudently torn up as soon as he had read it, was: *Definitely not. I have to be available all evening in case Mrs Boulton needs me. Presumably we will manage to dance with each other?*

Until that moment it hadn't occurred to him that Tizzie intended to attend the ball as a guest. He had pictured her as the efficient, quick-witted organiser, but behind the scenes – the power behind Mrs Boulton's throne. 'Are you having a ballgown, Tizzie,' he asked, concealing his surprise.

Mrs Ridings answered, her head turning from side to side like a clockwork toy, 'Of course she is, Mr Mayfield. We're collecting it tomorrow from the best dressmaker in Saltley. It's – '

'To be a surprise,' cut in Tizzie warningly. 'Mrs Boulton knows I intend to dance, Edward. Goodness knows I've worked hard enough making the arrangements. She says I must enjoy myself.'

Edward's mind raced. If he partnered Tizzie too often he might as well announce to all Saltley that his intentions towards the pawnbroker's daughter were serious, and he was still in the process of deciding whether they were or not. 'It's an absolute bore, Mrs Ridings,' he confessed, 'but I've been told by my superiors that I must pay attention to all the wives and daughters of the infirmary's main benefactors. Naturally I want to dance only with Tizzie, but I shall have to restrain myself, for business reasons.'

Mrs Ridings had looked doubtful, but old Abel merely nodded approval. Tizzie, however, had flashed him an openly suspicious look from the brilliant eyes. It was never easy to fool her.

They had seen him off with an invitation to come again

soon, and that night he had actually lost sleep wondering whether he was being a fool in not snapping her up. She was attractive in her own, unique, unpretty-pretty way; he liked her shape – narrow-hipped and high-breasted; he had a fondness for red-heads; she was the most exciting virgin he had ever met and she had a brain like a man – no, better than many of the men with whom he did business.

Oh yes, last Tuesday evening had set him thinking. Without apparent effort she had suggested two new ways of tackling his costing for the laying-out of the infirmary grounds. Without recourse to pencil and paper she had given him five, ten and fifteen per cent of the sums he had jotted down. It was making him think. He might have trained as an architect, but he had no gift for designing buildings – no vision. He knew it, and had been told so in no uncertain terms. What he did have was a flair for putting other people's ideas into operation. He would never make his name as an architect, but he had sometimes toyed with the idea of setting up on his own as a contractor – a building manager for creative architects – a business manager in big business. With his contacts and knowledge of construction, and Tizzie's clear head and ability with figures – not to mention a sizeable contribution from her dear Papa – he could for the first time think seriously about a business of his own. . . . Yes, he had a lot to decide in the next week or two.

'What's the matter, love? Has something at the mill upset you?' It was Friday, tea was over and they were in Sarah's bedroom, putting on their new ballgowns to show Charlie. Rachel was trying to hide her reluctance and Sarah was unexpectedly subdued.

'That woman's crushed hand was awful,' admitted Sarah soberly, thinking of an accident in the card room, 'and Johnny Barnes's back will take ages to heal, but it's not the accidents . . .' She stared down at the petticoats billowing over her hoop as Rachel eased the pale yellow crinoline over her head. 'Look, Mama,' she burst out, 'I know Ralph's a bit – a bit unusual, but why does he have to keep such a keen eye on my sick-bay? He's been in four times this week, examining the record book; and Lily Bracewell – she's one of the weavers – let slip that he's been checking with her overseer as to how she actually cut her arm, and whether it's healing properly. It's not fair, I'm older than him, but he takes no notice when I say that Papa has given me a free hand. And not only that – Polly's frightened of him.'

Rachel was fastening the tiny silver buttons down the back of her daughter's bodice, and she stared in dismay over one gleaming shoulder at the resentful young face in the mirror. Evidently Ralph's spell of cooperation had been too good to last. 'Your father knows about it, love,' she soothed, 'and he says he's going to have a word with Ralph. He's not easy – we all know that – but he's clever and still very young, so he thinks he can do everything better than anyone else. Leave it to your father, love, he'll sort it out.' She ignored the remark about Polly, who was a good girl and devoted to Sarah, but probably a bit on edge at seeing so much of the Schofield men. She unpinned Sarah's luxuriant hair. 'Now, shall we sweep this back with your silver combs, just as we've planned to do tomorrow night?'

They were almost ready when there was a tap at the door and Alice walked in, solidly middle-aged but wearing a frilly apron and a saucy ribboned cap suitable for a teenage maid. She smiled grimly at Rachel's astonishment. 'Only acting on instructions, Mum. Well, Miss Sarah – will I do?'

'It's only a joke, Mama!' laughed Sarah. 'You look just right, Alice. We won't be a minute.' So similar and yet so different, mother and daughter surveyed each other with satisfaction, and they all went downstairs.

Alice threw open the sitting-room door, marched

in, and announced at the top of her voice, 'Gentle-
men: presenting Mrs Rachel Schofield and Miss Sarah
Schofield, modelling gowns for the forthcoming ball at
Saltley Town Hall.'

Rachel just had time to tell herself that laughter might
well cover her feeling of awkwardness before Sarah
hissed in her ear, 'Walk like a model, Mama!' They
both stalked in, skirts swishing, shoulders gleaming,
and paced back and forth in front of Joshua, Sam and
Charlie.

Always one for a lark, Sam applauded, then jumped
up and kissed their hands, while Alice watched from
the doorway, shaking her head as if at the antics of
children. Ellie's bowlegged little form had been lurking
behind her, and now she peeped wide-eyed under Alice's
arm, while Hannah watched from the hall, mouth agape.
Sarah giggled and patted her new hairdo, while Rachel
waited for Joshua's approval. He walked round, eyeing
them both from every angle, and then gave each of them
a smacking kiss. 'I'm the luckiest man in Saltley,' he said
simply. 'What do you say, Charlie?'

'I say you are, at that,' agreed his friend quietly,
'without a doubt.'

Somehow the merriment evaporated, leaving Rachel
standing self-consciously in her blue gown, while Sam
waltzed Sarah dizzily round the room. He whirled her to
a stop in front of Charlie and she dropped a demure little
curtsey. 'End of fashion show, Mr Barnes,' she said.

The melancholy features were transformed by his
rare smile. 'You look quite beautiful, Sarah – every
inch a woman of fashion. It's the loveliest dress you've
ever worn.' The spaniel eyes turned on her mother,
'And Rachel, so do you. That cornflower blue is
exactly right.'

They went upstairs to take off their dresses, and then
Sam whisked Sarah off to play bagatelle in the dining
room, while Rachel took up the pattern that had been
woven throughout her married life: Joshua and his best

friend talking cotton, while she listened and did her needlework in the light of the lamp. She felt annoyed with herself for having imagined that everything was going to change. . . .

CHAPTER ELEVEN

A Night to Remember

TIZZIE'S BRIGHT HAIR AND leaf-green gown brought colour to the cream and gold of the Town Hall's public rooms as she marched on a tour of inspection before the first guests arrived. Everything was going according to plan, and she should have been feeling on top of the world, but a succession of things were taking the edge off her enjoyment.

She had arrived in style in the Boultons' carriage, but there had been nobody on hand to see her, apart from a straggle of labourers passing the steps on their way to the market. And at home she had looked forward to showing off just a bit in front of Mary and her parents. Instead they too were busy getting dressed to go out, because the Hartleys were holding a party to celebrate Mary and William's engagement. Tizzie had been expecting it, waiting for it, but she had never imagined it happening on the most important evening of her life.

It infuriated her that Mary seemed to see it as a stroke of genius on William's part, 'Isn't he thoughtful, Tizzie?' she gabbled happily. 'We would never have considered buying tickets for the ball ourselves, but he says he knew quite well I would be wishing I was there: as soon as we fixed the day he persuaded his mother to arrange this party, and it's all so much more exciting than that old ball. . . . Oh – sorry, Tizz, but you know what I mean.'

It had all been somewhat wearing, when she wanted to concentrate on her own appearance; depressing as well, because at this rate her scatterbrained little sister would be married before Edward so much as acknowledged his feelings in public. And whatever Bull-beef's shortcomings, he didn't conceal his love for Mary; he declared it openly, proudly. For the very first time Tizzie found herself questioning whether her sister, at her butcher's party, wearing her ordinary dress with the little pink bows, was better off than she was in her grand silk gown, trying to secure a couple of dances with the man she was desperate to marry.

At least the gown itself couldn't be faulted. It had cost more than three times as much as her most expensive dress to date, and its skirts were so full they dipped and swayed with her every movement. Bearing in mind that in the near future she might need more fine clothes, she had thanked her parents prettily, and been pleased to see her mother still dubious about the daringly-cut bodice. Her father had for once been provoked into praise. 'You do us all credit, Tizzie. I hope it's a grand do tonight, and that Mrs Boulton appreciates all your hard work.' He rubbed the dried wisps of his hair with a reflective hand. 'And that dress . . . well, it might be immodest but I suppose it's the fashion, and I will say it's worth every penny.'

Of course it was. Hadn't she pored over the fashion papers and dragged her mother all over Manchester to find exactly the right shade of green? Hadn't she practically stood over the dressmaker until it was finished? Mary had let out a shriek when she saw it. 'Ooh, Tizzie! It's lovely! You look like one of Lord Soar's guests, rather than just one of the organisers. Oh, I do *wish* I could arrange my hair like yours. Look, will you fasten it back for me like you usually do?'

Tizzie had been glad to get away when the carriage called for her, glad to pace beneath the silent chandeliers with only the caterers for company. Mary's words rankled – 'just one of the organisers' indeed. One day she would attend functions like this as the wife of a famous architect,

while Mary would be scrubbing the shop floor and sprinkling it with sawdust. . . . And then she was brought back
to the present by the arrival of the Waltons. Eli and his
Bessie were like twin barrels, she thought waspishly, and
darted a quick glance at the daughters to ensure that she
need fear no competition from them. Two more barrels,
she told herself dismissively, though to be sure they
conducted themselves like the slenderest beauties.

Mrs Walton's little eyes glinted in the vastness of
her face. 'Well, Tizzie,' she said coolly. 'Your mother's
managed a nice little dress for you, then.'

Tizzie smiled sweetly. 'Yes, thank you, Mrs Walton.
You and your daughters are looking lovely.' She went
on to explain who would be in the reception line, and
where they would all stand to greet the guests.

Eli strutted nearer, his face smaller than his wife's
but just as pink and shiny. 'Aye,' he said, giving her
a surprised stare from his little pig's eyes, 'this is how
they arranged it at that big do in Manchester, isn't it,
Bessie? Fancy you knowing that, Tizzie.'

'Yes, just fancy,' mocked Tizzie silently, 'and fancy
me spending hours studying accounts of society balls
and books on etiquette.' She smiled modestly into the
shrewd round face beneath its frizzy grey tonsure, and he
leaned closer. 'Well done, Tizzie,' he muttered. His eyes
flickered over her bare shoulders and glistening bosom,
as if merely admiring the creamy unfreckled skin, and
then lifted quickly and met hers. For a second she was
stunned. Well, well! The Mayor of Saltley and Master
of Bluebell Mill was unlike Edward in every conceivable
way, but his eyes conveyed the same hungry message.
Was this another reason why Bessie the barrel was so
cool with her? Maybe the little ape would ask her to
dance? It could do her no harm in the town, and it
would certainly please her mother. Then her attention
wandered from the Waltons. Surely it wouldn't be much
longer before Edward arrived?

*   *   *

They were heading back to Ledden Street after buying-in at the market, when Martha asked if they could go back past the Town Hall.

Matthew eyed her good-humouredly. 'It be the longest way round,' he pointed out, 'but why not if that's what you'd like?' He knew, as did all Saltley, that it was the night of the ball; if Martha wanted to watch the moneyed folk arrive in all their finery it was no surprise. He had realised long ago that she gained pleasure from seeing beautiful clothes and fine houses. She had a hunger for beauty and romance, had prim little Martha; she might as well find them where she was able, because there would be little of either in the weaving shed.

He found her a place in the group of watchers and then leaned against a lamp-post with his hat tilted over his eyes – a new hat at last, though similar in style to the old one. It was a festive, lamp-lit scene, with a uniformed doorman opening carriage doors and ushering guests up to the pillared entrance, and it provided him with a rare opportunity to study Martha unobserved. She was always on the move at Ledden Street, always wary of being the focus of attention, but here her mind was on the fine ladies in their fancy gowns. Her face seemed smaller than ever now that her summer bonnet had been replaced by a more substantial one of padded linen. He had watched her stitching away at it each evening in the peaceful hour before bed when Uncle Jack told his tales, and he found himself wondering what she would wear when the weather turned really cold. Many of the women were already in big shawls – grey, most of them, with criss-crossed overchecks. He found them very drab, because he'd always been attracted to a bit of colour. Life was dark enough without drab clothes.

'If it's as pretty as this outside what must it be like inside?' she whispered. 'Oh look – that's Mr Buckley and his daughter Esther . . . and young Mr James – they're going to be married. . . .' She looked prepared to stand there all night; eyes wide, lips slightly apart, drinking in the colour and brightness and gaiety. 'That's Mr and Mrs Dobbs, of Holden Mill,' she told him intently, 'and see, the Fairbrothers of Greenbank are arriving – just look at that dress! Oh, I hope we haven't missed the Schofields. . . .'

Matthew stayed propped against his lamp-post. There were worse ways of spending time than watching folk arrive and making his own private assessment of them. The Buckley girl, now, who was going to marry the Schofield son; she was pretty in a kittenish kind of way, but she had about her a look of the eldest Ryder girl, who had been a kitten with very sharp claws. Not a member of staff in that great house and all its grounds had had anything good to say about her.

His gaze returned to Martha. She was biting her lips, the lips he had kissed so briefly and so sweetly the night he gave her the rose. He hadn't touched her since; no, not even the tips of her fingers when he took his plate from her across the table, or when he helped her pack the heavy shopping in her basket. Because that was the way it must be. He had a longing to take her in his arms and hold her close, and then to kiss that soft, pretty mouth. But if he did that for a second time it would, in Martha's eyes at least, commit him to marriage. And that wasn't even to be considered while she earned more than he did: a man didn't let his wife keep him. His glance flickered over those gathered at the foot of the steps. He was quite sure that none of the men there earned less than their wives.

When the Schofields arrived he listened to the murmur of the crowd and watched Martha's saucer-like eyes with some understanding. There was a fairy-tale air about the family, he thought, a kind of golden aura that was only partly to do with the blonde hair. 'You've seen Mr Schofield, haven't you?' hissed Martha, 'well – the lady in blue with the white wrap is Mrs Schofield, and the others are Mr Sam and Miss Sarah. It doesn't look as if Mr Ralph is coming.'

Matthew recalled the beautiful youth with the empty
eyes in the yard at Jericho Mills, and then forgot him
in watching the father, who was evidently in high
good humour. 'Ne'then!' he called cheerfully to those
watching. 'We wouldn't have been gallivanting like this
twelve months back, would we?' His bright blue eyes
observed them all and Matthew stood up straight and
tried to look capable of a hard day's work. This was
Joshua of the golden trumpet, the man who might one
day employ him.

He took his wife's arm as they approached the steps,
and Matthew caught his expression as he looked down
at her. Rarely had he seen such open devotion on a
man's face. It was undisguised, for all to witness, and
he felt warmed, as if he stood by a glowing fire. So love
didn't always die when youth fled and lust was sated?
This couple seemed to be proof of that. Then he looked
at the brother and sister. 'Mr Sam,' whispered Martha
dotingly, 'and Miss Sarah, oh – isn't she lovely?'

Matthew eyed the Schofield daughter warily. She was
wearing a silvery fringed shawl over a dress the colour
of primroses, and the amazing blonde hair was looped
up in great coils behind her head and fastened with
silver combs. She waved to the onlookers and gave a
self-conscious little laugh, and he knew at once that
she felt uncomfortable to be seen in such finery when
the crowd were still in their grubby work clothes. He
caught a glimpse of a slim foot in a yellow silk slipper,
and then a flutter of frilled petticoats as she went up
the steps with her brother.

It seemed suddenly dark and bare when the four of
them had gone inside, and he gazed after them like a
hungry man whose meal is removed from the table in
front of him. Then he shrugged. A woman like that
wasn't for the likes of him, a man raised in the stables
of a third-rate coaching inn. But she seemed good as
well as beautiful, and life had taught him that the two
didn't always go together.

He looked down at Martha. She was staring up the deserted steps, and on her small face was a look that pulled at his heart – a look of wistful yearning, of longing for something more than could ever come her way at Ledden Street, with her mother and Uncle Jack to care for. One of his sudden impulses took control of his tongue, and he heard himself say, 'When you've seen as much as you want to here, come across to Dolly Redfern's with me for a cup of tea. I want to ask you something.'

It was cramped and steamy in the tea-hut, but they found a tiny table and two empty stools, and stacked their purchases in the corner. Dolly Redfern poured tea from a vast earthenware pot and took payment with a flash of her bird-bright eyes. When Matthew turned back to the counter and asked for two currant tea-cakes she looked at them both more closely, remembering them from a couple of weeks earlier. They were an odd pair, she decided, the man so striking and gypsyish and the woman so small and plain. She was a bit plumper now, though, and bonnier for it, but she wore no ring – was she his sister, or what?

Matthew laid his hat on the scrubbed table and watched Martha. She was impressed by his purchase of the tea-cakes, but only mildly curious as to what he was going to ask her. He was struck by her modesty. Obviously she hadn't the remotest expectation of a proposal of marriage. Suddenly his nerve went. What if she refused him? How could he combine the status of lodger with that of rejected suitor? Then he recalled the look on her face when he kissed her, and told himself that she surely had some sort of fondness for him.

And what of his long-held resolve not to marry until his forties? That was still twenty years away – almost a lifetime – and he no longer relished the wait. He wanted a house and a clean little wife who would cook for him and wash his clothes – yes, and warm his bed. A wife who would cleave only to him as long as they both lived. From under his lashes he watched her eating. He had a squeamish streak about people who gobbled or slobbered over their food, but all Martha's physical activities were deft and precise. She was a pretty eater, and he thought he could face her across the table for the rest of his life.

'Martha,' he said without preamble. 'I be mortal fond o' you. Will you marry me as soon as I'm earnin' more money?'

He saw her jaw drop, and she turned so pale he put out an arm in case she fell senseless from the stool. 'Hey,' he protested, trying to laugh, 'is it that bad'n idea?'

She took a gulp of tea, and at last said flatly, 'I'm twenty-six, and you're twenty-two, aren't you?'

'Yes. But I don't mind the difference, if you don't.'

Faint colour rose in her bony cheeks, but her eyes were flat and dead when they met his. 'Me mam and me uncle Jack – I couldn't leave them. They will have to – to stay with me.'

'Well, o'course they will,' he agreed. 'That goes without sayin'.'

'And what about your sisters and half-brothers?'

'They're settled where they are. I said I'd go to see 'en as soon as I was on my feet, and that's not yet, by a long way. I couldn't marry you until my pay equals yours.'

She eyed him intently. 'And when will that be?'

He shrugged. 'When I get taken on at the mill. Mr Broadhurst does his best, but he can't pay more than's laid down, and then the winter's comin'.' He wondered whether to tell her now that he sometimes gave money to Billy Warhurst and his family, but decided it was hardly the right moment.

'Did you know some of the mills are goin' back on short time, Matthew?'

'What?' he said in dismay. 'Jericho as well?'

'No, but only because Mr Schofield bought careful.

He's told the overlookers we've got cotton till Christmas, and buying should be back to normal again by then.' She pulled his hat across the table and absently ran her finger round the brim. 'I did hear that some of the Jericho labourers let themselves be shipped off to America to learn how to make glass.'

Matthew laughed. 'That's no good to me. I'm crossin' no ocean to find work.'

'No, I know that. But they're saying in Saltley that when their ship docked in New York they were press-ganged into the Yankee Army.'

Perplexed, he stared at her. 'I be sorry to hear that, but how could it affect me?'

Because their names aren't ahead of yours on Mr Schofield's waiting-list any longer.'

His spirits soared and he grasped her hand in full view of everyone in the hut. Dolly Redfern was so taken by it she spilt tea on her counter. 'Do you want to marry me, Martha?' he asked hoarsely. 'Do you?'

For only the second time he saw her truly beautiful smile, and not even the glint of her tears could dim its radiance. 'Oh yes,' she said. 'I want to, right enough.'

'Mama, why is Mrs Walton always so offhanded with me?'

Rachel could have hugged her daughter. She was so lacking in conceit it had never occurred to her that with two squat, over-plump daughters to marry off, the sight of a girl with Sarah's sort of looks must be a sore trial to Bessie Walton. 'Don't worry, love – she's apt to be a bit brisk at times,' she said gently. 'What did she want, anyway?'

'She says that man over there wants to meet me. He's called Edward Mayfield.'

Rachel inspected him across the dance floor. What a very presentable young man, and more mature than Sam and Sarah's friends. She smiled gently in his direction and bent her head in acknowledgment. It was high time her lovely girl met someone outside her immediate circle of cotton-masters' offspring. 'I think he has something to do with the new infirmary, pet, so you'd have a common interest. Are you booked for every dance?'

'Yes, but Sam could back out of a few. The trouble is I do *like* dancing with Sam. He's not frightened of whirling me round very fast.' She studied Edward from the corner of her eye. 'He's a bit different, isn't he?'

'Very different, I'd say. Oh, Mrs Boulton is bringing him across.'

Sarah bit her lips to redden them and twitched at her gown. 'Do I look all right, Mama?'

Rachel would have had to be blind not to see that her daughter eclipsed every woman in the room, but she gave no hint of it. 'You look very nice, dear,' she said mildly.

Clad in magenta silk, Eleanor Boulton sailed galleon-like across the room with Edward in tow. The Schofields irritated her intensely, what with Joshua's magnificent mills and the way he pampered his workers, and Rachel looking ten years younger than her age, and their children's amazing looks; the lot of them were just too good to be true. Still, if Edward was taken by Sarah — and what man in the room wasn't — then Bessie might well be right in saying it would be no bad thing for Tizzie and the committee; they'd then be free of the potential for scandal. Bessie, of course, was something of an expert at avoiding scandal — she'd had to be. As for Tizzie, she was a little madam, and far too strong-willed for her age and position. She was a real asset to the committee all the same, and if her own mother couldn't protect her good name, then she, Eleanor Bolton, was quite prepared to do it. Besides, she needed her herself for the next hour.

The attraction between Edward and Sarah was power-ful and immediate. He kissed her hand with easy self-assurance, and she stared at her fingers as if surprised to find them still attached to her hand.

He was stunned by her looks and charmed by her unassuming manner. She was captivated by his elegance and sophistication. Sam was asked to relinquish one of his dances; then they took to the floor, waltzing at the correct arm's length and oblivious to those around them as they made silent assessment of each other.

Her task accomplished, Eleanor Boulton made her excuses and went to join her husband Ezra, who was hovering near Lord Soar's party. Rachel eyed her departing figure and wondered if she'd been wrong in judging her to be a hard woman. She'd been so affable and kind when she brought Edward Mayfield across to be introduced, so friendly. And Sarah was taken with him – that was quite obvious. It might be wise to find out more about him, just in case. . . .

On the floor Edward's hunting instincts were in full cry. What skin! What a shape! Undoubtedly a virgin and as innocent as the day. She was the most beautiful girl he had ever seen, and he wouldn't throw the mother out of his bed, either, given the choice. He steeled himself not to pull her too close, and the effort of it made his fingers tremble behind her waist. He was amazed they hadn't met before. If she was a Schofield her father must be the master of Jericho Mills; the man who turned down an invitation to serve on the committee and then sent a huge donation; the man who generated that weird blend of envy and admiration from the other mill-owners. He would be *rolling*! There was more to this girl than her looks – and they were enough to be going on with, thank you very much.

Eli Walton bounced past with Tizzie, and at once Edward compared the two girls. His little red-head had looked so gorgeous when he arrived he'd tried to drag her out to Gatefield Lane on the spot. He had even slipped a stable-boy something in advance to leave the oat-room door open for them, but to his fury Tizzie was at the beck and call of that grey-faced old bag, and distinctly unavailable. Now, though, with Sarah Schofield only inches away, Tizzie didn't seem quite so desirable. Her taut, high-breasted body appeared hard and angular next to Sarah's soft slenderness; her abundant wavy red hair garish compared to Sarah's smooth blonde coils; the superb green gown bold and a trifle flashy against the exquisite silvery-primrose of the girl in his arms.

Tizzie was exciting – in fact she was unique – but he could have her any time. She would have to wait until after supper for her next dance with him. After all, he was merely obeying his company's orders to make himself pleasant to the wives and daughters of the fund's benefactors. Joshua Schofield was a benefactor, and a generous one, so that was that.

The young ones had gone to join their friends for supper at another table, while Rachel and Joshua had a quiet half-hour on their own at a table for two in an alcove. It was the first really big social event they'd attended for almost three years; they had loved dancing together again and watching their children enjoy themselves. There was a burst of laughter from their table, and Sam's voice could be heard above the others. 'He still likes a laugh,' said Rachel, 'but he's really growing up, isn't he? I feel I could rely on him if I needed anything when you weren't here.'

Joshua held her hand. 'I'm always here for you, love, and always will be, God willing. But you're right, he's maturing fast and he's a good lad. As for Sarah – they think the world of her at Jericho, especially since the to-do about Johnny Barnes. Some of 'em have started calling the sick-bay the "lamp room", you know, because of that drawing of Miss Nightingale's lamp that somebody did on the door. Sam's had the idea of making it permanent, and he's fixed up for a sign-writer to come in and enamel it. Now don't tell her – it's to be a surprise.'

She liked the idea of that, and wondered if Sam had inherited his father's flair for the popular gesture. And what of Ralph? What had he inherited? Her youngest son – her little boy – and what did she know of him? 'I would have liked Ralph here,' she said quietly, 'wouldn't you?'

'No. Not if he wasn't willing. He asked us in a proper manner about this twenty-first party, and his friend's mother wrote us a polite, sensible letter.' He flicked edgily at his whiskers. 'You know, love, I think we might have to face up to it that Ralph has his own ideas about things. I've made enquiries about this lad Richard. He's clever, and by all accounts he works hard at the Exchange. His parents are respectable, chapel-going folk, and comfortably off. If we'd made Ralph come here instead of Liverpool he might have put a blight on things – you know how he can, if he has a mind to. Try not to worry, love.'

She chewed on her lip, and then looked thoughtfully at her eldest son. He was no problem, never had been, unless being too good and too trusting could be termed a problem. He was laughing at Sam, but next to him his wife-to-be was unsmiling. It occurred to Rachel that she could look very sour at times. 'Have you booked a dance with Esther?' she asked.

'Yes. And James says he'll have the same one with you. How does it feel to dance with your sons, Mrs Schofield?'

'Wonderful,' she admitted, 'but not as good as dancing with their father.'

Joshua chuckled, highly pleased. 'That young architect fella,' he said suddenly. 'What do you make of him with all that hand-kissing and such? Oh aye, I saw it. I was chatting to Ezra, but I had one eye on you and Sarah.'

Rachel concealed a smile. The day he missed something she would faint clean away from the shock. 'He's different from the Saltley men, and very charming,' she said consideringly. 'He's had only one dance with her, so far, but I can tell she likes him.'

'Aye, and he likes her. If he'd had a knife and fork handy he'd have made a meal of her, he wouldn't part. Still, if he's a decent young fella it'll do her no harm to see a bit of somebody different. I did hear he was friendly with the Ridings girl – the red-head.'

'Yes, they've danced together, but I think they're both on the committee. Somebody was saying she's responsible for most of tonight's organisation, so she's intelligent. She's lovely as well, isn't she?'

Just then a pale young man from Lord Soar's party made his way through the tables and bowed to them both. 'His Lordship's compliments, and would Mr and Mrs Schofield care to join him during the speeches?'

Joshua hesitated for so long she had to nudge him under the table. He sighed audibly and she was worried in case the man had heard. 'Please thank his Lordship,' he said at last, 'and say we'll be across there directly.' The man departed and he attacked his port-wine jelly with a noisy clatter of spoon on glass. 'Damn me,' he said irritably, 'can't the old lad see I'm enjoying having you to myself for once?'

Sam edged away from the Walton girls and smiled vaguely at twittery Charlotte Dobbs. He'd done his duty by the lot of them, and felt a sudden urge to escape the giggling throng and their over-pleasant mothers. The last waltz of the evening was just beginning and he was in low spirits. He'd felt like it before when everybody was paired up except the girls he didn't particularly like.

James and Esther were taking to the floor, and to Sam's observant eye his brother looked tense and slightly resentful. Something had crossed dear Esther, and no doubt she'd been letting James know what it was. Over there was Francis Soar, red-faced and amiable, puffing around with that quiet little girl who was rumoured to be heiress to a fortune. He hoped she was good enough for Francis, because he was a decent lad, good-natured and always slightly embarrassed by the ancient family name.

The way he'd been questioning James about High Lee
he should have been a farmer.

Ah – here came Sarah, dancing with Edward Mayfield.
Sam leaned against a pillar and under the guise of surveying everyone on the floor, studied them both closely.
She liked him – oh yes, she liked him; and the elegant
Mr Mayfield liked her. That was fine. After jumping to
conclusions about his brother's choice of partner – never
mind that he was right – he would reserve judgement on
any of the men who fell for Sarah until she fell for them.
And even then he'd made her a promise.

Over there were his parents. His father grey-haired
but full of youthful energy, and his mother looking
lovely as she always did. He was ashamed now of his
past resentments, when he'd believed she had no time
for him. With the closing of the food centre and the
school at Jericho she had become again the mother of
his youth; she listened to accounts of his exploits each
day, chatted to them all at the dining table, brushed and
pressed their clothes herself rather than leaving it to one
of the women. How could he not have seen she'd been
run off her feet for years?

At the moment, though, she had eyes for nobody
but his father. They looked so well together, they
fitted each other – one of the rare couples it was
impossible to imagine with different partners. Sam felt
again the disturbing sensation that sometimes came to
him – a searching – a reaching out for he didn't know
what. With his parents whirling in front of him in each
other's arms, he began to see what might make him
feel that way. Maybe it was that unattractive emotion,
envy. All at once he knew he wanted somebody of his
own who meant as much to him as his mother meant
to his father.

He shrugged and half-smiled. He would have to do
something about it then, instead of moping about at the
edge of the dance-floor feeling sorry for himself. Turning
to walk on he almost collided with a young woman in

green who was hurrying in from the supper room. It was the pawnbroker's daughter, the eldest one.

She sidestepped quickly, and unaware of his regard looked eagerly at those who weren't dancing. She frowned, as if in perplexity, and then transferred her attention to the couples on the floor. For a moment she stood quite still, and Sam followed the direction of her gaze. Dear oh dear, she'd been hoping to have the last dance with the charming Mr Mayfield, but he was otherwise engaged. Hard lines, Miss Ridings. She was hardly the type to be devastated.

Or was she? He saw her lower lip tremble and her bare shoulders droop. He even had the absurd, the utterly mad conviction that her bright hair suddenly gave up its lustre. Young women often reacted badly when the man they liked met his sister, and he was accustomed to helping them over a bad few minutes.

'Ah Miss Ridings, there you are.' He came out with it as if he'd been wandering the Town Hall searching for her. 'I doubted whether I would find you free for this dance, but if it happens that you are, perhaps you would do me the honour?'

She turned to him, her magnificent green eyes dead as stones. 'Mr Schofield, how nice,' she said politely. 'Yes, I'm free – unexpectedly so. Thank you.'

She was graceful, attractive, and polite. She was hard, she was bony, and her mind was elsewhere. She was also amazingly stylish and self-possessed to be the sister of that brown-haired little bundle who was so besotted by Will Hartley. But he didn't like her, and couldn't think why he'd felt the urge to save her face. He dismissed the pleasantries he'd contemplated about the success of the occasion and the benefit to the fund, and managed a wink at Sarah when they neared each other.

For the first time in both their lives there was no flicker of response from his sister. She was miles away – up in the clouds. He held the taut, graceful form of Tizzie Ridings and followed the lilting music with the emptiness of loss inside him. Sarah – his lovely, funny little sister Sarah – was growing up and away from him. It had to happen sooner or later, but oh, it was a wrench.

He bade a brisk farewell to the pawnbroker's daughter, and she thanked him politely. Mrs Boulton was beckoning imperiously from across the room, but he made no move to escort her to the older woman. Straightbacked, the red-head walked away in obedience to the summons, and Sam went to find his family and prepare for home.

Almost everyone had left. Tizzie was to go home in a hired carriage ordered by Ezra Boulton, and she was not happy. Edward was with the Walton family and the daughters were drooling over him. Above their heads he mouthed a silent kiss at her, and she gave him a small, hard smile. It seemed to her that every female between sixteen and sixty had conspired to keep him from her, and they had managed only three dances together.

Eli insisted on handing her into the carriage. With his wife and daughters coming down the steps he was correctness itself, but his glance flicked down hungrily when she lifted her skirts to climb in. It seemed he couldn't bear to miss the sight of an ankle, or better still a leg. Over-bright with wine, his pig-like little eyes glittered into hers. 'Well done, Tizzie,' he muttered. 'You've worked hard, and it won't be forgotten.'

'Thank you, Mr Walton.' She said a polite farewell to Edward and the rest of them, then settled in her seat for the ride home. Once alone she took herself briskly to task. What, exactly, had she expected from the evening? That Edward would swoon when he saw her in her dress? That he would dance with nobody else? That he would announce to everybody in Saltley that he was madly in love with her? Common-sense denied that she'd expected anything of the sort, but the whirling emotions inside her confirmed it. She *had* expected Edward to declare himself, or at the very least make clear that they had an understanding.

Instead, when she'd refused to sneak out to the alley with him, he had treated her as no more than a fellow-member of the committee. She swayed back and forth as the cab clattered over the cobbles, telling herself bitterly that if she'd been the daughter of a gentleman – especially one with looks as well as expectations – she would be engaged to Edward at that very moment. As if to confirm her thoughts, once out of the carriage she heard the sound that had blighted her life: the creak of metal as the three brass balls swung on their bracket.

She looked up to see them glinting darkly in the moonlight, and was filled with sudden rage. Just let her father ask if she'd enjoyed the evening – just let him! Her skirt dipped and billowed in the breeze as she waited for her mother to come and let her in. Tizzie looked down at the gleaming silk and with a sudden reversal of feeling summoned a smile to her lips. Her parents had begun their married life sorting rags in Miller's shed. If they hadn't progressed to the pawnshop she wouldn't have had this dress; she wouldn't have been educated – she wouldn't have met Edward in the first place.

The door opened, and her mother stood there with a warm wrap over her nightgown. 'Come on up, and tell me all about it,' she whispered. 'I've got a hot drink ready for you, but don't make a noise – your father's asleep and he's not so well.'

Upstairs a single gas lamp was burning and the fire had fallen to a few dull embers, making the comfortable room seem drab and unwelcoming compared to the brilliance of the Town Hall. 'Well, how did you get on?' asked Maria eagerly.

'Oh – it was a great success. The committee are delighted and I had a marvellous time. I danced with Edward several times, and with Mr Walton and Mr Boulton and young Mr Schofield. Mrs Boulton says she can't possibly do without me as her assistant.'

Her mother sighed in relieved admiration. 'Oh, I'm

that proud of you, Tizzie. Now, here's your milk. Drink it up.'

If she hadn't been observing her mother's reactions so closely Tizzie might not have noticed that her smooth, strong-featured face was very pale, her body in some strange way deflated. 'Is everything all right?' she asked. 'What's wrong with Father?'

'He's had a bad breathless do, and the doctor's been. He was joining in a sing-song at William's, when he turned so short of breath he went blue around the mouth. We didn't make much of it in case we spoiled things for Mary, but I had to ask Mr Hartley to bring us home. I put him to bed and then sent Barney running for the doctor.'

Tizzie was so stunned at the idea of her father joining in a sing-song she stood there woodenly and stared at her mother. 'Don't get upset,' Maria said shortly, 'he seems a lot better now.'

'But what is it? His heart?'

Her mother nodded heavily. 'He's never been robust, as you know. He wasn't – he didn't have a healthy start in life. The doctor says his heart's out of rhythm, and it's affecting his lungs. He'll have to take things quietly.'

'But what about the business? Barney can't do it all – the shop and the cellar and the books.'

'No, I know. We wondered if you'd help out a bit until we can find a paid assistant.'

Tizzie looked down at her beautiful gown. The bright green silk looked almost black in the dim light, and she stroked it regretfully. Lovely, lovely dress, but what had it brought her? Nothing so far except a spell in the shop, by the look of things. 'You're tired out, Mother. Let's go to bed and talk about it in the morning, shall we?'

Maria nodded. 'Did they like your dress, Tizzie?'

'Everybody loved it,' she said with truth.

'Good. Let's have you out of it, then.' Maria took a clean bed sheet and laid it across the table. She put the dress on one half, and covered it loosely with the

other, then unfastened Tizzie's petticoats and helped her
to step out of her hoop. She untied her stays, and asked
delicately, 'Edward didn't – say anything at all?'

'No, Mother. Not yet. But he will, I'm sure of it.'

Her mother gave a tired nod, and seemed satisfied.
'Come on, then, time for bed.' She lit their candles and
turned out the gas, then led the way upstairs.

In her shimmy and pantalettes, Tizzie went up behind
her. What would it be like if she was on her way to bed
with Edward, in their own beautiful house? One thing
was sure – the pantalettes and shimmy and her pretty
new stays would be tossed aside in seconds. . . .

Maria turned and gave her a rare kiss on the cheek.
'Good-night, love.'

'Good-night, Mother.'

It was a relief to find Mary fast asleep in the big bed,
one hand twisted in her thick, shiny plait. Tizzie held
up her candle and looked at the plump, good-natured
face. In the morning she would no doubt relate every
boring detail of the engagement party, and then, just as
an afterthought, ask about the ball.

She had quite forgotten about her father by the time
she climbed into bed.

CHAPTER TWELVE

'It comes to all of us'

SUNDAY MORNINGS IN SALTLEY were quiet. Those with a choice of footwear forsook their clogs, and silenced the weekday clatter. There were no mill-hooters, no coal wagons rumbling from mine to mill, no horse-drawn carts rattling over the cobbles. There was just the far-off whistle of the trains, and maybe the hoof-beats of a horse or the swish of a carriage as those with transport made for church and chapel.

At Meadowbank House Joshua was having a last look through the week's newspapers in case he'd missed an item of news. He couldn't abide it when people mentioned events of which he knew nothing. Rachel was upstairs putting away the ballgowns and the men's evening suits, and trying to remember when she and Joshua last had the house to themselves, because for once everybody was out. James and Esther had taken Sam and Sarah up to High Lee Court to see the work being done on their house, and Ralph was still in Liverpool. It was Alice's day off, so she was visiting her sister in Oldham; Hannah had gone to morning instead of evening chapel; Ellie had scuttled off with a basket of food to the black cellar she called home. In the stables Will and young Davey had been given the morning off, and Benjamin the gardener never worked on Sundays anyway.

Once assured that he would still get his Sunday dinner, Joshua had been pleased to hear they'd be alone together. 'We're doing well,' he chuckled, 'supper for two last night and dinner for two today.'

'We'll be back to normal at tea-time,' Rachel reminded

him. 'Seven of us, counting Esther. I've arranged it for
five o'clock so we'll all be in time for chapel.'

Now she finished putting away the clothes and went
down to see if he wanted a cup of coffee. It would be a
good time to mention Ralph's attitude to the sick-bay.
Newspapers scattered around him, Joshua was in his
favourite seat by the window. It looked out over the
front garden, and beyond the gates he could see in the
distance Jericho's chimney and the top of its square
tower, with the great flag streaming out on the wind.
'Hello,' he said, 'there's an officer of the police coming
here. What on earth does he want?'

Rachel hurried to the window. Police only called on
law-abiding people if there was bad news. . . . Joshua
held up a reassuring hand. 'It's probably something to
do with the mill, love.' They watched the uniformed
figure hurry up the drive to the front steps, and when
the doorbell rang Rachel whirled round. What was she
thinking of? There was nobody to answer it!

'I'll go. You stay here,' said Joshua firmly. 'No, stay
here, Rachel.'

Obediently she sank into a chair. There'd been an
accident – she knew it. There were four of them in
the carriage going up to High Lee, and Zacky as well,
driving. Or perhaps it was Ralph – Liverpool was full of
thieves and robbers. Or maybe the train had come off
the rails, or he'd been on the Mersey and the boat had
sunk! Remorse stabbed at her because she hadn't been
closer to their youngest son. There was the murmur of
voices in the hall and she covered her ears. Bad news
would come better from Joshua's lips.

She felt the thud of the front door closing, and then
heard the policeman's feet going down the steps. Joshua
came back, his eyes stretched wide with unbelief. She
jumped up and said fearfully. 'What is it, love? Tell me,
Joshua; what's the matter?'

'It's Charlie,' he said limply. 'He's dead. Charlie's
dead.'

She almost said 'Thank God!', and was glad she hadn't, because she only meant thank God it wasn't one of the children. She went and put her arms round Joshua. 'Oh, love! What happened? Was he taken ill?'

'No. He was found in the alley at Mosley Street. Somebody on a top floor some distance away saw the hoist doors open at about half-past nine this morning. Being a Sunday, and with thieving in the area, they told the police. One of their men found Charlie lying there dead, and they telegraphed Saltley right away.' Joshua shook his head and passed a hand across his face. 'His neck was broken, and it seems he'd been dead for hours. The back door had been forced – and they think he surprised somebody as they were winching stuff down to the alley. They suggest he might have struggled with them and fallen – or – or been pushed out through the hoist doors.' He sat down heavily. 'And we had a night-watchman due to start to-morrow. Charlie said we needed him. He might have known, mightn't he?'

'A presentiment,' she agreed, horrified. 'Oh, it doesn't seem real, does it? Poor, poor Charlie.' She bent over Joshua, planting little kisses on his hair. 'Where is he now? The – the body, I mean.'

'At the police mortuary. They've asked about his next of kin, and I told that young officer he hasn't got any. I have to go and attest to his identity, and then tell them what's missing from the warehouse.'

'Will you know?'

'I'll know, right enough. The police will want to speak to everybody tomorrow. I'll see John Wagstaff, and he can tell the men from the floors. I wouldn't like them to hear it from elsewhere, or be surprised to find the police there in the morning.' He jumped up. 'Right. I'd better be off.'

'Hold on a minute. Let me leave a note for Hannah, and you'd better do one for the boys and Sarah, in case they're back before us.'

'You're coming?' He couldn't disguise his relief.

'There's no need, you know. Things might be in a bit of a mess – '

'I know. I'm coming. Oh, the carriage isn't here! Will there be a train?'

'That young police fella is sending a cab up to take us to the station. We'll catch the eleven-thirty, if we look sharp.'

Rachel printed a clear little note for Hannah, who was slow at reading, and lowered the heat of the kitchen stove. Then Joshua scribbled a message for his sons and Sarah while she ran upstairs for her bonnet and wrap. In minutes they were out of the house and being driven down to the station.

At the mortuary Rachel held Joshua's hand, and insisted on staying with him while he viewed the body, to the open disapproval of the officer in charge. There were three corpses in the room, two of them covered and with pencilled notes pinned to their sheets. One note said *Found Drowned in the Irwell 8 a.m.*, the other, on what could have been a new-born infant, said simply, *Abandoned Saturday night*. The third body was Charlie's.

He was in his night-shirt and a loose woollen robe, and apart from a startling blue-white pallor looked very much himself. There was a dent in his forehead that put her in mind of a boiled egg after being tapped by a spoon, and there were particles of grit embedded in one cheek. His hands were folded peacefully across his chest in a manner that should have seemed ludicrous in view of his violent end, but succeeded in looking dignified and appropriate. There was no visible sign of the broken neck.

Joshua's hand gripped hers, hard, but his control never wavered as he gazed down at his friend. The policeman stepped forward with a paper. 'Sir, do you attest that this is the body of your business associate, Charles Barnes?'

'I do,' said Joshua, and signed the paper.

It was over and done with in two minutes, At the door Joshua turned for a last look at Charlie on the slab, and Rachel marvelled at his calmness. 'Have you finished with the body?' he asked quietly.

'Yes, Sir. The doctor has made his report and the coroner has inspected it.'

'Then I want him removing from that room and transported to Saltley, to – ' he lifted questioning eyebrows at Rachel, who nodded at once, '– to my home. In a proper and respectful manner.'

As always, instinct directed Rachel, and she asked impulsively, 'Shall we travel back home with him, Joshua, when we've finished at Mosley Street?'

He turned to her. 'Aye, he'd like that, and so would I. Thanks, love.' To the officer he said. 'Please send out to the best undertaker in the city and ask him to wait on me at my Mosley Street establishment within the hour. Here's my card. And I want to speak to the officer in charge of this case.' Having seen the man's disapproval of Rachel, he eyed him bleakly. 'At the earliest convenient moment, if you please.'

Not for the first time, Rachel watched fascinated as her husband moved into action. The qualities that made him a success in business were clearly apparent: decisiveness, speed, authority, and the ability to make people yearn to please him; all harnessed under a keen mind that seemed to think faster than other minds. She ached with love and admiration, even as she felt unease at his amazing control.

The next hour was hectic. A cab was despatched to bring in John Wagstaff from his cottage at Hulme Locks. Joshua declared that no stock was missing; but the police had found the winch-chains fastened round a bale of fine shirting ready to lower it to the alley, which seemed to confirm that Charlie had interrupted the intruders. The undertaker received orders on transporting the body to Saltley, and requested the commission to handle the funeral itself as soon as the inquest was over. Charlie's lawyer was sent for, and arrived breathless from a rapid ride across the city; the senior policeman and Joshua went into deep discussions in Charlie's office. Pale with distress, John Wagstaff arrived, to be interviewed at once by the police.

In the midst of all this Rachel asked if it would be all right to make tea for everybody up in Charlie's rooms. 'I don't think he'd mind, would he, Joshua?'

He looked at her sombrely. 'If it was for us he wouldn't have minded giving his life's blood, so I don't think he'd mind you invading his kitchen to make a pot of tea,' he said quietly. 'Everything's in order up there, so they say. No theft or interference of any kind.'

Rachel hurried up the stairs. She didn't know what Joshua would make of the miniature. He was bound to see it sooner or later . . . but surely not now, when he was still numb from the shock? Should she hide it in a drawer or something, and rely on inspiration about what to do with it when they came across it?

The beautiful, masculine room revived painful memories. It seemed hours rather than weeks since she sat in that chair by the window and saw the little painting of herself. But it wasn't there now. Not on the little table, not on his desk, not anywhere in sight. She sighed in relief. Perhaps he'd moved it. Well, wherever it was, she would think about it later. In the kitchen she put the kettle on and set cups and saucers on a tray. Suddenly the tall, ungainly figure felt very close and real, and the mournful dog eyes seemed to hold hers from the darkest corners of his kitchen. She recalled how he had moved the miniature from sight so skilfully that day, under the impression she hadn't seen it. Poor, kind Charlie. Almost thirty years of hiding his feelings, of loving the wrong woman. She thought how he had told her he would leave the company rather than come between Ralph and his parents ever again. . . .

Afterwards, looking back, she found an odd satisfaction in the knowledge that she'd been the first to weep for him. She had the idea he would have been pleased. At the time she only knew that he had no wife to grieve for him, no children, no parents, no brothers or sisters: nobody except the Schofield family and their employees. She sat at his kitchen table and wept as if her heart was broken. She had no handkerchief with her, so she dried her tears on a blue and white pot towel.

It didn't last long. It couldn't, because they were all waiting for their tea downstairs. Mr Wagstaff accepted his cup as if it was the nectar of the gods, but Joshua took one look at her and suddenly turned aside, and she knew that the traces of her tears had moved him and made it impossible for him to perform the mundane act of drinking tea.

They went back to Saltley in what was actually a funeral carriage, with the driver seated above them wearing an everyday waterproof cape but Charlie lying behind them in a splendid oak coffin. The wind had dropped and rain poured steadily from a grey-black sky. Joshua looked so ghastly she wondered if they would reach home without him being taken ill, and all at once knew what she must do. She closed the black curtains and held out her arms. 'Cry, love,' she said gently. 'There's only me to see. Cry for Charlie, if you want to.'

Then, for the very first time in all the years they'd been together, Joshua wept. They were almost home before he was calm again, and he sat with his head on her breast, exhausted. The horses climbed the curved road up past Jericho, dipping their wet heads as if sensing that the journey was almost at an end. Rachel drew back the curtains. 'Look at the flag,' she said in surprise, 'it's already at half-mast. How can that be when nobody knows about it yet?'

'The boys know,' said Joshua with deep satisfaction. 'They've come back from High Lee. They've done it, for Charlie.'

* * *

You could get used to anything, given time, Rachel told herself, even a dead body lying in state in your husband's study. The undertaker had done his work on Charlie; now he was flower-decked and immaculate, ready for people to call and pay their respects. She'd been prepared for it to upset the household, but found that it seemed simply right, and unexceptional, that he should be staying with friends until his funeral.

The men were all in Manchester, and she was at her Monday morning task of checking her children's rooms and putting away their Sunday clothes. Her own mother had instilled into her that good clothes must be cared for, and now she had time to spare she brushed and tidied their outerwear and supervised the laundering of her menfolk's linen. She even ironed their best shirts herself.

Her mind was on the occupants as she went from room to room. In three weeks' time James would be married and gone for ever from the family home. She would miss him as she would an arm or a leg, but she had vowed never to cling, never to interfere in his marriage. Esther wouldn't find it difficult to look after him. He wasn't a fussy eater, he was careful of his clothes, he was moderately tidy. She looked around her. The room was restrained and tranquil, like its owner, echoing his love of country life with plants and pictures and his boyhood collections of moths and birds' eggs.

Sam wasn't so orderly. His desk was littered with samples of raw cotton, his used shirt was dropped on the floor, his muddy boots left out for Zacky to clean and his coat slung over the wardrobe door. She shook and brushed the fine worsted, examining it for marks. It had been James who thought of lowering the Jericho flag, but Sam who climbed out on the wet roof of the tower and worked the ropes of the great flagstaff.

Entering Ralph's room she felt a flattening of her spirits. It was as well-furnished as the others, but it always gave her the impression of being empty. It lacked something vital, but she couldn't have said what. All his personal items were in drawers and cupboards, or the desk where for years he had kept his notebooks and mathematical charts. These days it was locked, but the key was in open view on the window ledge. Thoughtfully she stared out at the damp, sloping meadows behind the house. It had been a strange homecoming for him yesterday. He had seemed relaxed and almost pleasant when he came in. He had even said, 'Hello Mother,' a sure sign of good spirits. Then he looked over her shoulder at Joshua. 'I see the mill flag is at half-mast, Father. There's nothing wrong at Jericho, is there?'

When told the news he was stunned. She had observed his reaction carefully, in view of the trouble between him and Charlie. It was a positive relief to see him as shaken as the other three. 'Where is he now?' he asked.

Joshua nodded his head at the study door. 'In there. He's being decently laid out at the moment.' When Ralph frowned in puzzlement he said heavily, 'Don't forget he has no family. He'll stay here until the funeral, and that's to be on Tuesday, unless the coroner delays it.'

'But what about the police? Surely they're investigating? Do they say it was an accident?'

'Yes, up to now. If they find he was pushed, then of course it's murder.'

It was the first time the word had been used among the family. Ralph's jaw sagged, his brothers stared in dismay, Sarah burst into tears and ran upstairs, and Rachel hurried after her, offering comfort.

Now she sighed and turned back into Ralph's room. It was so incredibly neat. Even his used shirts were folded on a chair by the door ready for laundering. In the wardrobe his evening coat and trousers were put away on their hangers. Her nose wrinkled and her stomach gave a familiar lurch. There was a faint whiff of tallow, a smell that had always sickened her, but surely not from his new evening clothes? She followed

her nose, and found a long smear of grease on the left
sleeve of his new coat. Where on earth had he picked
that up? She would take it down and get the fullers
earth on it, with a hot iron. They would be starting the
day's ironing soon.

The coat over her arm, she was half-way down the
stairs when a picture dropped into her mind, clear and
entire, like one of the framed oil-paintings in her parlour.
It was of the open doors of the hoist at Mosley Street and
the winding-wheel of the winch, its hub thick with reesty
tallow; Charlie was in his waistcoat stamping the rolls
and saying to her, 'Come away, and mind your dress
on the wheel behind you!' But Ralph couldn't have had
this particular sleeve near the wheel of the hoist, it was
his brand-new evening coat. He'd only worn it once, to
Richard's party in Liverpool. She must remember to
ask him if he'd been near any machinery on his night
out. . . .

At the foot of the stairs she stopped dead, her knees
suddenly reluctant to support her. *No!* How could she
think it? How could it even cross her mind? But Joshua's
words echoed emptily in her head. 'The arrogant young
devil said he'd have him replaced! Charlie! Replaced!'
Rachel clutched at the newel post as a pain identical to
that of childbirth gripped her pelvis.

Hannah came past and eyed her in alarm. 'What is
it, Mum? Are you poorly?'

Rachel straightened up and managed a faint smile.
'No, I'm all right, Hannah, just a bit tired. I didn't sleep
so well.'

'I'm not surprised at that, Mum. Perhaps you should
go and have a nice lie down, and I'll bring you a cup
of tea?'

'No, I must be on hand if anyone calls to pay their
respects to Mr Barnes. Please don't make a fuss. I'm
all right.'

She took Ralph's coat to the laundry and tackled the
greasy mark. She could hear Zacky cleaning the previous

day's mud from the carriage, and the laundry-woman was taking sheets and tablecloths in from the lines. Everything seemed reassuringly normal on this abnormal day. Rachel stroked her son's coat, sighing as the tension left her. She was wrong, thank God – she was wrong. If Joshua knew what she'd thought in that mad, dreadful moment, he would go down with a stroke. She wouldn't say anything to anybody about the grease stain – not even Ralph.

Joshua was still shattered, but the loss was slowly becoming bearable. Charlie had been laid to rest at a little country chapel out on the road where pack-horses once carried salt from Cheshire over the hills to Yorkshire. Only the family knew the full tale of why he'd arranged such a distant burial, but Joshua was in no state of mind to offer explanations to anyone else, and the mourners could hardly object.

Now, with the funeral procession rattling briskly back to Meadowbank House, he let the memory of a golden day from his youth ease his grief. He and Charlie had been seventeen. It was a Whit Saturday, and they had used the rare holiday to go walking in the hills. At mid-day they sat in the sun under a blackthorn hedge, day-dreaming together and planning a great mill for the spinning and weaving of cotton. 'You can be the owner,' laughed Charlie 'because you've enough go in you for both of us. And I'll be your manager – your agent if you like – and do the buying and selling.'

They had wandered past isolated farms and through the hamlet of High Holdwell, until their way back took them past a Methodist chapel, square and solid and with an amazing view. They drank from an ice-cold spring that issued from a rock-face nearby, and then sat on the chapel steps. Below them lay the plain that stretched to Manchester and beyond, its haze speared by tall chimneys, and they played a guessing game about whose mill each chimney belonged to.

Then Charlie took him behind the chapel to a silent burial ground, and showed him the grave where his mother and father lay. It was covered in bluebells and shaded by a gnarled old tree in fresh leaf. 'It's peaceful, isn't it?' he said contentedly. 'When my time comes I'd like to lie here, Joshua, next to them.'

Radiantly healthy and from a long-lived line, Joshua was uncomfortable at such talk and tried to laugh the remark aside. But Charlie just looked at him with the sad brown eyes that seemed so out of place in a teenage face. 'It comes to all of us, sooner or later,' he said gently, brushing the bluebells with his foot.

Well, it had come to Charlie with a vengeance, and the manner of it troubled Joshua. The inquest, such as it was, had recorded death by misadventure. There was no evidence of robbery, only of intent – a badly-forced rear door and winch-chains fastened to a roll of best quality shirting. There was also no evidence of personal attack, as his injuries had been quite consistent with a fall from such a height. The senior police officer had asked barely veiled questions about the state of Charlie's mind: had he been depressed, did he have money worries, was there a lady-friend, and so forth.

Joshua sighed, and at once five pairs of eyes swivelled in his direction. He gritted his teeth and stared at the yellowing trees. The family had been marvellous, especially Rachel, but he was getting weary of being handled with kid gloves. All right, he'd admit he hadn't been himself – that was only to be expected when a man lost his best friend – but he wasn't a blasted invalid, either. And neither was Charlie a man to trip over his own feet at an open hoist; nor was he one to throw himself out in a suicide bid.

Whatever the truth of his death, it had created an upheaval in the company, because apart from himself there was nobody with the experience and expertise to succeed him. He could see now he'd been lacking in foresight, expecting his business manager to live for ever; and in his own self-obsessed way Ralph had looked ahead when he tried to assert his authority. And give the lad his due, he'd shown proper restraint and good sense when they put their heads together to decide how to run things.

Time would show whether the new arrangement was any good. John Wagstaff was to be given a rise, and would take on a lot of Charlie's paper work. Ralph would now spend Monday to Friday at Mosley Street and Saturdays at Jericho, not visiting the mine at all; he himself was to spend half his week in Manchester supervising him. Sam's week was rearranged as well, and James – well, James had been willing to go where he was needed, but he had so many irons in the fire at High Lee that in the end Joshua had just asked him to spend Wednesdays at Mosley Street. That was their best selling day, and the customers liked him. The whole system was flexible; they would have to see how it went. One thing was certain: however helpful he proved, however brilliant his exploits on the Exchange, Master Ralph was not going to be put in charge of Mosley Street for a very long time.

The big funeral carriage sped on towards Saltley, with Joshua still deep in thought. At least he wasn't lacking in foresight about somebody to take over from him at Jericho – his successor was sitting right opposite him. Sam – the one who thought as he did, who had his values, the one he. . . . Joshua sat up straight and wriggled in his seat, consciously dismissing what he'd been about to say to himself. If he said that Sam was the one he could trust it implied that he couldn't trust the other two, and that wasn't the case at all. But the familiar warmth eased its way around his heart, and wouldn't be denied. Like Charlie, Sam was loyal all the way – he was sure of it.

Rachel was waiting to catch his eye, and she gave him the tender little look that was his alone. What a woman! He sent up a word of thanks for her, as he'd been doing for over thirty years. This little lot had taken it out of her. Black usually suited her, but today, for the first time ever, she looked her age.

'We didn't just stop work – they shut the engines down for a full half-hour! Nothing like that's ever happened before at Jericho.' Martha had come in from work highly pleased with her unexpected leisure, and as always, fiercely loyal to the master of Jericho. 'Mr Schofield said we could do what we liked as long as we were quiet and we gave thought to Mr Barnes while he was being laid to rest. Wasn't that lovely?'

'I can't see as it was all that generous, when most of you are on piece work,' snorted her mother. 'You'll all lose pay.'

'No, we won't. He says he'll make it up to us. He wanted the engines shut down as a mark of respect. He told us that he and Mr Barnes chose the engines together, and that Mr Barnes designed the engine house. . . .'

Matthew had followed her in, and he listened with interest and a touch of amusement. She had changed in the last three days, and for the better. She was more outgoing now, more lively. There was something new beneath her reserve, and to him it seemed like pride. Could she really be proud that they were to be married: a woman capable of supporting three people from her earnings, and with a clean, well-furnished home?

He had been secretly wary of Mrs Spencer's reaction, fearing she might consider a park labourer to be a poor catch for her daughter; but when they came in from the market and told her the news she had nodded her head so vigorously her cap fell off into the hearth. 'Well, I never did!' she gasped, as Martha rescued it. 'Well! I'm that pleased, and so's Jack, aren't you, Jack? If you make as good a husband as our Bella's Henry you'll do. Come here, and give me a kiss!' And to Martha's astonishment she lifted her pale cheek, and then grabbed Matthew's collar and kissed him back.

There were no such good wishes from Uncle Jack. He was picking listlessly at his shirt buttons and twisting his scrawny neck from side to side. 'Take no notice,' whispered Mrs Spencer, shaking her head, 'he's been shocking today. Here, Martha, bring me my red purse!'

Martha produced a tiny red purse, decorated with beads. Mrs Spencer took a shilling from it, and looked at Martha defiantly. 'I've had this put by for somethin' special,' she said with satisfaction. 'Go and get us some brandy, Matthew, and we'll have a tot to celebrate. I haven't tasted a drop in years, and it's good for my rheumatics.'

Matthew became very still. Martha's eyes were stretched wide with amazement at her mother hoarding money for drink, but her cheeks were pink with pleasure. For an instant he actually considered it. After all, it was a once in a lifetime occasion. Then he recovered himself, and sent a sad little glance at Martha. He had made a vow that he would never, ever break, no matter what the provocation. 'I'm sorry,' he said quietly. 'I can't join you in that. I never drink. Never.'

Mrs Spencer looked at her cherished shilling. 'If you don't, you don't, and that's all there is to it,' she said irritably. 'We can't drink without the bridegroom-to-be.' She put the shilling back and fastened the little purse. 'At least you're not like some, signing the pledge and forgetting it next day.'

The evening had gone flat, all at once. He looked at Martha in apology, but she gave him her little twitch of the lips and said, 'I'll make us all a cup of tea, then. We've brought you both a currant tea-cake, Mam.' Then quietly, to him, 'I think you must have your reasons, Matthew.'

'I have,' he agreed, 'and when we're married I'll tell you what they are.'

Now, he watched the new, more confident Martha, and told himself that the change in her could only be

because of him. Suddenly he was impatient to have
her for his wife. In the long years since Peggy-oh died
there had been nobody to talk to, nobody to confide
in. He could talk to Martha, and he felt she would try
to understand. He had a sort of idea that – that she
loved him.

Tizzie had decided that pawnbroking would be quite
agreeable if it took place in a clean, bright shop and
she didn't have to deal with the public. They depressed
her; in fact they nauseated her. The men resented her,
but the women seemed relieved to find her in charge,
until they realised she was no softer than her father.
As for her surroundings – well, she'd always hated the
gloom and the smell and the countless bundles, but it did
have a certain attraction when seen from the position of
power behind the counter.

Her mother had banned Mary from helping. 'No,
you're too soft-hearted for the shop, my girl. Let's see
how Tizzie gets on. She's willing, and she's more of a
business-woman than you'll ever be. If you help me up
here I can spend more time with your father, and there's
your bottom drawer to sew for, don't forget. I can't have
a daughter of mine getting married without enough sheets
and pillowcases, nor wearing nighties without a bit of
fancy-work.'

Tizzie had sniffed at that. Closer acquaintance with
the beef-slaughtering brigade had certainly banished
her mother's objections to the match. Any day now
she would be boasting about Mary marrying into the
family of 'Saltley's most prosperous meat purveyors,'
or some such pretentious drivel.

But she, Tizzie, was in charge of the shop. She was
often bored, but now and then something startling
happened, such as when a nervous little woman in an
out-of-date bonnet dragged a great ruby ring from her
finger, or when a fat, elderly man slapped a string of
real pearls on the counter. Estimating value had been

tricky at first, and she had climbed the stairs dozens of times a day to consult with her father; but she was a quick learner with an excellent memory, and now she troubled him only about good jewellery.

Barney Jellicoe was proving a great help, and she was seeing more of him in a single day than in all the previous year. At first she had found his close proximity repellant; but gradually the great moon face and top-heavy body had become acceptable to her, while his quiet intelligence saved her many a dash up to the sick-room. If she had to visit Mrs Boulton or attend a committee meeting, or if her mother demanded that she took a long break from the shop, Barney would come up from the cellar to take over. Reluctantly, she had to re-assess her father yet again. She had always scorned him for employing a grotesque numskull, but now she had to acknowledge his insight in seeing the potential of the lumbering dwarf.

In all she would have been surprisingly content, except for seeing Edward only twice since the ball: once at committee with no opportunity to be alone together, and yesterday morning, when he came into the shop just before noon and found her alone. What an encounter that had been! Inside sixty seconds he had her behind a coat rail and in his arms. It was such bliss to feel his urgent mouth and searching hands that for a moment she forgot the danger of discovery. But even as she slapped his fingers away from her bodice, part of her mind was assessing whether it might be no bad thing for her mother to walk in. Could her parents press him into marriage if they believed she'd been compromised?

He was muttering hoarsely, the familiar unfocussed glitter in his eyes. 'Tizzie, I can't bear it when I don't see you! Can't you lock the door or something?' She knew he was desperate for lovemaking – that was why he had arrived during his working morning. She had a lightning glimpse of what marriage could be like . . . she busy in their elegant house, and Edward dashing

home at any old time to toss her on the bed. She
felt quite sick with longing for such excitement, until
beyond their grappling she heard a heavy tread on the
ladder from the cellar, and a creak as the trapdoor was
pushed upwards.

'It's Barney!' she gasped. 'Quick!' Edward was safely
at the other side of the counter when the big pale face
and pelt of dark hair surfaced. She introduced him to
Edward, feeling a stab of pride at the contrast between
his tall elegance and Barney's squat form under the
hessian apron. Edward nodded coolly, and she noted
a scornful lift to the red mouth.

But then an unfamiliar sensation gripped her; she
couldn't have put a name to it, she only knew that it
pained her to see this odd confrontation. Barney nodded
politely, eyes moving alertly from her to Edward and
back again. She had to force herself not to finger her
bodice to check whether the buttons were all fastened.
'Mr Mayfield is on the fund-raising committee, Barney,'
she said brightly, 'but by profession he's an architect,
and in charge of the new infirmary.'

'Aye, I know,' said Barney quietly. 'I only come up
to check some cash in, Miss Tizzie. It's been busy down
below due to folk getting their relief this mornin'. Shall
I leave it till later?'

'Uh – no, you'd better do it now. Mr Mayfield is just
leaving, aren't you, Edward?'

'It would seem so,' he agreed tightly. 'You will have
to let me know when you're free to see me, Tizzie, or
it may be some time before our next meeting.' He put
on his hat, adjusted it carefully, flipped at his coat tails
and sauntered out.

It was a threat, thinly veiled. She stood behind the
counter and managed not to clasp her hands like some
weak-willed fool in an illustrated paper. He was resentful
at not seeing her alone any more, and suddenly she
knew that if she didn't take care she would lose him.
Her knees felt so weak she tottered to a chair and

sat down. Yesterday her father had hinted that a visit
to Manchester would soon be necessary, and that he
might ask her to deputise for him. Would he insist on
her being accompanied, and if so, by whom? Mary she
could manage, Barney she could deceive, but what if
he insisted on her mother going with her? If only she
could be free to meet Edward at some private spot in
the city she would allow him every liberty except the
final one. Heaven help her, she was besotted by him,
but she hadn't quite lost her wits.

Barney was behind her, apparently unaware that her
legs refused to support her. She could hear the clink
of coins as he sorted coppers into the smooth wooden
runnels of the cash drawer. It was a pleasant sound,
and one that calmed her racing mind.

Charlie's affairs were in immaculate order, his will
detailed and generous. There were dozens of small
bequests, but the bulk of his money was to be divided
equally between the six Schofields, and his furniture
and personal effects disposed of as Joshua and Rachel
saw fit.

They went through his belongings one Saturday, just
the two of them, with Zacky and Hannah waiting down
in Mosley Street with the carriage to help with bundles
and boxes. Rachel was on edge about what to say if
the miniature should come to light, her mind veering
between that and all the other concerns that seemed to
be crowding in on her. The wedding was almost upon
them, and should have brought her no worry, but she
had started to recall Sam's objections to Esther when
James first showed an interest in her. The new, mature
Sam was correctness itself, but his protests from more
outspoken days kept echoing in her head: 'Surely James
can find somebody better than her!' or 'Mother, do you
really like Esther? She seems a calculating little madam
to me. . . .' What if he should turn out to be right, and
the rest of them wrong? It was too late now to tackle

James; too late to do anything but hope that her good, her truly good first-born son had chosen a wife who would make him happy.

And what about Sarah, madly in love for the first time? After a lifetime of angelic behaviour, she was becoming increasingly wilful and uncooperative. Fortunately, Edward was considerate and scrupulously correct. He was a gentleman, who would never, ever, besmirch her daughter's good name; but only yesterday Sarah had burst into overwrought tears just because they refused to let her spend a whole day with him, unchaperoned. As if she hadn't enough on her mind, Ralph had asked if he could set up his own establishment, here in Charlie's splendid rooms, and there hadn't been time to discuss with Joshua how to refuse him.

The one spark of light relief would be Tuesday's musical evening at Alsing, ancestral home of Lord and Lady Soar. It was to be a quiet, informal evening, and she couldn't help looking forward to it. The invitation had arrived weeks ago, before the autumn ball, and she had persuaded a reluctant Joshua that they must accept at once. The pleasure and anticipation were now dimmed, and she knew he wished they'd never accepted. She'd heard nothing about the Boultons or the Waltons being invited, thank goodness, but his friend Joe Chadwick was going, and the Dobbs and the Fairbrothers would be there.

Now Joshua was pale and silent. It seemed horribly intrusive to be emptying Charlie's cupboards and drawers, with evidence of his love for them all being revealed by countless sketches and photographs of the family. She needn't have worried about the miniature – there was no sign of it. The lawyer had said Charlie's will was a recent one, so perhaps he had disposed of the tiny painting before putting his affairs in order.

They had sorted out the clothes and the personal belongings, but she hesitated when they started on the household linen. 'Joshua, it seems silly to take all this

back to Saltley if there's any chance of Ralph setting up
here, and we still haven't decided about the furniture,
apart from the pieces for James and Esther. What shall
we do? He's too young to live alone, isn't he?'

Joshua flicked at his whiskers. 'At his age I was
renting half a mill floor, and employing six workers,'
he reflected, 'but I was still living under my father's
roof. Let's tell him we're waiting to see what he makes
of himself in the next month or two, and that we'll talk
about it again when he's eighteen. They're still killing
each other in America, but they're sending us more and
more cotton, so it would make sense to have him here
on the spot. Many's the time Charlie was at the docks
as soon as a consignment arrived, checking the quality
before it was unloaded, and he had to make written
acceptance.'

'But Ralph hasn't the experience for that, surely? You
said yourself it would take years for him to learn all about
cotton.'

Joshua's vivid gaze held hers. 'Don't underestimate
your youngest, love. Like Charlie said, he's bright –
very bright. Quicker than I was at his age, quicker
than Sam or James. He has a brain, and he's being
a good lad. I think all that to-do a few months back
was just growing pains, because at present I can't fault
him, either in his work or his attitude. Let's leave the
place ready for occupation, covered in dust sheets and
so forth if you want, and kept aired now the winter's
coming. I have the feeling he'll be settled in here before
the spring.'

Rachel stared out at a rainswept Piccadilly, her finger-
tips stroking the little wine table next to Charlie's chair.
She knew she should have been pleased at Joshua's words
about their youngest; but all she could feel was a bleak
conviction that Charlie wouldn't have wanted Ralph to
handle his things, to sleep in his mahogany bed or dine
at his lovely old table. On the other hand, if he set
up here she wouldn't have to see so much of him at

home, would she? Her throat felt dry and she swallowed under a wave of nausea. What sort of mother was she, for heaven's sake?

With an effort she nodded and raised a faint smile. 'I'm sure you're right, love,' she agreed gently. 'Now, shall I get Zacky and Hannah up here to help us with these boxes?'

CHAPTER THIRTEEN

Revelations

IT HAD BEEN EASY, surprisingly easy after all those hours of plotting how to see Edward on his own. Tizzie sat in a corner seat on the train back to Saltley and wondered why she felt so deflated.

Yesterday her father had asked her to take a sealed package to a jobbing jeweller just off Deansgate. 'He's all on edge about it being delivered in the morning,' Maria told her wearily, 'but our Mary's going up to Holden to see William's uncle, and I can't leave him, so there's nothing else for it – you'll have to go on your own. You must take a cab from the station and make him wait to take you back again.'

'I'll be careful,' Tizzie assured her, 'but I'd like to look at the shops for once, Mother. Can't I have an extra hour or two to study the fashions? I feel like a bit of a change.'

Maria sighed, but gave her an approving pat on the hand. 'You deserve a break,' she admitted, 'because you've worked hard looking after things downstairs, and your father says he doesn't know what we'd have done without you. Now you must get straight back in the cab to go to the shops, and whatever you do keep to the main streets, and don't speak to strangers. Tell Barney you'll be away all morning, and I'll tell your father.'

Within minutes Tizzie had sent a note to Edward's rooms, saying she would be in the coffee house at the corner of Cross Street and King Street from ten-thirty until eleven next morning. So, the package safely delivered, all she had needed to do was sit by the window drinking her coffee and nibbling a cake, watching people go in and out of the Town Hall opposite.

At a quarter to eleven a cab stopped outside and Edward hurried in. It was wonderful to see him, and even more wonderful that he'd come running when she beckoned. In minutes he had her in the cab with the curtains drawn and was kissing her so ferociously she feared her lips would split. The driver stopped outside a tall house in a quiet street, and as if it were all arranged, Edward led her at once to a first-floor room.

It wasn't what she'd expected at all. In the wakeful night she had pictured them driving round the city in search of a deserted park, or even kissing in some dark alley. . . . But to sneak upstairs in a strange house, unchallenged, smacked of those women Mary spoke of so scornfully: the street women, the prostitutes who charged money for their favours. Her lips were bruised and sore and she wasn't pleased with the way things were going.

Edward opened the door of a room and thrust her inside, then turned the key in the lock, and she saw again his strange, unfocussed stare. 'Clever girl!' he said, grabbing her. 'My darling, clever little Tizzie. How did you know I was desperate for you? I spent all last night dreaming of your mouth and your adorable body. God, but I'm aching for you. No, don't waste time looking at the room. It's paltry, but all I could get at short notice.'

'Edward,' she said clearly. 'Edward, listen to me. I sent the note because I wanted us to be able to meet without half Saltley watching. Nothing has changed about what's permissible between us and what isn't.'

Ignoring her words, he untied the ribbons of her new winter bonnet and threw it on a chair, then thrust his fingers into her hair and plucked out the pins. He removed her warm cloak and tossed it aside; with a

grunt of impatience at there being no front fastening
to her bodice, he whirled her round and tackled the
tiny hooks and eyes that closed the back of her green
velvet dress. His fingers, unsteady with eagerness, were
fumbling between her shoulder blades, and for a moment
she stood quite still and observed the room. It was square
and clean, with a washstand and a wardrobe and a bed.
The bed was big, bigger than the one she shared with
Mary, with a pink satin counterpane and piles of soft
cushions instead of pillows, but – she twisted her head
from side to side in puzzlement – why were there so
many mirrors in the room? And why was that huge
gold chamberpot on a sort of raised platform in the
corner?

A tremor of fear plucked at her. It was one thing to
make love in the open air in Saltley, protected from
public view only by a thicket of trees; it was quite
another to be here in a locked room in a silent
house in a vast impersonal city, with Edward intent
on removing her clothes. Hadn't she always accepted
his ruthless streak, admired it even? All at once she
had a sensation of vertigo, as if she teetered unprotected
on the parapet of a tall building. She wasn't in control
now, as she'd been in Back Lane or Soar Park, and
it was clear he was determined on the full sexual act.
Her body demanded to be free of her clothes, to seize
this chance of learning what all the fuss was about, but
her mind registered that he had spoken no word of real
affection before starting to strip her.

Then she caught sight of herself in a vast mirror at
the other side of the bed. Hair cascading over one eye,
shoulders bare as he tugged her dress down below her
waist, and then her legs and pantalettes whirling in an
arc as he lifted her free of her hooped petticoat. What
struck her in that reflected image was not her body,
half-undressed; it was her face, white and stiff, the eyes
like great emeralds on a piece of linen.

Sudden rage filled her. Who did he think she was?

Some paid drab who would accept such treatment for coppers? She'd wanted excitement, and she'd got it, here and now, but she couldn't risk the full act – not even once. 'No!' she said flatly. 'Force me and I'll tell everybody you abducted me. Can't you get it into your head that if ever I have a child, it will be in wedlock? Edward – are you listening?'

Panting, he released her and began instead to remove his own clothes. 'I've written home to my parents, telling them all about you,' he assured her. 'It's only a matter of weeks before they give their consent. Come on, Tizzie, let's do it properly for once!'

'No,' she repeated. 'I'll only undress to my shimmy – you take off as much as you like. We'll satisfy you like we did in the park, or we'll do nothing at all!'

Red-faced, he stood there, half-out of his trousers, and gave a short, hard laugh. 'Tizzie Ridings, you're incredible! You're unique, do you know that? Strange as it may seem, though, I've never yet had to force a woman, and I'm not going to start with you.' He took a handkerchief from his pocket and threw it on the bed. 'Half a loaf is better than no bread,' he said. 'Now come here – let's unfasten those blasted stays.'

The train rattled on towards Saltley and Tizzie went over each word, each gesture, each intimate embrace. She'd won again, but she felt no satisfaction; because, like Edward, she wanted more. The difference between them was that she wanted it inside marriage, with – she sought the appropriate words – with affection and respect as well as desire. What a funny thing – she'd never craved respect from him until today. Surely, after what they'd done to each other in that extraordinary room, he would speak to his parents about them getting married?

Back at the pawnshop Barney was up on his special boardwalk behind the counter, dealing with a customer. His dark eyes observed her gravely and he gave a polite little nod as she headed for the stairs. Her mother was in the kitchen with the strings of her cap unfastened, looking flustered. 'It's all right,' Tizzie assured her. 'I delivered it safely and took cabs both ways like you said, and I had a lovely time looking at the shops.'

'Oh, good. Tell me about it later. Your father's had his lawyer here again, and I don't know whether it means he's better or worse, though it must be better, I suppose, because he's talking of going down to the shop this afternoon.'

Oh, marvellous, thought Tizzie. Her days of freedom down there were numbered, by the looks of it. 'He's getting better, that's obvious, but I thought the doctor said "no exertion". What about coming back up the stairs?'

'I don't know, I don't know. He's breathless if he crosses the room, but he says he can't lie around for ever. And he's writing, writing, writing, all the time. I'm that worried about him.'

Tizzie breathed out heavily through her nose. It infuriated her when strong, sensible, attractive Mother let herself be reduced to jelly by that shrunken little creature. Still, to give him his due he did show signs of acumen at times. If he'd seen his lawyer for the second time perhaps he'd been settling his affairs. 'Look Mother, try to keep calm. He'll probably be all right going down the stairs, and you and I can carry him back up between us, if need be, or we can ask Barney to help us; he might be stunted but he's as strong as an ox. Shall I go and suggest that to Father?'

'No, don't interrupt him when he's eating, you know what his appetite's like. Come and get your dinner and – oh, I forgot, here's a note for you – it was brought round earlier on.'

Tizzie smiled grimly when she saw it was from Mrs Boulton. What would she and Mrs Walton have to say if they knew how their assistant secretary had spent the morning? 'She wants to know if I can go round this afternoon to make final arrangements for the variety concert; she sends you and Father her best regards, and hopes he's feeling stronger.'

Maria flushed with pleasure. It still amazed her that Tizzie should mix with the top families. 'You must go,' she said at once. 'You're quite right, Barney can help to get your father upstairs. When you've finished your dinner go and tell him, will you?'

He took it calmly. 'That's all right, Miss Tizzie, I'll lock up downstairs and put the note on the door again, and if necessary carry your father up on me back – he can't weigh more than seven stone.' He fiddled needlessly with a pile of new pawn tickets. 'I saw Mr Mayfield yesterday, Miss Tizzie. He's a fine-looking man. . . .'

'Yes, he is.' She eyed him curiously. 'Is there something bothering you, Barney? Have you had trouble with a customer? Is – is it something to do with Mr Mayfield?' Without knowing it she ran her tongue over her sore lips.

'Er – yes. He – he gets around a bit in the town, so they say.'

Oh yes, he got around, with the Walton girls trailing him, and any other female he'd glanced at more than once. 'He works hard for the fund-raising committee, the same as I do,' she said shortly. 'That's why I'm going to the Boultons' this afternoon – on committee affairs. I'm not in the least concerned with Mr Mayfield's personal life.'

'Oh?' The word was undoubtedly a question. He stroked the front of his apron, and put out a hand. She'd noticed them the other day, those hands, and been surprised to see they were clean and well-shaped, with the finger-nails neatly clipped. But what on earth was he aiming to do? Not touch her, for heaven's sake?

He merely reached past her arm for the ball of string, and tied a label to the top button of the overcoat he'd just taken in. Eyes lowered, he said quietly, 'He seems a nice, well-spoken young fella.'

She wasn't imagining it – there was emphasis on the

'seems'. She turned away to the cash drawer, skirts swirling. Was he trying to tell her something? If so, he was getting above himself. 'You can go down to the cellar for a while,' she said coolly. 'I'll give you a knock when I'm ready to go out.'

Barney stumped to the trapdoor, and then hesitated, as if about to speak further. She told herself she had quite enough to think about without trying to fathom the mind of a dwarf, and ignored him.

It was the same resentful maid, the same grey-faced Mrs Boulton, the same lengthy ritual with the tea and cake. 'I'll have the jam sponge first, and help yourself, my dear.' The steel-grey eyes met hers, and something glinted briefly in their depths. 'I've been chatting to Mrs Walton, and we're both so very pleased you put a stop to any talk about you and Edward.'

'I only followed your advice, Mrs Boulton.'

'Yes, and I flatter myself it was sensible. What a blow if you'd lost your your good name only to find he's turned his attentions elsewhere.'

Tizzie took another sip of her tea. 'There are always young ladies vying for his attentions,' she said calmly.

'Of course there are – he's an attractive young man,' agreed the older woman silkily, 'but it's a bit different this time, don't you think? It's mutual, so I hear.'

Careful, Tizzie warned herself. Don't let her see you're puzzled. She helped herself to a slice of Madeira cake. 'I've been so busy helping my father in his business, Mrs Boulton, that I've hardly seen Edward.'

'She's lovely, I admit. Beautiful, some say, though I wouldn't go as far as that myself. Spoiled, of course, like her brothers – their every whim pandered to by the parents. Joshua's always acted as if he owns all Saltley, what with his showy mills and his coal-mine, and refusing to stand for the council, and his wife primping around like a woman half her age. . . .'

Tizzie put down her cup without it rattling on the

saucer. The Schofields – she was talking about Sarah Schofield! Something was blocking her throat, strangling her almost, so that she couldn't even attempt to bite the cake. She recalled how Edward had shared the last waltz with the silver-blonde Schofield girl. Why hadn't it dawned on her then?

'You do know they spend every spare minute together, my dear? I'd like to say it won't last, but little Miss Sarah always gets what she wants; there's open talk of an engagement.' The spark glinted again behind the dull, metallic eyes, and now Tizzie recognised it as malice. 'I hear he walks her home every day from that ridiculous sick-bay she runs up at Jericho, with that odd-looking assistant of hers trailing along behind them like an apology for a chaperone.'

But only three hours ago, in that weird pink room, he had touched her, Tizzie; handled her more intimately, she was sure, than many a husband handled his wife. She exerted every scrap of her considerable control and said with faint irritation, 'I knew they were seeing each other, because it began at the ball, didn't it? I hadn't heard about an engagement, though. You and Mrs Walton were so wise in warning me, so forward-looking. I can never thank you enough.'

Instantly mollified, Mrs Boulton brushed a few crumbs from her jutting bosom and held out her cup for a refill. 'He's a self-seeking nobody, Tizzie, and you're well rid of him,' she declared bluntly. 'If the Schofields agree to their only daughter marrying him they want their heads seeing to.'

She wasn't sure whether it was minutes or hours before she made her escape. All she knew was that her performance seemed to have convinced Mrs Boulton, because the older woman patted her hand and then squeezed it as she left. 'There are more fish in the sea than ever came out of it, Tizzie,' she said.

The revolting old windbag! Tizzie forgot about her before she reached the bottom step. She walked in the direction of home until she was out of sight of the house, and then back-tracked briskly towards the new infirmary. The big, solid building was nearing completion, and she spotted Edward's elegant form behind an upstairs window. He had seen her, and met her half-way up the main staircase.

'Well, well,' he grinned, 'what's this? Have you come for a second helping?'

She looked at him and her anger was swept away by loss and longing. He was so different, so very different from the men of Saltley. She noted his every feature – the silky hair, the hazel eyes in their distinctive sockets, the exciting red mouth; for a horrible moment she thought she was going to weep. How could he do this to her? How could he? She sought desperately for words that held some dignity, and asked quietly, 'Edward, I've been told that you and Sarah Schofield are almost engaged. Is it true?'

He shrugged. 'It's taken you long enough to hear of it. Yes, it's true.'

She stared at him stupidly. 'But what about this morning?'

He avoided her eyes. 'When you handed me the opportunity on a platter, how could I refuse?'

Rage came back. She wanted to shriek, to tear his face with her nails, but workmen were just below them, polishing the floor of the entrance hall. She forced herself to speak quietly, and the effort of it made her want to vomit. 'I admit she's beautiful, but apart from that, why do you prefer her to me?'

'She's malleable,' he said simply. 'Easier to handle than you, and her father owns a mill, not a pawnshop. It's over, Tizzie, unless you'd like to meet me on the quiet from time to time, though you'd have to promise to keep it a deep, dark secret.'

Was he serious? She didn't know. Would anybody ever know what went on in that smooth, elegant head? As for Joshua Schofield owning a mill rather than a pawnshop, well, she'd always expected the three brass balls to ruin her life. 'You're a ruthless swine, Edward,' she said emptily. 'And I'm thankful I kept you under control all these weeks.'

'Very prudent,' he agreed. 'You'll be able to put it down to experience, with no hard feelings.'

He was gripping the lapels of his frock coat in a kind of bravado, and she looked at his long white fingers, recalling how he had used them on her that morning. Her next words came unplanned from somewhere deep inside her. 'My sister will be thankful it's over between us,' she said. 'Good-bye, Edward.'

'Good-bye, my little Tizzie. Think of me with pleasure, if you can.'

She gave him a look compounded of anger and disgust, then went down the stairs and out into the November dusk. She was alone, but she wouldn't, she would *not* cry.

The shop was empty and there was no sign of Barney, but on the desk where she did the paperwork was a white china vase holding a spray of evergreen leaves starred with berries. At any other time she would have called down to the cellar to ask about it, but it wasn't important. Nothing was important, nothing mattered, except that Edward didn't want her. Sooner or later she would have to tell her parents and Mary. . . .

She felt exhausted, and knew she must pull herself together before she could face an evening behind the counter. The door at the bottom of the stairs was open, something unheard of, and as she closed it behind her she heard a high, keening wail of anguish from up above. There was a murmur of voices, and the doctor appeared on the landing, followed by Barney.

'Ah, at last!' The medical man beckoned impatiently. 'Come along, young lady – your mother needs you. I was too late to do anything for your father; it was a quick passing, and he wouldn't have felt the pain for long. Heart, of course – he's been living on borrowed time.' He turned to Barney. 'Remember to give the undertaker my name.' Then again to Tizzie, 'You have a sister, I believe? Well, the pair of you will have to keep an eye on your mother – she can't accept that he's dead. I've given her something that should put her to sleep till the morning. You've got a good man here; send him for me if you're desperate. Now go and settle her in bed – in another room, if she'll leave him.'

Tizzie pulled herself reluctantly upwards. She wasn't ready for this; she couldn't take it in, as her mind was still full of Edward. But Barney had turned on the medical man, almost as if he were his equal. 'That's no way to break it to Miss Tizzie!' he said sharply.

The doctor stared down in astonishment, then gave a shamefaced nod. 'Perhaps I was a bit brisk,' he agreed, 'but I've got many another to see today, don't forget.' He turned to Tizzie. 'I'm sorry, my dear. Take it quietly with your mother until she falls asleep, and try to be nearby when she wakes. Keep calm, calm and quiet, that's what's needed.' With a flip of the hand he hurried away, leaving them both on the landing.

Her mother's wailing continued, but Tizzie made no move to go to her. 'When, Barney?' she asked limply.

'About half-past three, Miss Tizzie. He was downstairs, bendin' over the safe, when he was took bad with a breathless do; without waitin' to ask your mother I carried him up to his bed.'

'What? On your back?'

'No, I picked him up like you would a child.' He held out his short thick arms. 'He's no weight at all. He improved for a minute or two up here, then clutched at his chest in agony, like. I ran for the doctor, but he was out on a call. By the time I got back with him, well, your mother had him sat up, talking to him and trying to give him a drink; he'd been gone twenty minutes or more, the doctor said.' Barney's great white face was haggard with grief. 'He's been good to me, you know, he has that. But your mother – she's in a bad way. What do you want me to do?'

Natural ability surfaced from beneath Tizzie's misery. 'First, put notices on both doors to say we're closed until tomorrow. Then go round to the Hartleys' house to see if my sister is back from Holden yet – she's due to spend the evening round there. If she hasn't arrived, leave a message asking her to return at once as Father is – is very ill. Go to the undertaker last; I'd like to have my mother out of that room before he gets here. And Barney – thank you.'

The dark eyes met hers briefly. 'I'll be as quick as I can, Miss Tizzie.'

The noise from the bedroom was now like that of a tired and injured animal. Tizzie took off her bonnet and cloak, and with a deep sigh, went in. Her mother was leaning over her father's body, clutching at his bare, bony chest, and from time to time slapping his cheeks as if trying to bring him round from a faint. Her hair was in a wild tangle, without pins, as though she had pulled and tugged at it in a frenzy.

Her father looked as he always did: face gaunt, grey wisps of hair flattened to his skull, the eyes now closed, but the mouth – his one attractive feature – stretched in the savage rictus of pain, lips drawn back from the even teeth. Tizzie touched her mother gently on the shoulder. 'Mother,' she said, 'he's gone. Don't try to wake him – he's dead. Father's dead.'

Her mother looked up, tear-drenched eyes already dulled from the drug. 'That's what the doctor told me,' she said plaintively. 'He didn't realise that Abel's just fainted. He has a weak heart, you know. He's never been a robust man – I've always had to be careful of his health.'

Tizzie looked at them both. Was death always like this? Ugly, painful, unacceptable? Did it always reduce sensible people to gibbering wrecks? She touched the bed sheet. 'Shall we just cover him up, Mother? Ever so gently?'

'Aah!' With a cry that was almost a snarl, Maria threw herself across her husband. 'Go away!' she cried. 'Leave me with him! He'll want me here when he comes round. Where's our Mary? Send her in – she has more feeling for him than you've ever had.'

That was true enough, Tizzie told herself. 'Barney's just gone to fetch her,' she soothed. 'She'll be here soon.'

Maria made no reply, but continued to slap the cheeks of the corpse and to pat the limp wrists. Tizzie watched, stunned that her mother should behave with such abandon. It put her in mind of the third-rate plays at the Theatre Royal, where bad actors overplayed their parts. Tight-lipped, she stood there for a moment, then turned on her heel and walked out. If she was determined to stay with him, let her. With luck she would fall asleep on his chest, and then they could lift her away.

The big room across the landing was chilly and dark, so she put coal on the fire and turned up the gas, then sat stiffly on the sofa. She didn't know what a person was expected to feel on the death of a father. At that moment she was nauseated by her mother's behaviour, but incapable of real feeling about anyone other than Edward. And there was still Mary to deal with. . . . One thing was certain: there would be little time to think about Edward in the next few days. She didn't know whether to be glad or sorry about that.

Twenty-four hours later Maria was more rational. She no longer expected her husband to revive, but sat by the open coffin, chatting quietly to him, and holding his hand. Kind and reassuring, Mary handled her gently and left Tizzie free for the shop, because with news of the pawnbroker's death, half of Saltley had made their way there, either to redeem their belongings or seek reassurance as to their safety.

The funeral had been arranged, but they hadn't been able to trace her father's only living relative, a niece called Milly Wardle, last heard of as a child in Marple. Maria had made a great scene about it, stamping her feet and saying that everyone should have their own flesh and blood at their funeral. In the end, they invited only a handful of acquaintances and a couple of business friends. Mourning clothes for the three of them had been bought, and the lawyer was calling by appointment before the funeral next morning. Now, after a busy day, Tizzie sat at her father's desk getting the books up to date and wondering when she would have time to think about her own affairs. She had informed Mary about Edward: 'It's all over between Edward and me,' she said simply. 'I'll tell you about it when we have time.'

Mary had given her a tearful squeeze. 'Oh, Tizz! Thank goodness! I thought you were looking awful because of Father, but it's that as well, isn't it? Tell me when you're ready, and only if you want to.'

Now, she added up a column for the second time. Visions of Edward and Sarah Schofield kept invading her mind, all mixed up with questions about her father. Was he entering the wonderful new life they preached about at Bethesda? Was he already up in Glory, waiting for her mother? She had never been close to him, but all at once she felt as if she were adrift in a leaking boat on a boundless ocean.

She was staring absently at the white china vase in front of her when Barney came up through the trapdoor, causing her to touch the evergreen leaves curiously. 'Barney, you didn't put this on the desk, did you?'

He emptied small change noisily into the cash tray. 'Yes, I did. It was just a thought, Miss Tizzie.'

'It's lovely,' she said, surprised. 'Thank you. How did you find time to do it between my father dying and me returning home?'

She was looking at his back, and saw the skin of his

neck flush. 'I did it earlier – just after you left,' he said without turning.

In a rare flash of intuition she knew that the gesture was connected with Edward. Barney had tried to warn her, hadn't he? Perhaps he had known about Sarah Schofield, and wondered if Mrs Boulton might tell her; or had he guessed she'd been with him in Manchester, noticed her swollen lips or the bite mark on her neck that she'd hoped to hide under her collar? She stared at the little white vase and told herself that one person at least had tried to offer consolation, and it made not the slightest difference that he was an odd-looking dwarf. She spoke to his broad back, and had no way of knowing that she sounded forlorn. 'Barney, I'm not involved with Edward Mayfield any longer.'

He swung round and stood by her chair, so that for once they faced each other eye to eye. 'I'm glad to hear that, Miss Tizzie,' he said, and went back to his cellar.

The revelation had sprung from her own angry words, and it shook Tizzie as nothing in her life had shaken her before – not even Edward's rejection. Mary had been upstairs in their bedroom, and Tizzie went across the landing to check on things in their parents' room. Her mother, a lifelong Nonconformist, was insisting on dozens of Popish candles round the coffin, and Tizzie had a dread of the corpse putrefying because of the warmth they created. She put her head round the door to see if her mother was using the extra ones she'd demanded, and caught her kissing her father's dead mouth.

'Mother!' she said in disgust. 'This time tomorrow he'll be in his grave. What will you do then, kiss his tombstone?'

Maria turned on her. 'He's my *husband*,' she said savagely.

'*Was* your husband, you mean. He was my father, but at least I'm not slobbering over his corpse.' It was strongly-put, but her mother's constant handling of the body irritated her beyond restraint. 'Why can't you accept it, Mother? He was living on borrowed time, anyway. The doctor said so.'

Maria's tone was deep and venomous. 'Since you were a child you've rejected your father, haven't you? I clattered your ear-hole for belittling the pawnshop when you were nine years old – do you remember that? Well, let me tell you something that might change your attitude. The man you never tried to respect, the man you secretly despised, might not even *be* your father. Think on that, my girl!'

Conviction lay behind the words. Tizzie stared at her. 'What do you mean?'

Maria picked up her husband's limp hand and wagged it at her. 'He had been after me for over a year, but fool that I was in them days, I wouldn't look twice at a rag-man. Yes, he worked fourteen hours a day collecting rags for Eddie Miller on an old hand cart. I'd decided to wait for somebody better-off, you see, because though I was skin and bone, I was bonny. I worked at the far side of Saltley Bog, for a man who grew vegetables for the markets; one night I was going home after cutting celery when I was set on and taken by force. I was raped, if you want the exact word. Raped and then thrown in a ditch like a bundle of old rubbish. Yes, you might well gawp, lady. You're not long turned twenty; well, it happened twenty years and ten months ago, give or take a few days, and though I was twenty-five no man had ever touched me, bar a kiss on the cheek from my uncle.

'The man held a knife to my throat, and then threatened to use it on my private parts, so I stopped struggling. My life was hard, but it was all I had. He hurt me that bad I thought hell had opened up here on earth, I can tell you. I daren't go home to my mother – she'd have said I asked for it – but I knew enough to worry about whether he'd given me something I could do without. Not that you'd know what I mean. . . . I was frightened he might have left me expecting a child, and I didn't want to be put away. So what did I do? I went to see the man who'd been wanting to marry me.' She looked down at the coffin, and said in a normal conversational tone, 'I'm sorry, Abel, I know what you've always said, but many's the time I've longed to tell this one the truth. A bit of a question-mark as to who fathered her might bring you some respect at last.'

Tizzie was gripping the edge of the door. This was the thing she'd glimpsed but never seen clearly during her childhood and teens, the unspoken something she'd been conscious of. 'Who was the man? Did you know him?'

'I'd never set eyes on him. He was tall and bony, he was dressed better than a bog labourer but not as if he had money, and he smelled of spirits. When I came round I set out to find Abel – he lived by himself in a wooden hut on one of the paths across the bog.'

'And what did he say?'

'Not much at first. He boiled a pan of water and found me some calico for the bleeding, and then went out while I got myself clean. Then – and mark this, lady – he offered to marry me right away. He said if I'd marry him, and agree to a – a coming together as soon as we were wed, and never again unless I wanted it, then if I'd fallen for a child we'd never know for sure whether it was his or that man's. He promised, he promised on his knees, that he would never, by look or word, treat such a child as other than his own.' Maria stared at her daughter. 'Well, there *was* a child, and she's facing me now, in this room. And she's a liar if she says he didn't keep that promise. Well? Did he? *Did he?*'

'He did,' muttered Tizzie.

'He made me happy. He showed me tenderness when I'd never known the meaning of the word. And I grew to admire him, and respect him, and then to love him as he loved me. And that's the man you despise, Tizzie, so give it some thought.' She looked round the room and yawned, patting her open mouth politely, as if they'd been making light conversation for the last five minutes. 'Blow the candles out except for this one here, will you, and I'll have a wash and go to bed. I'm tired, and I want to be well-rested for his funeral.'

Tizzie blew them all out, and the smoke made her eyes water. At the door she turned and looked at the body of the man who might, and might not, be her father. He looked smaller than ever in the light of the single candle.

Joshua told himself that the musical evening at Alsing wasn't as bad as he'd expected. The singing and piano playing had at least had a bit of a tune to it, the refreshments had been good, and there'd been a table to get his feet under; he couldn't abide standing around juggling with a plate and fork and a wineglass. These high-born folk were no different to anybody else when you got down to it, though they weren't behind the door at ordering their guests around; like when that flunkey asked them all to 'proceed to the picture gallery to view his Lordship's collections'! If they had a do at Meadowbank House he didn't tell folk to traipse down to the kitchens to see the new gas-stove, or up to the bedroom to look at his silver hairbrushes.

He was strolling through the Long Gallery with John Fairbrother, paying scant attention as the older man told him how he was going to change from spinning fine counts to middling. He was busy watching Rachel. She'd been a bit under the weather this last week or two; off her food, given to long silences, even snapping at Sarah once or twice. When he kept asking what was the matter she would try to put him off with a kiss, or say he was imagining it.

But look at her now. Her hair was swept back in a great shining coil and fastened with those mother-of-pearl clasps he'd given her a few years back, and she was laughing with Janey Dobbs, her cheeks pink and her eyes sparkling. Relief eased through his heart like oil on hot dry metal. Whatever had been wrong with her, she was over it, and coming here had done her good. She was her old self again, all peaches and cream in the severe silver-grey dress that acknowledged they were mourning Charlie; though he fancied she'd lost a bit of weight. If anything, though, she looked more beautiful than ever. Lord Soar had monopolised her earlier on, and having seen Lady Soar he wasn't surprised. But the man at his side had just repeated a remark, so he paid more 'attention as they walked the big lamp-lit room. He could still watch Rachel, and tell himself what a lucky devil he was.

Rachel in her turn was watching her husband. He was adjusting to being without Charlie, she thought. He'd lost that tightness across the upper lip, and the lines from nose to jaw were less pronounced. She was glad they'd come. It was such a novelty to be a guest of the Soars. The vast house was amazing, and there seemed to be dozens of servants. Still, you'd think the cook would have used butter for the pastry rather than lard, when they were entertaining.

She saw young Lord Alsing unlocking another show-case. Ordered to the task, he looked slightly sheepish to be showing off the family treasures. Poor lad, his mother spoke to him as if he were a mere acquaintance, and if he had a valet the man wanted ginning-up, because his master's clothes needed a good brushing.

Guests clustered round as he said, 'And these are my father's miniatures . . . mostly of the family, and some of them dating back to the early seventeenth century.' Rachel turned away and pretended to examine some silver paperweights. Miniatures were the last things she wanted to see, whether of the Soars or anybody else. Her mind wandered to the approaching wedding. What a shame if the weather didn't improve before Saturday, and suppose –

Janey's voice interrupted her musings. 'But what are

these little jewels, your Lordship? They're so pretty, such an unusual blue.'

'They're sapphires, Ma'am. One tends to expect all sapphires to be a deep, dark blue, but that isn't the case, they can be all shades of blue. These are cornflower sapphires, and quite rare. They complement the dress of the child in the painting – the young Eleanor Soar, painted in – let me see – yes, in 1747.'

It brought Rachel away from the paperweights. The miniature was of a pale child, unremarkable, but the frame. . . . She stared at the delicate gold scrolling, the pearls and the blue jewels, and felt a silly little stab of disappointment. She had imagined Charlie's frame to be unique – perhaps made specially – yet here was one exactly like it. She waited until Lord Soar's son was free, and with a quick glance at Joshua, talking now to Joe Chadwick, said, 'This lovely frame here, with the pearls and sapphires – I've been searching for something of the sort for a special present, a – a surprise for someone, but I don't know where to look for such a thing. I suppose this has been in your family for generations?'

'On the contrary, Ma'am. The miniature itself is quite old, but the frame is my father's most recent acquisition, and we think the workmanship might be quite modern.' Guileless brown eyes looked into hers. 'You see, he has contacts who know his tastes and keep a look-out for what might interest him. When a piece turns up – porcelain or jade or silver, or more rarely a miniature frame such as this – they write to him about it. Often he sends me to examine the piece, and sometimes he will purchase it.'

Rachel put a hand to the edge of the showcase to steady herself. 'Is that so, your Lordship? And could – '

He broke in, 'Please call me Francis.'

'Very well. Francis. I'd like that. You're of an age with my sons, I think. In fact, Sam speaks of you very highly.'

His fair, good-natured face flushed with pleasure.

'Does he indeed? And I have a high regard for him, Mrs Schofield. I'm sorry our paths don't cross more often.'

Rachel forced herself to examine the frame of the miniature more closely. It was the same. She was certain of it. 'I'd like to call on the man who acquired this for your father – er – Francis. Could you tell me where he's in business?'

'In Liverpool, Ma'am. Here, I'll give you the address, it isn't far from Lime Street station. I'll write it on my card, look, with a word from me, so he'll know I've sent you.'

Liverpool? Ralph was in Liverpool the night Charlie died. . . . Francis Soar was so helpful, so eager to oblige, that she smiled at him even though her mind was jerking and straining to reject wicked, far-fetched ideas. 'How very kind of you, Francis. Could I ask you as a special favour not to mention this little matter to anyone?'

He looked from side to side like a conspirator, and smiled back; a plump, amiable, shy young man, who carried wealth and an ancient pedigree like a burden. 'I won't say a word,' he assured her earnestly. 'And Mrs Schofield, would you pass on my respects to your – your family?'

Outside at last, it was wet and very cold, prompting Zacky to tuck the rug over their knees in the carriage. She clutched at Joshua and kissed him urgently, needing the comfort of his familiar mouth. 'Hey, steady on,' he laughed. 'You know I can't deal with you properly till we get home.' He nestled her against him, but at once felt the tension in her. 'What's the matter, love?'

'Nothing. I'm just cold, that's all, and a bit tired.'

'Well, you will mix with the aristocracy. That great house is enough to tire anybody. Did you enjoy yourself, though?'

'Yes, I did. It was lovely.' Well done Rachel, she told herself: that's two lies in less than a minute. But words were rarely enough to fool Joshua. He could sense when things weren't right with her, almost as if he were part of her, and she of him. . . . She closed her eyes and pretended to doze, but kept hold of his hand and ached with love for him; a new, protective love, born of foreboding.

A sleepless night brought Rachel to the conclusion that she would have to find out about the miniature, if only to quieten her mind. At breakfast she told the family she was going shopping in Manchester. Busy with their own affairs, they accepted it, even Joshua, who as a rule wanted to know every detail when she planned to go anywhere on her own. All he said was, 'A pity it's not one of my days at Mosley Street, love, I'd have taken you somewhere nice for your dinner. As it is I'll be at the mine all day. Production's down, after all we've spent on improvements, so we're having a good sorting-out to see what's wrong. And Sam, don't forget to look in on the doublers and winders as soon as you get to Jericho; I'll see you later, across at Low Lee.'

She set off as soon as they were all out of the house, wearing her black, both for Charlie and because the little half-veil would shield her from curious eyes. Once at Victoria she booked a return ticket to Liverpool Lime Street and boarded the next train. The country's busiest port, with sailors everywhere and the smell of the sea blowing from the Mersey, it nevertheless reminded her strongly of Manchester. There was the same air of prosperity and purpose. There were the same well-dressed men and women and grand new buildings; and behind the surface gloss she knew there would be the same stinking alleys and yards, the same countless children, barefoot in November.

Sitting in a cab she stared absently at the tall masts of sailing ships that could be seen lining the distant quays, and didn't even wonder if there was one of the fast blockade-runners in port; she was too intent on preparing what to say.

It was less of a shop than a dark little house, with
a plaque by the door saying: *H. Bracewell. Gold,
Silver, and Precious Stones Bought and Sold. Valuations.
Assessments.* She asked the cabbie to wait for her, and
went in. There was no shop counter, just an elegant
table backed by tall showcases and a large iron safe. A
calm elderly man stood by the end showcase, watching
her over his eyeglasses. 'Good morning, Madam,' he
said quietly. 'And what is your pleasure?'

Rachel relaxed a little. A polite man, and well-
spoken, when she'd half-expected a bumptious salesman.
'Do I have the pleasure of addressing Mr Bracewell
himself?'

'You do indeed, Madam.' A widow, he told himself,
left in debt by her husband. He got a lot of those, coming
in even before the funeral, some of them.

'I would be very grateful for your help, Mr Bracewell.
I have here a word of introduction from a – a close
friend.' She gave him Francis Soar's card. He read it,
bowed, and waited for her to proceed. 'Last evening he
showed me a miniature frame that you sold to his father
quite recently. It was identical to one that belonged to
a friend of my family – one that I believed had been
made specially for him. I can't help wondering if it's
the same frame, or merely a copy, or even one of a
bulk production.'

Harold Bracewell was relieved to see her composure.
This was no widow, desperate to sell her trinkets, but a
woman of intelligence, and behind the half-veil, one of
mature beauty and style. It was a genuine enquiry and
she'd been sent by a titled family who paid promptly – a
rarity in his experience. 'I can assure you, Madam, that
the frame is indeed hand-made, and to my knowledge,
unique. I found it an impressive piece, and knowing his
Lordship's tastes, contacted him at once.'

He sketched another little bow, whether out of respect
for the Soars, admiration of a goldsmith's workmanship,
or politeness to herself, she couldn't tell. 'I regret,

Madam, that I cannot divulge the value of the piece, except to say that it is considerable. Exquisite workmanship, high-grade gold, genuine pearls and perfectly matched sapphires.'

At once Rachel lowered her eyes. 'There was no picture in the frame when it came into your possession, Mr Bracewell?'

'No, Madam.'

She leaned forward and gripped the edge of the table. 'Please believe that I don't ask out of idle curiosity. Would it go against your principles of business to tell me who sold you the frame?'

Mr Bracewell hesitated. He would be a fool to pretend that he didn't touch goods whose origins were suspect, but he had never in his life done so knowingly. He had no wish to be even remotely involved in criminal proceedings, but he was sure that this lady in her mourning was here on a personal matter. He took a black ledger from the table drawer. 'This is confidential, Madam,' he warned gently. 'I have a name for the transaction. I always have names, for both purchases and sales.'

He ran a thin finger down a closely written page. 'Here we are, though to be sure I remember the gentleman well. The miniature was brought in by a Mr Charles Barnes, of Mosley Street, Manchester.' He put out a hand. 'Ma'am! My dear lady! Please take a seat!'

The relief was such that Rachel had sagged at the knees, and fell back gratefully on the proffered chair. Charlie, it was Charlie! Deep shame flooded her. Dear, dear God in Heaven, she'd suspected her son when it was Charlie. He'd guessed – no, he'd known she'd seen it that afternoon, and he'd decided then to sell it, as being too risky to keep if he wasn't to hurt Joshua. She threw back the little veil and smiled radiantly at Harold Bracewell. 'Thank you very much,' she said, nodding her head with each word. 'You've been so very helpful, Mr Bracewell. I shall know where to come when I want a special gift for someone.'

So, she was relieved. Harold Bracewell felt oddly uplifted to have given her a name that pleased her. He looked at her eyes, surrounded by the faintest of wrinkles but blue and lovely as those sapphires set among pearls. And he wondered. . . .

He offered his arm as she made for the door. 'An amazingly good-looking young man, as I recall,' he said pleasantly. 'Angelic, one might say, with that golden hair. Quite remarkable, I thought.'

Rachel stood quite still. 'You're speaking of Mr Barnes?' she said faintly.

'Yes, Madam. I thought you knew the gentleman? A born businessman, if ever I've seen one, in spite of his youth.' But what was wrong now? She was white as death. Such a change, in less than a moment. All at once he felt out of his depth. Was she perhaps fevered in the head? His mind rejected such terms as 'deranged' or 'unstable'.

Rachel forced her voice to calmness. 'Mr Bracewell, there is one thing I neglected to ask you. Could I trouble you for the date of the sale?'

He hurried back to his records, remembering the date quite well, but anxious to make sure, to have things go right for her. 'Here we are. It was October the 25th, Madam. Is there anything else? I say, Madam, are you quite well? Is that your cab waiting? Can I do anything more?'

Charlie had died in the early hours of the 22nd. It needed all her strength to speak intelligibly. 'Yes, one thing. This is a very private and personal matter. Could I ask you to treat my visit here as strictly confidential, just between the two of us? Please, Mr Bracewell?'

He felt the onset of panic. He could hardly keep it secret if she collapsed, here in his doorway. 'You have my word on it,' he assured her hastily. 'Nobody will ever know of it from me.'

'Thank you, Mr Bracewell. Good-day.'

He helped her to the waiting cab, and on impulse seized her hand and kissed it. Then he watched in dismay as she climbed aboard, her movements those of a tired old woman. Deeply troubled, he stood there and watched as the cab rattled away over the cobbles.

CHAPTER FOURTEEN

In the Mill

THE SMELL OF DAMP earth and wet leaves drifted through Soar Park as the men worked on a shed to house the steamer *Daisybelle*. Matthew was planing timber for the doors when Daniel Broadhurst came and spoke in his ear. 'Matthew, there's a young woman wants a word with you over by the railings. Don't linger, now, 'cos Mr Vessey's due on his rounds.'

'Thanks, Mr Broadhurst.' Matthew straightened up and saw Martha's small figure hovering outside the railings that edged the landing-stage, her shawl clutched at chest level. He was conscious of the others watching curiously as he hurried across to her. 'What's wrong, Martha? Why bain't 'ee at the mill?'

'It's the breakfast break,' she gasped, 'an' I've been runnin'.'

'Is it your mother?'

'No. Listen. It's all over Jericho that they're takin' on more labourers. I've seen Mr Holt – he's the setter-on – and what do you think, your name's on his list! He says he'll see what he thinks of you if you can be there by dinner-time. That's why I've come.'

The flush of exertion stained her pale cheeks, and deep in her eyes there was a question. He knew at once what it was. If he rushed to Jericho about the job then he really wanted to marry her. If he didn't, if he made excuses, then it was all a sham. She was so lacking in self-esteem he wanted to reassure her by picking her up, shawl and all, and whirling her round in his arms. That would convince her, right enough.

Instead he asked, 'Do you know what they're payin'?'

'No, but it shouldn't be less than seventeen shillin', because it's for the heavy gang, and only them who're fit and well can stand up to it. You have to be strong, he says, and intelligent, so the pay's bound to be good. You go to the lodge and ask for Mr Holt.'

'I'll be there,' he said, and smiled. 'I'll go across as soon as we knock off. And Martha – thank 'ee. Thank 'ee most kindly.' Excitement sang in his veins, and made him purse his mouth in the form of a kiss. With a blink of the eyes she was gone, clogs skimming the path that led to the nearest gate. He hurried back to his timber, and Daniel Broadhurst came across to him. 'Nothing amiss, I hope, lad?'

'No, Mr Broadhurst. I lodge with that young lady's mother.' He looked into the steady grey eyes and was certain he could tell this man the reason for Martha's visit, which was more than he could have attempted with Nuttall in a million years. 'She came to say there might be an openin' for me in the mill.'

The older man eyed him thoughtfully. 'You're not a trained cotton operative, are you?'

'No, 'twould be labourin', but better pay then here, I believe.'

'Yes, it would be. You're in need of more money?'

'I want to marry her, Mr Broadhurst. It's not that I don't like it here, but – '

'It's all right, Matthew, I understand. Don't forget, though, you're in God's fresh air here in the park. There's no fresh air in the mill, and if you aren't used to it. . . .'

'I've tried all sorts o' work, Mr Broadhurst. I'm what you might call hardened.'

'Aye, you can work, I'll grant you that. Well, the best of luck.'

Made bold by the foreman's kindly manner, Matthew removed his hat and asked, 'Mr Broadhurst, if I get taken on, would you give a friend o' mine the chance of my job here? He's a good worker, and desperate for it.'

Daniel Broadhurst looked at him sadly. 'If you go, Matthew, the job goes as well. Mr Vessey says I'll have to lose two of you before Christmas anyway, so there's no way I could replace you, nor give you the job back if you should want it. You must bear that in mind if you give your notice in.'

Matthew went on with his work. He could tell Billy he'd tried, though he didn't know what good that would do him, or his family. The last time he'd called round his wife had looked thinner than ever, and the old mother was out of bed and shuffling back and forth, making the inevitable porridge. If only he could find Billy a job he would have an easy mind, and be able to concentrate on his own affairs.

He said nothing to Jonas or the others, and at noon slipped away as they all made their way to the tack room for their snap. He wasn't aware that he was moving at a trot until he saw people staring at him. The sight of the great twin mills with the golden trumpet and the red rose shining on the gates brought memories of his first day in Saltley. He'd liked the master of Jericho from the start, and it seemed he'd been proved right in his judgement. Mr Schofield – Martha's hero – had kept his name in mind since midsummer, without once being reminded.

It was a blow to find seven or eight men already lined up and waiting, and by the time Mr Holt arrived there were thirteen. He interviewed them in the strict order of his list, and his method of selection was simple. He told each man to load a wicker skip with great bobbins of yarn, and then lift it on to a bogey. If they managed that, they had to add and subtract four sets of numbers and read one of the mill's printed notices. Those who could do all of it were asked to stand on one side; those who couldn't were sent on their way with a nod and a kind word.

It had been childishly easy. Matthew smiled in relief and he set his hat ferociously straight. Mr Holt eyed those who had passed the test. 'Right – you five have got yourselves a job! Six till six, and and your pay's seventeen and six a week. You'll all know that's good pay for mill labourin', but for that we expect speed, strength and stamina. You'll be on the heavy gang under Mr Maynard, fourteen of you in all. He's a fair man, but he likes quick movers. You'll start on Monday mornin'. Now, let's have your names and addresses. . . .'

He was in! 'I've done it, Peggy-oh,' breathed Matthew silently, and had to smother a triumphant laugh. The mill engines were shut down for the dinner hour, and there was no sign of Martha among those in the yard; he hurried back to the park to give Mr Broadhurst his notice, and then joined the others. Jonas was openly envious at the news. 'Seventeen and six a week,' he repeated, his voice rising. 'With another mouth to feed before long the wife could make short work o' that!'

One of the others overheard, and guffawed. 'Don't say number ten's on the way, Jonas. Been on the night shift again, have you?'

The grey-haired little man took it all in good part, but Matthew couldn't join in the laughter for the life of him. Like himself, Jonas had been lucky to be given this job. Without it he would be on relief, him and his wife and their seven surviving children, not to mention the one she must have been carrying even while he was working for Nuttall. There was one sure way of avoiding having another mouth to feed, and every man there knew what it was. It always amazed him that nobody ever seemed to try it.

At Ledden Street there was a clean calico cloth on the table and potato pie sizzling in the oven, with Martha bustling about pretending that she didn't feel sick with uncertainty. Matthew walked in with a straight face and clumped through to the back kitchen as he always did, without his usual bright greeting. He heard Mrs Spencer hiss, 'Go and ask him!' and when Martha appeared in the doorway he swung round with a laugh, swept off his hat and bowed low. 'Your humble servant, and a member of the heavy gang at Jericho as from Monday, at – wait for it – seventeen and six a week!'

She uttered a squeal and clapped a small rough hand to her mouth. 'You were havin' us on, Matthew Raike! Oh, I'm that proud of you!'

He took her hands and pulled her towards him. 'Can we set the day, Martha? Can we? Let's make it soon.'

'The sooner the better, for me,' she said, and blushed bright pink. Then, for the second time, he kissed her, breathing in her clean soap and water smell and crossing his hands behind her tiny waist. Her lips were as soft and sweet as he remembered, and with his eyes closed he didn't see her plain little face. He released her almost at once. 'Your mother's waitin',' he said. 'Let's tell her we want it to be soon.'

The potato pie was followed by baked apples, making a festive meal, and of the four of them only Uncle Jack had a serious face. He had little to say, but was as rational as Matthew had ever seen him. 'Come on, Uncle Jack, it be a happy day,' he coaxed. 'Bain't you pleased for us?'

'You'll soon lose your good healthy colour in the mill, lad,' was all the old man said.

He told Martha about the Warhurst family in the back kitchen, out of earshot of her mother. She stared at him as if he was demented. 'You what? How much have you been givin' 'em?'

'A shillin' or so a week. Half a crown now and again. They're desperate for it.'

'But so are half Saltley. If you gave to everybody in need you'd soon be in need yourself. They'll get relief, you know. And don't look at me like that – we've been livin' on bread and scrape and hand-outs from Jericho for over two years in this house; it's not goin' to happen

again if I can help it. I want somethin' better for us an'
– an' our children than you and me have had. I want to
put somethin' by for a rainy day.'

He couldn't fault her for that, and in any case he didn't
want an argument when they'd just decided to marry
within the month. 'I'm goin' round there now,' he said
quietly, 'and givin' them two shillin' I've been keepin'.'
He left her standing tight-lipped at the slop-stone, and
headed for the Warhurst house, telling himself there was
no need to be taken aback, because he'd known from
the start that she and her mother were keen ones with
the money.

The little back-to-back on the smelly street was empty,
bare black windows staring out at the overflowing drain.
He stood there with guilt stabbing that he hadn't been
near for more than a fortnight, and a woman called
across to him, 'If you're after the Warhursts they've
gone to live in Miller's Yard, off Gallgate. You can't
miss it – three-storey houses and a big black shed along
one side.' He touched his hat in thanks, and headed
apprehensively down the hill. By now he'd seen most
of the courts and yards of Saltley, and he knew they
were as bad as the vilest slums of Plymouth.

Martha stood over the tin bowl and stared at the washing
up until the greasy water lost its heat. She had often
wondered, but of course never asked, on what he spent
the rest of his wages after paying them his seven and six
a week. She'd hoped he was saving it towards getting
married, maybe even putting it in a savings bank; now
she recalled the first time he'd helped her home from
the market, when he retraced his steps to give money to
that woman and her children at the top of Rope Street.
They taught you at Sunday School and Chapel to give to
the poor, so it must be right, but what if you were poor
yourself? So poor that you had less than ten shillings in
the stone jar on the mantelpiece, and with an invalid
mother and a one-armed old uncle to care for.

She hadn't liked the look on Matthew's face when he went out. His mouth, so often smiling, had been set in a hard, determined line, and the dark eyes had seemed to look straight through her. She dried her hands and carried the candle across to the piece of looking glass propped on the pot shelf. Mercilessly she examined her face. Despair filled her and she gave the little glass a smack with the flat of her hand. There was nothing about her to hold any man, let alone one like Matthew. Everybody liked him. Even her mother forgot the habit of years and smiled and simpered when he was there, and Uncle Jack was clearer in the head since he came, talking sense more often. But she, Martha: she loved him. She adored him. He made her laugh. He made her feel like an attractive woman; he made her dream vivid, rather shocking dreams about what they would do when they were married and sharing the big bedroom.

If she went against him about giving money away she knew she might lose him. But there were married women in the weaving shed who sweated sixty-odd hours a week over their looms; who barely stopped work to give birth, and who lived in poky little houses with half their belongings in pawn. And for why? Because their husbands spent money as fast as they both earned it, and the wife must work to feed the children. Admitted, it usually went on drink, and she couldn't accuse Matthew of that. But could she ever agree to him giving their hard-earned money to a family who were already heading for the workhouse? She gave her reflection a last despairing stare, and went to the fire for another kettle of hot water.

'Haven't you finished them pots yet?' asked her mother, aggrieved. 'You're doin' some shafflin', aren't you? Come on, or you'll be ironin' at midnight, and I want to be settled in me bed before ten. And where's Matthew, anyway?'

'Out,' said Martha shortly. 'On his own affairs. On his own business.'

'Is he now?' snorted her mother. 'His business is your business, don't forget, or soon will be. And I hope you have the sense to talk to him about money before you get wed.'

Oh, so her ears had been working overtime again, had they? Martha sniffed. 'We'll talk money, don't you worry about that. And when I'm a married woman I'll be answerable to me husband, not me mother.'

Uncle Jack stopped pulling at his shirt buttons and looked on in disapproval. 'Ee, you do look sour, Martha. I thought you'd stopped givin' your old buck since Matthew come here.'

Irritation mounting, Martha looked at them both, then lifted the big kettle from the fire. She could think in peace in the back kitchen, and decide what to do about him giving his money away.

A street lamp shone high above Miller's Yard, and the black bulk of the shed loomed along one side of it. The sound of coughing and the cry of an infant came from beneath the shed, and Matthew guessed that the open foundations were used as night shelter by those with no homes.

An old woman smoking a pipe was about to descend the steps from the street, so he lifted his hat. 'Evenin', Missis. I'm lookin' for the Warhurst family who've just come here. Do 'ee happen to know which – er – which dwellin' they're in?'

The woman clenched the pipe between her gums and mumbled, 'Int' corner o'er yonder. Nearly undert' shed.'

'Thank'ee kindly.' Matthew jumped nimbly across a stagnant pool and knocked on the corner door. He could hear scuffling inside the cellar and the sound of coughing, and then the door was dragged open, its timbers groaning with damp.

Billy stood here, holding aloft a stump of candle in a tin saucer. A stale, rotten odour issued from behind him, and with a twitch of the nostrils Matthew recognised the smell of bugs. His stomach lurched. ''Tis only me, Billy.'

The man in the doorway peered out, the whites of his eyes gleaming in the flicker of the candle. 'Ne'then,' he said abruptly.

Matthew stared. It couldn't be plainer that he wasn't welcome. A cold sweat broke out under his collar. 'I bin a bit busy, Billy,' he said uncomfortably.

'You don't have to explain yoursel' to me,' replied the older man quietly. 'If you never call on us again, you've done more than we could ever have expected.' He jerked his head back. 'I can't ask you in. It's – it's pretty bad.'

So that was it. Belatedly, Matthew recognised the other man's deep shame. 'But what brought 'ee to this, Billy? I know things were hard, but you seemed to be keepin' body and soul together.'

'Aye, but whose body, and whose soul?' asked Billy with a mirthless laugh. 'Me mother's body parted company with her soul a week last Friday, and the little 'un followed her next day. It would 'a' been a pauper's burial for the pair of 'em, so we give up the house and used two weeks' relief on the funeral. Mr Miller paid me three shillin' in advance, and he's lettin' me have this place as part of me pay.'

'Very generous,' said Matthew blankly, 'an' I'm sorry about your mother and the baby.' Even as he uttered the trite words he knew he didn't mean them. He couldn't truly be sorry that the weak old woman and the listless baby in her wooden box would never be hungry again. He brought out the two separate shillings and pressed them into Billy's hand. 'I been savin' this for 'ee,' he said rapidly. 'I'll come again next week, you can count on it.'

The candle shook and spluttered, and the man holding it let out a strange, half-strangled cry. Billy was weeping. Matthew groaned in distress and put out a hand to grip the thin wrist, then hurried away, forgetting to leap over the pools and splashing through the filth. It was no use, he told himself desperately. If Martha wouldn't agree to him helping the Warhursts, he couldn't marry her. And that was that.

When he got back she was at the table, ironing, and he marched straight through to the back kitchen. She took one look at his face, clanked the heavy iron on its stand, and followed him. 'Don't say it, Matthew. If you feel that strongly about it I won't argue. How will it be if you keep three shillin' a week to spend on – on them who need it? I'll agree to that.'

She mistook his amazed stare for refusal. 'An' – an' a pan of broth on Mondays,' she threw in hastily. 'How about that?'

His head swam with relief, but he didn't say so. Instead he grabbed her and kissed her on the mouth, swinging her up in his arms so that her clogged feet left the kitchen floor. Her lips clung to his in what seemed like desperation, and when he set her down he saw the shine of tears on her cheeks. 'What's this? Did I hurt 'ee?'

She shook her head and straightened her pinafore. There was no need to tell him they were tears of relief.

It had been the biggest wedding of the year at St Joseph's. Some said that Ephraim Buckley was one of the church's wealthiest members, but others pointed out that he was far from its most generous. Whatever the truth of it, everyone agreed that the roller-maker hadn't stinted on his only child's wedding.

Those not at their work crowded along the railings, watching the carriages arrive and depart, intrigued by the novelty of this joining of church and chapel families. They gazed in awe at the six bridesmaids dressed in perfectly graduated shades from apricot to bronze; and those who had peeped inside the church said the flowers were beyond belief. It was the Town Hall, no less, for the reception, with a seven-course luncheon by a Manchester firm, known throughout the county for their superb wedding feasts. Even the weather was kind, having turned fine and sunny so that the bride and groom were able to drive from the ceremony in an open carriage, with Esther looking exquisite in a full crinoline of ivory silk beneath a fur-lined cloak.

The meal almost at an end, Sam leaned back in his chair and studied the assembled guests. Two hundred and fifty of them, proof that old Buckley had put his hand in his pocket with a vengeance. Out of the corner of his eye he saw the newly-weds touch hands beneath the table; he would perhaps have been persuaded that he was mistaken about Esther, had he not overheard a conversation between her and James a couple of days earlier.

It had concerned his mother, seated now next to Ephraim Buckley and wearing an elegant lilac gown and the latest fashion in hats. Apart from her extreme pallor, and a certain blankness in the gaze, there was little sign of the mysterious malady that had struck her as she travelled back from Manchester on Wednesday. He had returned from Low Lee with his father to find her being carried from a cab into the house, retching and apparently light-headed, with an official of the railway company at her side. His father had leapt from his horse with the speed of a youth. 'God in heaven, not the cholera!' he choked. Ralph was already home, as were Esther and James; at that moment Sarah arrived back from Jericho with Edward, trailed as always by the faithful Polly. For the first time in days, if not weeks, Sam saw his sister take her eyes off Edward Mayfield voluntarily, and she rushed to her mother's side.

Beside himself with anxiety, and after a gruelling day at the mine, his father nevertheless took over and organised everyone in sight, calming the rising pandemonium. He questioned the man from the railway, to find that she had collapsed on alighting from the Manchester train. He despatched Davey for the doctor, instructed Ellie to light the bedroom fire, Hannah to put hot bottles in the bed, and Alice to prepare a light invalid meal in case for some reason his wife hadn't eaten and was weak with hunger. Sam could smile at it now: his father always believed that a lack of food in the normally well-nourished caused rapid collapse, both physical and mental. He had carried her upstairs himself, and allowed Sarah into the room to undress her and help him put her to bed.

'We don't think it looks like the cholera,' Sarah told them all when she came down. 'He's sitting with her now, trying to find out if she's eaten anything that could have upset her, or if she's been in an accident or seen something horrible. She's just lying there wide awake, but not speaking. Oh, thank goodness, here's the doctor.'

Edward departed with a tactful word about being in the way, and they were all waiting for the diagnosis when Sam heard Esther's voice from the little sitting room across the hall. The tone of it made him edge nearer the door, and listen quite shamelessly. 'But I tell you she can't be ill,' she was saying. 'She can't be ill before Saturday!'

'I'm afraid she is ill, my love,' James replied. 'I've never seen her like this in my life. Don't get upset – I'm sure she'll be all right for the wedding.'

There was a pause, and in spite of his low opinion of Esther, Sam expected to hear an apology or maybe a word of comfort. He was disappointed. Her reply was venomous. 'She'd better be! She'd just better be! It's bad enough having her and Sarah in half-mourning for a mere business associate. We simply can't have her ill for the wedding. She's to sit next to Papa at the Town Hall!'

'I hardly think she's decided to be ill out of awkward-ness,' replied James shortly. 'I know you're on edge about Saturday, sweetheart, but it's still almost three days away. Mother's a strong healthy woman, and I'm sure – '

Sam had heard no more, because his father came down the stairs, tweaking edgily at his whiskers. 'The doctor says it's prostration due to engorgement of the blood and an upset stomach,' he announced, 'brought on by the exhaustion of a busy day, and possibly her age. He's bleeding her now.' They looked at him blankly. A day's shopping wasn't a busy day for their mother, and what had her age to do with it? 'A light diet,' he went on, 'and complete rest for a few days, then she should be all right. Go in to your meal, all of you. I'm having mine up in the room with her, when the doctor's finished.'

Remembering, Sam observed the dainty little bride with a bitter eye. 'Jimmy, Jimmy,' he said silently, 'why didn't you listen to me?' He had spoken his few words as best man with a show of good humour, but when the other speeches dragged on he paid scant attention. Why did he have this feeling that everything was about to change? This sense of threat to the family? He shot an anxious look at his mother, and saw her smiling at Ephraim Buckley. She was almost herself again, surely?

His gaze moved on to Sarah, sitting with Edward Mayfield. Beautiful in pale dove-grey trimmed with lavender, she was hanging on his every word. A sigh came from the very depths of Sam's being. His little sister was madly in love; too madly, he thought. Infatuated was a better word. The gentle common-sense, the feet-on-the-ground practicality bestowed by her parents had disappeared in the last month, leaving a wilful, emotional girl who seemed determined to hurl herself at this elegant man from Hampshire.

Mindful of his promise, Sam had as yet found no fault with him. He had made discreet enquiries, of course, and learned that the architect had flirted mildly with the daughters of the town's foremost families, but until the night of the ball had been closest to the pawnbroker's daughter. He had shrugged at that. Men were often close to somebody or other until they met his sister, and the Ridings were the very essence of respectability. The next thing he would do was find out about the man's background. No doubt he was solvent, but even taking into account the Schofields' reduced wealth, Sarah was a still quite a catch for a struggling architect.

Sam dragged his mind back to the present moment. Somebody was wishing the happy couple well for their honeymoon in Italy. They were to spend their wedding night at High Lee Court; he hoped, oh he did hope that James would find his bride loving and willing . . .

Exhaustion was dragging at Rachel as the speeches drew to a close. The effort of appearing well enough to attend her son's wedding and of forcing down the rich food had been almost too much to bear, but thank God she hadn't spoiled the day for James. Her first-born; her good first-born boy, married. . . . She listened to Ephraim's self-satisfied comments, and yearned for Joshua's comforting presence, but she couldn't even catch his eye. He was some distance away, next to Esther's formidable Aunt Margaret, who was playing hostess to Ephraim's host.

Ralph was almost opposite her, and though she had felt his eyes on her throughout the meal she had merely glanced at him as if her mind was elsewhere, which was very far from the truth. She watched the festive scene and recalled the endless black hours of the last few days and nights. Once she had calmed herself she had managed to back up the diagnosis of sudden, inexplicable illness, and spent the hours of supposed rest thinking about her youngest son. A thousand times she asked herself where they'd gone wrong with him. Had it been some sort of omen that in all their married life he had been the only subject they couldn't discuss with ease? She tried to convince herself that he had sold the frame legitimately, legally; that Charlie had given it to him, or asked him to arrange the sale. But if so, why had he gone ahead with it once Charlie was dead, without telling anyone? And why had he travelled to Liverpool, when Manchester had its own jewellery quarter? What about the grease on his sleeve? And the fact that he had known about a night-watchman starting at Mosley Street the following day?

In the end she had to accept what intuition told her: Ralph had been responsible for Charlie's death. Maybe he hadn't actually pushed him through the hoist doors, she told herself; maybe they struggled and Charlie fell. Whatever had happened, Ralph must have come back from Liverpool in the early hours – yes, there was a train, she'd checked on that during her nightmare journey back to Saltley. Then he must have gone back again, to return as planned on Sunday afternoon. Maybe the young man Richard was involved? She didn't know, and she wouldn't try to find out. Her mind was incapable of grappling with anything else just yet. Dimly she realised that there was more to come. She would have to consider her son's motives, his ultimate aims, but all she wanted now was to sleep. To sleep and then awake to find that it was all a nightmare. But though for Joshua's sake she pretended, sleep was impossible. She doubted if she would ever sleep again. But at least those hours of torment had brought her to a firm decision. Whatever the provocation, she could never blacken the name of her lovely, well-blessed family by revealing that they harboured a murderer in their midst.

But even more important than that was how the truth would affect Joshua. No matter how he might plead with her to share what was on her mind, she could never tell him that his youngest son had killed his best friend and then robbed him. And if she couldn't tell Joshua, she couldn't tell anyone. She certainly couldn't confront Ralph himself and then take no action, or he would believe she condoned murder. He would go unpunished, and she would carry the unspeakable knowledge to her grave.

They set off for the mill together, Martha in her clogs and thick plaid shawl, and Matthew in his wide felt hat and winter coat, wearing his boots because he had no clogs, and didn't particularly want any. They joined the crowds heading for the mills, where the firing-up of the boilers made red-tinged smoke belch from the great chimneys. Matthew looked up into the half-light and smiled. This was why he'd travelled to Lancashire – to join the best-paid work force in the land.

Beneath a distant lamp he could see the crossroads where he'd always met up with Jonas on his way to the park, and yes, there was a small figure, waving. He waved his hat in reply, long and hard, though he doubted whether the other man could see. He felt inordinately pleased that his friend was thinking of him. For an instant his step slowed as he recalled the companionship of the tack room, the smell of fresh earth and wet leaves, and the benign good humour of Daniel Broadhurst. But Martha was clattering along briskly, so he walked at her side with his long, easy stride, listening to the 'how-do' and 'ne'then' of the mill-workers' greetings. As they reached the gates a plump, motherly woman crossed the street towards them. 'This is me friend,' Martha whispered, and he saw the colour run up her pale cheeks. 'I'll introduce you, shall I?'

He agreed, half-amused, and Martha said breathlessly, 'Jessie, this is Matthew, you know – Matthew Raike. And this is Mrs Lane, Jessie. She's been a good friend to me.'

Matthew raised his hat and smiled his captivating smile. 'Mornin' Mrs Lane. I be pleased to meet a friend o' Martha's.'

The woman held out her hand and shook his warmly, observing him with hastily veiled surprise. 'I'm pleased to meet you, an'all,' she said. 'I hear you've fixed the day? Well, you'll have a good wife in this one, you won't part. I've known her for years.'

The three of them passed through the gates, where the trumpet and the rose shone with the beaded moisture of dawn. 'Good luck,' Martha whispered. 'I'll wait just over there for you at six o'clock – that's – that's if you want?'

'Oh, I want,' he assured her, with a smile. He watched the two women cross the cobbled yard towards the long, brick-built weaving-shed, then went to wait at the appointed place for Mr Maynard and the rest of the heavy gang. He felt so full of energy he could have done a couple of handsprings, just for the fun of it.

Two hours later, in the breakfast break, he wondered why he'd ever imagined he worked hard at the Mizzen Mast, or Ryder Hall or Soar Park. This – *this* was work, he told himself. No wonder they'd asked for strong, intelligent men. So far his strength had been called for in abundance; he would have to wait and see whether his intelligence would be put to the test. He munched his bread and dripping and compared his first sight of Jericho Mills with what he'd seen in the last two hours. Those bare, clean-swept rooms, with summer sunlight streaming through clean windows, and the men's voices echoing in the emptiness. He lifted his eyes to the six storeys of the West Side mill behind him; it was bedlam in there now, absolute bedlam. Five or six hundred men, women and children, and a similar number in the mill next door, the one they called East Side; and they all took it as a matter of course that the noise was deafening, the heat overpowering and the smell indescribable.

So far he'd been in the weaving shed and the blowing room, which was a hell-hole if ever he'd seen one. There were scutching machines that opened the bales of raw cotton and stripped them of leaves and seeds and such-like, and then the blowing machines that blew the cotton free of the dust. And what dust! You could barely see for it, let alone breathe, though to be sure there were big, steam-driven fans that sucked it out through vents in the wall. But what had staggered him most was the weaving shed. It was enormous, a single-storey building with a zig-zagged, partly glazed roof supported by iron pillars, and it smelled of hot oil and sweat. The noise had been deafening, overpowering, because there were hundreds, hundreds of power looms, all banging and clattering at once, four to each weaver; at last he understood why Martha sometimes spoke with exaggerated mouthing and used actions to suit the words, even when she was at home. He didn't see her though, because the gang were loading rolls of cotton cloth to take to the cut-lookers, and there was no time to linger.

Now, sitting by himself on a wicker skip in the damp cool air of the yard, he thought about Martha working from six till six on her looms, and then going home to more drudgery, and he shook his head in admiration of her stamina. When he'd worked his way up through the mill to good money he would see to it that she had some rest. . . .

The day wore on, and he found that the heavy gang were in demand in both mills, from the yard up to the spinning rooms and above them the attics. They moved like a squad of well-drilled soldiers; lifting, loading, weighing, winching, their movements governed by constant messages brought by errand boys from each floor, and the job-book that never left Maynard's hand.

The foreman was a short, heavy-set man reputed to have been a prize weight-lifter in his time. He was given to bawdy jokes and had a loud, ready laugh, but he harried his men relentlesly, and so was not given the mark of respect bestowed so affectionately on Daniel Broadhurst – a Mister behind his back as well as to his face. Matthew was reserving judgement on the man. He was no Mr Broadhurst, but neither was he a Norman Nuttall, thank God.

By six o'clock his body was weary and his mind over-full of new impressions. He arrived at the appointed place and felt a spurt of pleasure when Martha hurried to join him. Cotton fluff clung to her hair and wisps of it dotted the fringe of her shawl. 'How've you got on?' she asked anxiously.

'All right,' he said with a smile.

She let out her breath in relief. 'They've all been tellin' me it's horse-work under Maynard, an' I've been that worried! You must tell me all about it on the way home. Oh, look! They're givin' somethin' out at the gates!'

A trestle table was set up there, and women were handing small, paper-wrapped packages to every worker as they left. On each one was a small, printed label: *With all good wishes from Mr and Mrs James Schofield.*

'It's weddin' cake!' said Martha, highly delighted. 'That's just like Mr James.'

Twelve hundred pieces of wedding cake? All at once Matthew felt the first faint stirrings of the loyalty that so often amused him in Martha. It was a very big family at Jericho Mills, and he hoped he was going to enjoy being part of it.

CHAPTER FIFTEEN

'With this ring . . .'

THE PEOPLE OF SALTLEY observed Abel Ridings' funeral and declared it to be a poor affair, with only three or four good wreaths and less than a dozen mourners.

Maria Ridings had looked seventy if she looked a day, they said, and while the younger daughter wept and was supported by her intended, the other, the red-head, stayed erect and quite silent under her veil. Behind the four of them – yes, right behind the chief mourners – was the dwarf from the dolly-shop, dressed up like a normal person in a good black coat and with a black crepe band around his hat.

After the disappointing funeral, was there a time of quiet mourning behind the three brass balls? No, that very evening there were lamps lit all over the place, and the upstairs curtains not even drawn. Then next morning the dwarf was out first thing putting a home-made sign over the door, naming the licensed pawnbroker as Elizabeth Ridings. That was the eldest daughter – the red-head – the one who called herself Tizzie. Who ever heard of a young woman not yet twenty-one being a pawnbroker? Her father might have been spurned like all his kind, but he'd been known as a keen man of business, and no fool. It was clear now that he'd had a mind of his own, as well, and wasn't afraid to be different. Time would tell whether the daughter would match up to the father. . . .

The night before the funeral Mary had found her sister sitting grimly over a dying fire, taking in what her mother had just told her across the open coffin.

'What's wrong, Tizz? Has she been talking nonsense again?'

'No,' Tizzie said slowly, 'she's been telling the truth.' At that moment it didn't occur to her to keep silent about the fact that she might be the offspring of a rapist. She just looked into her sister's concerned brown eyes and told her everything.

Mary was horrified. 'Oh, poor Mother! But you aren't the daughter of that awful man, Tizzie. Father's hair was red in his youth, don't forget, and can't you see you've inherited his business ability? And look at your teeth and the shape of your mouth – anybody can see they're just like his. Come on, you're tired out. Off you go to bed, and when I've settled Mother I'll bring you a drink of hot milk. You're my full sister, Tizzie, I'm sure of it!' She gave her a squeeze and a smacking kiss, and then said sadly, 'You weren't all that fond of him, though, were you? I don't think he found it easy to show his feelings, you know, but I'm sure that in his own way he loved us both. And I'm certain he adored Mother.'

Sixteen hours later they were dressed for the funeral and listening to Abel's lawyer. Large, fleshy, talkative, he had faced the three of them and related with relish the terms of his client's last will and testament. Since that astounding recital Tizzie had studied a copy of the will until she knew it by heart, and two weeks later the various bequests were still leaping into her mind at random.

'And to my beloved wife, Maria Ridings, the residue of my estate, apportioned to provide the sum of four pounds a week for life, and whatsoever monies shall then remain to be taken as a lump sum. . . . My dear daughter Mary Ridings, the sum of five hundred pounds as a marriage settlement to be used for the founding of her husband's business and the setting up of their home, with the earnest request that their marriage is not postponed on account of my death. . . . The sum of fifty pounds to Barnabas Jellicoe in recognition of his

loyal and devoted service, on condition that he continues
in his present position for at least twelve months after
my death, if so requested. . . .'

Then had followed her own legacy, so startling and
unexpected her jaw had dropped open and stayed that
way until it started to ache. 'To my dear daughter
Elizabeth Ridings, the full rights, licence and premises
of my pawnbroking business, and the goods and chattels
therein, as pledged against monetary advances to sundry
persons listed in the business records, on condition that
she runs the said business for at least twelve months
after my death, and does not enter into a contract of
matrimony in that time. . . .'

He had known, she thought in amazement, he had
known he was about to die! And he had left hundreds
and hundreds of pounds, proof that he could have
afforded a move to Manchester long ago if he'd been
so minded. What was more he hadn't wanted her to
marry Edward! The feeling that had nudged at her in
recent months swept into her heart with the force of a
torrent. She had underestimated him, she had despised
him, and she had been wrong! He had left her his
smelly, flea-ridden pawnshop rather than an astounding
five hundred pounds like Mary, and she was glad, glad,
glad! She uttered a laugh that was more like a sob, then
put her hands to her face and wept.

Her mother stared, black-shadowed eyes narrowed
and assessing, but Mary jumped up and clasped her
sister to her bosom. 'Don't cry, Tizz! He knew you
were capable of running the business. Tizzie, are you
pleased, or what?'

'I'm pleased,' she said through her tears, and thought
of the shrunken, colourless little man who had so often
irritated her. A new emotion was welling up inside her
and she didn't recognise it. Much later she was to wonder
if it could be remorse.

The lawyer waited until she was calm again, then
pointed out that though her father had insisted on

the legalities of the transfer being prepared, the law required the shop to remain open, with the name of the new licensee openly displayed. That had been the start of the busiest time of her life – so busy that her grief about Edward was something she could only acknowledge in the silence of the night, with Mary slumbering at her side.

Her mother was quiet, pale, reflective. She cooked meals for the three of them, supervised the scuttling Biddy on her two half-days, listened politely when Mary spoke of the approaching wedding, and never referred to what she had revealed that night. But Tizzie had heard her. The drug might have loosened her mother's tongue, but the ring of truth was in her words, and now they were chiselled on Tizzie's mind as clearly as her father's name was chiselled on his headstone.

Life was very strange, she told herself. Six months ago she might have welcomed news that she wasn't Abel's flesh and blood, but with a doubt about her parentage she had to admit that as a father he was preferable to a drunken rapist. He had left her a stack of notes on the business – a beginner's guide to pawnbroking, each aspect dealt with in detail under its own separate heading. He must have spent countless hours on it when he should have been resting, and she had the oddest feeling that the pages of neat, spiky writing were offering her a message other than how to run the pawnshop.

There was little time for such reflection, though. Mary was in a ferment of joy about her wedding, and sometimes Tizzie was glad to go down to the shop, away from her constant chatter. 'Wasn't Father marvellous, Tizzie, leaving all that money to William and me? We can buy the shop we've always wanted on the corner of Holden Street, and it has a really lovely house, big enough to raise a family. And William can order stock for Christmas and afford an assistant butcher, and I'll be on the spot to help with plucking the Christmas poultry. Oh, I do think Father was lovely to say we

mustn't postpone the wedding, but I can't get Mother
to show any interest. I know she's still dreadfully upset,
but do you think I should ask her again if she thinks a
quiet meal at William's would be fitting? Tizzie, I don't
suppose you would ask her for me? Please, Tizz. . . .'

'All right. Leave it to me.' What was one more thing
to see to out of so many?

Later, with Mary busy elsewhere, Tizzie observed
her mother across the dinner table. She still looked
dreadful, but that unnerving blankness was fading from
her gaze, and she had eaten a little beef stew and a
mouthful of carrots. 'Mother,' she said carefully, 'Mary
and William are anxious to do nothing to upset you
regarding their wedding, but with only ten days to go
Mary must make arrangements for after the ceremony.
Would a quiet meal at the Hartleys' be agreeable to
you? Nothing noisy or ostentatious, just family and a
few close friends. Mrs Hartley is willing, if you are.'

'If it had been left to me they would have waited until
next summer,' said Maria, 'but as your father wanted it
like this they must do as they see fit. One thing I insist
on: I must meet all expenses. The bride's parents pay
for the wedding – it's the correct way of doing.'

Tizzie nodded gravely, concealing her relief. Surely
those few words heralded her mother's return to normality?

'And what about you, Tizzie,' she asked now, 'you
and Edward?'

Tizzie would have liked to shout out the truth. She
felt the urge to stand up and bellow: 'He's rotten! He
used me for his own enjoyment, and then pushed me
aside for Sarah Schofield!' Instead she said quietly,
'His interests have turned elsewhere, so I hear. I'm
not concerned about him, Mother. I have the business
to see to, and Father's will to follow.'

It was a shock to find her mother not even listening. 'I shall order a new black bonnet for the
wedding,' she declared with sudden animation. 'Tizzie,

will you have a selection sent round for me to choose
from?'

Tizzie glared at her, then marched out and ran down
to the shop. Let Mary come and find her if she wanted
to know about her wedding meal, she told herself, and
took over from Barney at the counter. There was a new
ease in her dealings with him, though she had expected
the opposite when he became her employee instead of
her father's. Mindful of his value to her, she had talked
at length with him during that long, busy evening after
the funeral; he had surprised her by asking whether she
wanted him to stay on.

'But of course I do,' she said blankly. 'How can you
doubt it?'

'Your father's will said "if so requested",' he pointed
out. 'I didn't know if you would request it, that's all.'

'All right, I request it,' she said briskly. 'Is that
better? Or perhaps you don't like the idea of working
for a woman of my age?'

His eyes, dark and guarded, met hers. 'I have no
objections, Miss Tizzie.'

'My father has left a pile of notes on how to run the
business,' she told him, 'but I'll need practical help,
and I think you can give it. I believe my father paid
you a pound a week? How would it suit you if I raised
that to twenty-five shillings, on the understanding that
you'll be my right-hand man, and take over when I go
to Manchester, or if I attend a meeting in Saltley?'

She was intrigued to see deep colour edge up from
his jawline. 'It will suit me very well, Miss Tizzie,' he
said quietly.

'And I might want a few changes in the shop. Nothing
startling, but just to make it a bit less – less dingy.'

'That's up to you, Miss Tizzie. It's your shop now.'

'And – and I'd like to think you'll speak out if you
see me doing something foo – uh – wrong. If we are to
work together we must be quite open with each other.
One more thing – I don't know anything about you,

Barney. Where you live, or whether you're married, for instance.'

'I have no wife,' he said, smiling faintly and shaking his big head, 'nor any family. I live in Rope Street, up at the market end. I have two rooms in a three-storey house there.'

She had the feeling he was laughing at her, but didn't know why. 'Then write down your address and leave it on the desk for me,' she said, somewhat put out. 'And now, what do you suggest we do about a temporary licensing notice for over the door?'

That exchange had been the start of the new relationship. She was the boss, he the employee, but between them was a mutual respect.

It was a cold day for a wedding. Too cold for her mother to go out, said Martha, coming in from the back yard. Mrs Spencer would have none of it. 'I'm going,' she snapped. 'If I can't get to me daughter's weddin' I might as well be dead. An' if Henry's bringin' me an invalid chair all the way from Rochdale I'm not disappointin' him. Don't worry yoursel', I'll wrap up warm.'

Martha exchanged a look with Matthew. They were both to finish work at noon, and after that surely it should be her day, hers and Matthew's, not her mother's? 'Wouldn't you be better staying here by the fire, Mother? The last time you got thoroughly chilled you couldn't move for a week, don't forget.'

'I know, I know, but I want to see you get wed, lass.'

For a fleeting moment it was there, that bond between mother and daughter. Martha softened. 'What do you think, Matthew?'

He straightened up from putting coal on the fire. 'My own mother can't come to our weddin'' he pointed out gently, 'so I'd be main pleased to have yours. So long as Henry brings you back here as quick as he can, Mrs Spencer.'

The older woman wagged her head, highly pleased. 'That's settled, then. Jack knows he's to stoke the oven before you get in from work, Martha, and they'll be arrivin' from Rochdale by that time. Here, have you changed the bed?'

Martha blushed. 'Yes. It's all clean and tidy up there. You know I've done everythin' I can think of in advance.'

'Aye, you can shift when you put your mind to it,' admitted her mother. She flapped her hands at them. 'Well, go on then! You don't want to be locked out of work on your weddin' mornin'.'

Out in the street the blast of the wind took their breath. From the north-east, thought Matthew, and cold enough to bring snow. Martha plodded at his side, head down, her clogs hitting the pavement with heavy thuds rather than the usual brisk clack. He knew she'd been up late night after night, sewing and cooking for today. 'You be tired, I expect, Martha?'

Her small face looked pale and very plain under the heavy shawl, but she smiled. 'Not too tired to enjoy me weddin' day,' she said. 'We'll be Mr and Mrs Raike the next time we come to Jericho.' He tucked her hand under his arm and squeezed it against his side as they headed up the hill. 'Matthew,' she said quietly, 'I am sorry you'll have nobody of your own, this afternoon.'

'Don't 'ee worry. I've written to my sisters, and they'll tell the boys. I looked after them all for long enough, so I don't doubt they'll be thinkin' of us. And Martha, there's one thing I want you to know.' Her eyes widened warily and he shook her arm, impatient at seeing her still unsure of him. 'When I'm on better money I want 'ee to take life a bit easier.'

'Easier?' she repeated, as if she'd never heard of the word.

'Yes, you know, not workin' so hard.'

The five-to-six blower sounded as they reached the gates, and she quickened her step. 'I expect to work,

Matthew. How can it be any different with four looms, a house, me mother, me Uncle Jack, and after today a husband?'

'If I can manage it, it *will* be different,' he said. 'You wait and see!' Then he bent and kissed her full on the mouth.

She blushed bright red. People were shoving past them and staring. 'I'll see you later,' she whispered, and hurried away to the weaving shed, finding that her feet were so light they seemed to skim the cobbles without really touching them. Who could ever have thought she would marry somebody like him? A laugh issued from deep inside her, and she swallowed it, allowing herself only a silent smile. What was a bit of hard work when she had a man such as Matthew?

It was all bustle when they got back to Ledden Street. Bella and her family had just arrived, and she was already at the oven in her pinafore. She was bigger and plumper than Martha, sharing the same fine hair and pale skin, but with a hearty laugh and a ready tongue. She greeted her sister with a kiss, and gave Matthew a keen assessing stare as they shook hands. Henry was broad and fair and good-natured, teasing Mrs Spencer and chatting to Uncle Jack as easily as if he saw him every day of the week. Something about him put Matthew in mind of Daniel Broadhurst, and he was relieved; he hadn't wanted somebody he didn't take to as his best man. The little girls looked clean and well-fed, sitting together on the settee and giggling. He was at ease with children, and they chattered to him without restraint, asking why he didn't talk the same as they did. 'These three have had the time of their life riding in that chair from the station,' laughed Bella. 'I've had to make sure they know it's their granny's when we go to the weddin'.'

They all had hot soup and a barm cake, and then Matthew put on his new shirt and necktie and his freshly-pressed jacket. It was the first time he'd worn a brand-new shirt, and it felt hard and uncomfortable round his neck. Martha was wearing her best blue dress and bonnet, and rare colour ran in her cheeks when she picked up her two pink chrysanthemums. 'Come here and give me a kiss, then,' instructed her mother, who was so wrapped up in blankets and wraps in her chair as to appear spherical, with only her nose and the sharp eyes visible.

Martha kissed her and muttered, 'Are you all right, Mam?'

Mrs Spencer nodded. 'Aye, lass. Let's be off to chapel.'

Martha reached for her heavy grey shawl, but Matthew said, 'Hold on a minute, then planted a chaste little kiss on her cheek and gave her his wedding gift. It was a new shawl in a deep rose-pink, soft and heavily fringed, with fine blue and mauve overchecks. The shop had put it by for him, and he'd been paying off on it every week.

The three women stared at it openmouthed, and when Martha swirled it round her shoulders it almost reached the ground. 'Matthew, it's lovely!' she said, eyes shining. 'Thank you, thank you – I've never seen anything so beautiful.'

He smiled and set his hat at an angle. 'Off we go, then,' he said.

In less than an hour they were man and wife. It was a quiet little ceremony in a Primitive Methodist chapel, which to Matthew's eyes seemed plain and bare compared to the village church he remembered from his early days. The minister who married them was a kindly man who wished them well when they signed his book, and smiled in congratulation that they could write their names instead of having to make their mark. Then they were walking back to Ledden Street arm in arm, with Henry hurrying ahead pushing the chair and the little girls holding hands in front of their mother.

'Are you happy, Mrs Raike?' asked Matthew as they bent against the wind.

'I am that, Mr Raike,' she said, looking almost

pretty in the reflected pink glow of the shawl. 'Are you?'

'At this minute I'm the happiest man in the world,' he said simply.

A bridal carriage swished past them from Bethesda chapel, and a rosy-cheeked bride looked out and waved at them, then laughed into her new husband's face. Matthew thought he recognised her, and then saw another face at the window of the second carriage – handsome but bony beneath glossy red hair and a stylish black hat, with wide alert eyes observing their little procession. The girls from the pawnshop, he thought, and the pleasant one newly-wed. He glanced at Martha, wondering if she felt bad about the contrast between their two weddings, but she was admiring her plain gold band with that new, contented curve to her mouth.

He lay in bed, waiting for Martha to come up when she'd settled her mother. From what he'd heard here and there it was always the new wife who sat in bed waiting for her husband, but it was different for him and Martha. It had to be.

His mind was so full of the day's happenings he could hardly contain himself to lie still. It had been a good day, he told himself, a lovely day, and he had the feeling that somewhere old Peggy-oh would be smiling. Bella had taken over the feeding of them all as soon as she walked in, and it had been a fine feast. Roast beef and what they called Yorkshire pudding, with roast potatoes and vegetables, followed by trifle and wedding cake – a real wedding cake made by Martha; small, admitted, but crammed with fruit. Henry and Uncle Jack had shared a jug of ale, and Mrs Spencer and Bella each had a tot of brandy. None of them remarked on it when he and Martha had ginger cordial – she did it without fuss, and he could have kissed her for it. The three little maids had been happy as could be, bringing back memories of his sisters Maggie and Liza in their childhood, yes – and Dorcas, too.

Martha's step sounded on the stairs, and she came in with her hair in a long plait over one shoulder, and carrying another candle and a piece of soft calico, folded. She was already wearing her nightgown, and he knew she had undressed down in the back kitchen. That pleased him, because he valued modesty; he had seen little enough of it at the Mizzen Mast. There was dainty frilling at her neck and wrists, and he wondered if it was the fine lace she'd been crocheting in the evenings for weeks past.

He turned back the covers and said quietly, 'First the bed was yours, and then it was mine, but it's ours now, Martha.'

She blew out the candles, and climbed in silently beside him. Then suddenly she turned to him and threw her arms around his neck. 'Oh – I'm that happy, Matthew!'

Her lips were as soft as ever, but he longed to feel her, skin to skin against him. She let him lift the cotton nightgown over her head, and for the first time in his life he held the unclad body of a woman. She was very small, but to his rough hands her skin felt smooth as silk; and she smelled very clean, of soap and lavender and something else that he didn't recognise, but which set his blood racing.

He knew he must be careful not to hurt her, but he couldn't hold back, and it seemed neither could she. When they came together he glimpsed her teeth bared in pain; then it was as if they were one creature, soaring together high above the front bedroom in Ledden Street, up through the snow-laden winter night, seeking the brightness of the moon and the stars. He felt release and relief and the most powerful joy; and underneath it a stab of surprise that it should be so clean and wholesome and natural. As clearly as if Peggy-oh Luke were in the room, he heard the echo of the old man's words from long ago: 'It's not always ugly

and lustful, Matthew. One day, God willing, it'll come
to you . . .'

Martha was very still in his arms, and sleep was
clutching at him, slowing his noisy breathing, making
him neglect her. He forced words to his lips and they
came out heavy and slurred. 'Have I hurt 'ee, Martha?
Martha – did I hurt 'ee?'

She was reaching out of bed for the piece of calico,
and he felt her patting herself dry with it before tucking
it between her legs. He was relieved that she knew about
the bleeding; but his eyes were weighted, he couldn't stay
awake. 'Martha,' he mumbled. 'Did I hurt 'ee?'

'Just a bit,' she whispered, 'but I'm all right now.
And Matthew . . . Matthew?' He was already asleep,
one hand still behind her shoulders, the other on her
buttocks. She edged closer into his arms and stared
into the darkness. So that was it. . . . It had hurt, just
as Jessie had been good enough to warn her when the
looms were silent at breakfast time. But he had tried
to think of her, of whether he had hurt her. She put
her face against his chest and kissed it. The hairs tickled
her nose, and she could hear the rhythmic beating of
his heart. When he became part of her she had almost
cried out that she loved him, but somehow it seemed
wrong for her to say it first.

She ran a hand down the length of his body, feeling
the long, relaxed thigh that was still half over her own,
and she gave a little sigh. Maybe he would say it,
one day.

He wakened in the early hours, telling himself it was
her presence that had disturbed him, but knowing it was
really the dream. Not the nightmare, thank heaven – at
least he'd been spared that on his wedding night; but
he'd been dreaming of the girls when they were as
small as Bella's three. There was an odd feeling in his
chest, as if something was enclosed there that demanded
release. . . .

'What is it, Matthew?' Martha was awake, lying

quite still against him. 'You've not had the nightmare?'

'No, you'd have known about it if I had. 'Twas a
dream about the girls – a happy dream. Strange, when
half the time we weren't happy at all.' He wondered
if she would ask about Dorcas, but she just lay close
and kept silent. And because she didn't ask, he was
overcome by the urge to tell her. He felt the words
rising to his lips of their own accord, and he had to
force himself to speak slowly.

'Martha,' he said carefully, 'thanks for makin' it easy
about the drink – you know, havin' the ginger cordial
an' that. It's all to do with my sister – I reckon you
guessed as much? She was a priddy liddle soul, with
big brown eyes and dark curly hair like my mother.
Always laughin', and heaven knows there wasn't much
to laugh about. She had a fondness for books and such.
We'd taught her to read an' she must have been clever,
because if ever she come across writin' – a newspaper or
a leaflet that somebody had put down – she would climb
into the hayloft an' read it under one of the skylights.

'The inn paid Fat Annie a wage, an' me as well, but
the rest of 'en just did what was needed, an' in return
they let us all live behind the stables. Fat Annie – well,
she drank a lot. Swam in it, given the chance. She would
send me to the bar with her jug an' coppers to pay for ale,
coppers that could have been better spent on clothes for
our backs, or a decent meal. When I was about fifteen I
took to drinkin' from her jug an' then toppin' it up from
the tap in the yard. It – it made me feel good, you see.
She used to complain to the barman about waterin' it
down, an' o' course I was found out. By then I was
too big to be leathered, but she took it out on me in
another way, knowin' if we had less food I would see
the little 'uns got enough even if I went hungry. But by
that time I had a taste for the drink.

'I wasn't content, you see. I wanted somethin' better
for us all than skivvyin' in a run-down inn, and the

drink kind o' took the edge off it. Things didn't seem
so bad with a pint of ale inside me. The girls knew I
used to cheat and cadge to make a bit, but till then I'd
always done it for them. Now I was doin' it for myself.
Anythin' for a jug of ale. Well, almost anythin'. I could
have earned shillin's rather than pence from some of the
customers – men who wanted a young boy. But the old
friend I told you about, Luke Fawcett, he warned me
somethin' powerful against 'en. He warned me against
the drink as well, an' so did Dorcas. She said I wasn't
her Mattie when I smelled of the barrels from the
cellar. . . .'

He faltered to a stop. What had come over him to
start relating all this when Martha had a fondness for
him? She would be disappointed in him, or worse, she
would be disgusted. He was mad to be telling this terrible
tale on their wedding night.

'I'm listenin' Matthew,' she said quietly. 'Go on, you
can tell me.'

After that it was a bit easier. 'Well, one day the inn
was busy because a passenger ship had put in. We were
run off our feet, the girls helpin' the maids, the boys
fetchin' an' carryin', an' Fat Annie – er – she was busy
lookin' after the sailors. Peggy-oh Luke was out at the
quay, as he liked watchin' the big ships. Then a customer
lost his papers – important papers in a stiff red envelope.
He was in a rare state, an' offered a shillin' to whoever
could find it. He didn't know I'd slipped the envelope
out of the straps of his trunk, just so I could give it back
an' maybe make a ha'penny out of him. I got a shillin'
instead; when we were quiet again in the afternoon
I gave the five young 'uns a penny apiece an' spent
fourpence on meself – on gin. I hadn't tried it before,
but I knew folk set store by it. Fat Annie and the rest
of 'em went for a sleep, all except Dorcas; she bought
a picture paper with her penny and took it up to a far
corner of the loft that nobody knew about except me.
We used to say it was our liddle secret. The gin I took

up to my own sleeping place, an' – an' I drank myself
senseless.

'Nobody knew how the fire started, but as darkness
fell the horses smelled the smoke an' went mad. There
was pandemonium. They got the horses out, but though
Fat Annie screamed an' carried on she couldn't rouse
me, so Peggy-oh slung me over his shoulder an' carried
me down to the yard, an' got his hair burned off for
his trouble. Then they saw Dorcas was missin', but
nobody knew where she was. The hayloft was goin'
up like tinder, an' I was lyin' senseless in the yard.
When I come to myself it was mornin', and the stables
were blackened and stinkin'. They'd all been rushin'
round searchin' for Dorcas, but she was long dead.
Burned to a cinder in her little hidey-hole among the
hay.' He held on to Martha's hand, though his own
was wet with sweat. 'I saw her liddle body – insisted
on it, I did. She looked like a side of lamb that had
been over-long on the spit; charred an' sticky an' quite
black. . . .'

There was silence for a moment. He had opened that
door in his mind with a vengeance, hadn't he? What
would she think? What would she say?

She held his hand more tightly. 'Oh, Matthew,
Matthew . . . what did you do?'

'Do?' He stared into the darkness. 'I sat and wondered
how best to kill myself. That's what I did.'

He felt her cringe. 'But you changed your mind?'

'Peggy-oh changed it for me. He talked to me for an
hour or more, holdin' me on his knee like I was a toddler.
It was months, though, before I put the idea of it from
me once an' for all. One thing I did do, though, with
my head still achin' from the gin; I vowed that as long
as I lived I would never touch alcohol again. That, at
least, I could do for her. That's the reason for me not
drinkin', Martha. That's the reason for my nightmares.
It's always Fat Annie screechin' an' carryin' on, tryin' to
get me up, but I can't rise from my bed, an' everybody's

screamin'. It must have sunk into my mind, though I knew nothing of it at the time.'

'I'm that sorry, Matthew,' she said simply. 'Have you talked about it to anybody else?'

'No. None of the others reproached me, though God knows why not, so the only person I talked to was Luke Fawcett. He saved my life twice over, did Luke.'

'What about your stepmother? Didn't she say anything?'

'No, how could she? It was her got me on the drink in the first place.'

Martha made no comment on that. Instead she pulled his head to her own small bosom, and stroked his cheek. 'Go to sleep again,' she commanded gently. 'It's still the middle of the night.'

Go to sleep he did, as peacefully as a child held close to its mother's breast; and even as sleep claimed him he felt the pressure inside him ease and disappear. With a contented little grunt he released his grip on Martha's hand and turned away from her, his breathing deep and even. And at his side she lay awake, thinking about what he had told her. Downstairs her mother was coughing, and she waited to be summoned, but it seemed she was to be spared that on her wedding night.

The Hartleys tried. Out of respect for the Ridings' bereavement they really tried to ban unseemly jollity. But the bride was bubbling with happiness, her husband on top of the world, and his family delighted with their union. Jollity showed itself and wouldn't be submerged.

Tizzie sat next to her mother, picking at the excellent food and observing her sister's new in-laws. She had to admit they were a fine-looking lot; beefy, like William, but clear-skinned and bright-eyed, and every one of them well-built. There was an ease among them, too, a robust good humour that was only partly dimmed by the black-clad widow in her seat by the fire.

'Try one of my dinky-pies, Mrs Ridings . . . and
Tizzie, perhaps I can tempt you as well?' It was William's
mother, quiet and solicitous, with more delicacies. Maria
smiled vaguely and took a tiny hot pie, dumping it on a
plate already filled to overflowing. Tizzie swallowed a
sigh. Surely she could gather her wits for her daughter's
wedding?

She shot an apologetic look at Mrs Hartley, and felt a
surprising rush of admiration for the woman. She might
be a butcher's wife, and no more than a town-dwelling
country bumpkin; but she had risen to an awkward
situation with grace and tact, providing splendid food
for over twenty people and a happy celebration for her
son and his bride. She moved away with her tray of pies
and Tizzie jumped up and followed her. 'This is a lovely
meal, Mrs Hartley,' she said quietly. 'I know my mother
appreciates it, but I'm afraid she isn't quite well enough
to express her gratitude just yet.'

Surprise showed on the good-natured face and was
hastily concealed. 'Thanks, Tizzie,' she said simply. 'We
think the world of Mary, you know, and anythin' we do
for her we do willin', and with pleasure. We're all sorry
about your father, yet we did want a bit of a do for
them both – somethin' they could look back on, what
with her havin' her weddin' dress all ready and the cake
ordered. . . .' She patted Tizzie's hand and moved on,
while Tizzie returned to her seat. Why had Mrs Hartley
been taken aback at her words when Mary must surely
have said as much already?

She recalled her previous dealings with the Hartleys,
and knew that at their rare meetings she'd been polite
and no more. They were tradesmen, she had thought
then, not in remotely the same category as Edward's
family. She flapped a big white napkin across her lap and
stabbed at a portion of jellied chicken. She had thought
a lot of things during the months she'd been besotted
by Edward, and she knew now that not all of them had
been wise, or right, or even remotely sensible. It riled

her to realise how gullible she'd been. And who must she thank that she wasn't even now carrying his child, shunned and humiliated and without a doubt unwed? She must thank the bride, that's who, for telling her things of which she'd been ignorant, facts that had guided her behaviour with Edward before it was too late. Her dear, her truly dear sister the bride, in her blush-pink gown with the pearl-buttoned bodice and the little head-dress of veiling and silk leaves. It had been her idea to anchor Mary's dark hair in a coronet of plaits on the crown of her head; her suggestion to thread black velvet ribbon through the bright leaves as a tribute to the man who had provided such a splendid start to her married life.

Everybody started to clap, and she realised that the happy couple had just cut the cake. She smiled and blew a kiss to her sister, but felt a return of the despair that had swamped her in Bethesda chapel. The days before the wedding had been so busy she had looked on the actual ceremony as just one more task to be dealt with. But hearing the 'with this ring', and 'with my body', and all the rest of it she was suddenly ripped apart by the most bitter regret. It had been bad enough weeks ago when she realised that Mary would beat her to the altar; it was infinitely worse to see the ring being slipped on her finger, and to know that nobody was clamouring to do the same for her.

In that instant, sitting next to her mother in the front pew, Tizzie had glimpsed her future. She would be a spinster, too proud to accept an ordinary man, but set apart from the life she coveted because of the pawnshop. Then, on their way back from the church, there had been that little wedding group following the invalid chair, with the bride in a vast pink shawl, carrying two pink flowers. She'd recognised her as a mill-worker from Ledden Street whose name was in the pawnshop books – Spencer, that was it. She was a tiny, plain little creature, but she had got herself that striking gypsyish man who worked in

Soar Park, the one who had come in on the cotton wagon.

As her sister laughed and chattered with her in-laws Tizzie reflected on the Spencer woman's wedding. There was something in her bearing that echoed Mary's. Perhaps it was the intense happiness of marrying for love? A different kind of love, perhaps, than she had felt for Edward. . . .

There, at her sister's wedding party, Tizzie made a decision. The seeds of it were sown before that moment, but since Edward threw her aside there hadn't been time to plan the way ahead. All at once she knew she would never allow herself to be hurt again by any man. Common sense told her she was truly the child of the rapist: her own enjoyment of sexual licence, her own dominant streak, the fact that like him she was tall and bony; they all pointed to that creature having fathered her. She'd been seduced by a rogue, she'd been fathered by a rogue, but by heaven she would make sure that no rogue would affect her life from now on. She would become a business woman, and in Saltley rather than Manchester. Better a big fish in a little pond than a small fish floundering in the ocean. And when –

'Tizzie!' It was Mary at her side. 'Tizz – you're miles away! It's the speeches next, when we've had the cake. Isn't it all lovely, Tizz? I say, do you think Mother's all right?'

Tizzie shrugged. 'She's just tired and depressed. I thought perhaps I'd take her home as soon as we've drunk your health. That way you can all enjoy yourselves without feeling awkward. What do you say to that?'

Mary gave her a kiss. 'I say it's a good idea. You always have the best ideas, Tizzie.'

CHAPTER SIXTEEN

Falling Apart

JOSHUA WAS ON THE train back to Saltley after a busy morning at Mosley Street and a couple of hours on the Exchange. He stared out at the snow-covered fields and shifted irritably in his seat when he found himself sighing, uneasily aware that he had a lot on his mind. A sudden drop in imports of raw cotton had put many a Lancashire mill on short time, but they'd managed to keep Jericho working; he hoped things would be back to normal by the new year.

Ralph had been the first of them to sense trouble. He'd acted like greased lightning, putting in immediate bids and then suggesting they bought heavily before prices rose to prohibitive levels; he'd saved them money more astutely than even Charlie could have done. The lad was quick, amazingly quick, but Joshua had noticed at the Exchange that some of his old friends were a bit on the quiet side when he greeted them; he couldn't help wondering if Master Ralph had been treading on their toes. He would have to watch him, he would that, and if neither he nor Sam were around he would ask John Wagstaff to let him know how Ralph conducted himself with the other manufacturers. It was one thing to be alert and business-like, but quite another to be so sharp you sullied the Schofield reputation for fair dealing. The lad would slow down in time – he just needed guidance. At the moment he was so full of himself he was asking again about living in Charlie's rooms.

Things at home were bothering him too. There was Sarah, his little Sarah, falling over herself to get engaged.

It was a bit too rushed for his liking, and as yet Edward hadn't formally asked for her hand. He was talking of going in for contracting on his own account, and apparently he'd had a few enquiries. Nothing wrong with that – he was a capable lad but when he said he might have to move a hundred miles away she'd started weeping and carrying on as if the world was coming to an end. Not that the house had been free of weeping and wailing just lately; in fact there hadn't been five minutes' peace since the pair of them first met at the Town Hall. She was in love, was his little girl, head over heels in love for the first time in her life, and she didn't know how to deal with it. Sometimes he thought Edward could have calmed her down if he'd had a mind to, but she was more excitable than ever when he was there. The only time she was tranquil was when she was in the bedroom with Rachel or in the sick-bay at Jericho. She and Polly ran that like clockwork, and the workers loved her for it. At all other times she was a difficult, emotional girl who was more of a trial than he'd ever known.

And there was James and Esther. They were back from their honeymoon, and though they said it had been wonderful in Italy, his eldest son was remarkably subdued. Polite of course, and pleasant enough, but somewhere in Italy he'd lost his quiet sense of humour and the easy conversation that had always been a delight to him and Rachel. He himself had believed that Esther didn't have too much of her father in her, because Ephraim was known in the town as a sharp-tongued old devil, and until the wedding she'd always been sweet as honey. But once or twice of late she'd spoken to James in a way that had shaken him and Rachel. It had upset them, but they'd talked it over and decided it was early days in the marriage, and they mustn't interfere. Let them settle in at High Lee, they had said, and then see how things were by Christmas.

But all those concerns were mere pinpricks compared

to his worry about Rachel, who was turning into an
invalid before his very eyes. Weight was dropping off
her bones. She was having difficulty eating, and when
she forced something down as often as not she vomited
it back. She had risen to the demands of the wedding,
though he suspected it had been an effort. Within ten
days of her catastrophic day out in Manchester he had
tackled the doctor about a second opinion, only to be
told the same old tale by the next one: the change of
life, or the climacteric, as they liked to call it. The
fool had even hinted that she was highly strung, and
had a 'nervous stomach'. There were mornings when
she would be up at seven, determined to take up her
normal routine, but when he came home at mid-day
she would be upstairs resting, with Alice and Hannah
worried to death and Sarah spending her dinner hour
at the bedside.

He'd talked to the children about it, of course, because
they had a right to know what was going on. She might
be his wife, and God knows he loved her more than life
itself, but she was their mother as well, and they were
worried about her. Even Ralph, who had never been
one for a display of affection, kept trotting up to the
bedroom when he thought nobody was looking.

Joshua wriggled in his seat again and tapped his stick
on the floor between his feet. He'd left Manchester early
in order to spend a quiet hour with her. A stomach
specialist was attending her at four-thirty, and he just
wanted her to himself for a bit before then. This man
was reputed to be the best in Manchester, but if he
didn't show gumption he'd summon the best in London,
or Edinburgh, or wherever they talked sense and knew
medicine.

It was quiet when he arrived home. Alice and the
rest of them were having their afternoon break in
the kitchen, and he found Rachel up and dressed
in front of the fire in the little sitting-room. Her
face lit up when he walked in. 'Joshua! What's this?

It's only half-past three. Do you want something to eat?'

'No. I had an early dinner at the chop-house, and then went on to the Exchange.' He gave her a kiss and hovered next to her chair.

'How's everything at Mosley Street?'

'Fine, now all the shemozzle's over, but I've come home to talk about you, not the cotton.' He pulled up a chair and sat facing her, very close. 'How are you, love?'

'Oh – not so bad,' she said lightly. 'I've had some chicken broth, and a bit of egg custard. Sarah watched over me like a hawk as I ate it, and she said I did well.'

It was welcome news and he tried to look pleased, but for her to regard shifting a drop of soup as a triumph. . . . Something was wrong. He knew it – he just knew there was something terribly wrong. Searchingly he stared into her face. The cheekbones were more pronounced, and her eyes seemed bigger than ever. She was still a beautiful woman, but was he imagining that she was closing her face against him? He'd been able to read it like an open book until these last few weeks.

'Are you in pain?' he asked suddenly. 'Is that what you're keeping from me? I'd rather know, love. If there's something hurting you, you must tell me, then I'll know what to do.'

She avoided his questioning gaze. 'And what *would* you do?' she asked gently.

'For a start get another doctor besides the one who's coming today. A whole battalion of 'em if necessary,' he said shortly. 'Is something giving you pain?'

She took hold of his hand. 'I feel no pain, love,' she said, and marvelled at her own capacity for deceit.

'Thank God for that!' he said heavily. 'Now this man who's coming; he has rooms on John Dalton Street, and he's some sort of top man at the Royal, so he should be able to sort you out. Have you written down the

foods that seem to suit you best, like I said? Has Alice
weighed you? Have you made a note of how heavy you
were before this lot started? It's easy to forget things if
he starts on about something different.'

'I've written everything down, just like you said, and
I'm all ready,' she soothed. 'I'll go up and get into bed
at a quarter past four. And Joshua, try not to worry.
Tell me what's going on in Manchester. Please, love.'

'Well, imports have picked up a bit, but bidding's still
high. Ralph's like a dog with two tails since he pulled
us out of the mire last week.'

'I'm sure he is,' agreed his mother quietly. 'But then,
you always said he was quick, didn't you?'

'Aye, he's quick, but I was thinking I mustn't give
him too much of a free hand just yet. He has an eye
for a quick profit, and I don't want folk saying the
firm of Joshua Schofield and Sons is straight as a die
– providing you watch your step with the youngest.'
He laughed to take the sting from his words, but he
meant them. 'He's been asking me again about taking
over Charlie's rooms. He says he'd like to be on the
spot like Charlie was, and then –

'*No!*' She interrupted him, two spots of colour standing
out on her cheeks like daubs from a child's paint-box.
'Don't let him, Joshua! Don't have him in there!'

He gave her a reproving little pat on the cheek. 'Steady
on, love. He'll be quite safe, you know, now there's a
night-watchman. He's keen on the idea, and I have to
admit it'd make sense.'

But she jumped up from her chair and began pacing
back and forth, 'I can't agree to it, Joshua. He's – he's
not old enough.'

'Hear me out,' he said, eyeing her in perplexity. 'I
was wondering if he could go to Mosley Street from
Monday morning till Friday afternoon, and sleep here
Friday, Saturday and Sunday nights. That'd be the best
of both worlds, wouldn't it? We could get Charlie's
cleaning woman in to see to his breakfasts, and he

could buy the rest of his meals wherever he wants. He
likes eating out, and there's no shortage of good food
in Manchester.'

She avoided his eyes and clenched her fists. 'No,' she
said flatly, 'I can't have it. I don't like the thought of
it. I can't see the necessity for it.'

'But I've told you it can be handy having a man
on the spot. Charlie used to pay a runner from the
Exchange, and another to bring word from the docks
when a new shipment was in. And he could always nip
off to Liverpool at short notice. Hey, what is it, love?
What have I said now?'

She had burst into tears at the word 'Liverpool', and
stood there with her hands clapped to her face. He stared
at her blankly. She'd never been one for weeping and
wailing. He knew what it was – lack of food! She needed
a few good meals inside her. 'Don't cry, love,' he urged.
'We'll leave it for now. Stay where you are – I'm going
to get you a drink of hot milk. You need nourishment,
that's what you need.'

Through her fingers she watched him leave the room.
She had almost replied, 'What I need is peace of mind,'
but of course she couldn't say it. She couldn't say half
the things that entered her head. She sat down again
and stared tensely into the fire. She didn't know how
long she could carry on like this. When she made the
decision to keep silent she had known it wouldn't be
easy to deceive Joshua. He might accept lies, because
she had never lied to him in all their married life and so
he didn't doubt her word; but he was alert, observant,
perceptive and he loved her. She'd expected difficulties
with him, she'd expected having to watch what she said,
and having to stop herself from shrinking when Ralph
came near her. What she hadn't expected was that
the strain of it all would lead to physical ailment –
if indeed strain was the cause of it. In the last week
or two she'd been wondering if perhaps she had a
cancer in her stomach. She'd heard of people with a

growth vomiting back their food at random, just like she did.

Her heart ached with love when he came back with a cup of hot milk on a tray. He always looked out of his element whenever he performed a domestic task. 'I'm sorry I was so silly,' she said calmly. 'I expect I'm a bit on edge about the doctor coming. I'll go up and get into bed as soon as I've drunk this.'

'Aye, that'll be best, love,' he said, and sat down at the other side of the fireplace. But the vivid blue eyes followed her every move, and he pulled at his whiskers without ceasing.

When the doctor came downstairs he led him at once into the study and eyed him with scant patience. 'Well, doctor? What do you make of her?'

The doctor laid his bill on Joshua's desk. 'At your convenience, Mr Schofield,' he murmured. 'Regarding your wife. She is a fine, healthy woman who is rapidly losing weight.'

'Yes, yes, I know that. But *why*? Do you know why?'

'I suspect ulceration of the stomach, a condition often brought on by an injudicious diet and the stress of a busy social life.'

'My wife doesn't have a busy social life, and until this lot started she ate moderately of good, nourishing food.'

'So she tells me. However, even the most temperate individuals have been known to develop ulcers in the stomach. It's to do with the digestive acids. I have left a diet sheet with your servant: bland foods containing little fibrous matter, no highly seasoned dishes, no overloading of the digestive tract.'

Joshua rocked back and forth on his heels and toes. 'She won't overload her digestive tract if she can barely get stuff down in the first place,' he said shortly. 'But we'll give it a try. Now, suppose you're wrong. What other diagnosis can you come up with?

The doctor smoothed his silver hair and stroked the soft leather gloves further down each finger. He didn't care for this Schofield. A bumptious self-made man, making a great to-do about his wife, who seemed to have little wrong with her. He didn't like his manner, either, it was lacking in deference. There would be no harm in shaking his confidence a little. 'I can come up with cancer of the stomach, or of the intestines, or of the gullet,' he said coolly. 'I can come up with a liver disorder, a nervous and depressive temperament, an indolent and inactive way of life that is not conducive to a regular evacuation of the bowels, to name but a few.' He was pleased to see the other's jaw tighten. 'But at this stage I incline to my first diagnosis. If your wife keeps strictly to the foods I suggest, daintily presented to tempt her appetite, I think you'll see an improvement. In any case I recommend another consultation in a fortnight's time.'

'Do you now? I'll see what I think of her in a week, never mind a fortnight. If there's no improvement I'll get another opinion.'

The doctor eyed him with barely concealed dislike. 'That is your privilege, Mr Schofield. I bid you good-day.'

'And good-day to you,' said Joshua grimly. 'Wait a minute, I'll settle your bill. I doubt if we'll meet again.' He laid two sovereigns on the desk, then marched to the door and called, 'Alice! Show the doctor to his carriage.'

Upstairs Rachel was propped against the pillows. 'You didn't like him,' she said, on seeing his face.

'I wasn't over-struck,' he admitted, 'but he seems to think his diet might help. What do you say?'

'I'll try it, of course,' she said brightly. 'And now I think I'll get dressed again.'

'Shall I call Alice?'

She smiled. 'No, you can lace me. You had enough practice when we were first married. Do you remember?'

He managed a laugh and it eased the sudden tightness in his throat.

'I'm not likely to forget. Let's have you, then.' It was no comfort to find that when tightened to the limit, her stays were still easy round the middle. 'That diet had better work,' he joked, 'or you'll cost me a fortune in new stays.'

The bedroom door burst open and Sarah rushed in, halting in amazement at the sight of her mother in her shimmy, with her father fastening her stays. 'Oh! Sorry!' She didn't leave the room, but grabbed Rachel's wrap and hustled her into it.'Quick, Papa! Edward's downstairs!'

'Well, what of it? We've just had a specialist here to examine your mother, in case you're interested. And what of the sick-bay, might I ask?'

Sarah's eyes brimmed with all-too-ready tears. 'I forgot about the specialist. I'm sorry, Papa. What did he say?'

'He's put me on a diet, love,' said Rachel calmly. 'I'll tell you about it later. Now, has Polly walked home with you and Edward? You know what your father and I said about that.'

Sarah did an irate little dance, feet stamping and hands wagging. 'No she didn't. I had to leave her in charge. Edward came into the mill just before five. He's got something to ask you, Papa. Oh, please go down now. He's desperate to speak to you.'

'All right. Calm down. I'm on my way.' Guessing what was coming, he kissed his daughter and gave her a squeeze, wishing he could feel more enthusiasm. It was hard to feel enthusiastic about anything at the moment, except possibly his wife in her pale pink shimmy.

As the door closed behind him Sarah flung her arms round her mother. 'He's asked me to marry him! Right away! He's accepted a marvellous contract in a little place to the north of Carlisle. Oh, do say you're pleased! We'll be moving around for the first year or two and then he's going to set up his own establishment and employ people. Isn't it wonderful, Mama?'

'It's – very exciting,' agreed Rachel slowly. 'But how soon is "right away"?'

'In three or four weeks.' Sarah whirled round the room, and catching sight of herself in the mirror, rushed to the door. 'I'm going to change into my pink velvet for when he's finished talking to Papa.'

'We'll need to meet his family,' warned Rachel. 'And your father will want to know about his prospects and whether he can support a wife.'

'You need have no worries about that! He's going to earn huge commissions and we'll end up in a magnificent house and have four beautiful children.'

Rachel had flopped down on the bedside chair. 'Sarah, come here a minute. Come to me.' She used the tone that all her children recognised, and Sarah ran to her at once. 'Listen, my pet, this is a big decision, and not to be rushed. We like Edward, but we don't really know a lot about him, do we? Do you feel he'll be a good husband to you and a good father to your children? Do you think he'll look after you? Does he – does he love you as much as you love him?'

'Of course he does, Mama! He's not a youth – he's almost thirty; a man of the world, a man of business. He says he's been waiting all his life for someone like me.'

Rachel looked down at her daughter and felt her heart thud with heavy, chest-shaking strokes. They were going to lose her. That was right and proper and only to be expected; it was good, as long as they lost her to the right man. She liked Edward, but he was very different from Joshua, or James, or Sam. . . . And was she herself fit to organise a wedding, physically fit? 'I've always looked forward to planning your wedding at leisure, love, not trying to fix up a rushed affair, as this would have to be. And in summer, not the depths of winter. . . .'

'Oh, fiddle! I don't care about any of that as long as it's quick. Papa will agree, won't he?'

'I don't know, but we'll soon find out.' She sent Sarah off with a hug, but remained seated limply in the chair. If she did indeed have a growth in her stomach, a quick wedding would at least let her see Sarah married. She would still be strong enough to supervise other people, to give orders. She could force herself to the Manchester shops to buy Sarah what she needed – her wedding gown, and maybe a fur-lined cloak like Esther's to wear over it, and warm clothes for the northern winter. And Joshua would be finding out right now about Edward's prospects. . . .

Instinct had put him behind his big desk. There had been little to surprise him in Edward's request except the proposed date of the wedding. 'Steady on, that's less than a month away,' he protested. 'We've not even met your parents yet!' He was pleased to see the younger man nervous, his hands never still for a second. And what hands – slender as a woman's, with long, manicured nails. Joshua breathed out heavily. He'd have preferred a Lancashire man to a dandy like this one, but you couldn't order who your daughter fell for.

Edward looked steadfastly at the broad figure behind the desk. He never made the mistake of underestimating Sarah's father. His achievements announced a keen and agile brain, and those eyes of his were like two damned razors, cutting through the careful little stratagems he employed to ease his way through life. 'My parents say they'll be delighted to welcome you and Mrs Schofield at any time convenient to you. They haven't as yet met Sarah, so perhaps we could all travel to Hampshire together?'

Joshua pulled at his whiskers. 'My wife isn't up to that kind of journey at present, Edward, but happen I could go without her, or maybe send Sam in my place. He thinks like me, does Sam.'

Oh yes, he would. Sam the big-head, Sarah's self-appointed bodyguard, would make sure he thought like the man who controlled the moneybags. Thank God he hadn't got the pair of them to deal with – one was quite sufficient.

'Let's get down to facts and figures,' went on Joshua. 'Sarah will get a marriage settlement from her mother and me, and she has means of her own, money that's been banked for her over the years; in addition to that she has a recent legacy. I daresay she's told you all this?'

'Yes, but only in general terms.'

'Well, I can be quite specific, if we get as far as that.' Joshua was reading a page of notes. 'Do you love my daughter?' he asked, and looked up suddenly from under his brows.

God, that was cunning. A good thing he was on his guard. Edward gazed straight into the shrewd eyes and spoke up earnestly, even managing a slight hoarseness to add weight to his words. 'I love her with all my heart, sir.'

The old fella sighed, perhaps in relief. 'Aye, well, you can cut out the "sir". "Mr Schofield" will do for now. Let's hear about your finances, your long-term plans. I couldn't let Sarah go to a man who hasn't got his future mapped out.'

Expecting that, Edward handed over two closely written pages. 'Here are details of my earnings, and a forecast of what I'll be doing in the next two years. At the end of that time I want to set up my own business establishment, maybe in Manchester or Birmingham; by then I'll be in a position to buy a sizeable house instead of renting, and we'll make it our permanent home.'

Joshua waved a hand. 'Sit back in your chair while I read this lot. If it's satisfactory I'll go up and have a word with her mother, and you can go and wait in the little sitting-room across the hall. I daresay Sarah's in there now, dancing with impatience. But I warn you, at this stage I'll be able to give you no more than qualified approval.'

Edward relaxed a little. The old fella wouldn't be able to fault his figures. He might be no genius as an architect, but he knew how to build from a good design, and how to run a building site. Sarah was as good as up the aisle, as good as in his bed – his first silver-blonde. The very thought of it made him shift restlessly in his seat. He'd never waited for any woman as long as he'd waited for her. The frustration of it was costing him good money in Manchester. Not that he was splashing out on any threesomes; Lottie, Bernice and Angelique were a rare treat these days. If he was to buy an engagement ring that would satisfy old razor-eyes here he must economise. . . .

In the bedroom Rachel was getting into her dress. Joshua sat himself on the bed and watched as she buttoned up her bodice. 'I haven't said yes or no, yet,' he reported. 'On paper his prospects are excellent, and you recall I heard good reports on him from the new management board of the infirmary. He says his parents have asked us down to Hampshire at our convenience, and there's no doubt they're in love, is there? What do you think about the date they're after?'

'It's so soon, Joshua, so quick.' She was fastening the ribbons of her lace cap. and by a trick of the gaslight her eyes were suddenly invisible in their sockets and her teeth showed and glinted, giving her face the appearance of a skull. He drew in his breath and then sighed with relief as she turned fully to the light and stared absently across the room. 'I'd like to see her married,' she said quietly.

For once speech deserted him. The implication of her words was clear: she thought she wouldn't be here to see it if the wedding was long delayed. He jumped up and took her in his arms, shaken to find himself unable to reassure her. God in heaven, what ailed him? What ailed her, that she could even hint at such a thing? What ailed them both that they should let it lie between them, unquestioned? In that instant he decided to allow the wedding, but he didn't tell her so. He just held her close and kissed her gently on the mouth.

'I'm not going to Hampshire without you,' he said, 'so what do you say to sending Sam? We could tell him what to look out for, and he could travel down with them both to keep it all proper and correct.' He put a finger under her chin and tipped her head back. 'And could we manage to arrange a wedding in less than a month? Are you up to it?'

'It will do me good,' she said firmly, 'and take my mind off my ailments. But let's not rush into a decision. Can you tell them you'll give final permission when they get back from Hampshire?'

'Yes, that'll be best.' He made for the door. 'No final consent. Just a qualified "yes" at this stage.'

'Joshua, is Sam back yet?'

'No. Don't worry, I'll tell him. He'll want us to put the brakes on, I shouldn't wonder. Are you having your tea up here?'

'No. I want us all at the table together. Except for James, of course.' Their eyes met and he gave a little sigh. They missed their eldest son, and weren't easy in their minds about him.

There was a knock at the door and Ralph came in, immaculate as ever and with his remarkable eyes swivelling from one to the other. 'Father,' he said, inclining his head politely, 'and Mother. I'm wondering if you've had chance to discuss my moving to Mosley Street?'

Lips compressed, Rachel observed him in silence, and Joshua lifted a hand, palm outwards. 'We're a bit busy at the moment, Ralph, but your mother's not so keen on the idea. I think we'll leave it for a week or two.'

Ralph turned his wide blue gaze on Rachel. 'Do you have any particular objections, Mother?'

She turned away. 'I'm not in favour, Ralph. I cannot approve. Leave it at that.'

The lips tightened over the perfect teeth. 'I am not a child,' he said quietly, 'to be forbidden what I want on a whim. I'm doing a man's work in a man's world. I demand to know the reason.'

She whirled to face him. 'Do you indeed? Well, I have a reason but I don't choose to enlarge on it, that's all.'

'Leave it for now,' said Joshua heavily. 'We have other things on our minds at the moment. Edward has asked for your sister's hand.'

'Really? With momentous events like that to discuss I can't expect you to waste time on my concerns, then.'

'That'll do, Ralph. Your mother isn't well. We've had a specialist attending her here at the house only an hour ago.'

Ralph stood there, eyes lowered. 'I'd quite forgotten that, I'm afraid. I'm terribly sorry.' He went to Rachel and kissed her cheek. 'I trust he can help you, Mother.'

She remained quite still and made no reply, while Joshua watched them both in perplexity. What was wrong with the pair of them, standing there like a couple of statues? The lad looked as if he'd been knocked on the head with a mallet. Well, he must learn he couldn't have everything his own way, though to be fair Rachel was being a bit sharp with him. She wasn't herself, of course. Why, she'd spent the last eighteen years trying to get close to this one; yet when he kissed her of his own accord she never moved a muscle.

When Ralph had gone he saw that she was very pale. 'You're tired, love. Why, you're all of a tremble. Look, hadn't you better have a word with Alice and Hannah about this diet?'

'I'll speak to them, Joshua. Stop worrying. Listen, is that Sam's voice?'

'Aye. I'll go and catch him before he sees Sarah.'

*   *   *

Edward had left the house to go and write letters, and the family were all at table. Sarah in her pink velvet was rosy-cheeked and talkative, but ignoring Sam. Ralph was even quieter than usual, his gaze rarely leaving his mother, who was pale and quite composed. Sam was picking at his food, something unheard-of, and at the head of the table Joshua cleared his plate in the manner of one of his own boilermen stoking the boilers – performing a necessary task with efficiency but little enjoyment. All at once Sarah stopped chattering. It had dawned on her that she was the only one overflowing with joy. 'This is the happiest day of my life,' she said defiantly, 'and I was hoping you'd all feel the same.'

Rachel leaned across and patted her wrist. 'We're just getting used to the idea, love.'

'It isn't decided, anyway,' said Sam belligerently. 'It would be far better for Edward to move up north and get settled, and then you could have your wedding in the spring or early summer, if you're still of the same mind.'

'I'm sorry you feel it's a bit rushed,' said Sarah unrepentantly. 'I shall miss you all like anything, and Saltley as well. Only the other day I was in Soar Park, thinking how lovely it was in the dell. . . .'

They all stared at her, slightly puzzled, but Sam put his knife and fork down on top of his unfinished meal, and gave an odd little smile. An awkward silence descended on the room, and Joshua looked round at them all, his spirits falling lower by the minute. His family, the lovely close-knit family he was so proud of – he was damned if it wasn't falling apart.

Sam spoke, and his attitude had changed. 'I think we're all a bit on edge at the speed of it, Funny-face. Let's look forward to that trip to Hampshire, and hold ourselves ready for a winter wedding.' Brother and sister exchanged looks, and she wrinkled her nose at him in the way that always used to mean they were thinking as one. If they were, Sam told himself soberly, it was for the first time since she met Edward Mayfield.

After the meal Joshua took him to the study and then paced restlesly in front of the fire. 'You're the only one I'd send in my place, Sam, but I must know you won't let your love for your sister bias you against the Mayfields. Can you reassure me on that?'

'I'll do my best to be impartial,' Sam told him. 'You can trust me on it.'

Joshua nodded, but eyed him curiously. 'What's the significance of the dell in Soar Park, then?'

Sam had to smile. Did he ever miss anything? 'Once, when we were walking there, I promised her I wouldn't raise objections to the man she chose to marry. You see, she knew that to some extent I spoiled things for James by finding fault with Esther. She mentioned the dell to remind me of that promise.'

Joshua halted in his pacing and flapped at his coat-tails. Should he tell Sam that he might well have been right about Esther? Their eyes met, and he knew he didn't need to say a word. Sam was perceptive. He'd been the only one of them not to be taken in by her. If there was anything amiss with Edward or his family he would spot it, and what was more he'd promised to be unbiased. Aye, he could breathe easy on the matter – for now. 'It's more of a rush job than I'd have liked,' he said, 'but what's the alternative? Having her going into a decline, or throwing one long tantrum till the spring?' He gazed into the fire. 'And then there's your mother. If she doesn't pick up a bit, or even gets worse, it'd happen be best if she sees Sarah married while she's still able to be in charge of things.'

Sam stared at him while the bile of sudden dread rose in his throat. 'You think it's bad, don't you?' he asked hoarsely. 'You think she might die. Why?' His voice rose. 'What's going on that I don't know about?'

'Nothing,' snapped Joshua. 'Keep your hair on.' How could he tell the lad that for a second his mother's face had taken on the look of a skull, a death's head? It had been his imagination, hadn't it? 'There *is* something wrong,' he admitted. 'I feel it in my bones, and I feel it in here,' he thumped his chest. 'I don't know what it is, and I'm damned if that fancy doctor knows, either. I've already got another chap in mind if she's no better by Christmas.

'Now, about Edward and his family. Weigh things up a bit, will you? On a journey of that length you'll have chance to see how he treats her, because I've no doubt he's been on his best behaviour in front of your mother and me. As for his parents, see what sort of folk they are, whether they're the same as us in their outlook and such. I've put down in black and white what she'll be worth in monetary terms. It goes without saying she's beyond price as a future wife and mother.

'Edward's nearly thirty, so it's not for his father to say yea or nay to the match, but as a courtesy we should let him know what Sarah would bring to the marriage; equally, as a courtesy to us he should tell you what Edward is worth, or at the very least what his expectations are. I'm not completely easy about contemplating such a rush job, so I think it prudent to tell them that her capital will come as only income for the first year or two, rather than as lump sums made over to Edward. Now, I'll give you a proper letter of introduction and authority. You know how I think and act, so conduct yourself in the same way, will you, on my behalf?'

'You can rely on me, Father. One thing has occurred to me. If it does come to a wedding, perhaps we'd all feel better if she took a personal maid with her.'

Joshua shot him a look. 'Oh aye? I'm not sure whether Edward's earnings will run to a lady's maid.'

'I was thinking I'd stand the cost of her.'

'If anybody but her husband stands the cost it'll be me,' Joshua assured him. 'It's a good idea, Sam. Have you any more where that came from?'

'Yes. I thought Polly might take the job. She's bright enough to pick up what's needed, and she's devoted to Sarah.'

Joshua smiled for the first time that day. 'You use it for something else besides putting your hat on,' he said.

Edward was in high spirits. Things were going his way with a vengeance, apart from an awkward spell on the journey when bodyguard Sam noticed him watching a pretty serving maid, and five minutes later a stylish woman in a black hat. He'd soon learned to keep his eyes only on Sarah, and after all, that was no penance. Her looks were amazing, even if it palled a bit when she kept agreeing with his every word. To give the bodyguard his due, he'd been pleasant enough, keeping in the background and following meekly behind them both when they changed trains or waited for a coach.

His parents had been so stunned by Sarah's looks and sunny nature, and by her blond muscle-man brother, that they'd ignored the accents and were grovelling in five minutes flat. Then when the old man read Papa Schofield's list of her assets – whew! Too bad his own didn't stand comparison: a hundred a year from Great Uncle George, a marriage settlement of three hundred from his father, and a couple of fields and a coppice to come when the old goat shuffled his coil. But at least his professional future looked bright. If he'd had no prospects there old Schofield would without doubt have given him short shrift. Still, he mustn't take Sam's approval for granted. He had the feeling that a brain lurked under all that muscle and good humour.

As for Sam, he watched and assessed and, as his father had requested, weighed things up a bit. The house was about the size of Meadowbank, but old, with a distinct, beautiful style; built in 1702, they'd told him, on the fringe of this small village not far from Wimborne. It was an area that to him seemed warm and lush and cosily genteel after the clamour of Saltley and the great limestone hills of the Pennines. The inside of the house was comfortable enough, but faded and a trifle shabby, and what they put on the table wouldn't have impressed anybody at home. Mr and Mrs Mayfield were old, far older than his own parents, but he'd expected as much because Edward was the youngest of six. It was obvious they thought themselves far above any Lancastrian, but Sarah had them eating out of her hand in no time. They were minor landowners and proud of it, and Edward had told him with a shrug that his father had never had to work for his living. They were what in Saltley would be called landed gentry. Well – it took all sorts.

He'd been keen to see how they dealt with their son. There was none of the easy affection of home, but then there wasn't much of it at the Boultons' or the Fairbrothers', for that matter. He detected an element of surprise in their treatment of Edward, and concluded it must be because he'd been lucky enough to find somebody like Sarah. As for Edward's attitude to them, he was extremely polite to his mother, and deferred to his father on everything. Respect was there, at any rate. Years ago he'd heard somebody say, 'If you want to see how a man will treat his wife after ten years of marriage, watch how he treats his parents.' If that were a reliable guide, Edward would be polite and considerate to Sarah, but with his true feelings hidden. Was that enough? He looked across the room at them both, and found it surprisingly easy to picture them married. They were holding hands, and she was gazing at Edward with open adoration. He sighed. Her judgement was suspended, maybe for good, her critical faculties non-existent.

In fairness, he could take no adverse report back to his father, but he could, and by God he would, warn the future husband. The opportunity came when Edward asked him out for a stroll around the village. Leaving Sarah indoors talking to Mrs Mayfield, they walked together in pale, watery sunshine. Edward tackled the subject at once. 'Well, Sam, what's the verdict to be? Do I get the seal of approval?'

'I can hardly refuse it, though I don't deny I'd have liked a longer wait. It's plain to see she thinks the world of you.'

'And I think the world of her. She's beautiful, she's virtuous, she has a lovely nature, and she's not without means. What more could I ask?'

At least he was honest about her money . . . 'What indeed? I'll make a report to my father, and it'll be for him to decide. But for myself, I want to warn you.'

Edward was two inches the taller, and he stretched up to take full advantage of them. The bodyguard took himself so seriously. He almost smiled, and then caught the blaze of the Schofield eyes. Good God, it was like looking at the father! 'Be good to her,' said Sam quietly. 'Be good to her and be faithful to her. She's never been away from home before, and everything will be strange and new for her. She's innocent, you know, innocent as a child, and she's good, truly good. If you hurt her in any way whatsoever – mentally, physically or emotionally – you'll have me to deal with.'

Take it with good grace, Edward warned himself; pat him on the arm and reassure him with a carefully chosen word, but for the life of him he couldn't summon one. There was something menacing about the younger man, and for a moment he was so intimidated he had to force himself not to step backwards. Threats seemed absurdly out of place as they stood next to the little village green, and he gave an uncomfortable twitch of the shoulders. In the end he managed a solemn nod of the head. 'You don't need to threaten, Sam,' he said with dignity. 'I'll look after her, of course I will. I love her. I'll guard her with my life.'

'Just see that you do,' said Sam, 'or I'll make sure you regret it for the rest of your days.'

CHAPTER SEVENTEEN

Departures

THE DOCTOR DREW MARTHA away from her mother's bed and spoke with brisk compassion. 'She's in a bad way,' he confirmed. 'Congestion of the lungs, pneumonia, call it what you will she's full of fluid, and made the worse by not being able to move without help. It's warm enough in here, but has she been out in the cold?'

'Yes. She would do it – she insisted. It was me weddin' day last Saturday. But we wrapped her up in everythin' we could lay our hands on.'

The doctor sighed. 'Blankets and wraps are no protection against breathing in the cold air,' he explained wearily. 'She's taken a chill deep inside her, in the lungs. You've poulticed her, I suppose?'

'Yes, three times a day, an' rubbed her chest with goose grease and camphorated oil. I've given her horehound as well.' She didn't mention the sweaty stocking she'd wrapped round her mother's neck in the night, having heard that doctors scorned such remedies.

'Send round at dinner-time and I'll make up a bottle for her. It should at least ease her breathing. Keep her propped up and don't let her get cold again. Give her plenty to drink if she'll take it, and Christmas Eve or no, I'll call on her tomorrow. What about your father here? He's all right, is he?'

'It's me uncle, an' he's not poorly, just worried about me mam. They've always been close. His mind comes and goes, like. Doctor, will she get better?'

'I have my doubts, lass. Time will tell, and good nursing. Dose her with the medicine, and move her

around a bit, if you can. Her fever's high, and I don't
doubt she'll reach a crisis before Christmas morning.
If she comes through that she'll recover, but don't set
store on it.' He looked curiously at Martha's child-like
form and young-old face. 'Just wed, you say? You could
have wished for a better start to married life than having
your mother in this state.'

She blushed slightly. The start to her married life
had been all she'd ever dreamed of, except in one
small respect and that only a few words unsaid. Her
wedding night had been the only one not interrupted
by her mother: now she had to sleep on the makeshift
at the other side of the hearth, and was away from her
looms as well as the marriage bed. 'At least we have a
wage comin' in,' she said. 'Me husband's at Jericho, the
same as me.'

The doctor made for the door and turned to observe
her. She was a mere slip of a thing, but then the little
ones were often the most hardy. 'Rest whenever you
can,' he advised, 'and keep an eye on your uncle.'

'I've been keepin' an eye on him for years,' said
Martha heavily. 'And thanks, doctor.'

She went back to the bed in the wall alcove. After a
lifetime of being chivvied by her mother's tongue she
felt almost bereft to hear no more than the odd hoarse
word. The bubbly rasp of her breathing sounded loud
in the silent room, and Martha sank to the bedside stool
and took hold of the hot, dry hand. 'I'm here, Mam,'
she said quietly. 'Do you think you could manage a
drink?'

The eyelids opened a fraction and the knobbled fingers
squeezed hers. 'Tea,' came the weak whisper.

Martha pressed the kettle into the fire and fetched
the teapot and the caddy. 'Do you want one as well,
Uncle Jack?'

'It's me sister, you know,' he informed her earnestly.
'Me sister Annie. Her tongue's a bit sharp but she looks
after me, does Annie.'

'While I stand and watch, I suppose,' thought Martha, and then reproached herself. It was no use getting annoyed when he was just as worried as she was, sitting there on the edge of his chair and plucking at his blessed buttons. She gave him a cup of tea and began spoon-feeding some to her mother. 'Come on, Mam, try and take a sip or two. The doctor says you must drink.'

'I think I'll have a nap,' said Mrs Spencer faintly. 'I'm that sleepy.'

'All right. I'll wipe your face and hands with the flannel. There, is that better?'

For an instant the bright spark of her mother's spirit showed in the once-sharp eyes, and then the transparent lids came down. 'It's me own fault, you warned me,' she acknowledged hoarsely, 'but I did want to see you wed. You looked that bonny in your pink shawl. An' listen, don't bother to send to Rochdale. They'll know soon enough.'

'Mam, what do you mean? I've already sent word to our Bella. She'll be here first thing in the morning, I expect.'

Her mother tutted with the old impatience, then turned to other matters. 'You're a good girl the way you've looked after me,' she mumbled, 'an' you've landed a good 'un in Matthew. Not many would've took on me an' our Jack when they got wed.'

Martha closed her eyes for an instant, stung by longing to hear her husband's soft-toned speech, to feel the touch of his fingers on her wrist. She hadn't long to wait – he'd be home just after twelve. She heaved her mother's frail form higher against her pillows; then she recalled her sitting swathed in wraps in the invalid chair, demanding a kiss for the first time in years, almost as if she'd known the outing to be the beginning of her end. . . .

The twisted fingers tightened on hers. 'Look after our Jack, won't you? He needs a firm hand now and again, but look after him.'

'Of course I will. Don't worry, Mam.'

The bubbling sound issued more loudly from her mother's chest, and all at once she let out a strident cry. 'Where's Mrs Woods's beddin', then? I promised it for three o'clock! An' Mr Bennet's towels? You'll have to take 'em round before you have your tea!'

Martha sighed. She was rambling again, back in the days when she took in washing. She patted the hot hand and eased a spoonful of warm tea between the dry lips. Behind her Uncle Jack rocked back and forth on his high-backed chair. 'I'm not on the wet shift, Annie,' he assured his sister dreamily. 'You'll have no wet clothes from me today.'

Martha looked at the clock. Only thirty-five minutes before Matthew came through the door. She could stand the two of them talking rubbish for that length of time. She could stand it for a full day, as long as he came home at the end of it. . . .

It was two o'clock in the morning, and Matthew was alone with Mrs Spencer. Uncle Jack was upstairs, muttering and groaning in his sleep, and Martha was in their bed, fully dressed under the covers. Before midnight he'd been making up the fire for her while she tried to stay awake in the wicker chair, and on a sudden impulse he picked her up in his arms and marched with her to the stairs. 'Bed!' he said. 'I'll sit with her, and call 'ee should there be any change.'

In spite of her exhaustion Martha had thought for one wild moment that he was carrying her upstairs to make love, but it was obvious such a thing had never crossed his mind. He laid her on the bed fully clothed, put the stone hot-bottle to her feet and covered her with the bedclothes. 'Do 'ee sleep, Martha. I'll see to her.'

Whoever heard of such a thing? Men didn't sit up with old women who might be about to breathe their last. 'You can't, Matthew,' she protested. 'She might need changin'. She's wettin' the bed.'

He nodded calmly, as if such things were well within his experience. 'I'll come for 'ee if that happens,' he said.

Thoughts stumbled through her tired mind. She'd never heard any of the weavers mention a husband who would lose his sleep to sit up with a sick mother-in-law. Matthew was different – so very, very different, and she was a mad fool to imagine he would make love to her with her mother at death's door in the room below; but oh, when they came together it was wonderful. Three times it had happened in less than a week, and each better than the last as they learned each other's needs.

She watched him with her tired eyes, and he bent and kissed her on the mouth. He was touched when she kissed him back with passion. Whoever would have thought her to be so loving? Plain, prim little Martha was blooming and blossoming with the pleasure of the marriage bed, in spite of her mother being so poorly. As for him, his clean, virginal little wife had banished for ever his misgivings about the act of love, because with her it was sweet and clean and altogether wholesome. The sordid unions he had witnessed in his youth might never have been. He tucked the blanket under her chin, blew out the candle and left her to her rest.

Now it was two o'clock in the morning, and he moistened Mrs Spencer's dry lips. The faded eyes opened slowly and stared hazily into his, and he caught his breath. He'd seen it before, that creeping of the upper and lower lids over the white of the eye, leaving only the iris visible. His mother-in-law was slipping away, with the fever still unbroken. On impulse he bent and kissed the thin cheek, then hurried upstairs for Martha. As they returned to the bed a rattling sound issued from the invalid's throat, and then all became silent and the busy tongue was stilled for ever.

'She's gone, Martha,' he said simply, and held out his arms, expecting tears.

But Martha was trying to conceal a shocking emotion. Shame made her face burn, and he observed her flushed cheeks with puzzlement. She buried her face against his chest, but the tears didn't come. God forgive her, all she could feel was relief! Silently she accepted it, and the guilt it brought. 'Bella will get here too late,' she said at last, 'and so I must lay her out on my own. She's always said we mustn't let anybody else do it. She's so thin, you see, like a little bag of bones. Leave me with her, will you, Matthew?'

She had barely finished when they heard Uncle Jack moving around his bedroom. Martha jumped up. 'We must warn him. Sometimes he comes down in the night. He might walk in an' see her.'

They found the old man climbing into his trousers by the light of a candle, using his one hand with the skill of long practice. 'Where are we off to, then?' he asked.

'What do you mean, Uncle? We're not goin' anywhere.'

'Annie's just been in an' said it's time we were off. "Come on, Jack", she said, "it's time to be goin'."'

The young ones exchanged a baffled stare. 'When was this?' asked Martha uneasily.

'A few minutes back,' he said impatiently. 'She walked in an' stood by the bed. I did wonder how ever she'd managed the stairs.'

Martha's pale cheeks glistened like wax. 'Uncle,' she said carefully, 'I think that must have been a dream. I'm sorry, but she died half an hour ago. I've just laid her out. Would you like to come and see her?'

The old man pushed past them and clattered down the dark stairs. They found him standing over his sister, patting the small hands that lay folded on her breast. They'd been prepared for his grief, but instead found full acceptance. 'She looks right peaceful,' he said approvingly. 'I think I'll sit with her for a bit '

Matthew pulled forward the long wicker chair. Uncle Jack sat in it and once again laid his hand on his sister's. 'I'm all right,' he said, 'don't worry on my account. I'll

just stay an' keep her company. You can both go to
your bed if you want.'

They hesitated in the doorway as he settled to his
vigil, the glow of the fire illuminating his fuzz of white
hair and the little lace cap that at last stayed firmly in
place on Mrs Spencer's head. 'She'd like a prayer from
the minister,' he said with certainty. 'Will you be askin'
him to call in?'

Martha nodded. 'We can't do much till it's daylight,
Uncle.'

'No. Well, off you go to your bed, then.' His manner
was so natural, his tone so laden with quiet authority that
they turned and went thankfully up the stairs, leaving
brother and sister sharing the firelight as they'd done
countless times over the years. Once in bed all thought
of lovemaking left Martha, and she turned to Matthew's
arms solely for comfort. She felt she should cry, but
the tears were locked away beneath the weight of that
deep relief.

They would have overslept but for the knocker-up at
quarter to five. Martha leapt out of bed and tapped a
response on the window, then grabbed her shawl. 'I'll
see how Uncle Jack is,' she said, 'and then get your
shavin' water.'

She found the fire very low and the candle guttering
in its holder, but Uncle Jack was still patiently holding
her mother's hand. 'It's gone cold in here, Uncle,' she
said guiltily. 'I should have given you a blanket to wrap
round you.'

He made no reply, and she decided to wake him when
she'd made a hot drink. Then by the flicker of the candle
she saw his open eyes, and the contented little smile that
was too set to be natural. 'Uncle,' she said fearfully, and
felt his hand. It was icy cold, like her mother's.

'Matthew!' she called. 'Matthew, come quick!'

He ran down barechested, and at once took in what
had happened. Gently he closed Uncle Jack's eyes. 'She
told him it was time to be goin', didn't she?' he said.

Martha stood there unmoving in her nightgown and shawl. How often had she felt the care of them pulling at her, dragging her down? It was funny, but her mother had been less trouble in the dying than she'd been in the living, summoning her brother to go with her. And he had slipped away content, if the little smile was any guide. She looked at the two of them so peacefully hand in hand in the faint light of the candle, and felt the burden of guilty relief slacken and ease. The worry of years was washed away as tears stung her eyes, and she opened her mouth wide to let out the first anguished sound of her grief.

It was Saturday, the afternoon of New Year's Eve, and Saltley Infirmary was on view to the public before the official opening by Lord Soar. The fund-raising committee would be there to examine the fruits of their labours; after a busy morning in the shop Tizzie was preparing to leave Barney in charge.

It was a fine clear day, though bitterly cold, but being in full mourning there was no question as to what she must wear. Stepping into her best crinoline petticoat she told herself that without doubt Edward would be there with his new fiancée, so it was a pity she couldn't wear the green velvet. It was her most elegant day dress, and if it had revived memories for him of that assignation in Manchester then well and good, because it might have caused him a moment's remorse. . . . She put on her heavy black gown and went in search of her mother to fasten it up the back, remembering Edward's impatience as he fumbled with the tiny buttons and loops of the green velvet. No doubt he would instruct the 'malleable' Sarah to wear front-fastening gowns for speed of removal.

Maria was writing in the living room, and slipped her papers into a linen folder when Tizzie walked in. She fastened her daughter's dress and then bent to pull the skirts into place. 'I might be out when you get back,' she said.

Tizzie gaped in astonishment. Her mother had left

the house only twice since the funeral, to attend her
daughter's wedding and to spend Christmas Day with
the newly-weds. 'Where are you going, Mother?'

'Oh, here and there,' said Maria vaguely. 'You
know, looking around. It's time I went out into the
world again.'

Tizzie hid her relief. Signs of normality at last! 'Well
done, Mother,' she said with a smile. Life might even
become enjoyable at some distant date, with Edward
out of Saltley and her mother as she used to be,
clear-headed and energetic. She gave her a searching
look. 'You won't go far, will you, as it's your first
outing since the funeral?'

A faint, almost derisive smile touched her mother's
mouth. 'I'm going out and about in the town, Tizzie, not
on an expedition into the unknown. Don't be stupid.'

Tizzie flipped at her skirts and left the room. So
much for the broken heart, she told herself, crushing an
upsurge of yearning for the mother she'd known before
her father died, the one who had been so proud of her,
who had really cared whether or not Edward asked her
to marry him.

But had that robust affection been real? She tied the
ribbons of her bonnet and examined her reflection. Did
she perhaps resemble the rapist? Was that the reason
for the gulf between them? Or was it that with her
father dead it was no longer necessary for her mother
to pretend a fondness that had never been?

She folded her lips in a straight, obstinate line and
went down to the shop. It was free of customers, so
Barney was down in the cellar, rearranging the countless
pots and pans and blankets of the poor. Tizzie had
hired an assistant for him, a boy of twelve; between
them they were moving the ill-lit jumble to a series of
orderly shelves and compartments. They had even, for
a time, banished the fleas.

Pulling her skirts to one side she went down the newly
built stairs. No longer did Barney ascend and descend

through a trapdoor. It had seemed to her demeaning that her second-in-command should emerge from a hole in the floor like a rodent, and now he was able to move with dignity from cellar to shop and back again. 'I want to thank you, Miss Tizzie,' he said when the carpenters had finished their task a week earlier. 'I had no complaints working for your father, but this is more than I ever dreamed of. I hope to show my appreciation by the way I work, an' such.'

She hadn't told him that it eased her mind to see his stunted form move smoothly on the shallow stairs, and smiled to think that at this rate she would soon be running neck and neck with Joshua Schofield in the good employer stakes.

Now, Barney ran forward with the lamp. 'You're off, Miss Tizzie,' he said, observing her bonnet and warm cloak with unreadable dark eyes. 'Me an' Albert are gettin' on with things down here while it's quiet.'

'It's looking better already,' she said, 'and I hope you'll find it easier to manage. I don't know what time I'll be back. If it gets late I'll call a cab rather than wait to be brought home by the Waltons, because we might get busy after tea.'

He fidgeted needlessly with a pile of dingy lace curtains. 'I expect Mr Mayfield will be congratulated at the openin',' he said quietly. 'They say it's a grand place, an' he's been in charge of it all.'

'Yes, that's true,' she said, eyeing him curiously.

His shapely hands pressed so hard on the edge of the low table that the tips of his fingers turned white. 'Uh – I've heard as how he's engaged to be married to young Miss Schofield,' he said, elaborately unconcerned.

So that was it. He was worried she might not know of it. 'Yes, I've heard that as well,' she said gently, 'but thanks, Barney.' She could never have explained to anyone why she felt so close to the man. Pity for his stunted shape was no part of her regard, nor was the fact that he was indispensable to the business. It was to do with the way he cared for her feelings. Throughout her entire life nobody, not even Mary, had ever credited her with the softness of a woman. She accepted that the blame for it rested on her; she had always been strong and self-sufficient, scorning the female wiles of tears and pretty pleading and helplessness. But in the last few weeks she had sensed that Barney saw beneath the surface. What he saw she didn't know – she herself wasn't all that sure what was there – but she knew he cared. And in return, she cared about him.

After much thought, she had bought him a Christmas present, a shirt of fine cream-coloured cotton that she'd had made with specially short sleeves, and when he turned up for work on Christmas Eve, he had brought her a posy of ivy and bright variegated holly. Afterwards, he had thanked her carefully for the shirt, and told her he had worn it on Christmas Day. She didn't ask how he had spent Christmas – it would have breached the bounds of their mutual reserve – but she wondered if he'd been alone in his two rooms at the top of Rope Street. Now she turned to climb the stairs again. 'You'll keep an ear open in case my mother should call you? She's going out on her own, later.'

'I'll listen,' he assured her. 'Don't worry, I'll see to things here.'

Tizzie went to watch for the Waltons' carriage. It was a relief to find only Bessie the Barrel sitting inside, because her husband was a nuisance. Since the night of the ball he had lost no opportunity of brushing against her, or openly laying a fatherly hand behind her waist and then digging his fingertips into the small of her back. It was laughable really, except that his wife might turn nasty if he made it too obvious.

He had even sent the odd sexual signal, yawning and elaborately covering his mouth with two fingers stiff and pointing upwards, or putting both hands behind his fat little rump and thrusting out his pelvis. All with a calm, faraway look in his eye, but darting furtive glances to see if she comprehended. She gave him only innocent smiles and puzzled stares, but inwardly she sighed. She'd been initiated into the signs and portents of sexual behaviour by an expert, not a fat, long-married philanderer with a spiteful wife. But she remained pleasant and polite to them both, as she was to Eleanor and Ezra Boulton. They were leading citizens of Saltley, and to offend them might hinder her future. Once she was established in business, with a certain position in the town, she would have a moment's fun at Eli Walton's expense, and then kick him, metaphorically of course, where it hurt most.

Mrs Walton gave her a cool, assessing smile. 'You're looking well, Tizzie. And how fortunate that black suits your colouring.'

Respect was there at last, thought Tizzie with satisfaction, and all because she owned the pawnshop. 'Thank you, Mrs Walton,' she said demurely.

'I hear we're to have the love-birds with us this afternoon. You'll know the wedding's a fortnight today?'

It was horribly difficult to appear unsurprised. 'I heard it was to be soon,' she managed. 'Why all the hurry?'

'That's what everybody wants to know.' Bessie Walton's eyes glittered in the vast pink moon of her face. 'I don't know what Joshua's thinking of, unless of course he has no option. No wonder Rachel's as thin as a rake.'

Her meaning was obvious, but Tizzie didn't give her the satisfaction of questions. Surely Edward and Sarah wouldn't flaunt themselves at the opening ceremony if she was expecting his child? She resolved to observe them closely and draw her own conclusions.

Steel-grey and stately, Mrs Boulton claimed her as soon as she shed her cloak. 'Tizzie, come and see the results of all our labours. Edward and Sarah are to take us on a tour of inspection.'

They were facing her before she could gather her breath, Edward elegant in striped black coat and waistcoat with a pale blue necktie, holding his fiancée by the forearm. In the pain of rejection Tizzie had nurtured the image of her as spoilt and overdressed, but pretty enough in a silvery, colourless kind of way. One stunned look dispelled that illusion. Sarah Schofield was alight with happiness, blue eyes lustrous, hair dazzling, the soft lips deep pink and her magnificent skin glowing like a peach. As for her dress – she was wearing half-mourning of unornamented dove-grey, and it merely emphasised her colourful beauty.

Conscious of Eleanor Boulton's regard, Tizzie gathered her resources and smiled warmly. 'Good afternoon, Edward. You've completed on time according to contract, I see. Congratulations on your engagement, as well. And to you, too, Miss Schofield.'

Eyes wary, Edward murmured a polite response, but Sarah beamed. 'Oh, thank you. Isn't it thrilling?' She gazed up at him in open adoration, even as she addressed Tizzie. 'You must call me Sarah, you know, and I'll call you Tizzie. Edward has been telling me how wonderful you've been on the committee.'

Tizzie shot him a look, and felt like asking if he'd also told her how wonderful she'd been with his hand up her skirts in Back Lane. There was no child on the way for Sarah Schofield, though, she was sure of it; no covering up of a shameful condition. The girl was brimming with joy and delight, so was it possible that he hadn't yet seduced her, besotted though she was?

Then Sarah dragged her eyes away from him to ask, 'What about you, Tizzie, how are you? I was so sorry about your father. And you're in business now, aren't you? You must be working awfully hard.'

'The last few weeks have been busy,' she conceded. 'I hear your wedding is to take place very soon?'

'A fortnight today! It's a mad rush, but Edward takes up a new position in three weeks' time. We're moving to the Carlisle area right after the wedding, so as to be settled in before he starts work.'

Mrs Boulton was listening avidly, but time was pressing. 'We'll have to talk as we go,' she told them weightily, 'or we'll be late for the opening. I'm to sit with Lady Soar, of course, so I must be there to greet her.'

The four of them moved on, and Edward's unaccustomed restraint fell away as he demonstrated the innovations of his firm's design. Tizzie asked questions in all the right places, murmured snippets of information in Mrs Boulton's ear, exclaimed, enthused, listened, and observed the happy couple; all the while she asked herself why she felt no bitterness towards the bride-to-be, no envy or resentment. Her sole emotion was pity for the girl; reluctant, it was true, but pity nonetheless. She put her in mind of Mary – there was an innocence in her, a softness that she herself had never possessed. Sarah Schofield deserved better than an unprincipled lecher like Edward.

Her mind raced with schemes to warn her against him, to speak to her parents, to write a letter to her brother Sam, but she rejected them all. The Schofields weren't fools. They must have satisfied themselves that he was a fit husband for their precious daughter; they certainly wouldn't welcome interference from an under-age pawnbroker who had narrowly avoided being the subject of scandal herself – and with the man she was warning them about, at that.

Tizzie excused herself at the first opportunity, and went to examine the seating arrangements for the opening ceremony. It seemed that even the mighty Board of Governors of the Infirmary had need of a good organiser, and in spite of her being in mourning they had approached her to be honorary secretary. Once she would have leapt at the job, but now she had a business to run and employed two people. What matter that they were a dwarf and a twelve-year-old? She paid them a wage, didn't she? Let the Board wait a while. She would agree to help them out at the third or fourth time of asking. . . .

Sam and Ralph were among the throng, representing

their parents. Joshua had asked it of them at mid-day over the dinner-table, as he carved pork with speedy expertise. 'It's your sister's first public outing since her engagement, and she should have the family behind her to demonstrate our approval. But your mother's up to her eyes in lists for the wedding, and I've a mind to stay at home and help her. We can have an early tea together while you young ones are at the bun-fight.'

'I'm willing,' said Sam at once. 'What about you, Ralph?'

Ralph inclined his golden head. 'Of course I'll represent you, Father. As for Mother, what do you make of her? Do you see any improvement?'

Joshua waved the carving knife irritably. 'No I do not! She's still vomiting her heart up at any old time of the day or night. But at least the wedding is giving her something to think about besides her ailments.' He looked round the table as if amazed to find one of them still missing. 'Is Sarah still with the dressmaker? She knows what time we have our dinner, doesn't she? But about your mother – I've got another doctor coming to examine her on Monday, so we'll see what he can come up with.'

Sam could think of nothing to say that was remotely helpful. Over Christmas he had begun to feel guilty about consuming a good meal if his mother was present; conscious of it, she now kept away from the dining room. Even his father ate mechanically these days, without relishing his meals. Sam watched him with concern. Two deep grooves scored his face from nose to jaw, and surely there was now more white than grey in his hair? Uncle Charlie's death had knocked the stuffing out of him, of course – especially as it had never been satisfactorily explained – and now there was all this worry about their mother.

Not that it seemed to affect his capacity for work. At present he was immersed in plans to build a great bath-house for the miners at Low Lee; even more revolutionary, he was thinking of closing Jericho at noon on Saturdays. If he hadn't been in such low spirits Sam would have laughed to think of the effect of such a move on Eli Walton and his cronies. They might even find themselves forced to follow suit.

Then Ralph spoke. 'Father, regarding my moving into Uncle Charlie's rooms. I think I'll postpone it for a while. I'd much rather come home every night while Mother is so ill.'

Knowing how much he wanted the move, Joshua was touched and somewhat surprised. 'Good lad,' he said simply. There was no point in telling him that Rachel was quite adamant that he was never to live there. 'I'm hoping she'll be on the improve before long, but with Sarah leaving us I'd be glad of both you and Sam at home till she's better.'

'I could go and read the daily paper to her when I get in each evening,' said Ralph thoughtfully, and Sam eyed him in silence. His brother had never before shown the slightest interest in anybody's welfare other than his own, so he must have a fondness for their mother, however well-concealed until now.

They ate in gloomy silence, each preoccupied, and when Sarah hurried in it felt like sun appearing through heavy cloud. 'It's gorgeous!' she said, giving her father a smacking kiss. 'The dress, I mean. I'm so lucky having a proper wedding at such short notice, with a beautiful dress and everything.'

'Well, we didn't fancy you going up the aisle in a hand-me-down carrying a bunch of dandelions,' said Joshua mildly, at which she collapsed into hiccuping giggles. Sam watched her, his innards tight with familiar anxiety. There was a feverishness to her gaiety of late, just as there was to her distress. He hoped to God she would calm down once she was married.

Later he moved through the crowds in the new building, and had to admit to a certain respect for his prospective brother-in-law. He knew his job, that was obvious, so at least Sarah would have a husband with the earning-power to keep her in material comfort. He could see them both across the room, surrounded by well-wishers, with Edward enjoying praise at the culmination of his work and Sarah beaming with pride and excitement. As always, the male members of the group were eyeing her like starving men confronted by a good meal, and he saw Edward tighten his hold and pull her closer.

Over there was Lady Soar – Lady Sour as he and Sarah used to call her – with her usual hangers-on, and at the other side of the room was Tizzie Ridings, listening to the Chairman of the Governors. He had a sudden recollection of her on the night of the autumn ball, staring in disbelief as Edward and Sarah danced the last waltz together. Sam had had the odd impression then that her hair had lost its brightness for a moment; he remembered asking her to dance out of sympathy, receiving little of either gratitude or pleasure for his pains.

The hair was bright enough now above the high-necked black dress, he noted – crisp and springy but sufficiently controlled to give a nod to current styling without slavish conformity. He wondered what was going on behind the emerald eyes . . . but at least she wasn't gazing soulfully at Edward. She was a woman of business now, of course, and very able, by all accounts. His musings were cut short by the sight of the Walton girls crossing the room with speed and purpose. 'Come on, Ralph, let's go and view the public wards,' he said hurriedly, and led the way with his brother close behind. He liked crowds, especially here in Saltley, acknowledging greetings from all sides with his customary good humour; he couldn't help wondering, though, why he should know so many folk, and Ralph so few. His brother might be talkative enough at Mosley Street but in Saltley he never let his face slip and seldom opened his mouth. He didn't miss much, though. Those eyes of his might appear empty, but they weren't set in an empty head – far from it.

'Hello, Sam, it's good to see you. And you also, Ralph.' Francis Soar approached, badly-groomed as ever but pleased to see them.

Sam shook him warmly by the hand. 'Francis, how are you?' He looked into the honest brown eyes, and wondered how on earth that stiff, acidulous old bag had ever produced such a son. 'How did you get on sorting out the boundaries of your hill-pasture?' he asked with interest. 'James was telling me it was all a bit tricky, but he was hoping to settle with your father direct rather than cause acrimony by using the lawyers.'

'I dined at High Lee Court last evening to go into it on my father's behalf. James and Esther have improved the old place no end, but of course you know that.'

'They've worked on it,' agreed Sam diplomatically. Francis would no doubt think the place delightful after living in the Alsing mausoleum; but Sam found his brother's house over-polished and ornate, and lacking the relaxed warmth of his own home.

'We discussed the boundaries at length.' Francis took care to include Ralph in the conversation, and appeared disconcerted by the expressionless stare. 'Er – uh – oh yes, in the end we came to an agreement that has satisfied my father, and which I hope will satisfy yours as well.'

'He doesn't interfere much with James, he lets him get on with things up there. He'll have the final word, of course, if it comes to it, but normally James only bothers him about matters concerning my mother's old home, the farm.'

'I was going to ask about your mother, Sam. I hear she's far from well.'

'She is *very* far from well,' broke in Ralph suddenly. 'But we're hoping for an improvement before long.'

'I was thinking of sending her some special delicacy from the kitchens at Alsing, but perhaps flowers from the hothouse would be better. What do you advise?'

'The flowers would be best, I think, because she's on a special diet,' said Sam. 'It's a kind thought.'

Francis leaned forward. 'I wonder if I could ask you to pass on my good wishes to your sister?' he muttered awkwardly. 'When is the wedding to be?'

Something about his manner caused Sam to observe him carefully. Not another thwarted admirer, surely? Hadn't there been talk of him marrying that dowdy little creature who was heiress to a fortune? He imagined he saw pain in the other's bent head and averted eyes; all at once he was swept by the most powerful regret that Sarah wasn't marrying this untidy, kindly young man instead of her elegant Edward. Family mausoleum or not, acid-faced old bag of a mother or not, Sam was quite certain that Francis Soar would have made her a good husband. 'It's in two weeks' time, Francis,' he said gently, 'and I'll pass on your message. I know Sarah will be delighted.'

'Do you think so?' There was incredulity there. Whatever the old misery had done to her son she hadn't taken away his natural modesty. It was somehow very touching to find the young Viscount surprised to hear that his good wishes would be well received.

Snow was whirling madly in the light that streamed from Jericho's tall windows. It was five o'clock on Friday afternoon, and in the lamp-room next to the mill tower Sarah and Polly were renewing dressings and seeing to minor injuries so as to leave everyone dealt with until the new nurse and her helper started work after the weekend.

Polly seemed obsessed by the weather. 'It's coming down harder than ever, Miss Sarah! Oh, suppose it's like this tomorrow, what will we do?'

Sarah smiled. 'We'll carry on as we've planned; stop worrying. Papa will have the road cleared outside Albion, and the pavement and steps of the Town Hall are always swept, anyway. Now, have we seen everybody? I don't recall young Johnny coming in, and what about Mrs Mason from the card room?'

By now Polly could read with ease and wrote a good, legible hand. 'Neither of them have been in today,' she agreed, checking the list.

Sarah looked at the clock. 'Send Tommy Booth to fetch them, will you? I've promised to go up on the floors to say good-bye to everybody at half-past. Just look at all these presents – aren't people kind?'

'If they hadn't got a soft spot for you they wouldn't give you a single present – boss's daughter or not – and here you are with something from every floor, and lots of individual ones, as well.'

Just then Johnny Barnes hurried in, and Sarah greeted him in relief, 'We were just going to send for you, Johnny, where have you been?'

The child shuffled awkwardly and unbuttoned his too-big shirt. 'I were busy cleanin' up, Miss Sarah, an' I didn't know what time it were. Mr Whitehead told me to come down.'

She peeled away the big dressing that covered his narrow shoulders. The wound was still ugly where flesh had been ripped from bone, but at last it was healing. 'We won't be seeing you any more after today,' she told him gently, 'you know that, don't you?'

'Yes, Miss. Me mam says she wishes you every happiness.'

'Tell her thanks, Johnny.' Polly helped her to place a clean cotton dressing on his back and they bandaged it into place. 'The new nurse will look after you from Monday. You'll do exactly what she tells you, won't you?'

'Yes, Miss.' He buttoned his shirt, and picking up a paper-wrapped package, gave it to her. 'Me mam's sent you this, Miss Sarah.' Pride surfaced briefly in the jut of his chin. 'It's a weddin' present.'

'Good gracious! Shall I open it now?'

The boy nodded, gnawing his lip intently. Sarah

unwrapped a white tablecloth, exquisitely worked in fine crochet. 'My goodness,' she said faintly. 'It's lovely, absolutely beautiful. But your mother should never have spent all this money.'

'She didn't buy it, she made it! She started it when you used to come to the house to see to me back. She said it were for your bottom drawer. Then after a bit we heard you were engaged an' gettin' married in three week, so she had to get a move on.'

Sarah examined the cloth with something like awe. His mother was a skinny, overworked little soul with six children, three of them younger than Johnny. 'It's really beautiful,' she repeated, deeply touched. 'I'll write her a special letter to say thank you. Oh, will she be able to read it, Johnny?'

'No, Miss, but our Bobby will. He learned to read at the school, wi' you an' Mrs Schofield.'

'Oh, of course, I remember him. Well, good-bye, Johnny. I hope your back heals really well.' She held out her hand to shake his, but seizing it he planted a kiss on the inside of her wrist, and then blushed scarlet. 'Thank you, Miss,' he said hoarsely, and bolted from the room.

Sarah stared after him and sniffled. 'Oh, Polly, I do hope I don't keep crying when I say good-bye to people.'

Polly's calm eyes surveyed her from their enormous dark sockets. 'It's only natural you should be a bit tearful, Miss Sarah. You've made a place for yourself here, after all.'

Sarah turned away. Until that moment she hadn't given a thought to how much she would miss the lamp-room and her work there. Her only worry had been about leaving her mother when she wasn't well. She retied her apron. 'We've just got time to see Mrs Mason before I go out on the floors,' she said briskly.

Followed by Polly she walked the gas-lit rooms, cheeks pink from the heat, eyes bright with excitement and unshed tears. From time to time she consulted the list in her apron pocket to make sure she was thanking people for the right gift, and at last reached the weaving shed. Once there she hesitated. It was the noisiest place in the whole of Jericho, and she couldn't understand the mouthing of the women, nor their rapid sign language. Bennet, the head overlooker, hurried to greet her, taking a wad of tobacco from his mouth. Seeing her by the door, a plump woman she recognised as Mrs Bracewell stepped into the alley and blew her a kiss before running back to her looms. Others copied her, until the huge, glass-roofed room was alive with pursed lips, outstretched palms and waving arms.

Beaming, she climbed on the overlooker's table and blew kisses back. Then a woman began to sing. Nobody could hear her, but by the strange, unspoken communion of the weavers, they followed her lips and joined in full-throated chorus against the clamour of the looms. Chapel-goers almost to the last woman, they sang the Doxology for her, as they did for any of their number about to make her marriage vows. 'Praise God from whom all blessings flow', the last verse of a hymn that was both a blessing and a thanksgiving.

There, standing on the table, with the sour-faced overlooker hovering nearby, Sarah looked at the faces behind the clattering looms, recognising most of them from either her classes or the food centre. Long working hours or no, there was a liveliness about them now that hadn't been there when they lived on hand-outs from the master of Jericho and the relief. She could see the little Spencer woman who had always taken home broth for her mother and the old uncle; she was married now, they said, and had buried both mother and uncle within ten days of the wedding. She was flitting about between her looms and singing with the rest of them, and there was a glow about her small face, as if to say she'd already had the Doxology sung for her. Behind her were the two sisters who had kept the class laughing at the way they made up what they couldn't decipher when they had to read aloud.

The last note fell away beneath the din of the looms, and deeply moved, Sarah blew a final kiss to them all and climbed down from the table. The boiler-house and the blowing-room next, and then she'd seen everybody. . . .

Joshua and Sam were at the office window as she and Polly crossed the snow-bordered yard. 'She's close to tears,' said her father, watching her in the light from the windows.

'Aye, and not the only one, I'll warrant,' agreed Sam.

Hard-frozen snow glittered between the railway lines as the newly-weds and Polly prepared to board the five-thirty train to Manchester. The family were all there to see them off, and so was Bessie Lomas, Polly's grandmother.

Sarah's blithe confidence had at last deserted her, and she clung to her parents as if she couldn't bear to leave them. 'Don't forget, Mama, let me know if you're going to keep on with the diet. And Papa, don't forget to tell me what this new doctor says. . . .'

At last, the flurry of farewells and kissing over, Rachel watched them climb aboard and was swamped by relief that she'd got through it without collapsing. Two weddings so close together, two of the most important days of her life, and she'd felt like death on both occasions. It was strange, but though they'd been so busy, the last three weeks had given her a measure of ease. Coping with caterers and florists, shopping for Sarah's trousseau, making arrangements for the ceremony and writing countless invitations and letters – it had all seemed uncannily restful compared to the turmoil that had filled her mind since Charlie's death.

Her daughter looked so lovely in the fur-lined cloak that had been their last gift before she relinquished the family name. And she had looked quite ravishing in her wedding gown – a full crinoline of stiff white silk, the sleeves edged with white fur, and on the shining hair a circlet of holly and Christmas roses. A hurried choice, all of it, and yet she'd looked as dazzling as if they'd spent twelve months in the planning of it. As Sarah's mother it had done her good to see Edward's face when he turned to greet his bride.

Joshua was having a quiet word with Polly before she climbed aboard, and then the girl ran to her grandma and gave her a hug. There was a hiss of steam from the engine, and the vapour hung motionless on the icy air. In that moment Rachel saw her family as if they too were frozen, etched in unmelting ice on the plate of her memory: Sarah weeping openly now that the parting had come, and her husband barely concealing his impatience; Ralph unmoved, his eyes glinting in the lamplight as he watched his sister and brothers; Sam trying to smile as he caught at Sarah's hand through the window. And what of James? She sighed. He was listening dutifully to Esther instead of bidding his sister a proper farewell. Her family, her lovely family was drifting apart; but here next to her, his arm round her waist, his breath warm on her cheek, was Joshua. She mustn't worry – he would hold them all together.

The whistle sounded, shrill and oddly plaintive, and everyone waved frenziedly as the train pulled out of the station. It's over, thank God, she thought, it's over and I haven't fainted, I haven't collapsed. Wearily she leaned against Joshua's solid chest. Her daughter was going away, and she was too tired to cry.

They all watched until the train was lost to sight, and Joshua cleared his throat. 'Come on, everybody,' he said hoarsely, 'let's get back to the warm.' They crossed the station yard towards the carriages, past the Saturday night stalls and the blacksmith's forge and the little shop that sold hot pies; by the light of a flaring gas-lamp, Rachel caught the look that her youngest directed at Sam. For a moment she neglected to breathe, and then took in air with a great wheezing hiss. Ralph's expression had been hostile, assessing, and quite malevolent.

Exhaustion cleared from her brain like fog before a strong sea-breeze. What an idiot she'd been, what a complacent fool! Ralph had got rid of Charlie because he stood between him and the power he craved at Mosley Street. Why had it never occurred to her that he might also wish to be rid of those who stood between him and the family money? He could harm Sam, or James, or even his father! With a quiet little sigh she slid through Joshua's encircling arm, and the last thing she heard was his urgent shout to the others as he bent to lift her from the cobblestones.

CHAPTER EIGHTEEN

Straight Talking

THE SHOP BELL PINGED and Mary came in. 'Oh goody, no customers,' she said, 'we can talk for a minute.'

Tizzie was pleased to see her, because she brought a breath of gaiety and good humour whenever she called in at the shop. Today she was rosy-cheeked from the cold, with the frills of her lacy house-cap peeping from beneath a new deep-red bonnet. 'You look blooming, Mary,' she said impulsively. 'Married life suits you.'

'Oh, it's just *lovely*! Just wait, you'll see what I mean when you meet the right man.'

Tizzie smiled grimly. 'I have no plans in that direction, I assure you.'

'Oh, fiddle! You can't mean to spend your whole life here in the shop?'

'Not my whole life, no, but maybe a few years of it. What do you think of the improvements?'

Mary whirled round, examining the newly painted walls, the counter that was now divided by partitions to preserve the privacy of customers, the rows of neat shelving, and the two plants in white china pots on top of the desk. 'Father would never do this, would he?' she said slowly. 'I remember I asked him once why he didn't brighten the place up, and he said that people felt comfortable in a shabby pawnshop, more easy in their minds that he wasn't making a fortune out of them. You think differently, I suppose?'

Tizzie shrugged. 'Father knew his business,' she admitted. 'The details he wrote out for me before he died have taught me as much as if I'd worked down here

for years. Maybe he had a point about shabby premises,
but you know as well as I do that the people who use this
place see it as a shameful necessity. I believe that if the
place looks brighter and cleaner it will seem respectable
to them rather than shameful, and so more of them will
be tempted to use it.'

Mary wrinkled her nose. 'You can always find good
reasons for doing what you want, Tizz. What does
Mother think about it?'

'She said, "It was good enough for your father", and
I said, "Well, it's not good enough for me". After that
she kept quiet. She doesn't interfere much.'

Mary's big brown eyes were watchful and concerned.
'I'm on my way to the shops, and I came round this way
to ask you both to Sunday dinner.'

Tizzie hesitated. Mary and William were always ready
to welcome them to Holden Street, and her mother
enjoyed the change; but the sparklingly clean house
and the open devotion between Bull-beef and her sister
had the strangest effect on her. No sooner had she wiped
her feet on the mat than her spirits fell with a bump. She
knew she should have been glad to see them so happy, but
black depression engulfed her whenever she went there.
'I'd planned to spend the day re-organising the books,'
she lied, 'but I'm sure Mother would love to come.'

'Oh, Tizz – you can't work seven days a week! Still,
it might be no bad thing for you to have a break from
each other. I'll go up and ask her.'

'She isn't there,' Tizzie said flatly.

'Not there? Where is she, then?'

'I don't know. She's taken to going out on the town
just lately. Don't ask me why.'

Mary gnawed at her lip. 'She's a grown woman, so
we can hardly stop her, can we? Is she – you know –
is she all right?'

'In the head, you mean? She's rational enough, but
not exactly forthcoming. I have no idea what she's
thinking.'

'Well, I can't wait around for her to come back, I have to do my shopping. Will you ask her to come on Sunday? She knows what time we eat. And Tizz, I do think you're doing marvellously here. Are you – are you happy?'

Their eyes met. The name Edward Mayfield remained unspoken, but Tizzie knew what lay behind the question. In a rare gesture of affection she leaned over the counter and touched her sister's cheek. 'Happy – what's happy?' she asked lightly. 'I'm no longer bored, and that's a kind of happiness – having something to exercise my mind. I've arranged to have the three brass balls removed this afternoon.'

'You always hated them, didn't you? But surely you need them to announce that you're a pawnbroker?'

'Of course I do, so I'm having new ones. At least they won't be tarnished, and they certainly won't squeak whenever the wind blows.'

Mary went off to do her shopping and left Tizzie to the routine tasks of the morning.

Barney had been a bit put-out when she told him about the three brass balls . . . 'You don't need to pay a man to do it,' he'd protested, colour rising in his flat, pale cheeks. 'There's the big ladder downstairs – I could have used that and put them up for you meself.'

She didn't like to see him climbing, his short legs and arms straining at tasks that would have been simple for a full-grown man, but she didn't tell him so. 'I'm sure you and Albert have enough to see to downstairs, Barney, but thanks for the offer.'

Later that morning she had taken in a heavy gold fob watch from a stranger; hardly had the man left the shop than the Waltons' carriage drew up outside. Eli stumped in, looking shorter and fatter than ever in a brown caped coat and a short-crowned hat to match. His sharp little eyes observed the empty shop and he adopted a slight swagger as he approached the counter. 'Morning, Tizzie. I'm just heading for the Bluebell on my way from the station, so I thought I'd drop in as I was passing.'

Did he think she wasn't aware that her shop was nowhere near the road that linked the station and Bluebell Mill? She swallowed an irritated sigh. 'It's nice of you to call, Mr Walton. We don't meet so often since the fund-raising committee was disbanded.'

He pursed his moist little mouth. 'That could be remedied, Tizzie.'

'Oh? How, Mr Walton?'

'I could arrange for you and me to meet in private. To discuss the business matters of the town, and maybe get to know each other better.'

Ah, so he was coming out with it at last. She lowered her lashes. 'I doubt if Mrs Walton would approve of that,' she said mildly, 'or Mrs Boulton, for that matter.'

He drummed stubby fingers on the edge of the counter. 'Eleanor Boulton wouldn't know of it,' he said shortly, 'and as for Bessie – she'll accommodate me.'

'That sounds as if she's used to it,' murmured Tizzie.

His lower lip jutted and his eyes glinted. 'Aye,' he agreed, 'she is. She has everything she wants, does Bessie, and I work damned hard to provide it. But all work and no play makes Eli a dull boy, and she knows that when I'm a dull boy I'm not easy to live with. So – she accommodates me.' He leaned forward impatiently. 'What about it, Tizzie? There's a little house on the far side of Saltley Bog where they're very discreet, and you'll find me a generous man – though of course not as open-handed as I'd be for a young woman who was, shall we say, untouched.'

As his words sank in a wave of sickness and humiliation almost brought Tizzie to her knees, and then her rock-hard common-sense asserted itself. Behave like a trollop and you get treated like a trollop, she told herself bitterly, and decided on the instant that nothing, *nothing*, would make her protest her virginity to this little toad. She took a deep breath and gave him the benefit of her

wide green stare. How could she ever have contemplated
staying on friendly terms until she was established in the
town? A new sensation stirred in her, pushing shame and
regret to one side. She thought it must be self-respect,
and felt it rise like armour around her. 'Are you asking
me to be your kept woman, Mr Walton?'

Walton shot a glance at the open stairway leading to
the cellar. 'Keep your voice down,' he warned, then put
his hands on his buttocks, thrusting out his pelvis and
grinning in admiration. 'You don't mince your words,
do you, Tizzie? What about it, then?'

Remnants of prudence urged her to frame her refusal
politely. 'I'm a businesswoman now, Mr Walton, with
a position to maintain in the town. I'm afraid I can't
risk the scandal.'

He blinked. 'Scandal didn't bother you when you
skipped down Back Lane with young Mayfield!'

'No, it didn't,' she agreed evenly. 'That was my
mistake, as your wife and Mrs Boulton pointed out
in no uncertain manner.'

'Are you turning me down?' he asked blankly. 'Me?
Master of Bluebell and mayor of Saltley?'

'Yes, I am, Mr Walton. Good day to you.'

'Just a minute. I can influence your business, Miss –
surely you see that? I employ nine hundred operatives,
and if I tell them not to pawn their stuff here then they'll
do as I say.'

'No doubt they will, the same as they do when you
tell them to buy their groceries at your tommy-shop.
Everybody in Saltley knows about Walton's tommy-rot.
I'll just have to struggle along without their custom,
won't I?'

He gaped at her, jaw sagging open, and when he spoke
his saliva spattered across the counter. 'You'll struggle,'
he said venomously, 'oh, you'll struggle, right enough.
I'll see to that.'

He walked out very slowly, and she knew he was
striving for an air of menace. She felt she should have

been able to laugh at his fat little form treading in slow measure towards his carriage, but there was an unpleasant sinking sensation beneath her stays. How much influence did he have in the town? Could he really affect the pawnshop? She made herself wait five minutes before going down to the cellar, where she found Albert stacking pots and pans and Barney sorting his ticket-stubs.

'Do you happen to know if we deal with many of those who work for Mr Walton at the Bluebell, Barney?'

He considered the question. 'A fair number, I'd say, but mostly down here. Workers at the Bluebell don't have much of value to pawn, Miss Tizzie. Was that Mr Walton's carriage just now?'

There was no hint of familiarity in his tone, no sign of awareness in the dark eyes, but Tizzie had the strongest feeling that he knew, or at least guessed, what had passed between her and the mayor. She was infuriated to feel the warmth of colour in her cheeks – she, who never blushed. 'I think that in future we may not have as much custom from Mr Walton's workers,' she said quietly.

'I reckon we'll survive without it,' he replied, and from the way he tucked in the corners of his mouth, she judged that he concealed a smile.

There was no hot meal ready when she went upstairs at mid-day, though her mother had come in half an hour earlier. She was sitting in her chair in front of the fire, with a notebook on her lap. Tizzie eyed her in puzzlement. 'Are you quite well, Mother?'

'Perfectly, thank you,' said Maria. 'I may as well tell you right away, Tizzie. I'm leaving at the end of the week.'

'Leaving? Moving out? But where are you going?'

'I'm taking that empty shop at the top of Farthing Lane. There's a snug little house to it, and it's in a nice area. I have the means to buy property, as you know. My husband left me well provided for.'

'My husband' rather than 'your father', Tizzie noted.

She felt as if the floor had opened up under her feet and left a gaping hole. This was her mother, who had guarded her every move and watched over her like a clucking hen for twenty years, calmly announcing that she was moving out and leaving her alone. 'You don't want to be here with me, do you, Mother?' she asked emptily.

'No, I don't. You have no need of me – you're more than capable of looking after yourself, as you've made plain over the years. I'm still in my prime and healthy, so I'm going to set myself up in business – a dress shop, aimed at the middle classes. Whenever we bought your clothes I always thought there was a gap just waiting to be filled in the Saltley shops. Ready-made dresses of quality, for those on a comfortable income rather than rolling in it. I'll be taking the furniture out of our bedroom with me. The rest of it you can keep.'

'Farthing Lane . . . you'll be near Mary and William, won't you? She called in earlier to ask you to dinner on Sunday.'

'Did she? Good. It'll save me cooking on my first day,' said her mother calmly. 'You'll have to get your own meal – I had mine while I was out. Now I have to get on; I'm making a list of what I need for the shop.'

'Then I won't interrupt you further,' said Tizzie quietly, and headed for the kitchen.

Martha was pregnant. Seven weeks married and expecting; one minute she was pleased and the next dismayed. If she needed final proof that she was a proper woman – proof beyond that of the marriage-bed – then here it was. That pleased her, and she saw it as a blessing on their union.

The dismay came because she didn't want to share him – oh, she didn't. She'd only had him to herself since the funeral, less than six weeks, and already she would have to share him. Of course it was always the mother who looked after a child; none-the-less it would have a claim on him, and happen he would grow to love it. The thought of it tightened her innards so that she clapped a hand to her abdomen as she turned back and forth between the looms, causing Jessie to flash an enquiring look across the racing shuttles. She would tell her when they had their breakfast, because with five of her own the older woman could put her right on many a point that puzzled her.

To think she'd been wary of telling Matthew, actually wondering how he would take it. She'd been meaning to tell him in bed, after they'd made love, because she wanted one more time without him knowing. Instead she found herself blurting it out as they approached the market for the Saturday night buying-in, and all because he'd seen that scarecrow woman and her daughter.

'Do 'ee wait a minute, Martha, while I give the liddle maid a copper,' he said as they neared the top of Rope Street. She had watched him hand a coin to the child, and seen the mother gaze at him as if at the Archangel Gabriel; the child, wearing a few rags and a motheaten headshawl, squeezed the coin on her palm and gave a little bounce of pleasure, like any other child might have done. Then Matthew, smiling that smile, tipped his hat to them both, as if to a pair of grand ladies.

When he rejoined her he had the same look on his face as when he'd been to see Billy Warhurst: defensive but relieved, as if a weight had been lifted from his shoulders, and all at once she couldn't put up with it.

'You'll have to stop these handouts to all an' sundry, Matthew,' she said sharply. 'We're goin' to need every penny by the autumn.'

Relief gave way to puzzlement. 'Why? What be happenin' in the autumn?'

'A baby'll happen, that's what! I'm expectin'.' She stared up at him, suddenly anxious. What a way to break it to him.

'Already? You're sure?' Delight shone from him like a beacon. 'Clever girl!' he cried, 'clever, clever girl!' He swung her up in his arms, shopping basket and all, there in the midst of the market-goers. They eyed him with tolerant calm, as if telling themselves it was that gypsyish fella from foreign parts, so he was bound to have funny ways.

Martha was embarrassed, but not enough to smother a feeling of pride that he should show his feelings for her in a public place. Over his shoulder she could see the woman and child watching them, and she wriggled to be put down. He set her on her feet carefully, and she straightened her bonnet. It was clever girl, was it? What about clever boy? 'I always thought it took two to put a woman in the family way,' she said, and Matthew laughed as if she'd made the cleverest of jokes.

'Come on, this calls for a celebration,' he said, and hustled her to Dolly Redfern's for a cup of tea and a spice bun. They sat at the same little table as when he asked her to marry him, under the owner's bright, inquisitive gaze. All at once he became serious. 'I'll have to keep well-in with Maynard,' he said thoughtfully. 'As a family man I must aim for promotion, ready for when there's only one wage comin' in.'

She smiled, half-puzzled. 'One wage? But I'll carry on workin', Matthew.'

He nodded. 'Yes, for now. I'm meanin' later on when you're near your time, an' after, when the liddle 'un's here.'

'But all the weavers carry on workin'. Why, some of 'em go into labour at their looms, an' take the babies to the minders before they're a fortnight old. Then go back in the mill.' She decided not to tell him that Miss Sarah used to try and persuade women to stop work at eight months, because he was sitting there with his hat dead straight across his brow, and an expression she recognised hardening his jaw. 'It's what they all do,' she said defiantly. 'It's – it's accepted.'

'Not by me, Martha,' he said quietly.

'Well, it is by me,' she retorted. 'I want to see us set

up, with more than just bare necessities in the house, an' I'm prepared to work for it.'

He put down his mug of tea and thought of his mother in her big white apron, looking after him and Maggie and Liza, seeing to their every need, until she became ill after Dorcas was born. And it came to him quite suddenly that Fat Annie had never gone out to work and left the young ones. True, she'd carried on her trade – if you could call it such – almost under their noses, but there was never a time when she hadn't been within call. Not that she came running if they wanted her – oh, no – but at least she'd been there. It pained him to be setting her of all people against his clean, conscientious little wife, and favourably at that; yet he had a childhood memory of Fat Annie holding his little half-brother against her shoulder with one hand, and slapping bread and dripping on the table for them all with the other. He frowned, and dismissed it from his mind.

Martha was watching him, blinking rapidly. She made no mention of the money he gave to the Warhursts or what he'd just given to the child, but it was as if the coins lay red-hot on the table between them, branding the rough boards. He tipped his hat forward and put his chin on his hands. A few months ago he'd been prepared to sleep beneath the railway arches, with only a home-made cupboard and a bundle to his name; now he had a wife, a loving wife, a home, a clean bed and well-cooked meals, and plenty more besides. If Martha had been like him, free with her money, she wouldn't have been able to support her mother and her uncle, or keep the house going through the cotton famine, or redeem their belongings from the pawn. . . . Was he perhaps comin' the gentleman a bit in thinking that his wife mustn't go out to work and put their child to the minder? It depressed him to acknowledge that he might be wrong on such an issue, and so he kept silent.

From outside the hut came the sound of a drunken argument – a man bellowing, thick of speech, and a woman shrieking in anger and maybe despair. Hearing it, Martha told herself there was many a man in Saltley who spent three or four times as much on drink as Matthew gave to the Warhursts; she was a fool not to give him credit for it. She was also an absolute imbecile to resent the way that woman looked at him. He was a handsome man and he had a way with him, and she must face up to the fact that women might take a fancy to him. But whether they took a fancy to him or not, it was her he had married, in chapel, in front of witnesses – and she'd snapped at him for giving a copper to a little girl. Her mind raced, seeking a way to make amends for her sharpness. 'That woman and her daughter, Matthew. I thought she had two girls, and a baby?'

Matthew's dark eyes were watching her carefully, and she wondered if he could have followed her thoughts. 'The baby died some months back,' he said gently, 'and not long after so did the youngest girl, of the fever. But let's not talk of 'em now; this is our night, an' we're supposed to be celebratin', not arguin'. There's months ahead of us to make decisions and plan for the liddle 'un.' He took hold of her hand in full view of everybody in the hut. 'Clever girl' he said again, and mouthed a kiss at her.

Joshua and Sam were leaving Albion after morning service, when Bessie Lomas caught at Joshua's sleeve as they made for the gate. 'Can I 'ave a word, Mr Schofield?'

'Aye, Bessie, what is it? Have you heard from Polly?'

'Yes, I 'ave. She tells me they're settlin' in up there, but that's not what I'm after.'

'Well, go on then. I'm listening.' It wouldn't be the winding room – everybody at Jericho knew that matters of work were dealt with at the mill, not at Meadowbank House, and certainly not at Albion.

Bessie tweaked at the faded bonnet-ribbons under her chin. 'I'm not askin' out of idle curiosity, but is Mrs Schofield improvin' a bit?'

Joshua eyed her narrowly. This was a sensible woman, responsible for a tribe of grandchildren, and in charge of six younger winders at Jericho. He didn't see her as one to gossip and spread gloom and doom about Rachel. 'She's not improving at all, Bessie, and that's a fact. I've had one medical opinion after another, and nobody does her any good.'

Bessie nodded. 'Aye, that's what they're sayin' on the floors. I – I keep wonderin' if you've heard of Dr Buckle in Ancoats. The free doctor, they call him, 'cos he only treats them wi' no money, an' earns what he needs from sellin' Buckle's Tonic – you'll 'ave heard of that, I reckon? Our Jane told me once it was him who'd kept her alive long enough to see her youngest on his feet, though as you know she didn't last much longer. They say the Royal's been after him to be a diagnoser or summat – you know, one as sorts out what's ailin' you. An' they say – you might think it's daft – they do say he has a third eye, one as can see inside you an' spot what's wrong.'

Joshua said nothing, and she stared up at him and chewed her lips in embarrassment. 'I just had the feelin' I should tell you about 'im, that's all. I think a lot of Mrs Schofield, I do that. She's been good to me an' all the little 'uns, an' our Polly swears by Miss Sarah – Mrs Mayfield, I should say.'

Joshua turned to Sam. 'Have you heard of him?'

'No, but if he only treats those without means, he's not likely to see Mother, is he?'

Joshua gazed absently at the departing congregation, waving his stick at those who called out in farewell. Then he nodded. 'Thanks, Bessie, I appreciate your concern. I'll look into it, and let you know how we get on.'

Satisfied, she pulled her shawl tighter and set off for home, leaving the two men heading for the carriage. 'We'll have a word with John Wagstaff at Mosley Street,' said Joshua heavily. 'Happen he'll know more about this fella. And Sam, if there's a chance he might help her I'll get him to see your mother if I have to drag him to the house; if he's all that good to the destitute, though, I can't see him refusing a donation towards his work. I'll appeal to him, man to man.'

Later that afternoon he sat in his study, staring out at the rain-soaked shrubbery. It was more than a month since she had collapsed after seeing Sarah and Edward off at the station; even now she was sitting in her chair in front of the bedroom fire, still in a nightgown and robe at three o'clock on a Sunday afternoon. She'd seen two more doctors and they'd both come up with the same answer – light diet, plenty of rest, nothing organically wrong except an irritation of the stomach. Oh, she was still trying to reassure him, but she couldn't always hide the expression in her eyes. Those eyes . . . bigger and lovelier than ever in the too-thin face. He likened it to the stare of somebody who'd experienced a nightmare and couldn't shake off the horror of it, even in broad daylight.

One thing, though, she seemed to be losing her distaste for Ralph, thank God. She'd asked if she could have a quiet half-hour with him this afternoon, but had quite forgotten the lad was away for the weekend in Liverpool. That alone proved the state of her – Rachel of all people forgetting when one of the children was away from home. He would see about getting this Doctor Buckle to look at her, he would that. Talk about clutching at straws. . . .

It was nine o'clock the next morning, with Joshua and Sam long gone to Jericho. Rachel was up and dressed, sitting in front of the bedroom fire waiting for Ralph, her head reeling with unspoken arguments about why she had postponed the confrontation for so long; whether she was right to be tackling him, and if it was some mad delusion that was leading her to accuse her own son of murder. But if the endless hours of enforced rest had done nothing else, they had clarified her mind; at last she was acknowledging that it was no delusion.

Wearily she shifted against the carefully placed cushions, easing one of them behind her neck. Headaches, vomiting, pains in her chest and shoulders. . . . The last two doctors had insisted on her resting, so it stood to sense that lack of exercise was giving her rheumatism.

There was a restrained knock at the door, and Ralph came in to stand solicitously in front of her. 'Good morning, Mother. Father tells me you've been wanting a talk with me.'

Quietly now, keep calm, take it steady. . . . She waved him to a chair opposite her. 'Yes. I wonder if you can guess what about, Ralph?'

The hint of a smile revealed his perfect teeth. 'I thought perhaps you've reconsidered me taking over Uncle Charlie's rooms?'

At that a great calm descended on Rachel, as if a cool, heavy blanket was blotting out excitement and emotion. 'No, Ralph, I can assure you I haven't changed my mind about that. I'm surprised you haven't realised why I feel so strongly about it.' The beautiful eyes wavered slightly, but he waited for her to continue.

'You see, I think it hardly fitting that the person who killed Uncle Charlie should take over his rooms.' Strength from a lifetime of moral discipline surged forth in Rachel at that moment. Weakness and lassitude disappeared but the calmness stayed with her while she assessed her son's reaction. This was what would tell her if she was a deluded fool not fit to be a mother, or if her deepest instincts could be trusted.

The expressionless mask-face came down, but not before she caught a flash of something in his eyes. Her heart turned over with such weight it felt like ten pounds of butter being tipped from the churn. She'd seen that expression too often to mistake it. God help them all – it was scorn, scorn and derision. He showed no amazement, made no shocked denial, and in that instant her suspicions were confirmed. Then he smiled gently, as if humouring a dotard. 'You wouldn't make such an accusation without proof, Mother? Let's hear it, and then we can tell Father and the others, can't we? Where's the evidence?'

'I cleaned it away with Fuller's Earth,' she told him. He blinked just once. 'Cleaned what away?'

'Grease – tallow – from the wheel of the hoist. It was on the left sleeve of your new evening coat. I smelled it when I checked your clothes.'

'I see. There was grease on my sleeve, so you immediately decide I'm a murderer. I wonder if dear James or darling Sam would be given such a label so quickly? Suppose I tell you that I brushed against the chains as I boarded the ferry across the Mersey? I was in Liverpool, in case you've forgotten.'

Rachel shook her head. 'I haven't forgotten. In fact, I have a note of the times of the night trains between Lime Street and Manchester Victoria.'

'Well, well, quite the investigator,' he said tightly. 'And have you uncovered any more so-called evidence?'

'Yes. By accident I came across the frame of Uncle Charlie's miniature of – of me. I traced it back to a Mr Bracewell in Liverpool, who gave me a very telling description of the young man who sold it to him, a young man who said his name was Charles Barnes. The description fitted you, Ralph.' The weight was in her chest again, but this time it was a hundredweight of coal being tipped off a wagon.

Only the eyes moved in the expressionless face, flickering back and forth in the manner of a clerk balancing columns of figures in a ledger. 'Uncle Charlie gave me the frame,' he said flatly. 'He knew I'd discovered his secret, his and yours. He offered the frame as a bribe to keep my mouth shut, so I wouldn't tell Father.'

'Tell him what?'

'Oh, really! That you were his mistress, of course. I

saw the miniature when I went up to his rooms on what you might call an errand of curiosity. Then when he was away I went through his desk and his bedroom drawers. Tut-tut. The letters, the sketches, the photographs. . . . So revealing, so indiscreet, so nauseating.'

Words trembled on Rachel's lips, and she fought them all back as inadequate. Just one stupefied phrase escaped: 'You're my son!'

'Yes,' said Ralph, 'and unfortunately you're my mother. Now, madam, listen to me. You've been storing this up for months in that cess-pit you call a mind, so why haven't you confided in my father, or the other two?'

'Because I couldn't bear him to know that his son had killed his best friend.' The words hung desolately against the cheerful crackling of the fire.

'Then why have you brought it up now?'

'Because I saw the way you looked at Sam, and I realised you might harm either him or James.'

'What? Harm dear Sam, the comedian of the family? The incestuous bully-boy who all but slavers over his sister? What a wrench for him when she upped and married the licentious Edward.'

Rachel gaped at him. Somebody was throwing sacks of coal around inside her chest, but she wouldn't be cowed by this creature who was flesh of her flesh – hers and Joshua's. Her neck creaked, and she realised she was shaking her head without ceasing. 'You're disgusting,' she said heavily, 'disgusting, sick, evil. But now you can listen to me. I have placed a letter with my lawyer, my personal lawyer who handles the High Lee affairs. If any member of my family, or any employee in a position of authority, dies in a way that is not immediately certifiable as being due to natural causes, one copy of the letter goes to your father, or James, or Sam – whoever is head of the family at that time – and the other to the police. So, Master Ralph, do not harm your father, or your brothers, or anyone else – ever.'

'Hm. There's life in the old crone yet! Very well – it's a bargain. I won't harm anyone, and I won't tell Father about you and Charlie Barnes. But I *will* take over his rooms. At Easter I move in permanently. Agree to that, madam, or your life – what's left of it – won't be worth that!' He clicked his fingers disdainfully.

Such was the horror of the confrontation, so unbelievable the words that issued from her son's perfect mouth, so noisy the banging and thudding inside her chest, that Rachel found herself nodding in agreement; she didn't even see him leave the room.

His father did, though. Joshua was halfway up the stairs when Ralph came out of the bedroom looking composed but somewhat paler than usual. He made to pass his father without speaking, but Joshua was having none of that. 'Hold on, lad,' he said affably. 'How did you get on with your mother? She's pretty sprightly this morning, isn't she?'

Ralph smiled slightly. 'Yes, but she was looking a little tired when I left her just now. She's withdrawn her objections to me having Uncle Charlie's rooms.'

Joshua pulled at his whiskers. 'Has she now?' He was damned if he could understand that. She'd been set against it from the start, and nothing he said would shift her. . . . Still, maybe it was a sign she was on the mend. The knot of anguish inside him eased a little, and he made to carry on climbing, but Ralph took his arm.

'We've settled – depending on your agreement – that I'll move in after Easter,' he said quietly. 'Could you see your way to approving that, Father?'

'Aye,' said Joshua, relieved. 'I'll have a word with John Wagstaff about getting Charlie's cleaning woman back, and such. We'll see you settled in there for Easter, lad.' He shot a glance at the tiny beads of sweat on Ralph's upper lip. Funny, that, considering he wasn't flushed or anything; in fact, he was very pale. But he had things to tell Rachel, and

meladdo here would be itching to get down to Mosley
Street.

'See you tonight,' he said, and ran up the stairs
like a boy.

She turned in her chair as he went in, and the
expression on her face tore at him. She looked haggard,
old, *ancient* – and she looked frightened. He ran to her
chair and put his arms around her. 'What is it, love?
Are you in pain?'

'Joshua,' she said thankfully, 'it's you! I love you,
Joshua! I do – I love you.'

'Of course you do,' he soothed, 'and I love you. You're
the light of my life, you know that.' In spite of himself his
voice broke on the words. God in heaven, he was going
to lose her – he knew it – he could sense it. Dragging
up a chair he sat opposite her, patting her hands. He
jumped up and took off his coat, then sat down again
in waistcoat and shirtsleeves, eyeing her carefully. 'Has
Ralph upset you?'

'What? Oh, no. We – we had a long talk. I decided
I was being a bit obstinate and – and silly about him
having Charlie's rooms. You could say we understand
each other now.'

He made no reply. She was concealing something, he
was sure of it. What was going on?

'Why aren't you at the mill, love?' she asked gently.

'I've been to Ancoats. Bessie Lomas told me about
a Dr Buckle down there who treats the poor and the
destitute. He's well known, even to those at the Royal,
as a good doctor who's an expert on diagnosis. I've been
down to ask if he'll see you. He won't come here but
he'll set aside half an hour for us before his evening
surgery tonight.'

She stifled an exhausted sigh. Not another one. . . .
But the bright blue eyes were gazing into hers, the
devotion in their depths reaching to her heart. Suddenly
she was filled with rage, forgetting such horrors as a
growth in her stomach. Ralph was doing this to his

father. Her own son was killing her and at the same
time making a wreck of his father. Well, she wasn't going
to fade away to please that young man! She smiled at her
husband. 'I feel stronger already,' she said, and for once
it was the truth.

Doctor Buckle's housekeeper showed them into the
front parlour rather than the waiting-room. Rachel, still
buoyed up by anger and defiance, was telling herself that
two speedy carriage rides and a train journey hadn't tired
her in the least. Joshua, outwardly calm, was worried
that the scrawny, shabby little doctor might well be
his last resort. Was he a fool to bring her here?
The crowd overflowing to the dirt road outside were
wheezing and coughing, quarrelling and screaming. It
was pandemonium.

The doctor himself had been calm but brisk when he
caught him at eight o'clock that morning. 'Schofield,
you say, from Saltley? Good-morning to you – sorry I
can't linger. My morning patients are waiting, as you'll
have seen.'

He'd listened to what Joshua had to say, not looking
into his face but gazing over his shoulder, as if at some
distant scene. 'An interesting case,' he said thoughtfully,
'but Mr Schofield, I don't treat those with the means to
pay, as I'm sure you've heard. I take it you've had other
opinions on your wife's condition?'

'Nine of them,' said Joshua heavily. 'Name your fee,
man, you're my last hope. She's not fifty yet and I – I
love her with all my heart.'

He looked back on the scene. God above – he'd nearly
shamed himself in front of the man then and shed tears!
He'd have to keep himself in hand better than that.

Buckle had put out a hand and gripped his arm. 'I've
heard you look after your workers,' he said, 'so that being
the case, I'll see her. Two guineas for a consultation, and
no promise I'll come up with anything better than the
other nine. Five-thirty till six this evening, here at the

house. Have her ready on the couch when I come in –
my housekeeper will see to you.'

So here they were: Rachel on the couch in the parlour,
and him pacing the hall, getting to know the pattern of
the carpet. At five to six Buckle came out and led him
to a small dining room. 'Sit you down, Mr Schofield.'

Obediently, Joshua sat. If he must sit to hear the
verdict it was bound to be bad. 'Well?' he said hoarsely.
'What do you think?'

Buckle faced him: an undersized, wrinkled gnome of
a man. 'What's worrying her?' he asked bluntly.

'Well, her health, man. The way she's failing, and
can't keep anything down. The fact she can't run the
house.'

Buckle's large dark eyes – the only attractive feature
in either his face or form – surveyed him with what might
have been compassion. 'Your wife is worried almost
to death,' he said gently. 'Oh, she hasn't admitted as
much, even under keen questioning, but I *know*. She's
concealing something, and the strain of it is killing her.
Yes, I'm sorry to say it, but she'll die if she can't ease
her mind; maybe she'll still die if she bares her soul in
the next hour.'

Joshua edged back in his seat and put up a protesting
hand. He'd known it, he'd known there was something,
but it had taken a stranger to tell him what was wrong
with his own wife. 'Her stomach,' he protested, 'she
can't keep anything down!'

The little man nodded. 'That's part of it. With some
it's the bowels that rebel, with others it's crippling
headaches, or aches and pains elsewhere in the body.
I have to tell you that her heart's affected by the strain
of all this – there's an irregularity there that bodes no
good. If she hadn't had a strong constitution she'd be
dead and buried by now.'

Joshua had to moisten his lips before he could speak.
'So it's not a case of diet, or medicine, or rest?'

'No. Ease her mind and you'll ease her body, and do

it quickly. That's all she needs, I'm certain of it. I'll have to leave you now, I'm afraid.'

Joshua stood up. He took five guineas from his waistcoat pocket and laid them on the table. 'Towards your work here, Dr Buckle,' he said, and held out a hand. 'Good-bye, and thank you.'

'Good-bye, Mr Schofield,' said the other, 'and God bless.'

They travelled home by cab, train and carriage, saying little. When she asked him the doctor's verdict Joshua hugged her and said lightly, 'He's given me food for thought, love. I'll tell you all about it in the morning. You need a good night's sleep, so I'll use the spare room. I have work to do that'll keep me up till late. Let's get you home and give you your tea, and then settle you in bed.'

Later, the carriage was climbing the hill from the station towards Jericho, while snowflakes whirled in the light from Zacky's lantern. 'Joshua,' she said thoughtfully, 'do you think Sarah's happy?'

With an effort he dragged his thoughts towards his daughter. 'Her letters are bright enough, love. She's got what she wanted in Edward, so why shouldn't she be happy? If she isn't I'll want to know the reason why not.'

Rachel stared towards the distant mill tower with its splendid flag, but it was invisible in the snowfilled darkness. Ralph had called Edward licentious. Please God, she prayed tiredly, let that be just his malice – like the terrible things he said about Charlie and me. She leaned against Joshua's shoulder and closed her eyes. She wasn't easy in her mind about Sarah, but that unease was as nothing compared to the situation with Ralph. Her interview with Dr Buckle, the speed with which he had deduced what was wrong with her, had caused a sudden reverse in her intentions – that, and the pain she saw in Joshua. All at once she knew she was wrong in trying to protect him. He was her husband, the boy's father. He was the strongest man she'd ever known, and he would never, ever, expect her to shoulder such a burden alone. She almost groaned aloud. She would have to tell him.

CHAPTER NINETEEN

Parting and Punishment

JOSHUA SETTLED FOR THE night, not in the spare room but in his study, and not to sleep but to think; he told himself that it was time he used his head for something else besides putting his hat on. He could think anywhere, of course – on his feet, in the mill, at the pit-head – but when matters were urgent the masculine calm of his study seemed to clarify his mind; he needed a clear mind now as never before.

Rachel had settled in bed, giving him a goodnight kiss and what she must have thought was a reassuring smile. He'd told Sam and Ralph that he would join her after working downstairs for an hour or two, and he'd sent Alice and the others to bed. Now, he was in his big armchair in front of the fire, with coal in the scuttle to last the night, determined not to take to his own bed until he'd fathomed what was worrying her. If she either wouldn't or couldn't tell him, he'd work it out for himself, and then whatever it was he'd put it right. Throughout their marriage they'd shared everything, yes everything, so what could it be that she must bind it to herself with a string of lies? God above, she'd never lied to him in her life until now, and if these weren't deliberate untruths they were at the very least lies of omission and misdirection. He gazed into the flames and summoned the alert, analytical state of mind that he relied on and that had always solved his business problems: brain power, instinct and inspiration.

Now when had she first been under the weather? Why, the day she came back from Manchester in a state of collapse, of course. No – go back further than that, he urged himself, because she'd not been herself for a while. He'd been at rock bottom because of Charlie, neglecting her a bit, so he'd thought, and, wait a minute. . . . A picture dropped into his mind: Rachel sitting opposite him in the funeral carriage as it sped back to Saltley, and the children treating him with kid gloves as if he was an invalid. Hadn't he thought then that for the first time she looked her age? Aye, and he'd put it down to the upheaval of losing Charlie.

But had she seemed poorly before that? At the ball, for instance? No, she'd been radiant that night, and afterwards they'd made love with the fire of their younger days and the accomplishment of a long marriage. And what about next morning when she went with him to identify Charlie's body? She'd been the strong one then; by God, she'd supported him and he'd been damned glad of it. She'd been a comfort to him, she had that, and all through the following week, what with police enquiries and the suggestion of murder. . . .

His eyes stung as he stared unblinking into the fire. Suggestion of murder? Memories marched through his mind like troops assembling for battle. She'd been absent-minded all that week, hadn't she, and irritable? Not with him, but with everybody else except perhaps Ralph, and he recalled she'd all but ignored their youngest.

Now, when had he first sensed she was retreating inside herself, cutting herself off from him? After the bun-fight at the Soars', that was when. She'd been shivering when Zacky tucked them under the rug to come home, and he'd felt the tension in her. And she'd kissed him with – with what? Passion? No, with a strange desperate urgency that she tried to laugh away. Next morning she'd gone off on that disastrous outing to Manchester – except that he'd been so worried about her he'd never actually checked that it *was* Manchester. . . . She hadn't even been able to remember where she'd eaten, or if she had had anything to drink. But it was after that outing she started vomiting. After that she'd closed her face to him. She had struggled through two weddings in nine weeks, and all the time he'd known, he'd *known* something was wrong. And then she'd been odd – more, she'd been awkward as the devil – about Ralph having Charlie's rooms. And that day when the lad kissed her she hadn't moved a muscle . . . Ralph, mind, kissing his mother. . . .

Joshua sat on in the firelight, eyes narrowed in concentration, recalling every word she'd uttered, every move she'd made, while upstairs Rachel abandoned the pretence of sleep and crossed the bedroom to her writing desk, her head aching almost unbearably. Ralph could walk in and put the pillow over my face, she thought wearily. He could trip Sam up at the hoist doors in the mill, he could lie in wait for James when he does the rounds of the properties up at High Lee. He could push his father into the mill reservoir. Far-fetched ideas, all of them, but no more far-fetched than what he'd done to Charlie. She reached for the paper and pen. Write it down, she told herself urgently. Write down everything you found out, but for Joshua's eyes only, in case you don't manage to tell him first thing in the morning.

Rachel turned up the gaslight and opened the inkwell. She loved him, more than the children, more than life itself. She would go to him now, in the spare room, and tell him while she held him in her arms. No – she would give him the piece of paper, and hold him while he read it – that way she wouldn't have to speak the words, because she doubted if her lips could frame them.

The compulsion to unburden herself was so strong her pen seemed to race unguided across the page, forming brief, bald sentences that told what she'd discovered; she ended with Ralph not even attempting to deny it. She saw Joshua's face rather than the paper as she added three final words: I love you.

But all at once her vision clouded and something

seemed to be blocking her throat. The pen fell from her fingers. What was this? What was wrong? Her eyes cleared, but her hand was quite numb, and when she tried to rise from her chair her right leg refused to bear her weight. What was it? Her mind raced, but her body refused to obey her. She must go to him before she collapsed – she must go downstairs, because she saw him quite clearly in her mind, not asleep in the spare room but in his study, fully dressed.

At that same moment Joshua was on his feet, hunched over his desk, hands gripping the edge of it. God in heaven, it was all to do with Ralph and Charlie. It couldn't – it couldn't be that his son had anything to do with Charlie's death? But facts were being marshalled in his mind and he couldn't push them aside. Last August his son, at seventeen, had told Charlie to address him as Mr Schofield. That had been the first thing. The last had been this morning when he came out of the bedroom after seeing his mother; he'd been calm, that bewildering unnatural calm, but there were beads of sweat on his upper lip. And Rachel, when he went in to her, had looked an old, old woman, and frightened. His dearest love was frightened in her own home.

Was he *blind* that he hadn't fathomed long ago what ailed her? Blind? He was a bloody mental defective not to have seen she was collapsing under a burden too terrible to be borne. God forgive him! His heart and his mind reached out to her; for the first time in months they were fully attuned, though in separate rooms, thinking and feeling as one. He knew no details as yet, but he did know she'd suffered because of Ralph, and he knew why she'd endured it for so long. 'My love,' he muttered, bending his head, 'my own little love, forgive me for not seeing it.'

There was a thud against the door, and when he opened it Rachel fell into the room, the long silver-gold plait of her hair swinging through the air like a rope. He caught her, and knew that the linking of their minds had brought her to him. He lifted her to the chair and at once closed the door. 'I know,' he said quickly. 'You don't have to tell me, I know.'

She spoke at the same moment, but the words were thick and lisping. 'Ralph,' she said. 'Sorry – sorry – sorry – ' And then he saw her face. The mouth he knew so well was pulled to one side, and the right eyelid was dragged down over the eye. He stared at her in horror. She'd had a stroke! He'd seen it before, in the elderly. But it wasn't a bad one because she'd come downstairs, and she could speak after a fashion, though her hand hung like a weight over the arm of the chair. He put her feet on a stool and a cushion behind her, and made to rush out to get help and send for the doctor; but with her good hand she gave him a sheet of paper, and then clutched at his arm. Tears welled in her eyes and oozed from under the half-closed lid. 'Don't go,' she said thickly. 'Read – hold me.'

Heart pounding with dread, he bent over her with his arms circling her shoulders. He wanted to run for Sam, to send Zacky hurtling for the doctor, but the twisted face pleaded with him to stay. 'Read,' she repeated.

So he read, and his worst fears were realised. What had he fathered, he asked himself, but she was watching him, waiting for his reaction. 'I'd worked it out,' he told her gently, 'but I didn't know how you found out that he did it. Forgive me, my darling, my little love, for not taking the weight of it from you. I'll deal with him later, never fear, but right now I must get the doctor. You've had a – you're not well. I must get help.'

Her mouth trembled and a dribble of saliva ran down her chin and wet her nightgown. 'S-sorry . . . d-d-didn't . . .'

'You're sorry you didn't tell me before,' he finished for her. 'I know why you didn't, love. It was to spare me, wasn't it?' He folded the paper and put it in his waistcoat pocket, and as he did so the last vestige of colour drained from his face. 'Leave it all to me, now.

I'll carry it as I should have done months ago. Don't try to move, I'll be back in a minute to put you to bed.'

She watched him, filled with remorse and love and fear – a new fear of what was wrong with her now, that she couldn't speak or stand. She saw the deep grooves that ran from his nose to his jaw; the pallid blue-white of his cheeks, and gripped his hand. 'I – love – you,' she said clearly.

'And I love you,' he said, kissing her fingers. Then the hand went rigid beneath his mouth. Her eyes opened fully, staring from their sockets, and the twisted lips drew back, baring her teeth like those of a skull.

Joshua cried out, unbelieving, but she was gone. For a moment he stared at her, then checked a howl of pain by biting his clenched fist. Blood ran salty against his lips, and he wiped it away unthinking. Then he closed the lids of her deep blue eyes, but didn't leave her. There was no more need for haste. She was dead. The pain inside him was so intense he thought he would never survive it, and minutes later was stunned to hear his own laboured breathing.

And then a different emotion stirred in him – that of anger. She had sacrificed her life in struggling to spare him the knowledge that their youngest son was a murderer. Ralph, blood of his blood, flesh of his flesh, his and Rachel's, had killed his dearest friend – as good as admitted it. It was a double horror, but nothing like the one that faced him now.

There was a noise inside his head like timber under the saw, and he found it came from the grinding of his teeth. He gave himself long minutes to calm down and to plan his next moves; then, still with his arm around her shoulders, he reached out and rang the bell to summon the servants.

'Mr Sam!' cried the manservant at High Lee Court, taken aback by a visit at three in the morning. 'You'll want the master?'

'Yes,' said Sam shortly. 'If you please.'

The man ushered him into the drawing room and then rushed to summon James, leaving Sam staring unseeingly at the intricate decor. It would be bad enough breaking it to James, but what about Sarah? She'd been torn apart when it came to the final farewell at the station, and now this, barely six weeks later.

James rushed into the room with a robe thrown over his nightshirt; behind him came Esther, wearing a fur-trimmed velvet wrap and a huge frilled cap over her curl-papers. She looked mystified.

'Is it something at Jericho, Sam?' James saw his brother's face and his jaw dropped. 'My God – it's Mother.'

'I'm sorry, Jimmy. She died at one o'clock. It was a stroke – well, two strokes, one after the other.' In the pain of the moment Sam spoke directly to James and ignored Esther. 'She must have been taken ill and struggled downstairs to find Father, who was working late in the study.' Sam, aware that he sounded calm and quite rational, felt as if he were speaking of a casual acquaintance rather than his mother. James looked ill, grasping the back of a chair for support and croaking to the servant, 'Tea, coffee, something hot for Mr Sam and the coachman. Brandy! Wine!'

As if reminded of the obligations of hospitality Esther stirred herself and followed the man from the room, giving instructions in her high, tinkling voice. 'Go on, Sam,' said James.

'She'd already lost her speech and the use of one side, but then she had a second stroke, much worse, and died in Father's arms.'

James reached out and embraced him. 'Thanks for coming to tell us yourself, Sam. She's been going down, I know, but this is a shock. How's Father?'

'Peculiar,' said Sam awkwardly. 'They were so close, you see.'

'Unique,' agreed James, seemingly unaware that by

a single word he revealed something of his own marriage. 'But how do you mean, peculiar? Is he beside himself?'

'No, far from it. He's very businesslike, giving instructions to all and sundry. He brushes aside sympathy and just watches everyone like a hawk – you know how he does. He came up and wakened me and told me very quietly, looking terribly pale but otherwise much as usual; five minutes later he was making a list of who to invite to the funeral.'

James flopped down on a sofa. 'I thought he'd have been shattered. But then they say it doesn't always sink in at first with those who're closest.'

'His one obsession is that everything must be done correctly for the funeral. It's on Thursday, by the way. The undertaker's at the house now, seeing to her.'

'And how's Ralph taking it?'

'Oh, you know him. Face like a slab of marble, doesn't speak unless he has to. I'd thought lately that he'd been showing signs of being worried about her, but I have to admit he doesn't seem heartbroken.'

'And Sarah? Who will tell her?'

'Me,' said Sam simply. 'I'm setting off first thing.'

Esther came back and busied herself offering wine or tea. James drank his quickly, and said, 'I've just been thanking Sam for coming to tell us himself, Esther.'

She observed her brother-in-law over the top of her cup. 'It *is* good of you to turn out, Sam,' she agreed promptly, 'but was it worth it? I mean, we can't do anything, can we?' There was an awkward silence, and she looked from one to the other with the same mystified expression on her pretty, kittenish face.

'We all thought James should be told at once that his mother has died,' said Sam shortly. 'I didn't ask your man to waken you, Esther, just my brother.'

James was holding his mouth in the way that meant he was upset. 'Esther, what are you thinking of?' he asked sadly. 'My mother is dead. I'm about to get dressed to go back with Sam for as long as I'm needed. I won't be a minute, Sam.' He left the room quickly, and Esther jumped up, ready to follow him.

'Obviously I'm forgetting myself,' she whispered furiously, clutching the furred edges of her wrap. 'But then, I was only six years old when *my* mother died.' And with a swirl of pink velvet she pattered after her husband.

Sam watched their retreating backs. This was the most horrible night of his life, and everybody was behaving out of character. Come to think of it, though, Esther wasn't out of character at all. More like running true to form. He looked round the ornately gilded room with distaste, then turned and made for the door. He would wait out in the fresh air with Zacky.

Forewarned by the Jericho Rose flying at half-mast, the entire workforce knew of Mrs Schofield's death by ten past six. Five minutes later notices were being posted on every floor, stating that the engines would be shut down for the funeral from noon on Thursday, with no loss of the afternoon's earnings for anybody.

There were those who declared that Mr Schofield would be prostrate with grief; they were proved wrong when he was seen making his customary rounds and then talking to Bessie Lomas in the winding room – one of the very few people to bring speech from him that morning.

Matthew, sweating with the heavy gang as they took in bales through the third-floor hoist, looked down on the silent figure striding across the yard, and knew a stab of pity for the man. He'd seen him with his wife when they arrived at the Town Hall for that autumn ball; a mature, lovely woman she was then, and if ever he'd seen a couple who had managed to hold fast to true love it was those two. A golden family, he'd called the Schofields in his mind: blessed with good looks, affection and wealth. Yet from what he heard from the gang the eldest son was married to a shrew and the youngest detested by the workers for his arrogance and tight-fistedness. Miss Sarah, though, was loved by everybody; but *he* knew, because he'd seen, that her fine architect husband had behaved badly with the pawnbroker's daughter only weeks before the wedding. . . . He could remember Miss Sarah arriving at the ball, a trifle self-conscious in her finery, looking quite lovely in her sparkling crinoline and her little silk slippers. Well, the golden family was a mite tarnished, it seemed, and bereft of a mother, at that. He stared down at the white-haired figure in the distance and felt real pain for his employer.

'Raike! Pull your weight, man, never mind watching your betters!' Maynard never missed a moment's inattention on the part of his men. Just then a runner came up with a note, which the foreman read and initialled. 'Raike! Take a bogey to the weaving-shed. Ten rolls to go to the cut-looker!'

Matthew tried to look downcast. If Maynard suspected he was pleased to visit the weaving-shed he would never be sent there again. Pulling the iron-wheeled bogey he crossed the yard, his heart lifting as it always did when he left the confines of the mill. A sudden change in the weather was heralding spring and the half-mast flag blew out on a fresh breeze.

He didn't dare linger to try and spot Martha, but Jessie Lane caught his eye and turned to the next set of looms. A moment later his little wife climbed on a base-rail and gave him a wave. Boldly he blew her a kiss, and when the overlooker glanced his way pretended to be wiping his brow. He felt a surge of pride because pregnancy suited her; she was pink-cheeked and no longer quite so plain. She had no morning sickness, no tiredness, and no lessening of her appetite for lovemaking; in fact, she sometimes took the lead. . . .

Matthews noted that for once the weavers were neither singing nor talking in their sign-language. At some time or other every woman there had taken from the open hand of Rachel Schofield, and now it was as if a blight had silenced them all. The mind-numbing clatter of the looms proceeded apace, pale sunbeams shone through the glass roof, but the weavers stayed silent.

Bending to move the rolls of cloth he was somewhat relieved that there would be no call to speak to the head cut-looker. His part was merely to stack the rolls, and the cut-room labourers would take them to the tables in rotation. Martha had told him of Harry Lingard's reputation, and he had no wish to exchange so much as a word with him.

In the cut-room he unloaded the bogey, half his mind pondering on a man who gained pleasure from fondling unwilling women, when a plump young weaver pushed past him, fastening the buttons of her bodice as she went. He glimpsed tears on her flushed cheeks, and caught a hint of one of Jericho's permanent smells – human sweat. At the other end of the room was Lingard, scrawny, bald-headed, with his hands outstretched as if still squeezing that full young bosom. Lips tight, Matthew bent over the next roll. 'Tis no concern o' yours, he told himself firmly, and wondered why he should have worried about Sarah Schofield when acts such as this happened daily in her father's employ.

In the kitchen of the neat rented house Sarah was preparing supper, pretending to concentrate on a recipe in order to avoid talking to Polly and revealing her low spirits. She'd come down to earth again, she told herself wearily, a descent that began on her wedding night. No more living up in the clouds, dizzy with love and fevered with desire. It had been innocent desire though, she thought protestingly; bubbles in the blood, nerve-ends pulsing so that she trembled at Edward's touch – the touch that she now knew to be that of an expert. Looking back, she was amazed at his restraint during their courtship. It certainly hadn't been out of respect for her virginity, so it must have been for fear of her menfolk; that, and the ever-present Polly as chaperone.

Now, feet on the ground again, the sturdy self-respect bestowed by her parents was fighting a losing battle against shame and humiliation. No wonder he had objected to her bringing Polly up north. A maid in this little house was a distinct handicap when he chose to forego supper in order to hustle his wife to bed, or to pull her down on the hearthrug to make love when it was time for an embarrassed young woman to make up the fire.

She had tried to give Polly the impression that she and Edward were so passionately in love that they sometimes forgot themselves, and the girl had been quiet and very polite. 'What you and your husband do is no concern of mine, Miss Sarah – I mean Madam. Happen you could get a bell, so I'd know when you're – when you want me?'

And so Polly was confined to her own little room or the kitchen unless they rang for her; that left the rest of the house free for behaviour that Sarah had never even imagined, let alone seen at Meadowbank House.

Her mother, daughter of a farmer, had explained gently and clearly the facts of sexual intercourse; Sarah knew from her friends that such outspoken talk was almost unheard of, even in enlightened times such as theirs. But her mother had said nothing about sexual intimacy outside the bedroom, or even outside the marriage bed. She had never so much as hinted that a husband would expect his wife to go without pantalettes while indoors, yet Edward had spelled it out for her as if instructing a dullard. Perhaps her mother and father were unnaturally chaste? She didn't know, she couldn't tell, but she was determined on one thing: she would not be shamed in front of Polly, who was more like a friend than a maid, and might be outraged on her behalf. So she removed her undergarments after Polly had helped her to dress, and then hid them away secretly, so that if Edward came home mid-morning, as he often did, he could give himself the pleasure of touching her, probing her innermost parts while Polly bustled about, cleaning or washing within earshot. Sometimes he would announce in advance the time of his arrival, and then she was able to send Polly out on some long, complicated errand in order to be available for him.

Once he lifted her skirts in the kitchen without checking that they were alone, and Polly saw it. That night in bed she had wept bitter tears, but he laughed derisively. 'She's a servant, Sarah! A nobody! Who cares what she thinks? Now come on, let's do that again, how I showed you this morning.'

She knew now that she was frigid. A frigid prude, he'd called her once. 'You're experienced, Edward,' she said after the first exhausting week, 'even I can see that. So will you take a little time to teach me how to please you? I'm sure I'll learn more quickly if you don't get so impatient.'

'I've been patient long enough, my pet,' he replied smoothly, 'while you teased and tormented me with your well-protected curves. Well, they're mine now, the same as with all husbands. And if you mention that hollow-eyed little gargoyle in the kitchen once more I'll bring her in to watch me in action. A threesome might bring a smile to your face instead of the look of a frightened rabbit!'

It had been more than six weeks, and she wasn't getting used to it, not at all; forty-six days to be precise, and she'd known for forty-five of them that she was a disappointment to him. His first silver-blonde, he'd called her, so the others must have been brunettes, red-heads, medium-fair, mid-brown. . . . She crossed the kitchen and took a cut of beef from the larder, telling herself rebelliously that perhaps it would encourage him to enjoy a piece of meat other than his wife. Then came a silent cry from her heart: Sammy, oh Sammy, you were right!

At the thought of her brother the other misery surfaced, that of homesickness. She wrote home so often and received so many letters in reply that Edward teased her about it. He was always in a good mood after being satisfied, and at such times could almost convince her that she imagined herself to be degraded. And then the next day, or even within the hour, it would happen again, like the time they were on their way home after a civic dinner. He was flushed with wine and the pleasure of seeing local businessmen admiring her, when on a whim he told the cabbie to drop them off in a deserted road. He pulled her into a coppice of trees and then tore her very best dress in his haste; when she washed herself at home there was earth and rotten leaves sticking to her buttocks. Truly, it was degrading.

Mama, she thought now, in desperation. Could I mention it to Mama? I could ask her not to even hint of it to Papa, or to Sam. No, certainly not to Sam, not to Sammy. . . .

As it happened the roast beef didn't make Edward enjoy a piece of meat other than his wife. He didn't come home that evening; due, so his note said, to an unexpected conference with a client. But somebody else came, at a quarter to ten: brother Sam.

They followed the coffin out of Albion in the order decreed by Joshua. He went first, alone, then James and Esther, Sarah and Edward, and Sam and Ralph, followed by mourners invited because of their regard for Rachel rather than their standing in the town. Sam observed the mixed gathering and thought that his father never hesitated to be different. It was all very dignified though, as he imagined his mother would have wanted it. The chapel had been packed, with flowers everywhere; once past the Old Cross and into Peter Street it seemed that all Saltley was lining the road to the cemetery, though it could have been no more than the Jericho workforce and those without a job of work to go to.

In the first carriage Sam kept a close eye on his father, convinced that such self-control couldn't last.

Flesh was dropping from his bones. For the first time
in family memory he wasn't eating, yet he was using
the energy of a man half his age: riding off with James
to see the lawyers regarding his wife's property at High
Lee, disappearing to the railway station at all hours and
coming home late in the evening; then shutting himself
in the study until two or three o'clock in the morning.

'Bear with me, lad,' he said quietly when Sam got back
from up north and took him aside in concern. 'What I'm
engaged in is necessary – tying up loose ends, you might
call it. Just do as I asked and keep an eye on things at
Jericho and Low Lee. Ralph tells me he's got Mosley
Street under control, and I don't doubt him on that.
I think by Thursday evening I'll be able to settle down
a bit. But there is one thing I haven't the time to do
myself. Try and gauge whether your sister's all right,
will you? Your mother wasn't easy in her mind about
her the day before she died, I don't know why. You
know her better than any of us, so perhaps you'd give
me your conclusions.'

Now, as the horses tossed their funeral plumes and
the carriages went at the walk past the silent crowds,
Sam's mind switched from his father to his sister. He'd
hoped that marriage would calm her down, hadn't he?
Well, that hope had been realised in full measure. Apart
from her greeting when he arrived: a cry of 'Sammy!'
and a quite frenzied hug, she had been quiet, restrained,
affectionate, and blankly despairing about her mother's
death. She hadn't wept. The old Sarah, his little sister,
would have been weeping and wailing in true anguish;
but the married woman just seemed to shrink, her lips
tightening into a white line across her lovely face.

Edward, arriving home elegant and good-humoured
not long after, had fussed over her, then hurried
away to delegate responsibility at the building site
so they could all take the early coach next morning.
Long before his father's request Sam had watched the
newly-weds closely, seeing at once that Sarah was over

her infatuation. It was a relief to find her no longer so mindlessly besotted, and after all, it had been too extreme to last. Perhaps they were now going through a period of adjustment to each other and to married life? He noticed, though, that young Polly was very subdued. Still as dutiful as ever to Sarah, of course, but never once, on that long journey home, did she so much as glance at Edward. He in his turn gave her orders in the curt, careless tones of a belted earl addressing a minion.

Now Polly was in a carriage at the rear of the funeral procession with her grandmother, Bessie Lomas. And then later, by chance, as the mourners congregated at the grave, Sam's gaze let on her through the throng. She looked up from under her black bonnet and their eyes met, then she turned to her grandmother, who was weeping silently. He had been responsible for hiring Polly as Sarah's maid, he thought now, and he was almost sure she liked him. Certainly she trusted him, so happen he would have a word with her back at the house when things were quieter. Not to ask questions that might upset her sense of loyalty, but merely to say he was there, if she needed to contact him. Something of that sort.

Then he lost track of events. His mother's coffin was being lowered into the grave, the minister was saying the 'Ashes to ashes' words, and it was beyond him not to ask 'Why? Why must it be my mother, at her age?' Pain hit him like a knife-thrust at this final parting, and the tightness in his throat made him fear he might weep. His father sprinkled earth on the fine oak coffin; for some reason as he did so he shot a look from under his brows at Ralph, who was staring impassively at the preacher. In that instant Sam felt tension in the air as surely as if a rope was stretched taut across the open grave; he sensed antagonism but didn't know where it came from. Sarah looked ready to collapse, but Edward was supporting her. James was also holding his wife, who was crying into a black-bordered handkerchief. He had an arm about her waist and a face like stone.

And then they were all back at the house, with Alice and the others waiting to serve the funeral tea. The Dobbs and the Fairbrothers mingled with a sprinkling of workers from Jericho, and Sam was relieved that they hadn't invited the Waltons or the Boultons. The two women who had helped his mother at the food centre were chatting quietly to John Wagstaff, and the retired schoolmaster who had run the reading class was trying to look as if he wasn't overjoyed to be having a good meal. A right mixed lot they were, because Francis Soar was there as well, talking to Joe Chadwick. His father had insisted on inviting him. 'I don't give a damn if he is a Viscount – he was fond of her,' he had declared flatly. 'He sent her flowers, and food from their fancy kitchens, even though we eat better here in the middle of the week than they do up at Alsing on high days and holidays. It was good of him. And in any case, she liked him.'

When it was all over his father stood at the door seeing them off, dry-eyed and sombre. A bereaved husband, behaving correctly. So why should he, Sam, have the feeling that his father was marking time, waiting?

The young ones moved into the little sitting room while Hannah and Ellie cleared up elsewhere. Sarah was pleased to see the flowers still in place; they had flanked the coffin while people called to pay their last respects to her mother, and now they seemed to bring that warm maternal presence back among them. With the exception of Ralph, silent by the window, they chatted aimlessly, uncertain what to do next.

Sam was watching her again, and she wondered how much he guessed, how much he knew. The strange thing was that she now felt better about Edward. Her mother was dead and events of that magnitude lessened other miseries. In any case, she suspected that her own special misery had been intensified by homesickness, and coming back had filled her with new resolve. Lots of women must find that side of marriage unwelcome, so she would do what they did: buckle to and get used to it. She would try harder to enjoy it, to be more of the mistress and less of the prude; in the process maybe she would rekindle what she'd felt for Edward before the wedding. And she would surely start with a baby very soon. If frequency of intimacy was any guide she was probably expecting at this very moment. . . . She looked at Sam and managed a smile. Seeing it, relief lightened his grim features, and at that moment their father came in.

'Good, you're all here,' he said briskly. 'I thought you might be wondering about your mother's will. You'll know she's always had property in her own right, mainly at High Lee? We hung on to that through the bad times, as I think I've told you before. Also, there are several personal bequests, and so I've arranged for her lawyer to see us here at nine in the morning. That'll leave the rest of the day free for you two to travel back up north if you want, and for you and Esther to catch up at home, James.'

They all stared at him, baffled and uneasy at the thrusting, energetic manner that went so oddly with his ravaged face. Then he turned to his youngest son. 'Ralph, I have something to discuss with you. A proposition, I suppose you'd call it. It involves a bit of a journey, so get your hat and coat and we'll be off. Zacky's waiting outside. The rest of you, carry on, carry on!'

He nodded and turned to go, but Sarah ran across to him. 'Papa! Do you have to go now, this minute? Can't you stay and relax, with us? You look a – a little tired.'

'Tired?' The vivid eyes widened, as if the word astounded him. Then he gave her a kiss and a hug. 'You're a good girl,' he said, 'but this is something I'd like to see settled.' He nodded to Ralph and a minute later they heard the front door close behind him.

Sam followed his brother out of the room. 'Keep a close eye on him, Ralph,' he urged. 'I'm worried. He's not himself at all.'

'I should say he's very much himself,' Ralph said

coolly. 'Giving orders and expecting everybody to jump to it and obey them without question. I'm just curious to know what it's all about.'

'It's a surprise, lad,' said Joshua affably when he faced Ralph in the carriage, 'a bit of a scheme I've worked out. I've thought a lot about you just lately, and I've realised you've got more brains than the other three put together. You've worked hard this last eight months, and this – well – I suppose you could call it a reward.'

'Is it the rooms at Mosley Street, Father?'

They were going down the hill past Jericho, and Joshua gazed thoughtfully at the flag, flying at half-mast against a darkening sky. 'No, Ralph, no; but believe me, I haven't forgotten how much you want to move in there. Just wait and see. If I were a wagering man I'd wager it's something not even you will have thought of.'

With no further words they boarded the Manchester train and when it reached Victoria Ralph made for the main entrance, as if to head towards Mosley Street.

'Hold on,' said Joshua, touching his arm. 'That's our train over there – the six o'clock for Lime Street. I've already got the tickets.'

Ralph's beautiful eyes stared blankly into his father's, and his neck twisted from side to side, as if confined by a too-tight collar. 'Liverpool? This is all very mysterious, Father.'

'Aye, the best surprises always are – especially the big ones,' agreed Joshua pleasantly. 'You can spend the journey trying to work out what I've got lined up for you. One hint I'll give you, and then not another word, because I think I'll nod off for a bit: we're not going to the Excha – dammit – we're not going to the most important place first.'

All at once Ralph's collar ceased to bother him, and he settled back in his seat: a handsome blond youth accompanying a white-haired man, who though alert and upright, looked old – very old.

It was busy as always at Lime Street station, crowds jostling, steam hissing, porters sweating; Joshua threaded his way confidently towards a private carriage that waited some distance from the ranked cabs. They headed in the direction of the docks; for a moment or two Ralph's calm gaze wavered. But as they sped on without slowing he relaxed; his expression was as blank as ever, but he had what a casual observer might have thought was a scornful curl to his lip.

It was dark at the quay. A fresh breeze blew from the water, and there was the creak of rigging and the distant sound of laughter from a dockside tavern. They stopped by the gangplank of a seagoing merchant ship, where a burly seaman seemed to be expecting them. 'Mr Schofield, sir, and Mr Ralph. Welcome aboard! This way, if you please.'

'After you, lad,' said Joshua. 'This is where we do the talking.'

They were shown into a cabin, lined in dark wood. Two empty chairs faced each other across a table littered with charts. 'Sit you down,' said Joshua calmly; as his son obeyed him the burly seaman was joined by another, and the two of them grabbed Ralph's arms and tied them securely to the chair. 'Thanks,' said Joshua shortly. 'That's all for now. Leave us until I call, will you?' Then he leaned forward and looked at his youngest son. 'Outwitted, Ralph?' he asked wearily. 'Surely not – not by your old fool of a father?'

Eyes bulging, Ralph struggled against his bonds, but they had been tied by sailors and didn't give an inch. 'What on earth is going on?' he asked furiously. 'What is this, Father? Sam told me you're not yourself! You're not well! You can't do this sort of thing!'

'Oh, but I can, Ralph. The captain of this ship has carried my cargoes for years, and he's only too ready to oblige me. Being so very bright, it'll have dawned on you already that I *know*. I know everything. I put two and two together, and made four.' Ralph gaped at him, slack-jawed, the blank face suddenly alive with bafflement, anger and surprise. 'Yes, I can add up, but your mother might still be alive if I'd done my sums a bit sooner. As it was she suffered months of anguish and ill-health because she couldn't bear to tell me that my son had murdered my best and oldest friend. At the end she confirmed what I'd guessed.'

'But you said she'd lost the power of speech!'

'Oh, I've said a lot of things in the last few days that were somewhat short of the truth. It's amazing how your standards fall when you're dealing with a murderer. But your mother managed a few, shall we say, telling phrases before she said good-bye. Also, she gave me a letter that she must have finished just as the first stroke hit her. You killed Charlie, Ralph, and you killed your mother. In addition you've used my name for shady dealings at the Manchester Exchange – oh yes, I've checked on that. I've been doing a lot of checking since the early hours of Tuesday.'

'But it was all a cover-up! Barnes gave me the frame to keep my mouth shut about him and her! Your faithful friend was besotted with her!'

'I know he was,' said Joshua heavily. 'I'd known it for years. How did I know? Because he told me. Once when I berated him about staying single, he told me he could never marry because he would never find anybody to match up to your mother. I was so accustomed to it that at times I forgot all about it. For close on thirty years she knew nothing of such devotion, until the day she called unexpectedly and saw the miniature.'

'You old fool, they were lovers!' Ralph hissed savagely. 'That dog-faced baboon and my mother cuckolded you, can't you see it?'

'No, I can't. They were good people, Ralph, truly good. Your mother loved me as I loved her, and God only knows how we came to have you. Why did you do it, Ralph? I know you resented Charlie, but he'd never done you an injury – he was teaching you all he knew of cotton. One day you'd have taken over at Mosley Street.'

'When?' asked Ralph venomously. 'When you were both in your graves? He could have gone on for years, and I wasn't prepared to wait. The opportunity arose, and I took it, that's all. Prove it if you can – there's no evidence!'

'I know there isn't. And even if there were I wouldn't blacken the family name by presenting my own son to the hangman.'

Ralph stared at the nautical charts on the table. 'So you're taking the easy way out and shipping me off to America?'

'Not all that easy. And not to America: to Australia.'

Ralph ran his tongue over his lips as if they were suddenly dry. 'I'll set up in business,' he said contemptuously. 'I'll make a fortune and then come back and buy you out, you and your precious Jericho.'

'You'd need capital to set up in business. I've traced your bank accounts; as you're a minor I've used my authority as your father to close them and transfer the capital to the mill. Quite a little fortune you had tucked away, wasn't it? Though of course there'd have been no bequest from your mother to add to it. Still, Australia's a new country. Hard, they say, but with lots of opportunities. . . .'

'Just a minute, Father, let's talk. I can explain everything – how I found out that Barnes had been lining his own pockets, how he would call in at home when you were at the mill. . . .'

'Save your breath, Ralph, we're limited for time. This ship goes out on the tide. Now, I've recovered the letter that your mother left with her lawyer, and I've re-written it in the form of a confession. Do you recall I said I had a proposition for you? It's this: sign the confession in front of witnesses, and I'll let you sail out as a passenger. Without means, admittedly, but not as a common deck-hand.'

'And if I don't?'

'You work your passage,' said Joshua grimly, 'and it'll make the hardest job in Saltley seem like a cake-walk by comparison.'

'You're deranged. You're in your dotage! I'll never sign a confession!'

'Very well.' Joshua went to the door and called in the two seamen. 'My son has taken the option of becoming a member of the crew, so you know what to do.'

Ralph eyed his father with venom as they untied him; but when he struggled the shorter of the two knocked him to the floor with a single back-handed blow to the head. Then they knelt beside him and silently removed his clothes down to his soft cotton singlet and under-drawers. 'Those as well,' said Joshua stonily.

And then, completely naked, Ralph began to weep. 'You can't mean it, Father,' he sobbed wildly. 'You don't really mean it.'

'Oh, I mean it,' his father assured him. 'From this moment I disown you, Ralph. You are no son of mine. I've put you in the custody of Captain Bridewell. He's a strict man, but fair, and not unduly brutal. And unlike you he's loyal – very loyal – to me. Right,' he picked up his hat and cane. 'I've done what I came to do, so I'll be off.'

But Ralph was at his feet, clinging to his ankles. 'Mother wouldn't have wanted this,' he gabbled. 'She wouldn't! I know it!'

'You know nothing about your mother, and you've always made sure she knew nothing about you, until you overlooked a smear of tallow on your sleeve.' Joshua pulled his leg free of Ralph's frenzied clasp, and looked down at him. He was weeping hysterically, a high-pitched wailing noise such as a child might make. His body looked white against the dark floorboards, and he covered his genitals with shaking hands. 'Think of your mother as you work your passage,' said Joshua bleakly; then, bundling together his son's clothes, he nodded to the two men and left the cabin.

Once ashore, he signalled to the waiting carriage but made no move to climb in. Long minutes passed and then the gang-plank was pulled aboard and the ship prepared to sail. Lights were lit on the bridge, men swarmed on deck, ropes hissed and rigging creaked. There was a harsh crackle of sail, two little tugs busied themselves under the bows, and the vessel eased away from the quay.

Joshua watched until it was swallowed by the darkness, then he spoke aloud to the damp dockside air. 'I hope you approve of that, love? I might have cheated the hangman, but at least he can't harm his brothers nor blacken our name any longer.' The quiet words echoed emptily along the quay, then piece by piece he threw his son's funeral clothes into the black water; with set face he watched as the garments either floated or sank.

After the train emptied at Victoria the guard made his customary check of the carriages. In the corner of one was a well-dressed elderly man, fast asleep. 'I say, sir, this is Manchester Victoria. All change here, sir.'

Joshua stirred and stumbled to his feet. Too early for sleep such as that, he admonished himself, and made for the Saltley train. They were all at the supper table when he got home. 'Papa!' Sarah rushed to kiss him, and Sam jumped up and grasped his arm in relief. He patted Sarah's cheek and gripped Sam by the shoulder. 'James, Sam – I'd like a word,' he said quietly, and led them to the little sitting-room.

'Where's Ralph, Father?' asked James, watching in puzzlement as Joshua flopped into a chair.

His father took a white carnation from the vase that had stood by Rachel's head, then bent forward with his elbows on his knees and twirled the flower between his fingers, examining it as if he'd never seen anything like it before.

'Father, where's Ralph?' repeated James.

'On board ship, bound for Australia,' said Joshua simply. 'I've disowned him, lads. He's no longer a son of mine.'

They stared at him, dumbfounded. 'Listen,' he said, 'and don't question me till I've done. Then, if you want confirmation, read this. It's based on a statement written by your mother half an hour before she died, and another that she left with her lawyer. Ralph admitted it verbally, but he wouldn't sign a confession. He said I was insane, a dotard, that your mother was unfaithful to me, and a great deal more besides.

'I'm sorry to have to tell you this, but he murdered your Uncle Charlie. Your mother found out. All these months she tried to keep it from me, and the worry of it killed her. There was no stomach cancer, no ulcer. She was worried, literally, to death. I've dealt with him to the best of my ability, short of handing him over to the police. He's gone – without a penny to his name or a rag to his back.'

They asked no questions, made no protests, because his very bearing swept aside all doubt. 'I had to wait until after the funeral, because that was the last thing I could do for her, and it had to be done properly. Sam, I can't face Sarah at the moment. If you think she's up to hearing it, will you tell her for me? You must decide between yourselves whether to tell Esther and Edward the truth. I want everybody else to be told he's gone abroad after a disagreement. And now I'm going to my bed.'

'But Father – ' protested James. Sam held up a hand and silenced him. 'Let him go,' he mouthed silently.

Without another word Joshua went out and mounted the stairs. At the top he turned and looked down on them both. 'We carry on,' he said flatly, 'though I've little heart for it, and that's a fact. Business as usual, tomorrow.'

A moment later the bedroom door closed behind him.

CHAPTER TWENTY

Going Home

TIZZIE WAS FEELING ODD. Not bored, not unhappy, just odd. It was a new kind of feeling and she didn't like it; it only came on when the shop was closed and she was in the silent rooms upstairs. Common sense declared it to be loneliness, but Mary's constant chatter had often irritated her and she'd resented her mother's managing ways, so could she really be missing them so much as to be lonely?

Admittedly it was very quiet on her own, and she didn't like having to cook her own meals. Sometimes she went into the town for a late supper; it meant ordering a cab in advance, though, because walking alone after dark didn't fit her new station in life. Not only that, there were few decent eating houses in Saltley, and the better-class inns looked askance at a young woman eating alone in the evening.

So she was highly pleased to be dressing for a supper party at the Boultons' – not for an infirmary board meeting where she would have to take notes, but purely a social event. She told herself that if the monumental Eleanor did live in an ill-lit mausoleum, the food there could only be an improvement on the re-heated hash she'd eaten the previous day.

She was wearing her new half-mourning dress. It was pale grey, a colour she found boring and nondescript, but which showed off her bright hair and eyes; she'd made sure that the bodice was close-fitting, to emphasise her high bosom and small waist. Decidedly fetching, she told herself in front of the mirror, yet severe enough for a woman of business. She was finding it very agreeable to be accepted as a businesswoman in her own right. There had even been a Sunday tea when Mrs Boulton had tried a spot of heavy-handed matchmaking. . . . The son of a distant Boulton cousin was there, a spindly young man with spectacles and a nervous stutter, and Tizzie saw at once that she was being shown off as a possible wife. It was laughable; even if the spindleshanks had had the looks of a Greek god, and been other than the fourth son of a mediocre grocer in Openshaw, she had no intention of getting involved with another man until she was well into middle-age and owned half Saltley. Then, maybe, she might think of marriage. On her terms. To a man of distinction. It had taken some skill to convince Mrs Boulton that she must work on her business before she let herself be tempted into matrimony.

When she arrived at the supper party there were nine other couples and her, the only unaccompanied woman. She wondered if she should feel demeaned by it, but if anything she was relieved to be beholden to no man, to be no man's kept woman. Because what was a wife, she asked herself, except her husband's kept woman?

That thought drew her eyes to Eli Walton, at that moment seated beneath a vast aspidistra, stuffing himself with jellied pork pie and ignoring Bessie at his side. He had lost no time in carrying out his threats to affect business in the pawnshop. Within three days of his visit Barney had reported that fewer Bluebell workers were using the dolly-shop; those who did came after dark, concealed beneath shawls or mufflers. Now the little pig-eyes were watching her narrowly, so she let her wide green gaze slide over him as if he were invisible, turning to the chairman of the infirmary board, who was demanding attention. The Mayor of Saltley caused her no worries, she thought dismissively.

Guests went back and forth to the buffet and then sat at small tables set around the walls. It was a way of eating that appealed to Tizzie, because it spared her being landed permanently with a bore. Talk was general, and went from Francis Soar inheriting the Earldom, to indignation at Joshua Schofield closing his mills on Saturday afternoons, to shock at the assassination of Abraham Lincoln. News of this event had reached London the previous week. Mrs Boulton used even that to vent her feelings about the Schofields, her voice rising easily above the chatter.

'Well, it gave Joshua another chance to lower his precious flag, didn't it? It was right and proper when Lord Soar died, because he was a benefactor to the town, and it was understandable when Rachel passed on, poor woman – though whether he was as cut-up as they made out I have my doubts, because he was at Jericho first thing the morning she died. And that youngest boy of theirs . . . have any of you heard news of him since he vanished from Saltley? He always had too high an opinion of himself, of course, like his father. I had to smile, though, when I saw that flag lowered *again*. . . .'

'But for Mr Lincoln, Eleanor,' protested her husband, for once managing to insert a word. 'Joshua was always one for Lincoln.'

There was a murmur of disapproval, and Tizzie listened with interest. The war had been over for less than a month, after dragging interminably to its end, and from the start of it a great deal had been said about the cotton masters supporting the North. Not all of them, she thought cynically. Certainly not the Boultons or the Waltons, or Ephraim Buckley, who had made a fortune out of rollers when the Indian surat had to be used. For herself, she was sick of hearing about it. But Abraham Lincoln was different, somehow. His speeches revealed him as a man who could deliver a message of some power, and power appealed to her – power of any kind. He'd been nothing to look at, of course – a long ungainly creature according to his pictures – but he'd had power; President of America, and killed now,

by an assassin. She found herself approving of Joshua
Schofield for paying his respects to such a man.

'Tizzie, here! A word. . . .' Eleanor Boulton drew her
to one side, eyes glinting like polished steel. 'This might
interest you, if only because it shows how wise you were
to pay heed to me and Bessie last autumn. There's a
housemaid at the place where Edward Mayfield had his
rooms, you remember?'

'I never went there,' Tizzie reminded her.

'No. Very wise. Well, the girl tried to kill herself this
morning – threw herself off the railway viaduct and into
the canal.'

'Tried? I should have thought she'd succeed, doing
that.'

'No, somebody saw her and pulled her out. It's all
been hushed up and they're putting it about that she's
mad; but I've got it on very good authority that the little
madam was found to be in the family way, and named
Edward as the father. She's lost the child, apparently,
and of course she's been dismissed from her post and
will be packed off to an aunt up in the hills if she escapes
a prison sentence. Now, what do you think of that?'

Tizzie tried to look mildly interested. 'When do they
think – I mean, how far on was she?'

Mrs Boulton clasped her hands beneath her enormous
bosom. 'You're a single girl, Tizzie, so I can't say
too much, but she was well over half-way. She must
have fallen around Christmas, after you stopped seeing
him but about the time he became engaged to Sarah
Schofield. I've talked it over with Bessie, and we see it
as our duty to write and tell Sarah, just to warn her in
case she hears of it from somebody who hasn't got her
welfare at heart.'

Tizzie stared at her. 'Pardon? What was that?'

'I say we're going to write to Sarah. Bessie's girls
will have her address. We feel we should tell her,
out of kindness, before she hears it from somebody
else.'

Tizzie kept silent. This woman had influence, influence that had improved her own standing so that she was not only a businesswoman and honorary secretary to charitable causes, but she was a friend of the town's foremost families. But she could do without it. She no longer needed to dance attendance on this malicious, well-corseted mountain of flesh. She looked round the room. There wasn't a single person there that she liked – not one. And Eleanor Boulton had enjoyed telling her, oh yes, enjoyed every word.

She wasn't shocked; she wasn't really surprised. Edward was Edward: an unprincipled libertine, and it was some sort of consolation to know she wasn't the only one to be taken in by him. She wondered how soon the pathetic little housemaid had come to her senses. . . . But the older woman was trying to judge her reaction. Steady, she warned herself, don't show that you care. 'I'm sure you won't shrink from telling Sarah, Mrs Boulton,' she said drily.

'Oh, I won't,' said the other with satisfaction. 'You can rest assured on that, Tizzie.'

The next two hours passed in a blur. After the meal a rather good contralto sang two solos, and the spindle-shanks arrived and played the piano interminably. And all the time Tizzie's mind raced. Against her expectations she had liked Sarah Schofield. When they met at the opening of the infirmary it had been obvious that she was far too good for Edward. And she, Tizzie, had contemplated warning her about him – speaking to her father or her brother Sam.

She was still deep in thought on the way home. Why hadn't she followed her impulse to speak to the Schofields, instead of making excuses to herself? He had admitted he was marrying Sarah because of her father's wealth and because she was malleable, and now she was miles away from home, with only that young girl to look after her. . . .

With Tizzie, the thought was the deed. She asked the

cabbie to wait and deliver a letter for her, then dashed
upstairs and wrote to Sam Schofield.

> Dear Mr Schofield,
> I would be greatly obliged if you could call on me
> here at the shop at your earliest convenience. The
> matter is confidential, and concerns your sister.
> Yours sincerely,
> Tizzie Ridings

The early morning was always quiet, but she warned
Barney in advance that she might need him on the
counter if a visitor should call to see her.

The shop had been open for only five minutes when
Sam Schofield came in. He removed his hat and said
quietly, 'Good morning, Miss Ridings. Thank you for
your note.'

She inclined her head. 'Mr Schofield. It's quieter
upstairs in my sitting room, if you'd follow me.'

She called down to Barney and led the way upstairs,
thankful that she'd almost banished the smell of unwashed
clothes and camphor. Already she had misgivings. This
broad, clear-eyed, wholesome individual didn't look the
kind of man she could tell about a seduced housemaid,
nor to understand her own relationship with Edward,
should she have to reveal it. Be brief, she thought. Say
what you've planned, and no more.

'Take a chair, Mr Schofield, thought I won't keep
you for long. I'm sorry to speak of such matters, and
I do realise that you might already know. . . .' It was
difficult to begin, with those brilliant eyes watching her
like that. 'It's this: last evening Mrs Boulton told me of
a young woman who tried to commit suicide yesterday
morning by jumping off the railway viaduct. Maybe
you've heard of it? No? Well, she was a maid at the big
house where your sister's husband, Edward Mayfield,
used to rent rooms. It seems she was expecting a child,
conceived last December, and she has named Edward –

Mr Mayfield – as the father. It's being hushed up, and the girl prosecuted or sent away; but what concerns me and may also concern you, is that Mrs Boulton intends to write to your sister to tell her about it.'

Colour left Sam Schofield's face as if wiped from a painting with turpentine. He didn't speak for a moment, but stared over her shoulder at the rainwashed rooftops opposite.

'I – I contacted you rather than your father because I – '

'Yes, yes,' he interrupted impatiently. 'That was right. Thank you. Did Mrs Boulton tell anyone else?'

'Not that I'm aware of, but Mrs Walton knows already. They plan a joint letter to Sarah.'

'Pardon the impertinence, Miss Ridings, but is there some reason why she should tell you?'

Tizzie studied her fingernails closely. 'She's a malicious woman, and she knows I used to be fond of Edward before he became engaged to your sister.'

Sam looked at the bent head with its springy, red-gold hair, and recalled the night of the ball when he imagined that hair to have lost its brightness. 'I'm sorry to pursue this, Miss Ridings, but I have no idea how close you were to my brother-in-law. Having known him, do you see there being any truth in what the girl says?'

Tizzie wasn't one to study her nails indefinitely. She stared him straight in the eye. 'I'm sorry to say it, but yes, I think she's probably telling the truth.'

Once again he fell silent, and she thought she saw disbelief in his face, or disgust, anything but acceptance. 'It's up to you whether you believe it,' she said briskly. 'I just didn't want her to hear it from Mrs Boulton. I realise she might know of it already.'

'No,' he said slowly. 'No, I'm sure she doesn't know. I never liked him, but I can't believe that while he was engaged to Sarah, or even before then, for that matter. . . .'

'He's without principles!' she burst out angrily. 'I

almost warned you or your father about him when they got engaged, but it didn't seem right to do it, and now I regret not making myself speak. You see, he tried very hard to put me in the same condition as that young woman.'

Sam lowered his gaze hastily. What an admission! Then she said, 'I was very young then, you see.'

The forlorn little phrase caught at him. She spoke as if her youth was past and done with. For perhaps half a minute his mind dwelt on her rather than on Sarah, on what it must have cost her to contact him . . . and he'd always thought her hard! 'I'm deeply grateful to you,' he said gently. 'It can't have been easy to speak of it to me. Do you think Mrs Boulton will write to Sarah at once?'

'Yes. She can't wait. She's jealous of your family, you see.'

'My family?' The remarkable eyes darkened. 'What's left of it, you mean.' He held out a large, cold hand and shook hers firmly, as if striking a bargain in business. 'Thank you again, on behalf of Sarah.'

'What will you do?' she asked curiously.

'See the girl to check that it's really true,' he said heavily, 'and then go up there myself to beat the postman, so she'll hear it from somebody who loves her.' Tizzie saw him out under Barney's dark polite gaze; when he had gone, the dwarf made no mention of his visit.

It was Biddy's second morning, the one for the rough cleaning, and Tizzie had resolved to speak to her. She went upstairs and stopped the girl as she scuttled around the kitchen. 'Biddy, how are you fixed to come in every morning instead of twice a week, to do the washing and cleaning and to cook my dinner every day?'

The girl gulped and pulled at her straw-coloured hair. 'I was goin' to tell you, Miss Tizzie. I can't come in again after today. I'm gettin' set on at the Greenbank on Monday. They're busy again now, you know.'

'Oh,' said Tizzie blankly. 'Congratulations. I suppose you don't know of somebody reliable who could take your place?'

Biddy stood on one leg and twined the other foot around it, a habit of hers when asked to think. 'There's a woman near us wants work. Respectable she is, a widow. She can't go in the mill because of her chest, like.'

Years of smelling the unwashed of Saltley had made Tizzie cautious. 'Is she clean?'

'Ooh, yes, Miss. She hangs washin' out.'

Tizzie sighed impatiently. The girl probably saw anyone who hung out washing voluntarily as being immaculate. 'Ask her to call in and see me as soon as she can, will you? And give the stairs a good brushing before you go. I'll have your wages ready at twelve o'clock.'

The morning proceeded with Tizzie going through the books. She could afford a live-in housekeeper rather than a daily, she decided, and then she might just take a stroll along the top end of Rope Street to see where Barney lived. He was intelligent, he had opinions on matters of the day, he was – well, he was quite good company, really.

There were two customers redeeming goods at the counter when the florist's delivery boy came in with a bouquet of roses. 'For Miss Ridings,' he announced, and handed them over with a flourish.

Wondering if they could be from the spindleshanks, Tizzie put them aside while she dealt with the customers; then read the handwritten card that was with them: *Once again, my sincere thanks. Sam Schofield.*

She stared at the card and then at the flowers, and felt the unfamiliar warmth of a blush on her cheeks. They were the first flowers she had ever received from a man. They were perfect pale apricot blooms, not yet fully open, threaded with narrow gold ribbons that trailed across the counter; the scent of them conquered that of camphor and flea powder. Tizzie chewed her

lips thoughtfully. It was her misfortune that they were
in recognition of a service, rather than a gesture of
regard.

She took them upstairs and left them in water to
arrange at her leisure, not sure why she didn't want
Barney to see them.

Sam had time for thought on the first leg of his journey
north, and looked back thankfully on the brief exchange
with his father. There had been no questions from him,
no probing, just: 'All right – don't tell me anything you
don't want to. It's a poor do if I can't trust you where
your sister's concerned. Go up there if you must; you
wouldn't ask if it wasn't necessary, I know that. Go on
my behalf and see she's all right, but be circumspect,
lad – she's a married woman and her first duty is to
her husband. Get back as quick as you can, though;
you know how we're fixed here.'

Actually they were fixed better than at any time since
Ralph left the country. Schofields now employed an
agent in Manchester to see to the imports; between
them Sam and James covered the week at Mosley Street,
taking orders for cotton cloth and spun yarn, buying and
selling at the Exchange; generally they were repairing
the damage done by Ralph to the firm's reputation. Sam
leaned back and sighed. He had never worked as hard in
his life as in the last couple of months, and now he was
off to see Sarah again, bearing news that was almost as
bad as the death of their mother.

He had seen the girl, the housemaid. For most of his
life he had known that the Schofield name could unfasten
many a door that was closed to others in Saltley. He
had known it and yet been reluctant to use the name
for advantage. But this morning he had brandished it,
bludgeoned with it, until the little room with bars on
the windows on the top floor of the infirmary had been
opened to him.

She was a bonny girl, not yet seventeen; full-bosomed

and curly-haired, with the ruined hands of her kind.
She was frightened to death both of the police and of
being sent home to her parents, and bitterly, desperately
resentful of the well-meaning boatman who had pulled
her out of the canal.

In plain speech Sam explained who he was, and she
had looked at him with eyes too old for her years.
'Bring me a Bible an' I'll swear on it, if that's what
you're here for,' she said tiredly, and he saw she was
long past the stage of shame and embarrassment. 'He'd
said all along he'd see to it that I didn't have a baby,
an' I'd live like a lady as his wife. Oh, I knew he were
gettin' engaged to – to your sister, but he said it were
only to please his parents, and he'd marry me instead
as soon as he persuaded them to accept me. He had
a way with him, you see. I didn't believe it when Cook
told me the weddin' were goin' ahead, then I sneaked
out of the house and saw them comin' out of Albion, I
did. . . .'

The little train puffed its way between the hills and
Sam shifted restlessly in his seat. He'd left her a sum of
money, but it hadn't eased his mind. He couldn't have
felt much worse if he'd seduced the girl himself! But
now, how to tell Sarah? How to deal with Mayfield?
He stared balefully across the carriage and a mild young
man opposite moved hastily to another seat.

Guilt pulled at him. He had inspected the Mayfields,
given approval of the family. Only now was it clear why
there had been an element of surprise in their attitude.
They'd known their son, known of his reputation with
women, and been surprised that a decent family had
accepted him. And he, Sam, as good as handed her over,
handed his little sister over to a loose-living womaniser
with no more than a warning. But he'd meant the warning
– oh aye, he'd meant it. . . .

He had left Saltley later than last time but was arriving
earlier, thanks to a new stretch of railway line that had
come into use since his last visit; by nine o'clock he was

taking a cab to the house. Weary of travel, undecided whether to speak first to Sarah or Edward, he knocked at the door.

Polly opened it and gave a smothered shriek on seeing him. 'Mr Sam! But I only sent it this mornin'!' She stepped outside and pulled the door to behind her. 'The letter, I mean,' she whispered. 'Oh, Mr Sam, I'm that glad to see you. I had to write it when she wasn't there, you see, 'cos she said nobody at home had to know, an' I'm beside meself wi' worry!'

Sam put down his overnight bag. This was calm, loyal, sensible Polly, not an overwrought old woman. He took her by the forearms. 'Polly, listen to me. I haven't received your letter. Tell me quickly, before I go in. What's happened?'

'He's a pig!' she said wildly. 'I hate him. He's cruel to her! He shows her up an' makes her cry! She wouldn't let me tell you. He treats her like – ' she bent her head, '– like a trollop.'

He tightened his grip. 'You mean he has no regard for – for her modesty?'

'*Modesty!* He's never heard of the word! Last night he brought a woman home an' took her in the bedroom with Miss Sarah an' locked the door. The – the three of them were in there all night. This mornin' I told him it wasn't right, an' he said – ' tears spilled into the huge sockets of her eyes and streamed down her cheeks, '– he said what was the matter with me, was I jealous that I hadn't been asked to join in!'

Sam let out a sound that was both a squeal of pain and a groan, and clapped a hand to his mouth to silence it. 'Go on,' he said hoarsely.

'So I wrote to you when I was supposed to be doin' the ironin'. She doesn't know, though. Miss Sarah doesn't know.'

'Right,' said Sam, pushing past her. 'Where is he?'

'Out. At a meeting of the elders. Elders – Presbyterians – they're offerin' him a contract for some model almshouses. They'll be the best for miles around because somebody's left the church a lot of money for it, but what about – '

'Start packing, Polly. As much as you can manage for my sister and yourself. We're going home. Where is she?'

Polly let him in. 'She's in there,' she whispered. 'She's very quiet, sort of.'

Pushing open the door he saw Sarah. She was in a high-backed chair facing the door, wearing a black dress with a pink shawl around her shoulders. She didn't look up but sat as if in a trance, her hands folded loosely in her lap.

'Sarah,' he said quietly. 'It's me, Sammy.'

She put out a groping hand like a blind woman, shaking her head from side to side in disbelief. 'I'm taking you home,' he said gently. 'Polly's packing your things. You're leaving him.'

She gave a small, polite smile, took his hand in hers, and slid neatly to the floor in a dead faint. He scooped her up and carried her to the sofa. 'I'll see to her,' said Polly from the door.

Distraught, Sam was patting her wrists, kissing her cheeks. 'What is it? Has she fainted?'

'Yes. It's not the first time. She'll come round all right.'

'Look after her till I get back,' he said urgently. 'We can't travel if she's not fit. I'm going to find him.'

She saw his face. 'Don't do it, Mr Sam, don't injure him. He's not worth it, honest he's not!'

Sam grabbed his hat. 'Polly, my sister's lucky in you, if in nothing else. I won't be long.' He raced from the house and picked up a cab in the little main square. Five minutes later he was at the Presbytery, eyeing a row of lighted windows to one side of the entrance. He walked in and made for a set of double doors and then whirled round, feeling someone at his shoulder. There was nobody there, but the instant's delay brought a breath of caution, and he

seemed to hear the voice of his father: 'No violence . . .
no bloodshed . . . there are other ways.' He paused for
another second, then threw open the doors and faced
twenty or more surprised, soberly clad men. They were
seated round a huge table with Edward standing at its
head, displaying a building plan.

Calling on more self-control than he'd needed in his
entire life, Sam circled the big table and stood next to his
brother-in-law, who gaped at him as if at a visitation from
the devil himself. 'I warned you,' said Sam quietly, and
then to the assembly, 'Excuse this intrusion, gentlemen.
I won't disturb you for more than a moment. You are all
church-goers, I gather? Elders, Ministers, God-fearing
men? I must tell you that Edward Mayfield, here to
solicit your patronage, is married to my sister. Some of
you may have met her. He has shamed and humiliated
her to such an extent she is about to leave him for good
after only four months of marriage. He is – and I have
proof, gentlemen – a fornicator, an adulterer, a lecher
and a libertine!'

Edward turned on him furiously. 'Wait a minute! You
can't make allegations like that, you great oaf! I have
my reputation to think of!'

Sam laughed, and it wasn't a pleasant sound. 'Reputation?' he grabbed Edward by the back of his coat collar,
and in spite of the difference in their height, lifted him
so that his heels left the floor and he teetered on tiptoe,
then he stared grimly at the assembly. 'An unfortunate
choice of word, reputation. Yesterday, in my home town
of Saltley in Lancashire, a sixteen-year-old girl tried to
kill herself because she was expecting this man's child –
conceived when he became engaged to be married to my
sister. Yes, I have proof and witnesses. I leave it to your
consciences whether you give work to such a man.'

He released Edward, who assumed an air of injured
amazement, straightening his collar and stroking his
shining hair. Watching him, Sam could restrain himself
no longer. He shot out a fist and hit his brother-in-law's

finely-chiselled nose. There was a satisfying crunch of smashed bone, blood spurted over the grey silk necktie and fine white shirt, and Edward cannoned across the table and lay on its surface, moaning.

Sam turned to the shocked elders. They were still round the table but by now on their feet, uncertain what to do next. 'I shall of course be contacting any professional bodies of which he is a member,' he said calmly. 'Please don't allow him back to his house tonight. We're packing to go home to Saltley.'

Then without another glance at the bloodsoaked man on the table, he walked briskly from the room to the waiting cab.

Joshua was delaying going to bed. He could manage to get through the day, but sleep in that empty bed was beyond him unless he was quite exhausted. Alice and the others were aloft long since; he sat by a dying fire pulling at his whiskers and wondering what was going on up at Sarah's. He'd asked Hannah to prepare her old room, telling himself she might come back for a few days' holiday if she was a bit homesick, but in reality he was worried by Sam's hurried departure. Something else nagged at him as well: he'd come face-to-face with the Walton women when he left the station at six o'clock. Bessie had been rolling along like a bladder of lard followed by her daughters, and as they drew level she took his arm. 'We're all thinking of you and your family, Joshua,' she said, and was hard put to it to conceal a smile.

He had merely raised his hat and walked on, thinking she referred to them losing Rachel, but on reflection he wasn't 'so sure. She couldn't possibly have found out the truth about Ralph? Nobody knew the full story except Sam, James and Sarah; that in itself was odd, with both the married ones electing to keep it from their spouses. . . . His mind veered to the son he'd disowned; was he toughened up by the life at sea,

hard and sinewy and sunburnt? Joshua thought of the
lonely double bed upstairs, the great wardrobe empty
of his wife's clothes, the silent meal times, and shook
his head. Let him work his fingers to the bone, let him
climb the mast, knock weevils from his food, scrape a
living in that vast, empty continent; but let him, please
God, feel a flicker of remorse for what he'd done.

There was the sound of voices outside, and a tapping
at the front door. When he opened it he found Sam
carrying Sarah in his arms, luggage piled around his
feet, and Polly behind him paying off a private carriage.
Sarah was fast asleep by the looks of her, but pale, with
one hand against her cheek like a little girl. 'Her bed's
ready,' he said.

'I had to bring her home – there was no option,'
said Sam briefly. 'I'll tell you everything when she's in
bed. And Polly here is an absolute God-send. I want a
comfortable bed for her.'

'She'll have it. I'll wake Hannah.'

They hovered on the landing while the womenfolk
undressed Sarah and put her to bed, and she slept
through it all as if drugged. Then Joshua took Sam
downstairs and gave him a glass of brandy and water.
'Drink this,' he said, 'you look as if you could do with
it. Now, let's hear it.'

Sam sighed deeply and then tossed back the brandy,
spluttering and choking. He was no drinker, but he hoped
it would help him say what must be said. He couldn't
whitewash the facts even if he'd wanted to, because his
father deserved the truth; in any case he would know
if he tried to conceal anything. So he stared fixedly in
front of him and related everything that had happened
since he spoke to Tizzie, and only when he'd finished
did he at last remove his coat.

Joshua paced the floor in a ferment of grief and anger.
'Did you lay hands on him?'

'Not as much as I'd have liked. I might have broken
his nose, that's all.'

Joshua sighed in relief. 'There's other ways than violence,' he said, eyes glittering. 'You did well to use restraint, Sam. She's back home with us, that's the main thing. Happen we should keep Polly here with her?'

Sam nodded in relief. 'She's devoted to Sarah, she's loyal, and she understands what she's been through. Yes, let's ask her to stay. I have a feeling Sarah might be shunned in the town, you know. Folk don't believe a wife should leave her husband; in fact, she didn't believe it herself. For better, for worse, she kept muttering whenever she woke up, for better for worse.'

'That's why she stuck it, you reckon?'

Sam removed his necktie and massaged the back of his neck wearily. 'Aye, that's why,' he agreed. 'That, and the fact she didn't want us to have the worry of it, after Mother and Ralph.'

'She's a good girl. God only knows I blame myself for letting that swine have her.'

'No, *I* blame *myself*,' Sam said bitterly.

'We'll share it then,' Joshua told him heavily. 'We'll share the blame between us, lad. One thing we will do, we'll have her holding her head high in Saltley before the week's out, or I'll know the reason why not!'

Tizzie was out doing her Saturday morning shopping, and was passing the bank when Sam Schofield came out and saw her. He stopped at once. 'Good morning, Miss Ridings.'

'Good morning, Mr Schofield. Thank you for the flowers. They're lovely.'

'Thank *you*. I'm on mill business at the moment, but I was going to call in at the shop later this morning to tell you I brought Sarah home last night. She's left him for good.'

He wasn't one to let grass grow under his feet, was he? 'Because of the girl?'

'No. I didn't tell her about that until we were well on the way home.'

'Oh.' She could have spared herself the soul-baring, then.

'But I'm thankful you told me,' he said earnestly. 'It sent me up there at top speed, and when I arrived things were bad. Awful. The details are Sarah's business, and you'll understand I can't discuss them. Suffice to say he's all you said of him and worse, much worse.'

She opened her mouth and closed it again. He could do without her questions. But to leave Edward after four months? Poor Sarah – a separated wife at twenty years of age. Wives who left their husbands received scant sympathy, whatever the cause. 'How is she?'

'Exhausted,' he said briefly. 'She slept nearly all the way home, and was still asleep when I left the house this morning. My father's stayed with her to be there when she wakes.'

'I'm sorry,' she said, 'so very sorry.' And then words came out of their own volition, without her even thinking, let alone planning them. 'I blame myself.'

He shook his head. 'Everybody blames themselves,' he said wearily. 'Why don't we all blame that depraved creature who calls himself a man? My father and I are concerned as to how people will treat her after this, and I expect she might not want to face them. Everybody knows she was head over heels about him, don't they?'

Tizzie had been thinking the same thing. 'Tell her to go out, to mix, to hold her head high,' she said urgently. 'Society frowns on a wife who leaves her husband, even if he's a swine.' She saw Sam's eyes widen at her choice of words, but didn't let it stop her. 'Sarah's the innocent one – don't let her hide away indoors.'

'You're a fighter,' he said, as if she was in full armour and waving a double-edged sword. 'Sarah's not so forceful.'

Eyes glinting like emeralds, Tizzie glared at him. He could think what he liked as long as he didn't see her as a doormat. 'Don't underestimate the respect felt for the Schofields in Saltley,' she said firmly, 'but if you're really concerned I could make a suggestion. I've had a little experience in not being accepted, because of my background. Find somebody with influence, somebody well known and highly respectable, to be seen in public with the whole family. They'll accept her back soon enough then, I'm sure.'

The look he gave her was unreadable, and she guessed he found her abrasive. 'I'll think about it,' he said abruptly. 'Thank you.' With another punctilious raising of his hat he walked rapidly away, leaving her frustrated and on edge. Sarah might have been unlucky in her choice of husband, but she was fortunate in her brother. Too bad he had none of that care and concern left over for lesser mortals. It would be interesting to know how he'd dealt with Edward.

Skirting the market she continued towards the grocer's, telling herself that with luck this might be the last time she had to shop for food like a conscientious little housewife. She approached Rope Street, and on impulse turned into it. It was the bottom end that was almost in Gallgate, so she would be quite safe at the top.

The contrast between the open market square and the dark thoroughfare was startling. Tall narrow houses faced each other across the dirt street, which was littered with rubbish of every description. Dark ginnels ran between the houses, and barefoot children played listlessly in the mud. This was the *better* end of Rope Street? Where Barney lived? Was there piped water in these dreadful houses, or proper drainage? Not by the looks of it. An open sough ran from each dwelling and joined the stinking stream that gushed down the hill. She didn't linger to find which house he lived in. Skirts gathered in one hand, shopping basket in the other, Tizzie retraced her steps.

Back at the pawnshop she put away her purchases before taking over from Barney, then she sat at her desk to talk to him. It was easier for them both if she faced him at eye level. 'Barney, I'm thinking of taking on a housekeeper. Somebody's coming to see me after the weekend.'

His rare smile flashed out. 'I'm pleased to hear that, Miss Tizzie. It'll save you shopping and cooking and such. Will she live in?'

'Yes, if she's satisfactory. If she isn't, I'll look for somebody else. I've been wondering whether you'd be interested in moving in here, once she's settled in?'

His jaw dropped. '*Live* here?'

'Yes. Why not?'

'An' sleep in the cellar, you mean?'

'Sleeping in the cellar wouldn't be an improvement on two rooms of your own, would it?' she said. 'No, the housekeeper can have the attic, which could soon be cleared out and made decent, and you could have my parents' old room. It's unfurnished, so you could bring in your own bits and pieces.'

He shifted around on his short thick legs. 'I appreciate the offer more than I can say,' he muttered, avoiding her eyes, 'but there's no call to feel sorry for me, Miss Tizzie. I'm well-suited where I am.'

She'd offended him, made him think she pitied him. 'I'm not at all sorry for you, Barney,' she said briskly. 'I regard you as a colleague, a – a friend. I saw it as a good move for the business.'

'An' what do you think they'd say about you in the town? Havin' a dwarf in your house as well as in your shop?'

She eyed him curiously. Did he mean what he seemed to mean? 'Oh, I think the presence of a housekeeper would protect our reputations,' she said drily.

The big moon-face flushed scarlet, and he put out a protesting hand. 'Nay, I didn't mean anythin' like that. I'm not quite a fool, an' neither are the folk in Saltley. I just meant that it'd seem a bit funny if you had somebody like me around all the time. Not the court jester, the pawnshop dwarf, sort of.'

Tizzie drummed her fingers on the desk. The minds of men – who was capable of reading them? Who could be bothered to read them? He was as taut as a trip wire, and it was abundantly clear that her offer held no attractions for him. 'I had no intention of embarrassing you,' she said, striving for lightness. 'Obviously I was mistaken in thinking it might appeal.' She held out a hand to shake his. 'Forget it if you can, Barney.'

He shook her hand politely, his own large and cool. 'Oh, it appealed,' he said quietly, 'it appealed all right. You weren't mistaken in that. It's just that I have good reasons for refusing.' He turned and went down the stairs, and a minute later she heard him giving orders to Albert.

'So much for your great idea, Tizzie Ridings,' she said aloud.

'I can't stay,' said Mary, arriving unexpectedly the next afternoon. 'William's picking me up in twenty minutes – he's just calling at the yard for something.'

Tizzie eyed her sister narrowly. 'No luck yet?'

'No. But William says I mustn't keep worrying about it, He says we must enjoy trying for a baby and leave the rest to nature.'

Tizzie was in full agreement there. She found Mary's obsessive desire for a child ridiculous, and her monthly reports of progress quite wearing. As for Bull-beef saying they must enjoy it. . . . She crushed an odd little tremor in her chest, just in case it was envy.

'Tizz, have you seen Mother lately?'

'I called in at Farthing Lane last week. There's no doubt the shop's a success – there were five customers waiting, in spite of that new assistant she's hired. As usual she had no time to talk – not that we have much to say to each other.'

'I'm sure it's all to do with losing Father, Tizzie. Give her time and she'll be calling here every week, the same as she does with William and me. Perhaps she can't

bear to be in these rooms, where they were together
for so long?'

Tizzie shrugged. 'It's true she couldn't get away from
here quick enough.' She wasn't going to admit to Mary
or anyone else how shaken she'd been by her mother's
departure, or how upset at her lack of concern.

'*Tizz!* Who are these from?' Mary had noticed the
roses, faded now and their petals falling, but still in the
heavy glass vase.

'Sam Schofield sent them,' she admitted reluctantly.
'I – I warned him that Mrs Boulton intended to write
to Sarah about the girl who threw herself off the
viaduct.'

Mary breathed out in relief. 'You know what they're
saying about the girl, then? Mrs Boulton's horrible,
isn't she?'

'Oh, she took care to tell me all about it. He was going
to try and see the girl before he went up to Sarah's.'

But Mary was eyeing the faded blooms thoughtfully.
'They must have been gorgeous.'

'They were a thank you for telling him. You know, I
could have warned the Schofields about Edward before
the wedding, but I gave them credit for having the sense
to check on him. I saw him, yesterday.'

'Edward?' squeaked Mary. 'Where?'

'No, Sam Schofield, while I was out shopping. She's
left Edward for good. Not just because of the girl, but
because he's what Sam Schofield called "a depraved
creature".'

'But everybody knows she was mad about him! And
she's so lovely, Tizz. Surely he adored her?'

'Apparently not, and she's mad about him no longer.
The family are worried about her having to face people
again, so I told him to take her out and about at once
to show she has nothing to be ashamed of, and to get
someone with influence to be seen in public with the
family.'

'Oh, he did that,' said Mary. 'Word had already gone

round that she'd left him when they all rolled up for
morning service at Albion: Mr Schofield with Sarah,
and Sam and James with young Lord Soar – you know,
the new Earl. He sat in the family pew with them all.
There was no lack of people speaking to Sarah, I can
tell you.'

Tizzie was somewhat stunned. Sam Schofield had
taken her advice with a vengeance, and called in the
aristocracy; now that really was bringing in the heavy
artillery. With a friend like that and a devoted family,
Sarah didn't need anybody else worrying about her. As
for brother Sam – there was no need to have anything
more to do with him. Life was simpler if you didn't get
too involved with people, wasn't it?

CHAPTER TWENTY-ONE

An Unbreakable Rule

MATTHEW LOOKED OUT OVER Saltley from the spot where, on first arriving, he had decided to stay in the town for at least six weeks. Since the anniversary of that day he had wanted to come back to this same hillside, just to sit and reflect on the past fourteen months and be thankful: it was hard, though, to leave Martha now she was tiring more easily.

She was a determined liddle soul, he told himself admiringly. She liked everything in order: house spotless, the meals on time, the washing and ironing done to a set pattern, the front step and flagstones mopped on the dot of one-thirty each Saturday. For the most part he thrived on the order of it, the respectability – it was what he'd wanted since he was a child, after all – but if he was honest he did sometimes miss the freedom to come and go as he pleased.

It gave him pleasure to walk with his little wife through Soar Park on Sunday afternoons, wearing a clean shirt and his good coat, greeting friends and workmates who like them had managed an hour or two of leisure; but it pleased him even more to stride the solitary pathways of the hills with only the sigh of the wind and the song of the birds for company.

Today the opportunity had come after their Sunday dinner – roast beef, no less, followed by rice pudding and wimberry pie. She could cook like a little angel, could Martha. She'd bustled about, clearing up at her new slower pace; he persuaded her to sit in the long wicker chair that had been her mother's, placing a cushion behind her back and another under her feet. 'Do 'ee rest, Martha,' he insisted, 'there be liddle enough chance in the week.'

She made no protest as she settled herself, and when he hovered restlessly above her, said, 'Why don't you go for one of your walks, Matthew? You always used to like goin' up in the hills. I'll just sit here an' do a bit of sewin'.'

He tried not to look delighted, not to hurry away, and she added, 'I've done a plate of sliced beef for the Warhursts instead of startin' the broth – it was easier. You can take it round to them if you want. They can have it cold tomorrow, an' I've put a jar of mustard pickle for them to have with it.'

He lingered for a while just to please her, and then set off for Miller's Yard. It looked little better in late summer than it had done when he first saw it in the depths of winter, and the sweet-stale smell of bugs met him at the Warhursts' door as it always did. Billy, though, was brighter. He was still working for Eddie Miller, but had been put in charge of the shoddy-mixer at ten and six a week. Not only that, his eldest child, a boy of twelve, had been taken on as a little piecer at Fairbrother's mill, They talked at the door as Billy related all this, it being understood that Matthew never went inside; but when he made to depart Billy put out a hand. 'Hold on a minute, lad, the wife wants a word.'

Matthew's heart sank. He always compared the weak, shuffling Mrs Warhurst with Martha, and it left him grieved for the woman. Now she came to the door with a brisker step. Her hair was newly-washed and shining, drawn back from a centre parting in the manner of the day, and she wore a clean lace cap. 'Mrs Warhurst,' he muttered in surprise, touching his hat. 'Pleased to see you lookin' so well.

She smiled, revealing her poor discoloured teeth. 'Your wife's all right, I hope, Mr Raike?'

'Yes, thank'ee kindly.'

'Billy tells me she's finishin' work when the baby comes?'

'That's right, Missis.'

'Well, things are pickin' up here, as you've heard, but I wanted to tell you meself that I've found a job early mornin's, cleanin' at the Salters Arms, an' they might give me a couple of hours in the evenin', washin' up. What with that an' Billy's rise an' our Arthur at Fairbrothers, I want to say we'll be able to manage very well without what you've been givin' us.' Her faded blue eyes filled with tears. 'We'll never forget what you've done for us if we live to be a hundred, will we, Billy?'

Billy laughed – a genuine laugh. 'There's not much chance of us reachin' that age, love, nor of us forgettin'.'

Matthew smiled at them both, deeply relieved. ''Twas a bit to help 'ee keep goin',' he said, 'and you know where I be if you need me.'

'Aye, lad, we know,' said Billy, 'but we're on the way up again now, I can feel it, an aimin' to get out of this stinkin' hole as soon as we're able. What's more I've heard they'll be lookin' for builders' labourers when they start on Boulton's new mill, so I'm keepin' an eye open there, as well. Mr Miller's shed's all right, an' I'm glad of it, but I've always liked a bit of fresh air at me work.' He shook Matthew by the hand, and gripped his shoulder for an instant. 'We'll be seein' you, lad.'

Matthew had leapt up the steps of the yard as if he had wings on his heels. Life was good, life was marvellous, they could manage without him! His conscience was clear at last, and Martha would be delighted. He strode rapidly up the hill towards Jericho, past the Schofields' house and then up the narrow road that led out of the town; now he could see the barn where he used to sleep. There was no sign of the cheerful farmer, nor of the long-haired wife who had met her lover within sight and hearing of the trespasser. . . .

He recalled that his boots had been falling apart that night. Now, he could wiggle his toes inside clean socks and his boots were of good strong leather. He told himself that coming to Peggy-oh's home town had been the best decision of his adult life. If the liddle 'un should be a boy they were to call him Luke after the man who had been both friend and father to him. They'd decided on names months ago: he was to choose if it was a boy, and Martha if it was a girl; there had been no hesitation on his part. 'Luke,' he had said, 'after Luke Fawcett; and what will you choose, Martha?'

Her cheeks were deep pink as she said quietly. 'Rose. Rose Dorcas Raike.'

He was touched by the Dorcas, and gave her a warm kiss of thanks for it, but Rose? 'That flag do mean a powerful lot to 'ee,' he said.

She'd flashed him a strange look, unreadable, yet he had the idea he'd disappointed her in some way. She made no reply, but gave that little twitch of her lips and then touched his hair.

The wind was picking up, bringing rain clouds from the west, but he sat on, relishing the rare spell of solitary thought. Six weeks more before the baby was due, and she meant to carry on at her looms until a fortnight before her time, and then finish for good. She had given way to him on that. There was work a-plenty in the mills at last, but her looms being Schofield's there were women ready and waiting to take them on. With two wages coming in and no elderly dependants, the last few months had seen new curtains in Ledden Street, a rug at the side of the bed, two glass vases on the mantelpiece, a new set of iron pans for the fire; there was also money in the little stone jar against a rainy day.

At work he'd tried his hardest to keep on the right side of Maynard, because a second heavy gang was to be started up so as to have one in each mill, and he was eager to be put in charge of it – under Maynard, of course. Sometimes it seemed they even breathed in and out at the foreman's command; the men joked that the Schofields didn't really run the place, but took their orders from Maynard, on the quiet.

At home they'd been busy too, Martha sewing and crocheting for the baby, while he spent countless hours making a wooden cradle. He was mindful of Peggy-oh's lessons in carpentry, and used a thrilling new aptitude he'd discovered in himself – woodcarving. Boy or girl, a rose was suitable for either, he decided, and at the head of the cradle carved a fine little bloom with a stem and three leaves, and above it the letter 'R' for their surname. Martha had been lost in admiration when he showed it to her, and he told himself that was reward enough for the time being. He lay back on the grass of the hedgerow, and knew that the real reward would be to see the child, healthy and content beneath the rose.

It was nearing the time for Martha to finish work when he nerved himself to ask Maynard whether he stood a chance of being put in charge of the second gang. He was mortified when the foreman laughed in his face.

'You, Raike? What on earth makes you think I'd recommend you?'

'Why, my work, Mr Maynard. I can pull my weight with anybody, and read an' write with the best of 'en.'

'There's two reasons why I wouldn't even consider you. One – you're too soft for a ganger, I've seen it in you from the start; an' two – you're from foreign parts. I want a Saltley man in charge, one as talks plain English, not your namby-pamby Devon twang.'

Matthew felt the blood rise hotly from his neck. 'Twang or no, I got took on by Mr Holt,' he said, 'an' on Mr Schofield's say-so, what's more!'

Maynard hesitated at the name of his employer, then pushed back his hat and stuck his chin out. 'Mr Holt might be the setter-on, but it's me as runs the heavy gang. Me, Raike, an' I can tell you that a local man'll get the ganger's job. You can work, I'll grant you that, an' if you do as you're told an' keep your trap shut we'll get along all right. You'd be very unwise, though, to get ideas above your station.'

Martha had been indignant when he told her. 'Maynard!' she said scornfully, 'he's nothing but a jumped-up bully who works the gang to their knees. He's a loud-mouth as well. They'll know who to use if the mill hooter breaks down, they won't part! Never mind him, Matthew, your time'll come. Mr Schofield knows who you are. He spoke to you that time, didn't he?'

Yes, he did at that. It had been months back, after Mrs Schofield died, after Miss Sarah left her husband. He'd been pulling a bogey of empty skips across the yard when he came face to face with Joshua Schofield. All in a moment he took in the deeply lined face that made his employer seem an old, old man, and touched his hat as they neared each other, but the mill-owner held up a hand to halt him. 'It's the fella from Devon, isn't it? Don't tell me the name . . . I've got it – Raike! I noticed a while back you were on the heavy gang, and they tell me you're not frightened of hard work. Well, are you suited here at Jericho, or are you hankering to be back in Plymouth?'

'I'm well suited, Mr Schofield, an' I'd like to thank 'ee kindly for keepin' me name in front o' Mr Holt.' Matthew felt he should mention Mrs Schofield, express his sympathy, but she was long gone and he couldn't bring himself to speak her name.

Mr Schofield flipped a hand at his word of thanks. 'Carry on, carry on,' he said briskly; he went on his way across the yard, his mind no doubt elsewhere before he'd gone a dozen steps.

Matthew sat on in the sunshine, thinking of the people who had influenced his life since he came to Saltley. Martha and her mother and Uncle Jack, Norman Nuttall, Billy and his family, Daniel Broadhurst, good man of the chapel, and, of course, Joshua of the golden trumpet.

As always, they walked to the mill together, with

Matthew thankful that his wife had only another day
and a half to work. Each evening her ankles were so
puffed up that she had to unfasten her clogs to walk
home, and she could hardly speak for weariness. None
of this was surprising, because the weaving shed was hot
and she was so big the other women pulled her leg and
said she'd get jammed between her looms.

It promised to be one of the golden days of late
September, with the scent of autumn on the air and a
fresh breeze blowing from the hills; it made him more
reluctant than usual to enter the damp heat of the mill
with its smell of machine-oil and yesterday's sweat, but
he saw Martha to the door of the weaving shed and
went off to join the gang. By five past six Maynard was
in full voice. 'Raike! To the weavin' shed! A sample
order to go to the cut-room for immediate inspection!
Take 'em straight to Mr Lingard's table. Come on, man
– move!'

As expected, Matthew set off at the trot. Maynard
thought himself so clever, but it had never once dawned
on him that he liked to be sent to the weaving shed.
There was no chance to wave to Martha, though; the
tobacco-chewing Bennet had the cuts of cotton waiting,
and just nodded to Matthew while changing his wad
from one cheek to the other.

Unusually, the cut-room was empty. No Lingard, no
assistants, no labourers; perhaps because they hadn't
yet started the routine tasks of the day. But Lingard's
bad book was open on his desk, while on the floor –
Matthew stared – on the floor but half hidden behind
the stacks of cloth was a cotton chemise. He knew what
it was because Martha wore one for work – a half-shimmy
that was only waist length, worn over her stays, with a
thinner one under them, for coolness.

Then he heard the sound. From behind the racks, it
came. A feminine sound – not a groan, not a shout,
but a whimper, which all at once became a cry of pain.
Matthew leapt over the cut-table and pushed behind

the piles of cloth. Lingard had a young woman there, his hands on her bare breasts, fingers digging into the soft flesh.

The girl let out a squeal at being seen in such a situation, and Lingard swung round on Matthew and snarled, 'Get out!'

Matthew acted on impulse. With a blow to the jaw he felled Lingard, and the girl burst into tears of shame and relief. He picked up her shimmy and tossed it across to her, ignoring the man who lay senseless. Dread was filling him. Everyone knew the consequences of striking another worker: whatever the provocation you were sacked on the spot. No physical violence in the mill; it was an unbreakable rule. The woman turned her back on him and slipped the half-shimmy over her head, plump shoulders quivering, and then put on her blouse.

'Why did 'ee take it off?' he asked angrily.

She shot him a look over her shoulder. 'It were that or bein' put in his book again. He sent word to come an' see him before I switched on, but I'd never have come if I'd known he'd be on his own.' She swallowed and looked as if she might vomit. 'I'm a married woman. What if he's marked me?'

'Tell your husband to come to me,' said Matthew wearily. 'I'll vouch for it bein' forced on 'ee. Go on, back to your looms.'

He bent over Lingard, who was still motionless. He – he wasn't dead? No – there was a rise and fall of the narrow chest, and the fingers of one hand twitched, as if still enjoying what they'd handled. Matthew gave him a look of disgust, and went back to the gang filled with foreboding.

By twelve o'clock he was pacing from the front door to the kitchen and back again, waiting for Martha to come home in her dinner hour. Because she would know. News of any kind spread through Jericho like wildfire.

Within minutes of the incident Maynard was sent for

from the cut-room, and when he had gone Matthew told the others. Their reactions ranged from amazement to satisfaction. 'You're mad!' said one. 'There isn't a chance in hell you'll be kept on.' Another man clapped him on the back. 'Serve the bugger right! He's always had a name for maulin' the women, but prepare yoursel' lad, there's no arguin' against it.' A couple of the men stayed silent, and in spite of his misery, Matthew knew why. They had often mocked his accent, and mentioned Saltley men who were out of work. Like Maynard, they resented him as an outsider.

The foreman came back tight-lipped. 'You're sacked, Raike,' he said at once. 'Collect your pay at the office, they'll be expectin' you.'

Matthew wasn't going to take it meekly. 'I'm to lose me job because that lecherous old swine messes about with a married woman an' I hit him for it? That's justice, is it?'

Maynard looked at him. 'It's justice of a kind. If every man in Jericho used his fists when he saw somethin' he didn't like, there'd be blows struck every day of the week. It's a rule of the mill – no arguin', no redress. Go an' collect your pay. An' Raike, I can't give you a reference.'

'What, not even one sayin' I'm too soft, an' talk with a namby-pamby Devon twang?' It eased him to throw caution to the winds where Maynard was concerned. 'Well, I'll be glad to get away from *you*, Maynard.'

Jaw set, the other said through his teeth, 'Tell that to your wife.'

At ten past twelve Martha came in, shawl over one arm, her face pale but with sweat standing out on her forehead. He went to take her in his arms, but she pushed him away. 'Fool!' she cried bitterly. 'Fool, to lose your job over Lingard. We've got two pound in the jar, you know, not two hundred. I knew it were too good to last, I knew it!'

'I'll get another job, an' stop shoutin',' he snapped,

anger wiping away his guilt. 'There's more work than ever in Saltley.'

'Oh aye? An' they'll come runnin' to give it you, will they, when word gets out you knocked the cut-looker unconscious?'

He glared at her. 'What did you want me to do? Pat him on the back an' say "well done"?'

'It's been goin' on for years,' she said wearily. 'All the weavers who're on the plump side know what to expect if they let a float down. He's just a mauler, a feeler. He doesn't go any further.'

'Oh, we must all be grateful for that, then, mustn't we? Look, I'm powerful sorry it happened but I've never been able to stand that sort o' thing. I saw enough of it at the Mizzen to last me a lifetime.'

She thudded down on a chair. 'They're lettin' me work an extra week,' she said, 'an' I can have me job back when the baby's a fortnight old. That's a week later than some of 'em start back. We've enough saved for three weeks, four at a pinch.'

He'd half-expected it, and now remorse sharpened his tongue. 'You've got what you wanted all along, then, haven't you?'

She looked at him, her plain little face puffy from pregnancy, and her eyes wide with hurt and accusation. 'Think what you like,' she said, and went to make a cup of tea.

'I've already made it,' he said, and poured it for her.

She took out her snap of bread and cheese and sat up to the table, but after a few mouthfuls pushed it away. 'I'm not hungry,' she said. 'I'll go an' see if I can get booked in with a child-minder. They'll all be busy at six o'clock with women collectin' their babies.'

When she had gone he sat with his head in his hands, knowing he could make no protest about the baby going to a minder. He couldn't walk the town looking for work or wait on the tally bridge with a new-born baby in his arms. He thought back to the scene in the cut-room, and found it strange that he didn't regret hitting Lingard. He might have lost his job, but at least he hadn't lost his self-respect.

Matthew was getting to know them all on the tally bridge: the slow-witted, the crippled, those with poor eyesight, and the boys, dozens of boys ready to go running if a spinner or self-acting minder should send down to the bridge for a piecer. Martha had been right; word had gone round that he'd knocked Jericho's cut-looker senseless, and though he'd sought work in every mill, every shop, every public house, there wasn't an employer in the town who would have him.

That would have been bad enough, but things hadn't improved between him and Martha. They spoke, but only when it was unavoidable, and then it was stilted and over-polite; and at night they lay silently side by side without touching each other. He would dash home during the day to see if she had started with the baby, to find her busy with some household task; she would look at him as if wondering why he'd left the bridge and maybe missed the chance of work.

One day he was sitting on the parapet, the only able-bodied man among them all, when a small girl in a navy-blue dress under a clean white pinafore walked sedately across the bridge. She was pretty, very pretty, with curly brown hair peeping from under a cotton bonnet, and he was thinking idly that she must be a young parlourmaid from one of the big houses, when to his surprise she stopped in front of him. 'Hello, Mister,' she said shyly.

It was the liddle maid who had followed the cotton wagon with her sister! But she looked so clean, she looked lovely! And he'd been worrying what had happened to her and her mother. 'You're priddy as a picture,' he said, highly pleased. 'Has your mother found work, then?'

'Yes. She's housekeeper to Miss Ridings at the pawn-shop,' she said proudly, 'an' I'm the learner. We live in, we're not in the cellar in Gallgate.'

'I be glad to hear that,' he said, smiling. Then the reversal in their situations hit him, and the smile was wiped from his face.

'Me mam saw you here on Saturday,' said the child. 'She says I have to ask if you an' your wife are managin'?'

'We're all right up to now,' said Matthew awkwardly. 'I lost me job because I hit a man who was doing somethin' – somethin' bad. I'm hopin' to get work any day now.'

'I'll come an' see you again, shall I, next time I come this way?'

'I'd like that,' he said gently, 'but what be you called, liddle miss?' All at once he felt the need to put a name to her.

She beamed at him. 'Naomi,' she said. 'It's from the Bible.' Then, suddenly serious and without a hint of mockery, she dipped the knee to him in a curtsey, and went on her way.

Touched and yet horribly unsettled, Matthew watched her small neat figure until she was out of sight. The bossy Miss Ridings must have mellowed somethin' powerful to give work to that raggety, half-starved woman and her daughter. Still, if they could find work, so could he. Perhaps he should do the rounds of the street-menders and drain-layers again?

At noon Tizzie went upstairs for her dinner, and for the hundredth time told herself she was glad she'd changed her mind: clean rooms, washing and ironing beautifully done, and meals cooked to perfection. Who would have thought the creature who turned up that day to be capable of it? Sent by Biddy, she had entered the shop with her daughter and they stood just inside the door, looking so forlorn, so destitute, that Tizzie almost sent them down the outside stairs to the dolly-shop without

giving them chance to say a word. But the woman
forestalled her. 'Miss Ridings?' she said. 'Beg pardon,
Miss, but I've come about the housekeeper's job.'

From a distance of nine or ten paces Tizzie could
smell them; it was not body odour, like those who
never washed, nor the sourness of dirty underclothes,
but the smell that was common to Saltley's very poor –
the flat, dead odour that always accompanied sickness
and hunger and despair. It was what from childhood
she'd always termed 'the poor smell'. Don't even let
her hope for the job, she told herself briskly. Don't
give an inch – she isn't what you need.

Just then Barney came up the stairs with a bag of loose
change. He saw the woman and child, and nodded his
big head at them pleasantly before emptying the coins
into the wooden runnels of the drawer. The woman
turned her head at the clink of money. As Barney went
back downstairs she returned her tired, dark gaze to
Tizzie, who said briskly, 'I'm sorry, but I'm looking
for a clean, respectable woman with no dependants –
one with experience of running a house – to cook and
clean and so forth.'

'I can do that,' said the woman. 'I've run a house
for nine people in me time, cookin', washin', ironin'
– everythin'. Me daughter here – she'd work full-time
an' all, not for wages, just for her dinner, like.'

Tizzie hesitated. Free labour was not to be lightly
dismissed. . . . But no, she didn't want to see that
gaunt face about the house, nor those vast dark eyes.
They made her feel uncomfortable. She took a shilling
from the drawer and laid it on the counter. 'I don't think
you're quite what I'm looking for,' she said, 'but here's
a little to help you along.'

The woman stared at the coin, and for an instant Tizzie
had the feeling she would refuse to pick it up, but the thin
fingers closed over it and she bowed her head meekly.
'Thank you, Miss. You're very kind, Miss.'

When they had gone Tizzie found herself pacing up

and down behind the counter. Why, why did such people
have to impinge on her life? Most of those who came
to pledge their bits and pieces were like those two
– under-nourished, under-employed, under – what –
undervalued? With an impatient sigh she went down
the stairs to have a word with Barney.

'That woman had come for the job of housekeeper,'
she said lightly, 'but I didn't think she was what I'm
looking for. And she has the child, as well.'

He nodded. 'I've seen her about, Miss Tizzie. She
lives in a yard in Gallgate. A widow, she is – her
husband died of the fever a couple of years back. She
had a baby after he died, an' lost the others, one by
one, except for the girl. They do say she was a fine
respectable body, once.'

Tizzie fancied there was condemnation in his tone,
and tossed her gleaming head. 'She certainly doesn't
look it now,' she said shortly.

At six o'clock she went upstairs for her tea, leaving
Barney in charge. She was having a kipper, cooked in hot
water the way she liked it, but for once the succulent oily
flesh seemed lacking in taste. She opened the newspaper
to read while she ate – one of the few pleasures she'd
found in living alone – and turned to an article about
Abraham Lincoln. The papers all seemed to like him
now he was dead, and yet she recalled that the London
Times had once called him a baboon. Whatever they
said of him, he'd been a humane sort of man for one
who held such power; a man of principle, as well. And
here again they were quoting that address he gave at
Gettysburg. . . .

She jumped up from the table and ran down to the
shop. 'Barney, that woman – do you think I should
give her a trial? A week, say, just to see if she's
any good.'

For the second time in three days he gave his rare,
brilliant smile. 'Yes, I do, Miss Tizzie. Happen I could
go an' tell her for you? An' happen you could spare a

couple of dresses from the cupboards? There's several
of 'em unredeemed, aren't there?'

That had been the start of it: a more relaxed, more
pleasurable life for her, and a transformation in the life
of Rebecca and young Naomi. All because she'd changed
her mind.

By mid-afternoon the shop was quiet, and Tizzie
sat at her desk, checking the books and jotting down
figures that confirmed what she suspected – business
was slowing down a little. Prosperity was returning to
Saltley, and with more people in work there were less
who needed the pawnshop. It wasn't dramatic – merely a
slight decline in trade – but she would have to think very
carefully about her next moves in business. Life as an
impoverished pawnbroker with no live-in housekeeper
held no appeal whatsoever.

She heard a carriage stop outside, and a moment later
Sarah Mayfield entered the shop, still black-clad for her
mother but lovely as ever, with the glistening hair swept
back under a neat little black velvet hat. There wasn't
a vestige of life or animation in either her expression
or bearing; she put Tizzie in mind of a beautiful lamp
that someone had forgotten to light. Usually she hated
people calling in at the shop to see her, but she held
out both her hands and said warmly, 'Sarah! It's lovely
to see you.'

The deep pink mouth trembled ever so slightly, and
Sarah asked, 'Could you possibly spare me a moment,
Tizzie?'

'Come upstairs. I'll get Barney to keep an eye on the
counter.'

Once in the big sitting-room she gave her visitor the
best chair and offered tea, which was gently refused.
'I wanted to have a word in private, Tizzie. You see,
although I've been home for ages it was only yesterday
that I pressed Sam for the full story of why he set off
up north in such a hurry that day. I knew it was to tell
me about the girl – the one who threw herself off the

viaduct – but I didn't – that is, I mean – ' She floundered,
pulling off her gloves finger by finger, seeking words that
were lost to her. Tizzie forced herself to stay silent. Let
her get it off her chest, she told herself. Let her say her
piece without help.

'When I knew it was because of what you told Sam, I
realised at once that it couldn't have been easy for you
to talk about it. Tizzie, it would have been dreadful if
I'd heard of it from Mrs Boulton. You spared me that,
and I want you to know I'm grateful for it. Sam says
he tried to thank you at the time, but I had to come
and say it too. And thanks for suggesting we should
be seen in public with a well-known figure. That's why
Sam asked his friend Francis Soar to go to chapel with
us that day. You know him, I expect?'

Tizzie hid an ironic smile. 'No. I met him once or
twice at fund-raising meetings, that's all.'

'He's kind,' said Sarah, 'he's really kind.'

Her tone revealed that she saw a kind man as a rarity,
but surely, thought Tizzie, her father and brothers were
proof that that wasn't the case. One man, though, had
not been in the least kind to her; for an instant Tizzie
– the least fanciful of mortals – imagined that he waited
unseen in the shadows of the room, tall and elegant in his
well-cut clothes. She moved her shoulders impatiently,
and decided to give him a mention. 'I'm truly sorry about
you and Edward,' she said. 'Really I am.'

Sarah regarded her sadly. Her eyes were weary, like
those of a middle-aged woman who has had her fill of
life's troubles, and they looked horribly out of place in
that young, unlined face. 'I wasn't right for Edward,'
she admitted gravely, 'and he wasn't right for me.
Somewhere, there's a woman who could make him
happy.'

Tizzie thought back to that hired room in Manchester,
to her own face glimpsed in the mirror: paper-white,
shocked and – yes, frightened. 'Maybe there is,' she
agreed matter-of-factly, 'but she'd be a very unusual

one. She'd have to be rich, for a start, and very attractive; from a respectable family, but with the sexual appetite of an alley cat and the experience of a forty-year-old prostitute!'

Sarah stared at her, and then the faintest of smiles touched her mouth. 'Oh, Tizzie,' she said in relief, 'you're like a breath of fresh air! Do you think we could meet again?'

'Why not?'

'Would you come to tea with me one day? I'm at home now with Polly, in charge of the house until I decide what to do with my life.'

'I work six days a week,' Tizzie reminded her. 'My only free afternoons are Sundays, and I expect your father and brother are at home then. You can come here any Sunday afternoon you like. How will that suit you?'

'It will suit me very well,' said Sarah. 'Thanks, Tizzie.'

Martha was in labour, and at last she knew why they called it by that name. It was agonising, gruelling work, with the midwife wearing an apron bloodstained from her last delivery, and Matthew pacing about downstairs. In moments of quiet she could hear his footsteps on the kitchen flagstones.

At least she was only one day late, she told herself between pains. That meant she'd be away from her looms for only three weeks and a day in all, so the money in the jar would last.

'Come on,' said the midwife; she was a kindly woman, but overworked at her calling, and tired now by her third confinement in twelve hours. 'We want no daydreamin'. You've got a big baby comin', an' you're only a little 'un. You'll have to work at it.'

Labour, work – when had she ever done anything else? But in some strange way this work was a joy, the pain a pleasure, because she and Matthew had made their peace with each other. He had come in for his dinner after a morning's casual work helping to clear out a mill reservoir, and had found her about to set off for the midwife. He grabbed her and kissed her face and her hair and even her rough little hands. He reeked of stagnant water but to her it seemed like the sweetest of perfumes. 'Martha, I'm sorry! God help me I be awful sorry to have brought us down to this, an' I'm sorry I snapped at you like I did.'

The relief was such that she had sagged at the knees, and big as she was he picked her up in his arms and carried her to her mother's chair. She had kissed him back, her mouth melting with remorse. 'I'm sorry an' all, Matthew. I couldn't seem to stop bein' short with you. An' oh – you smell awful!'

He smiled – the captivating smile that had always made her heart sing. 'Smell or not, I'm off for the midwife an' I'll be back before you know it.'

When he had gone she lay back, savouring their brief peacemaking until the next pain came; in the lull that followed it she knew a stab of keen regret that her mother wouldn't be there to see her fourth grandchild.

It was early evening. She'd been determined not to cry out, but in the final moments she did let out a scream. She couldn't help it. Matthew came hammering on the door. 'What's goin' on?' he bellowed. 'Martha, be 'ee all right?'

The midwife bellowed back. 'Of course she is! She's doin' well, but she's only the size of two pennorth o' copper. Go down an' make us all a cup o' tea. It won't be long now.'

Then the pain was over, and she was filled by the great peace of achievement. It was a boy. 'A fine little lad,' said the midwife with satisfaction. 'A bit short of beef on his bones, but he'll soon put that on. Here, put him to the breast. Look at that – he's losin' no time in suckin'. You've got a hungry little lad there, you haven't part.'

His hair was dark like Matthew's, and it lay in wet little whorls all over his head, and when he opened his eyes they were dark blue, tinged with brown. Matthew held her hand while he looked at him. 'Luke,' he said softly, 'liddle Luke. Thank'ee, Martha, from the bottom o' my heart.'

And it was all right. The doubts that had bedevilled her pregnancy, the fears that he would love the baby more than he loved her disappeared, never to return. For the second time in her life Martha fell in love: with a miniature version of her husband.

CHAPTER TWENTY-TWO

Going Up and Going Down

MARTHA HAD NEVER KNOWN two weeks to pass so quickly. As the midwife had prophesied, Luke was a hungry baby, demanding his feeds with an ear-piercing cry but settling contentedly once he'd been fed. Bella and her family had been across from Rochdale; the little girls hung over the cradle adoringly, while their mother declared Luke to be a handsome little fella with a good pair of lungs.

At first Martha was bowed down by the responsibility of being his sole source of nourishment. As she settled to the routine of frequent feeds, though, she relaxed a little; the conviction came to her that looking after a baby full-time and losing sleep with it was easier than running four looms full time and losing sleep with her mother and Uncle Jack. It was certainly more enjoyable, and of course she had a husband to help her. When she fed Luke in the night Matthew would go down and make her a cup of tea, and then sit up in bed at her side with his arm around her.

In spite of the fall in their income she was happier than she'd ever been in her life; she tried not to think about going back to work and leaving Luke. Such thoughts always brought a stab of resentment, and she didn't want anything of that sort to spoil the tender new relationship between the three of them. She couldn't fault Matthew on trying to find work. He had worn the soles of his good strong boots right through in tramping the town and its outskirts, but throughout the baby's short life had managed only a half-day unloading canal boats and two hours stacking bricks on the site of Walton's new mill.

The time of her return to Jericho drew nearer, and for Matthew's sake she had to banish all signs of reluctance; she didn't even allow herself to show unease about the child-minder. 'He'll be all right,' she said firmly. 'I'll feed him just before I set out and again in my dinner hour, and I'll be back home with him by ten past six. I'm not worried, and neither should you be. He's going longer between his feeds already.' She crushed the thought that he'd never gone longer than three hours in his life.

On the Monday morning Matthew was very quiet as she dressed Luke, and hovered at her side while she fed him. 'Stop worryin',' she told him calmly. 'Mrs Hill seems a decent woman, an' she has two helpers, so between them they should be able to manage ten or eleven babies. Only three of 'em are really small, anyway.'

They walked together as far as Peter Street, then Matthew had to leave them to go to the bridge. He touched the baby's cheek and dropped a kiss on his forehead; without a word of farewell he walked away, his lips clamped tightly together. Martha hurried on to the child-minder's, carrying Luke inside her shawl. He was fast asleep, and a wisp of dark hair showed under his bonnet.

There was a basket of sorts ready for him, and a girl of about twelve laid him in it very gently. Mrs Hill bustled up, smoothing her clean white apron. 'Off you go, an' don't worry,' she said briskly. 'We'll look after him, won't we, girls? Yes, we'll change him. . . . No, we won't leave him screamin'. . . . Don't worry, Mrs Raike. . . .'

And then Martha experienced a strange sensation, one that was to recur many times in the coming weeks. She turned to leave the house but her feet wouldn't move. They seemed to be glued to the floor. She gave Mrs Hill an apologetic little smile and forced herself towards the door, but it was as if her clogs were made

of lead. Outside she forged on grimly towards the mill.
The five-to-six blower would be going any minute.

It was almost a surprise when things began to fall into
place. Luke was usually gnawing his fist when she dashed
in at dinner time, but he was always freshly changed.
What was more he began to settle down, no longer
crying so much in the night, and not so ravenous for
his feeds. Mrs Hill and the girls seemed to find him
no more demanding than the other babies, and Martha
knew she should have been relieved. She *was* relieved,
but relief didn't make it any easier to leave him.

As for work, well, it was as it had always been. She
had taken over her own looms, near Jessie, and at last
she felt a complete woman; married to a handsome
husband with a beautiful baby son, and working, like
the other mothers. Knowing the reason she was back
among them the women took an interest in her, made
a fuss of her and kept asking about Matthew's efforts
to find work. She told herself that things could have
been much worse, that if she didn't feel so tired all the
time she wouldn't get that ridiculous feeling of being
unable to move her feet whenever she left Luke with
Mrs Hill.

For his part, Matthew was suffering from boredom,
frustration and unused energy. The hours on the bridge
were tedious, and the glum silence of the men and women
there set his teeth on edge; beneath his iritation lay deep
remorse and self-loathing. How could he have pretended
he didn't regret striking Lingard? The moment he saw
his son, felt that tiny hand in his, he knew he would
have watched Lingard maul a dozen weavers a day if
it would have spared Martha going back to work and
leaving Luke with a minder.

He thought of Luke constantly through the long,
dreary days, and it was like the sun coming out from
behind clouds when he went home and saw him. He
noted every movement of the perfect little hands, every
blink, every parting of the soft mouth, every windy smile.

Often he was tempted to go to Mrs Hill's to see how he was, or to carry him out for an airing; but one day he was leaving the bridge to do just that when a foreman bricklayer came up on horseback and hired him for a full afternoon.

Work of that kind was a rarity, of course, and he found his self-respect dwindling, his confidence faltering. What sort of man let his wife support both him and his son? Money was tight, because Mrs Hill's four shillings had to come out of Martha's seventeen and six a week; then there was rent, and with winter coming on they would need fuel for warmth as well as for cooking – there was no free coal since Uncle Jack died.

The infuriating thing was that Harry Lingard still reigned supreme over the cut-room, and Martha reported that the plump young weaver had left Jericho for good. Nobody knew whether her husband had seen the marks of Lingard handling her, or merely heard talk of why Matthew had hit him. Whatever his reasons, he had insisted on his wife leaving, and now she ran four looms at Boultons, and earned ninepence a week less. It had all been pointless, Matthew told himself in his darker moments; but sometimes a small, calm voice inside him said: 'No, it wasn't pointless – your point was made and you knocked Lingard senseless in proving it.'

One morning he was pacing back and forth across the bridge when the child Naomi came along, wearing a small shoulder-shawl over her dress and apron. 'Hello,' she said, beaming.

Glad to have his boredom eased, he swept off his hat with a flourish. 'Why, it's a young lady! Miss Naomi, or I'm much mistaken.'

Cheeks pink, she giggled, and said, 'Hold out your hand, Mr Raike.'

He held it out, and she laid a sixpence on his palm. 'Me mam's sent it,' she said proudly, 'an' she says you're not to refuse it. She's been savin' it up.'

Matthew stared down at the coin and felt the blood

drain from his face. Charity – that was what he'd sunk to, charity! Well, he wasn't having it! He couldn't accept hand-outs from Naomi's mother; she'd been destitute herself only a couple of months back. But the child was looking at him with such delight. . . . It was their turn now, he realised, their turn to give.

The silence between them lengthened. What did it say in the Bible? It is more blessed to give than to receive? That was true, he'd proved it, hadn't he? But now he was finding that it was harder to receive than to give. Much harder. He forced a smile to his face. 'Tell your mother thank'ee kindly. I'm – I'm very grateful.'

Highly pleased, she went on her way swinging her shopping basket, leaving Matthew in lower spirits than at any time since he came to Saltley. He put the sixpence in his waistcoat pocket, resolving to use it to buy extra milk each day for Martha. She always said she was all right, but sometimes she looked awful pale and washed out.

'Excuse me callin', Miss Tizzie, but I had to move fast. It's just somethin' I heard, an' I thought – well – it's just an idea, an' I'm sorry if I'm out of order. . . .' Barney had knocked on the sitting-room door at nine o'clock on a Sunday morning, dressed in his best, but plucking self-consciously at his necktie.

Tizzie was finishing her breakfast after her Sunday lie-over, and Rebecca and Naomi were busy in the kitchen. 'Come on in,' she said shortly. It always irritated her to see him on edge and apologising. Was she so unapproachable that he hesitated to call outside working hours? 'Do you want a cup of tea or coffee, Barney? A slice of bacon, perhaps, or a fried egg?'

'Oh no, Miss Tizzie. I had me breakfast a while back.'

'What is it then? Here, take a seat.'

With an effort he hoisted himself on to a chair. 'You know you were sayin' the takin's are down a bit? I've been thinkin' that perhaps we're in for a slack time, like, in the next twelve month.'

'So have I,' she admitted. 'I'm a bit concerned about it, to be honest.'

'I don't know how you're fixed for capital, but last night I heard of somethin' that might be an investment, sort of.' He glanced round the comfortable room, and with a straight face added, 'To keep you in the manner you're accustomed to, if business falls off even more. It's only a suggestion, you know, an' I don't want to presume.'

'Oh, out with it, Barney, and stop apologising! If you don't know by now that I value your opinion then you never will. A small amount of capital came with the business, you know that, and in spite of the alterations to the shop I've managed to increase it a bit. It's in my name, so I can do what I like with it. Why?'

'I hear what goes on in Saltley, you know. Men talk and forget I'm there, or they think I'm slow and don't watch what they say in front of me. It's just that I've heard there's a plot of land that'll be up for sale any day. It's good flat land; solid, an' there's a stream flows through it to the East Brook, as well as a natural pond. The canal's not far off, and more important, it's only quarter of a mile from the railway yard.'

Tizzie's eyes gleamed like emeralds. 'A mill! Land for a mill, you mean.'

Barney eyed her in the manner of a proud parent observing a brilliant offspring. 'Aye, a mill. There's several folk hankerin' to build now things are pickin' up a bit. I thought if you could buy a prime site for buildin', and then either lease it or sell to one of the cotton masters at a small profit. . . .'

'Surely the big cotton men will get in before me? Who owns it?'

'A woman,' he said, lips twitching towards a smile. 'A spinster, Elizabeth Baguley, out Park Bridge way. She has no family, no dependants. She's almost a hermit, they say. Has odd ideas, but she's good-hearted. I heard a fella as does odd jobs for her talking about it last night when I went for a drink. She's started sellin' off bits and pieces of her property to raise money to apprentice a tribe of the workhouse boys in engineerin'.'

So a good cause was involved. 'What action do you recommend, Barney?'

'A letter? You'd write a good letter, Miss Tizzie. How about putting it to her that you're a woman making her way in Saltley, and will she give you first refusal? There's nothing lost in that. I'll deliver it for you, if you like. Today.'

Tizzie smiled. His physical movements might be awkward, but mentally he moved at her speed, and she liked that. She drummed her fingers on the table. 'She'd need references?'

'Happen so. You're friendly with Mrs Mayfield, so I thought perhaps the Schofields?'

'Hah!' Tizzie ate her last piece of toast and jumped up to pace the room. 'I've finished, Naomi,' she called.

The child came in to clear the table and hesitated on seeing Barney. Tizzie held up a finger and said expectantly. 'Mr Jellicoe has called on a matter of business, Naomi.' The child bent her head and respectfully dipped the knee, then started to clear away.

Barney wriggled on the chair, his short legs inches from the floor, and Tizzie didn't know whether he was pleased or annoyed at the mark of respect. With an awkward shuffle he slid to the floor and gave her a slip of paper. 'Here's her address, Miss Tizzie, and details of all I've been able to find out about the land. If you'd like me to deliver the letter for you, I'll wait.'

'No,' she said at that. 'It's too far out to Park Bridge. I'll send it by messenger. But first I think I should have a look at the plot, don't you? Will you come with me now?'

He stared at her. 'What, out on the streets?'

Unspoken thoughts hung between them, words remained unsaid. Fool not to have guessed he might be embarrassed to be seen out with her. He was so very touchy – a strange combination of humility and what she suspected was pride. 'We'll have to go through the streets to get there, whether we walk or use a cab,' she said calmly, 'but it's a nice day, so let's walk, shall we? That's if you can spare the time?'

'I have nothing else planned, Miss Tizzie.'

'Then how about coming back here for your dinner, so we can talk it over and I can draft out the letter?'

'That'll be very nice, Miss Tizzie. A business meal, like.'

'Purely business,' she agreed gravely. 'I'll just tell Rebecca we'll be one extra, then get my things and we'll be off.' Upstairs in her room, she paused in front of the mirror, eyes glinting with excitement. Perhaps this would be the start of owning half Saltley, as she'd promised herself, of going up in the world? Half the town must be the limit of her ambition, though, because Lord Soar owned the other half, didn't he?

Joshua and Sam were sitting by the fire at Meadowbank. Sarah had gone to evening service at Albion, and under pretence of studying papers from Low Lee, Sam was worrying about her. She had announced over tea that she wanted to go to chapel on her own. 'I can't have you nursemaiding me for ever, Sammy,' she said quietly. 'If I'm to make any sort of life for myself I've got to stand on my own feet a bit. Zacky can take me and bring me home, if you like, but I must go on my own.'

It was all to do with Tizzie Ridings, Sam told himself. Since Sarah had become so friendly with her she had lost that dead look, and begun to take an interest in things again. At one time he would have been jealous that an outsider could do for his sister what he himself couldn't manage, but not now. All he could offer was support, love, and a strong arm to lean on, but he hadn't been able to repair her self-esteem, her self-respect. It had taken another woman, of similar age but a different way of life, to do that. Sarah said Tizzie was like a breath of fresh air that had blown away the horror of her brief married life. She was a strong character, was Miss Tizzie, he thought; a complex character. He couldn't read her as easily as he read most people – but oh, he was grateful to her.

Under guise of studying his papers he watched his father gazing at the blue velvet chair under the lamp, eyes filled with memories, his mouth tender. Not for the first time Sam wondered if they would all be better off without his mother's empty chair, and had once gently suggested it.

'Leave it where it is,' said his father. 'You can sit in it if you want – it's not a shrine – but I'm not having all sign of her obliterated from the house, not in my lifetime. I bought her that chair for her fortieth birthday, and she always loved it. In any case, I'd think of her whether the chair was there or not. That's one thing a good marriage gives you – plenty to look back on.'

Now the vivid eyes studied his son. 'Stop fiddling about with those figures, Sam. Sarah's right, you know. We can't keep her wrapped in cotton-wool if she's to live any sort of life. I've felt a lot better about her these last few weeks. I won't say she's like her old self – I don't think she'll ever be that – but there's a bit of go in her again. You got to her in time that night, lad. Any longer and he'd have damaged her beyond repair.'

Sam agreed with him. His own red-hot rage and disgust had cooled, and now he felt only a sick despair at Sarah's ruined life. Typically, his father had taken action within an hour of her waking on that first morning back home; he visited the bank manager, lawyers in Saltley and Manchester, and the Salford architects who had designed Jericho. Within a week the biggest part of Sarah's capital was back in the Schofield name, mainly due to the care with which he'd devised the financial arrangements before her marriage.

Knowing his father's strict moral code, Sam had

been taken aback by his lack of surprise at Edward's behaviour. A day or so after they returned home he said: 'I'm trying to look at it objectively, Sam, as if he wasn't married to our Sarah. You can't get to my age without knowing about the under-side of life; you only have to walk Manchester to see it, and parts of our own town, for that matter. The way I look at it is that we're all made different: what's unthinkable to some is accepted by others as normal, and behaviour that's a crying compulsion for some doesn't even occur to others. Married men in this town – some of them well known to you and me – are no better than Edward. I might not agree with what they do, but I try not to judge them.

'What I can't forgive is that he treated her without regard for her innocence; without patience, or respect, or even the pretence of affection, and used her worse than a paid trollop. He reduced her to that wreck of a girl you brought home on Friday night. There's such a thing as decent self-control, but by what she managed to tell me, and from what Polly says, he never so much as attempted restraint. How he thought he'd get away with such treatment of her I'll never know. Somewhere overseas he might have managed it, but the other side of Carlisle? We'd have found out sooner or later.

'No, I can't forgive him his lack of concern for her well-being, and because of that I'll ruin him.' He said it quite calmly, but hearing the words Sam had known there was no need to plan his own vengeance. It was his father's place to do it, with his contacts and the Schofield name and reputation. He went on, 'I've seen to it that he won't last much longer professionally, and his way of life will put paid to his health in the end. I've arranged for a man to keep track of him, and to let me know from time to time how he's faring. She's back with us, that's the main thing, and the doctor's almost sure she's not infected with some vile disease. I thank God with all my heart that she isn't in the family way, I do that.'

Now, months later, still holding the Low Lee returns like a shield, Sam was reflecting on all that had happened, when his father said suddenly: 'James! What about your brother, Sam? I've lost your mother and my best friend, Ralph is no longer my son, and my daughter's living apart from her swine of a husband, so I'd like to think that at least you and James are well set. I'm not such a fool as to think he's happy with Esther, though. I suppose he hasn't said anything to you?'

Sam sighed, reluctant to burden his father with more troubles, but it was difficult to hedge with him. He never expected you to conceal anything, and so you very rarely did. 'Yes, he confided in me a bit, after the funeral, when he was trying to decide whether to tell Esther the truth about Ralph. He suddenly said I'd been right to have doubts about her! What I'd give to have been wrong, Father. . . . He didn't exactly bare his soul or go into details, as I think he'd have seen it as disloyal; he went on about her never having had a loving home and so forth. What it boiled down to was that she's obsessed by the house and their social position, and above everything she wants to be accepted by the landed gentry and even the aristocracy. More important than all that, though, is that she finds it hard to put James first, and be a loving wife.'

Joshua sighed. 'Aye, that's more or less what I'd figured out.'

'You know what he's like – he was having difficulty in asserting himself.'

'Did he ask for advice?'

'No, but I gave him some.'

Joshua almost smiled. Sometimes Sam was so like himself at the same age. . . . They both cut through the clap-trap and called a spade a spade. 'What did you tell him?'

'I said he should have a straight talk with her; sit her down and insist she listened, and tell her he wouldn't put up with a nagging wife, that he wanted a normal

married life and a large family. I said he should tell
her that if she wasn't willing to at least try he'd have
to think about a separation.'

Joshua pursed his lips and raised his eyebrows. 'Not
bad for unasked advice. A bit drastic, perhaps?'

'Aye, maybe. But he took me aside a couple of
weeks back and told me they're getting on a bit better.
Underneath it all I suspect she knows she's lucky to have
landed old Jimmy; since Sarah came home as a separated
wife I think she's taken a good look at herself and their
marriage, and decided to pull her socks up.'

'Well, that's something, I suppose. I can't get over
how I always used to think she was such a good little
thing, and so did your mother, though I know she did
have a few doubts before the wedding. Perhaps you
won't mind if I ask you for a progress report now and
again?'

Sam smiled. 'Of course I won't. You're our father.
Who better to ask, and who better to report to? Oh,
another thing before Sarah gets back. What about her
request for a reference for Tizzie Ridings regarding that
plot of land?'

'I don't know anything about the girl,' protested
Joshua, 'except that she's a good friend to our Sarah.
What's her character? Would she keep her word? Does
she intend to pay cash? Can we say she won't go for an
exorbitant profit if she sells?'

Sam gazed thoughtfully into the fire. 'Character – she
was taken in by Edward, but didn't let him seduce her,
so we can't fault her on that, can we? Otherwise she's
straight as a die, and bossy as they come. Yes, I should
say she'd keep her word, out of pride if nothing else.
Yes, Sarah says she'd pay cash, and if she can't raise
enough she won't borrow. Profit – I'm not sure on that
one. She's ambitious – you can sense it. The thing is,
Father, we're in her debt because of Sarah, and somehow
I feel a bit sorry for her. She's not twenty-one yet, but
she runs that shop all on her own except for Jellicoe,

the dwarf, you know. Sometimes I have the feeling that under her brisk, capable exterior there's a soft-hearted woman.'

Joshua surveyed his son with interest. Was there something in the wind there? Sam and the young pawnbroker? One thing, the lad was so good at spotting an unsuitable match he was hardly likely to make one himself. 'All right,' he said, 'I'll give Tizzie as good a reference as even Elizabeth Baguley could demand. It might count for a bit if it's from me, because I knew Elizabeth once – before I met your mother. She was a bonny young woman then, but she never did get married. I don't know why not.'

'This beef is perfect,' declared Maria, and Mary laughed. 'It'd be a poor do if you couldn't have good beef at a butcher's table, Mother.'

'Even the best beef needs a good cook,' said William, with a wink at his wife. 'How are you getting on with your housekeeper, Tizzie? Is she as good a cook as Mary?'

Tizzie smiled. 'She's excellent. A treasure, in fact, and so is her young daughter.'

Cheeks bright pink, Mary said earnestly, 'Oh, I do think it's lovely, you having a housekeeper, Tizz. You never did like cooking and housework.'

They were having a festive Sunday dinner, because Mary was expecting a baby at last. There was port-wine trifle for pudding, and then she bustled out to make a cup of tea for everybody, giving William a meaning look as she went. At once he excused himself to go down to the shop, saying he had to check on his knives for the next morning.

Such a weak excuse could only be a ploy to leave her and her mother together, but Tizzie didn't comment on it. She tried to look relaxed and carefree, as if being alone with her mother was no novelty; in fact it was the first time for ten months or more. She looked at the woman who had ruled her life for almost twenty years, and knew that she still felt as if she'd been forsaken by her. She – a businesswoman and a landowner, going up in the world – why should she care what her mother did or didn't do?

But Maria was leaning forward intently. 'Tizzie, while we're on our own, I want a word with you. I nearly called in at the shop the other day, but I couldn't bring myself to it, it's been so long. . . .'

'So long since you were there, you mean?' Tizzie traced a pattern with her fingernail on the snow-white cloth. 'What's a mere ten months? You've been busy building up your business, by all accounts.'

'Yes. It's doing well, and I'm enjoying it. Tizzie, I've been thinking.'

'Oh?'

'It's come to me lately that I wasn't quite myself when I upped and left you on your own.'

Tizzie gave her mother a wide, expressionless green stare. 'Is that a fact?'

'Yes, it is. I've realised, gradually like, that it wasn't right leaving you like that. I can hardly believe I did it. I told our Mary so last week. I said, Mary, I can hardly believe I cleared off and left our Tizzie like that. And do you know what she said?'

'No.'

'She said, I couldn't believe it either, and I daresay Tizzie couldn't, but you don't need to worry, she's managing very well without you.'

Tizzie would have smiled at that if she'd been in a smiling mood. Good old Mary! But it was strange that her mother should repeat it. She looked into the plump, familiar face, and smothering all resentment, said, 'We all do and say things we regret, Mother. If it's any consolation to you, I've realised more and more that I didn't appreciate my – your husband as I should have done.'

Maria nodded. 'That's what turned me against you,

that you never liked him while he was alive, and you didn't seem to care that he was dead. But still, you're my daughter and I left you. I think a lot of you, Tizzie, even though I might not always have shown it. So – I apologise.'

It wasn't a gracious apology, but it was one Tizzie hadn't expected. Her mother did care about her, and – she had to admit it – she cared about her mother. But she wasn't going to fall down and grovel. 'Thanks, Mother, for that,' she said coolly. 'And I'll say this: I'm sorry for all the times I've upset you by not being closer to him. My only excuse is that he didn't encourage it.'

Surprise showed in her mother's eyes, and the hint of a tear. Tizzie braced herself to receive a kiss, but Maria made no such gesture, 'It's a start,' she said briskly. 'We'll have another go, shall we? Take it slowly?'

Tizzie nodded. 'All right, Mother.'

With a clatter of cups and saucers Mary came back and exchanged a glance with her mother. Tizzie pretended not to see it. Did they think she didn't know it was prearranged? She gave her sister a special smile, though, because all at once she felt as if a weight had been eased inside her chest – not taken away completely, just made lighter. Mary was a love. 'What names are you thinking of for my little niece or nephew?' she asked.

Luke had just turned four weeks old when they began to be uneasy about him. It should have been a happy occasion, because for the first time he slept through the night; but Martha knew he hadn't been hungry when she got home with him at ten past six, and she had to waken him for his bedtime feed, which he took very slowly. She sat with him by the dying fire, feeling him gently sucking, and thought back to his first two weeks, when he was so hungry he worried the breast like a little terrier. Now, sucking seemed to tire him, and she fancied that the crease which had formed around his wrists was disappearing, and that his fingers were looking long and thin again, as they did when he was new-born.

'What is it? What's worryin' 'ee?' Matthew was hovering, as always. 'He be too sleepy, is that it?'

Martha forgot to be calm and reassuring. 'I'm not easy about him,' she said worriedly. 'Do you think he's comin' on as he should? He isn't hungry.'

Matthew studied his son and shook his head. 'He looks much the same to me. He bain't cryin' as much, surely? Let's see how he is in the night.'

But for the first time Luke slept right through. Neither of them wakened until the knocker-up came, and Martha leapt from the bed to find him fast asleep in his cradle with one small fist against his chin. Breasts over-full, she scooped him up and fed him at once; he was hungry enough to reassure Matthew, but not her, so she questioned the child-minder when she took him in at ten to six.

'Was he all right yesterday, Mrs Hill? He seemed tired last night and he was off his feed.'

'He was right as rain, Mrs Raike. Don't you worry. He had a cry like he always does in the middle of the afternoon, but you always say not to leave him screamin'.'

'So do you pick him up and nurse him, or do you give him something?' Everybody knew that babies had to be given a sip of syrup to quieten them now and again.

Mrs Hill waved a plump hand. 'Oh, the girls walk him for half an hour at a time, or we give him a drop of water if he's thirsty.'

'Yes, but what about a quietener? Do you give him Child's Cordial or Godfrey Mixture or something?'

'Well, only a drop of Godfrey, an' not too often at that. Now, off you go an' leave him to me. I've minded hundreds in me time, an' this is your first, don't forget. Janey! Here, take baby Raike.'

Martha relinquished Luke, and went through the process of forcing her feet towards the door. He *was*

her first, and he *was* settling down. It was just that
she had the feeling he was sickening for something.
She would see what Jessie thought when they stopped
for their breakfast. She'd had five of her own, and she
asked about him every day. . . .'

'He's ever so quiet, Jessie, an' he's not so hungry. He
slept right through last night, an' we didn't wake up till
the knocker-up came.'

The older woman laughed. 'There's not many as worry
when that happens, Martha. Some of mine didn't sleep
through till they were nearly a twelve-month.'

'But your mother minded them during the day, didn't
she? It must be a relief if you can leave them with
somebody you can trust.'

Jessie stopped with her bread and jam half-way to her
mouth. 'You trust Mrs Hill, don't you?'

'I'm not sure whether I do or not,' Martha admitted.
'She's very experienced, an' I'm not, so I can't say much,
can I? He cried a lot when I first left him and for a day
or two after that, and then he quietened down. I daren't
say too much to Matthew – he's worried already about
him goin' to a minder, so I can't add to it. One of his
sisters died when she was little, so I expect that's on his
mind, an' all.'

'Do any of the others leave their childer with her?'
asked Jessie, nodding towards the weavers as they sat
by their looms.

'Not that I know of. All the minders near Jericho
were full up when I tried to get him booked in.'

'I'll ask around them all at dinner time when you go
off to feed him, and see what I can find out.' Jessie was
determinedly cheerful. 'I expect he's settlin' down. Have
you had him weighed at all?'

'No. Me sister said she never bothered, because she
could see hers comin' on. Luke seems just the same size
all the time, to me.'

'Well, you see him every day, that's why. I saw him
at a week old, didn't I, when I called at your house?

I'll come with you when you pick him up tonight. He'll probably be yellin' for his feed when you go in at twelve o'clock.'

Sure enough he was yelling. Red-faced and outraged, he was in Mrs Hill's arms when Martha dashed through the door. 'Off his feed, Mrs Raike?' the minder said briskly. 'I see no signs of it!'

With a sigh of relief, Martha reached out for him and unbuttoned her blouse. She would get used to his little ways in time.

At six o'clock Jessie walked with her to collect him, and took him from her at the corner of the street. 'Come here little fella, let's have hold of you.' She inspected him carefully in the light of the street lamp, and he opened peaceful dark eyes and stared up at her.

'What do you think, Jessie? Is he comin' on?'

'Well, he's bigger than when I last saw him, an' that's a fact. He doesn't seem desperate for his tea, though, does he?'

'No. He's been like this many a time.'

'Listen, love, I've asked around and none of the women know anythin' against Mrs Hill. They all say, though, that any child-minder'll dole out the syrups if they have a cryin' baby on their hands; the mothers'll use it themselves if they're desperate for a sleep. Most of 'em admit, though, that overdosin' upsets their stomachs. Mother's Quietness, Soothing Syrup, Godfrey Mixture – they're all laudanum when you've done. One of 'em thinks her eldest is a bit simple because of it.'

Horrified, Martha snatched Luke back and cuddled him, and they faced each other under the lamp, shawls flapping in the wind. 'Listen,' said Jessie. 'First of all, get him weighed. He was seven an' a half born, wasn't he? Well, Mrs Ranson from the bakehouse lends her big scales out for baby-weighin' every Friday night at eight o'clock. You pay a ha'penny and she'll weigh your baby to within half an ounce. Get him weighed on Friday, wearin' near enough what he had on when the midwife weighed him. A little lad who was seven an' a half at birth an' fed by a strong young mother should be eight an' a half to nine pound at the very least by the time he's over a month old. Give him as much as he'll take whenever he'll take it, an' try not to worry. Oh, another thing, are they all cryin' when you go in at six o'clock?'

'Some of 'em are, yes.'

'Well, she can't be all that free with the Godfrey or they'd be too doped to cry, wouldn't they? So feed him up when he'll have it, and take him to Ranson's on Friday.'

'Jessie says he looks all right to her,' Martha said cheerfully when she got in. 'But just to be on the safe side I'm havin' him weighed on Friday night. That'll give us somethin' to go by.' She made no mention of the Godfrey. What would be the point? Matthew had enough to blame himself for without that.

Luke settled down to feed, but fell asleep half way through, and again Martha had to waken him at bedtime. The worry of it all, the long day at the mill with so much on her mind had exhausted her, and she fell asleep in Matthew's arms as soon as she climbed into bed.

He lay awake, though, holding her. *Was* the liddle lad thriving? If there'd been anybody with a ha'porth of sense on the bridge he would have asked them what they thought; they were a slow-witted lot though, and he would no more ask them about his son than jump from his place on the parapet into the canal. He liked Jessie Lane, and was sure they could do worse than listen to advice from her.

He'd been so downhearted about Luke during the day that he went into Soar Park, just to see the men and make sure that nothing had changed regarding the chance of work. Daniel Broadhurst had greeted him warmly, but shook his head about the chance of a job. 'I did warn you, lad, when you left us. It's autumn again, and I'll have to lay off some of the lads before long. You'll have heard about Jonah? Went labourin' at the Greenbank a couple of weeks back and he's off already, bad with his chest. I warned him, same as I did you. We might get rained on here at the park, but at least we're in God's fresh air.'

Now, Matthew eased his arm from around Martha, and slipped out of bed to see whether Luke was all right. He lay placidly beneath the little carving of the rose, and Matthew bent lower to make sure he was breathing. The rise and fall of the tiny chest reassured him, and he got back into bed next to Martha. But he didn't sleep. Last week he had earned three shillings in casual work, the week before that two and threepence. If it wasn't that he might miss the chance of full-time work they'd be better off with him staying at home and caring for Luke himself.

Still dubious about Mrs Hill, Martha went round the child-minders nearer Jericho; in those with room for another baby she found old women and little girls doing the minding, and they weren't clean, like Mrs Hill. One of them was using her pinny to wipe sicked-up milk from a baby's neck. No, he would have to stay where he was.

On Friday night two other women were waiting to weigh their babies, neither of them mill-workers. One was a well-dressed woman who said her household scales were broken, and the other a wet-nurse, out to prove that her charge was getting enough. Sick with nerves, Martha handed over her ha'penny and laid Luke on the scale. He had refused his six o'clock feed, although Mrs Hill assured her she'd given him only a sip of water all afternoon.

'He's a quiet one,' said Mrs Ranson cheerfully, adjusting her weights. 'Nine pounds one and a half ounces exactly! Next, please.'

Martha carried him out to Matthew, who was waiting at the bakehouse door. 'He's comin' on after all, an' puttin' on weight,' she told him, eyes shining, 'so I'm not worryin' any more, an' you mustn't either.'

He dropped a kiss on her cheek, there, out on the street, and they headed back home. 'I've been thinkin',' he said, 'if I haven't landed a job by the time he's, say, seven or eight weeks old, how would it be if I looked after him for a spell instead of him goin' to the minder? We could try it for two or three weeks to see if he's less sleepy, and we'd be no worse off for money than we are now. If he's no different we'll let him go back to Mrs Hill, and I'll go to the bridge again.'

In spite of it maybe costing him the chance of a job, she'd been thinking the same thing, though how could she have suggested it? She'd never heard of a man who looked after a baby on his own. There was something else that bothered her about Mrs Hill and the girls besides the Godfrey, and she hadn't mentioned that to Matthew, either. Sometimes they smelled of drink. So did some of the overlookers, come to that, and a couple of the weavers if they'd been out in their dinner hour. But none of them were looking after her baby, were they?

'Right,' she said, squeezing his hand. 'We'll give it another couple of weeks, an' if we're still worried you can look after him at home!'

CHAPTER TWENTY-THREE

'We look to the future . . .'

ALBERT HAD GONE HOME and Barney was counting the money when the shop bell pinged and Maria came in. Tizzie looked up in surprise. 'Mother! I was just going to lock up. Would you like to come upstairs to have some supper with me?'

The two of them were on warmer terms, but it was the first time Maria had been back to the shop. She circled the floor impatiently, barely greeting Barney and not even glancing at the alterations, her mind intent on other matters. Once upstairs she said, 'I've been waiting for closing time, Tizzie, to get you on your own. I have something to tell you.'

Tizzie clicked her tongue in frustration. She would have liked her mother to remark on the clean curtains, the well-polished furniture and the supper-table neatly laid for one; she was clearly on edge about something, however. The ribbons of her bonnet had been tied in haste, and the fashionable short coat wasn't pulled down properly at the back. Tizzie's heart rocked in dismay. 'Mary? Is she all right?'

'What? Of course she is. Tizzie, I'm doing well at the shop, you know. I have two assistants now, and I've started advertising in the *Saltley Chronicle*.'

'I know you have. I've seen it.'

'Yes, and so has somebody else – Milly Wardle. Her mother was your father's sister, you remember, a widow with one child; when she died Milly was only three or four, and they bundled her off to the Wardles, over Marple way. She was Abel's only flesh and blood, but we never saw her again. Do you remember we tried to get in touch with her for the funeral, but we couldn't trace her? Well, she's a married woman now, living in Hyde, and yesterday she saw a copy of the *Chronicle* in her dinner hour; by seven o'clock she was at the shop, straight from the mill and covered in cotton.'

'Oh dear. She mustn't have known it was such a high-class establishment,' murmured Tizzie drily, but it was lost on Maria.

'She'd reasoned I must be prospering, and wanted to borrow a pound, but when I saw her I gave her five.'

'Five pounds! Why?'

Maria stood up to give full weight to her words. 'Because she looks *just like you!*'

Tizzie stared at her blankly, and then the meaning of it hit her. A member of the Ridings family looked just like her, so Abel Ridings must have fathered her. She saw the glint of tears in her mother's eyes, and said: '*He* was my father, then, and not the man on Saltley Bog?'

'Aye, there's no doubt of it. Abel had said so all along. He always tried to reassure me, said your mouth and teeth were like the Ridings, and your hair like an auntie he'd seen when he was a child. I used to think he was saying it just to put my mind at rest. I'm very pleased, Tizzie.'

Oh, she was pleased, was she? Pleased: not sorry for burdening her daughter with something she need never have known. Tizzie could see she must expect no more than unshed tears from her mother, but at least she'd lost no time in coming to tell her the news. And what news! She jumped to her feet with the joy of it. Since her mother's revelations across the candlelit corpse she had often reminded herself that she was the daughter of a rapist; now here was proof that in fact she was the child of a puny, insignificant pawnbroker; a man unable to generate affection in his own daughter, but with a kind and generous heart. She wanted to weep, to run up to her room to throw herself on the bed or to tell some kindred spirit the good news; but there was only her mother, sitting there looking satisfied and somewhat smug.

Her eyes swivelled from side to side in search of an excuse to escape. 'We'll drink a toast in celebration, Mother! I have a bottle of Madeira in the sideboard. I'll just tell Rebecca to fetch us some cake to have with it, and then I must go down to have a word with Barney about something before he goes home.'

She went to summon Rebecca from the scullery, and then ran downstairs, because the person she wanted to share in her joy was down in the dolly-shop. The lamp was still lit, and for some reason Barney was standing behind his table, gazing emptily at the neatly-stacked chattels of the poor. He turned when he heard her on the stairs, and with skirts whirling she stopped in front of him and bent to grasp his hands. 'Barney!' she gasped, 'Barney, wonderful news! I *am* my father's daughter – we've just had proof of it!'

He didn't know what she was talking about, but looked at their clasped hands in bewilderment. Then he gazed up into her face. 'Why, of course you're your father's daughter. Did you ever doubt it?'

'Yes, since the night before the funeral. Oh, I'm so happy!' And with his hands in hers she whirled him round the cellar, her skirts bouncing and dipping, her bright hair escaping from its pins and his short legs racing to keep pace with her. When they came to a stop he disengaged his hands, looking down at them as if he were seeing them for the first time. She said breathlessly. 'I just – just wanted you to know, Barney.'

'Why me, Miss Tizzie?' The big flat face was even paler than usual.

'Why? Because – oh – because we're friends, aren't we?'

The dark eyes stared guardedly into hers. 'Oh yes, we're friends right enough, Miss Tizzie. I'm your friend for life, I am that.'

With a little laugh she stuck the loose pins back in her hair and then went upstairs to her mother, who was running a questioning finger along the back of the sideboard, seeking dust. 'She's a good woman you've got, Tizzie,' she conceded. 'Did she make this cake?'

'Yes.'

'And what about the child? Is she all right in the head?'

'Of course she is. I'm teaching her to read and write.'

'Well, well. You've changed, Tizzie, and for the better. You're not so wrapped up in yourself.' It was a back-handed compliment, but Tizzie merely smiled. At that moment she felt she could have smiled at anything.

It was later, in bed, that a more sober mood took her. She stared through the open curtains at the distant stars and felt the deep chill of loneliness again. She liked Barney, she respected him – she had even let him buy a share in her land; but it would have been lovely if there had been somebody else to share the news with, somebody special.

It all happened so quickly, quicker than any nightmare. Five days after he'd been weighed at the bakehouse Luke was much the same, taking the odd feed with a semblance of appetite, but for the most part sucking lazily with his eyes closed; sometimes he cried endlessly for no obvious reason. Martha put on a calm face for Matthew, but in reality she became more and more worried. Suppose – just suppose he'd been *more* than nine pounds one and a half ounces earlier on, and had already lost weight when she had him on the scale at Ranson's?

'I'm takin' him to be weighed again tomorrow, Jessie, an' if he's only the same, or maybe lost a bit, Matthew's goin' to stay at home to look after him,' she told the older woman at breakfast time. 'Yesterday I told Mrs Hill I'd give her another sixpence a week if she keeps him off the Godfrey, and she agreed, but she won't admit to giving him more than a sip, anyway.'

'I'll come round with you to pick him up,' comforted Jessie. 'I've not seen him for a bit, so happen I can spot it if there's any change.'

At six o'clock Mrs Hill was her usual capable self, handing babies and young children back to their mothers, but with a word of warning here and there. 'He's a bit loose in the bowels, you know,' she said to one, and to another, 'Her bottom's sore with this diarrhoea.'

Martha hurried out with Luke wrapped in her shawl. 'It sounds as if there's diarrhoea in there, Jessie. It must be catchin'.'

Jessie took hold of him and together they made for the lamp at the corner. Wrapped against the cold, Luke lay limply in her arms, and she bent her head and studied him closely. 'He's goin' down the nick, Martha,' she said quietly. 'He didn't have those little dints at the sides of his nose last week. An' he's too quiet. Does he still cry?'

''Course he does. Sometimes he won't stop wailin', though he doesn't seem hungry.'

'Don't take him back there tomorrow,' Jessie said urgently. 'There's no telling what she gives him to shut him up. Let Matthew have him till you get him weighed.'

Martha hurried home, to find Matthew with the kettle on and their fry-ups ready for the pan. He was in high spirits. 'I've got two days' work as a hod-carrier, starting tomorrow,' he said. 'What about that? If I work like a cart-horse they might keep me on.'

'How much?' she asked abruptly.

He looked at her sharply. 'What be wrong?'

Martha put Luke in his cradle at the side of the hearth. 'He's just not right, Matthew. I don't want him to go back to Mrs Hill. I was hopin' you'd look after him tomorrow, then I'll have him weighed at eight o'clock.'

Matthew sat down and stared at the baby. 'Twas true he didn't look so good, he told himself. He was takin' on the look of a liddle old man, rather than a baby close on six weeks, and his eyes seemed to bulge from their sockets under the pale, closed lids. But to lose the hod-carryin' job? Bitterly he bowed his head in agreement. Better to lose two shillings a day than what Martha could earn at her looms. Besides, he could cuddle Luke all day long if he was at home.

Martha settled to feed Luke before they started their meal, and he sucked lazily, and then gave a dutiful burp. She put him down in his cradle and then saw to the meal; they had barely begun to eat before he let out a gurgling cry. He had brought back his milk, and the vomit was stained with brown. Martha cleaned him up and examined his nappy. 'Matthew! Look – he's bleedin'! Go on, get the doctor. We've enough in the jar to pay for a visit. Quick! Run!'

He needed no urging. He ran from the house coatless, away up the hill, and caught the doctor as he finished his evening meal but before he started his surgery. It was the brisk, kindly practitioner who had attended Mrs Spencer before she died. 'All right, keep calm!' he said shortly. 'I'll be with the little lad in five minutes. Keep him warm.'

The doctor arrived at Ledden Street almost as soon as Matthew, bringing his own bright lamp into the room, as if expecting to find no more than a single candle. Gently he took Luke from his cradle and laid him on the table among the tea things. Lips tight, he examined him carefully and listened to his chest, then he let out a growl of anger. 'Bah, you women are all alike! He's got the diarrhoea that's going round, and that'd be bad enough, but the child's drugged! His stomach's bleeding. What have you been giving him, eh? Godfrey? When will you mothers learn that babies cry, even the best of 'em. They cry if they're hungry, they cry if they're thirsty, they cry if they're wet, if they're too cold, if they're too warm. They cry so you'll help them, for God's sake – and you shut them up with laudanum!'

They stared at him across the table, Matthew open-mouthed with horror, Martha sick at the confirmation of her fears. 'We haven't shut him up with drugs,' Matthew protested angrily. 'We watch over him. We guard him with our lives!'

The doctor shot a look at Martha, and saw the fluff of the weaving shed still clinging to her hair. 'Don't try to deny it,' he said wearily. 'I've seen too many like him. His stomach will be shredded to ribbons, do you know that? If he wasn't a strong baby he'd be dead already. As it is this could finish him, because he'll have no resistance. Give him sips of warm water and small feeds of breast milk. And expect the worst.'

'The worst?' They both spoke in unison.

'He might live, he might die. Do as I tell you, give him sips of water and frequent small feeds of milk, and keep him off your blasted syrups!' With that he slammed out of the house, leaving then staring at the child, who lay quietly on the table in the midst of their unfinished meal.

Matthew looked at her, bewildered. 'Did 'ee know he was havin' this – this syrup?'

Martha opened her mouth to form the hardest word she'd ever had to utter. 'Yes,' she said quietly, 'I knew. I asked Mrs Hill about it last week, when we were worried. All the child-minders use it, Matthew, an' so do some of the mothers. Anybody can buy it. Matthew, don't look like that!'

'You didn't think to mention to me, then, that my son was bein' dosed with laudanum?' His voice was no more than a low whisper.

'Yes, I *did* think of it,' she said bitterly, 'but you were so busy feelin' sorry for yourself goin' to the bridge to twiddle your thumbs I thought it would only add to your worries. I offered Mrs Hill another sixpence a week to cut out the Godfrey, in case it was that that was makin' him so sleepy an' puttin' him off his feeds. She's a clean woman, I never thought she'd overdose him.'

'Clean!' Matthew flung himself round the table and swiped his arm along the mantelpiece, sending the two sparkling glass vases and the money jar crashing to the floor. '*They're* all clean!' he roared, then snatched two freshly-ironed sheets from the clothes-horse. 'So are they!' He stamped on them with his heavy boots, while she gaped at him in terror. 'Clean, clean, clean! You're obsessed with bein' clean, woman! I don't give a bloody damn how clean she is – she's dosed my son with her bloody Godfrey an' nearly killed him!'

'She wouldn't have needed to touch him, let alone dose him, if you hadn't played the knight in shinin' armour for a woman you didn't even know,' she cried. 'If you'd kept your job I'd have been at home lookin' after him.'

He bared his teeth at her. 'Is – that – so? Well, you took some persuadin' to agree to that, in case you've forgotten! As I recall it you were more intent on havin' a grand house than stayin' at home with your son!'

So engrossed were they in shouting at each other, that they never heard a little mew of distress from the baby, never saw a small fist clench in pain and then loosen. They hurled angry words at each other across the table, and when he stumbled over the sheets he'd trampled, Matthew picked them up and hurled them across the room in fury.

At last they fell silent, each afraid of their own anger, and it was then that Martha bent over Luke. He was dead. She could tell. His pale little face had a waxy sheen, and his upper lip and the sides of his nose had turned blue. He was quite still and he looked very tranquil. She let out a wail of anguish and picked him up from the table, but Matthew snatched him away from her, unbelieving.

There was no doubting it. Luke was dead. His liddle son dead, while they quarrelled. He looked at Martha and spoke with venom. 'I didn't even have chance to say good-bye to him 'ee were so busy shriekin'! Well go on,

wash him! Make him *clean*! That's what ee's concerned
about, isn't it? If ee'd noticed him breathin' his last 'ee
could 'a stuck another dose o' Godfrey down his throat
afore he went!'

Martha stared at him while one thought hammered in
her brain. She'd known it, hadn't she? She'd known all
along it was too good to last. The silence between them
stretched on, with Matthew still clutching the baby to
his chest. 'I will wash him,' she agreed quietly. 'I'll lay
him out, and nobody's askin' you to watch, Matthew,
so you can clear off!'

The funeral was on Saturday at three o'clock, the day
before Luke would have been christened. Matthew had
never felt so ill in his life. He didn't know how Martha
was feeling, because they hadn't exchanged more than
two words since she told him to clear off while she laid
out the baby; that same night she moved out of their
bed and into Uncle Jack's.

They had enough money to pay for a black horse
with a plume to pull a cart for the coffin, and for
the Spencer grave to be opened up for him. It was in
the Nonconformist graveyard, which relieved Matthew's
mind. He couldn't have borne his son to be buried in the
place he'd seen on his first day in Saltley, where the two
sextons were calmly digging up those rotting remains. It
was a very small cart, bare, except for Luke's coffin. They
walked behind it, side by side, untouching; their steps
keeping time to the clopping of the horse's hooves.

Bella and Henry were there, having left the girls at
home with a neighbour. So was Jessie, and by the
graveyard wall was a cluster of weavers in their best
shawls and black bonnets or head-wraps. The minister
was kind and gentle, but his attitude made clear that
babies died every day of the week: it was sad, but just
another of life's trials. 'Suffer the little children . . .' he
recited in his best pulpit tones.

When it was over Jessie touched Matthew on the arm.

'Get her to cry if you can, Matthew,' she advised gently, 'an' shed a tear yourself if you want. It's nowt to be ashamed of.'

He shot her a look of such hostility she moved back a pace. 'I bain't ashamed o' weepin' for my son,' he said abruptly. 'Why should'ee think it? What do shame me is that he died o' bein' dosed up with laudanum, when I knew nothin' of it!'

That night his nightmare returned for the first time since he unburdened himself about Dorcas on their wedding night, only it was much worse than before. This time it was Luke in the burning loft, and Mrs Hill shouting to wake him, rather than Fat Annie,

Martha, lying awake in Uncle Jack's bed, heard his gasps and then his cries, and finally his screams, and thought: he can get himself through it, the same as I'm getting myself through *my* nightmare. Later, she crept downstairs to put warm cloths on her aching breasts, and pressed out just enough milk to ease them a little. Jessie had told her that the milk would dry up in time, now there was no demand for it.

She wondered how long it would be before Matthew left her for good. It was always a surprise when she came in from the mill and found him still there, making up the fire, or putting the kettle on. She took to visiting Luke's grave in her dinner hour, or on the way home, having found she was able to weep in the quiet of the graveyard; it eased her to do it. She never mentioned it to Matthew, though. She never mentioned anything to him unless it was unavoidable. In any case, she sensed that if he realised her anguish it would somehow worsen his own, and she didn't want that.

She stayed on in Uncle Jack's room, and Matthew was glad of it. Her small body next to his would have led him to recall their lovemaking, the conceiving of Luke, and he wanted no such memories. The ache inside him was for the loss of his son, not the loss of his wife. . . .

* * *

Tizzie dressed with care. Sarah had asked her to Sunday dinner at Meadowbank House, and the carriage was coming for her. She found it ironic that she used to put up with the Boultons and the Waltons because they had influence in the town; yet now she was invited to the table of the most respected man in Saltley as an equal, a true friend of his daughter.

Out of mourning at last, she was wearing a new dress, a ready-made, purchased at a good discount from her mother's shop. It was of deep turquoise velvet, with a high collar studded with tiny imitation pearls, and twenty little pearl buttons fastened with loops down the front of the bodice. Freshly-washed, her hair was glinting and crackling with life, and she'd subdued it by sweeping it up at the back and fastening it with a positive army of pins. Rebecca and Noami had gone off to chapel; when she heard the carriage outside she went down with her cloak, ready to set off.

But it was Sam Schofield at the door, not Zacky the coachman. 'Mr Schofield! I didn't expect you.'

'No, I know, and it's Sam, don't forget. Could I have a word before we set off?'

'Of course. Will you come upstairs? Is Sarah all right?'

'She's fine, but I wanted to ask your advice about her.' He followed her into the room. 'It's about Edward, as well.'

She saw that he was deliberately giving her a moment to prepare herself. For what? Sarah was making a new life: travelling to the Royal twice a week as an observer, helping at Saltley Infirmary on the children's ward, running Meadowbank House. . . . 'He mustn't be allowed near her!' she said urgently. 'She's so much better!'

'I know she is, and I believe some of that's due to you, and I'm grateful. So is my father.' He saw colour rise in her cheeks: not the lovely rose-pink blush that happened so frequently with Sarah, but a reluctant red stain beneath the distinctive cheek-bones.

Aware that she was blushing and annoyed by it, Tizzie spoke briskly. 'I showed her she wasn't unique in having such a husband, and tried to get rid of her unnecessary guilt, that's all. What about Edward, anyway?'

The deep voice was oddly hesitant. 'He's – he's dead, Tizzie. My father heard last night. Ever since the separation he's paid a man to keep track of Edward's movements, and to send him reports from time to time. I – we – I haven't told you that before, Tizzie. I didn't know whether you – uh – '

'Whether I still had a regard for him?'

'Yes. Perhaps I needn't have been concerned about that?'

It was news to her that he was concerned about anybody other than his sister and his father and older brother, but the vivid blue eyes demanded a straight answer. 'No, there was no need for you to be concerned, though I admit I was besotted with Edward for many months. It was what they call infatuation, I suppose – the suspension of good sense.' Sam's broad, blond figure had the effect of blotting out her memories of the elegant, red-lipped man who had once filled her every thought. Blotted him out as he'd been blotted out of life itself. 'How did he die?' she asked calmly.

'Stabbed in a pawnshop near the waterfront in Portsmouth,' said Sam bluntly. 'He was ruined pro-fessionally – my father had seen to that – and left with very little of my sister's money, so eventually he drifted back to Hampshire. From what we can gather his family shunned him, and over the months he sank down among the low-life of the port, living on – uh – on the earnings of women, and selling or pawning his belongings. It wasn't a respectable pawnshop like this, and he was knifed there by a sailor who followed him in and said Edward had stolen his woman.'

'That sounds like Edward,' she agreed quietly. A

pawnshop. He wouldn't marry a daughter of the pawn-shop, but he'd died in one. . . . 'How has Sarah taken it?'

'She doesn't know yet. That's what I came to ask you. What should we tell her? The truth, the whole truth, or a watered-down version?'

They were still standing on the hearthrug, so she gestured to the chairs, deep in thought. 'I see no point in distressing her any more than you need,' she said at last. 'You know as well as I do that she's always believed she broke her solemn marriage vows – for better for worse, till death us do part, and so forth. If she knows the full story she'll be eaten up with guilt all over again. If I were you I wouldn't tell her anything at all until after he's buried. She might feel she should go to the funeral, and that could do her harm. He isn't – wasn't – worth the risk of spoiling her life all over again.'

Sam sat facing her, and now he leaned back in relief. 'That confirms my own instincts, Tizzie, but you've put it in a nutshell. Thanks. I'll tell my father what you say. He has a high regard for your views, you know.'

She smiled. 'Come to that, I have a high regard for his.'

'Oh, about your land. He was saying last night that everybody's overproducing again in cotton, because manufacturers are intent on using all the expensive machinery they installed before the cotton famine. He predicts a glut by next year, but he'll be telling you all about it over dinner.'

'Do you mean nobody will want to buy building land?'

'That's about it. Except perhaps John Fairbrother, who wants land for a social club and bowling greens and a swimming bath for his workers, the same as my father's. That'll outlive any glut, or any shortage, for that matter. And your land is quite near Fairbrother's mill.'

'Do you think he would be interested in it?'

'It's a possibility, and in spite of the fluctuations in

trade, he's not short of capital. You can ask my father's opinion. And we won't say anything to Sarah about Edward just yet. Right?'

'Right,' she agreed, leading the way downstairs.

They travelled in silence to Meadowbank House, with Tizzie reflecting on the Schofield family. Sarah was her friend – a bonding together of opposites, and maybe they were the closer for that very difference in their natures. Brother James was like her, gentle and kind and sensitive, and his wife, the pretty, kittenish Esther who was expecting a baby? Tizzie didn't know much about her, except that Sarah had said she was quite furious at being sick because of the pregnancy.

What of the head of the family? She liked Joshua Schofield, thought him distinguished. He had power and wealth, but he also had principles; he was humane, looking after his innumerable workers, and yet he was quite unconcerned by what was fashionable or acceptable to everyone else. Not only that, he loved his family, and was highly delighted at the prospect of a grandchild. As for the man at her side . . . it wasn't easy to weigh him up, but as far as she could tell he was a chip off the old block.

The carriage was waiting when Joshua came out of Saltley station after a long session at Mosley Street. It was bitterly cold, with a heavy, yellowish sky that heralded the first snow of winter. 'Take me to the Greenbank, Zacky,' said Joshua, waving aside the proffered rug, 'I promised to see Mr Fairbrother at his office. You can leave me there, and I'll walk home when I've done.'

They bowled along over new roads and dirt streets, then across the tally bridge that spanned the canal. Joshua eyed the restless crowd there, all of them on the move to keep warm, but standing back to let the carriage pass. They had crossed the bridge when he leaned forward and told Zacky to stop. He had noticed a tall, lean man standing apart from

the others, hat over his eyes, the collar of his coat
turned up.

'Wait here for me, Zacky. I'll have a word with
yond' mon.'

He walked back, telling himself he was disappointed in
the man from Devon. Disappointed in his own judgment,
as well. He hadn't seen him as a troublemaker, yet his
name had been on the list of sackings a couple of months
back, and for striking the head cut-looker, at that. He
stopped in front of the silent figure, and was stunned
at the change in him. The young fool, not to keep his
fists to himself!

'Raike? I thought it was you. What's all this, then?' He
blinked when he met the dark, empty blast of Matthew's
eyes. The man looked terrible, like a walking corpse. 'I
thought you told me you were well-suited at Jericho?'

'Oh, I was, Mr Schofield. I was.'

'Well, then? You're a family man now, so I heard.
You'd have done better to keep your fists to yourself,
surely?'

'I be well aware o' that.' If the mill-owner hadn't been
downright decent with him, Matthew wouldn't even have
bothered to reply.

Joshua swung his stick thoughtfully. The man's attitude
was hardly repentant. 'You knew the rules of the mill,
didn't you?'

'Oh, I knew the rules right enough. 'Twas the provocation that made me forget 'en. Only for a matter o'
seconds, mind, but by then the damage was done.'

'Well, I'm disappointed in you, Raike, I am that.'

Matthew leaned forward and stuck his face within
inches of the other's. 'You're disappointed in me?' he
repeated, showing his teeth. 'Well, I be disappointed in
you, how about that? Disappointed that you employ a
lecherous old swine like Lingard in your fine cotton mill.
Disappointed that your weavers have to put up with a
maulin' if they let a float down – oh, only if they're
nice an' plump, o' course – the skinny 'uns get away

with a fine, or havin' their name put in his bad book.
I call condonin' that sort o' thing *very* disappointin' in
a pillar o' the chapel.

'But I'll tell you this, it's not as disappointin' as the
death o' my son. Dosed to his death with quietin' syrup
at the child-minder's because my wife had to go back to
her looms when I got the sack. Mark that, Mr Schofield.
It's powerful disappointin' to lose your son just because
you hit a man for shamin' a married woman!'

He had spoken so seldom in the last ten days he felt
hoarse after the outburst, but it gave him a twinge of satisfaction to see Joshua Schofield's expression. He looked
– what? Dazed? Mortified? Horrified? All three.

'Just a minute,' the older man said quietly. 'Would
you repeat all that for me?'

Somewhat calmer, Matthew went through it again, but
this time without mention of Luke. He couldn't think
why he had brought his son into it, though to be sure
it hurt less to speak of him than it did to keep silent,
with the grief burning and smarting inside his chest.

The cotton-master faced him, clutching his silver-
topped stick. Matthew expected him to go back to
his carriage rather than bandy words with a sacked
employee, but such a course didn't seem to occur to
him. 'Do you say all the weavers know this goes on?'
he asked, eyes narrowed.

'Yes. My wife says it's gone on for years, but the
women aren't in a position to speak out against the man
who could dock their pay or even get them sacked. An' if
the weavers know about it, then so does half Jericho!'

The mill-owner was staring into the black depths of
the canal. There was an odd twist to his lips, like a man
with a mouthful of evil-tasting food. 'You've been out
of work ever since?' he asked quietly.

Matthew nodded. 'Nobody wants a man who knocked
the Jericho cut-looker senseless.'

'No, I don't suppose they do. You might not believe
it, but I knew nothing of this, nothing! I'll look into it

right away. Go home at once, and I'll be in touch. Wait,
– have you a trade? What did you do in Plymouth?'

'Gardenin',' said Matthew. 'I be trained to it. Mr
Broadhurst at Soar Park would speak for me if 'ee
should hear of a job.'

'Daniel Broadhurst? I know Daniel. He's another
pillar of the chapel, as it happens.'

Matthew shifted his shoulders uncomfortably. 'That
remark, it sort o' slipped out, Mr Schofield.'

'I'm not surprised. Right, leave it with me. Go off
home now.'

So it was Matthew who moved away from the bridge
first, leaving the older man still staring into the canal. It
was snowing by the time he reached Ledden Street. He
made up the fire and pulled out the oven damper ready to
heat up a tater-pie-without-meat that Martha had made
the previous night. A speck of coal dust landed on the
blanket of Luke's cradle, and he removed it with care.
They hardly spoke, yet by mutual consent they had left
the cradle in its place next to the hearth. He wondered
when she would move it, because he certainly couldn't
bring himself to do it.

He decided not to tell her about the encounter with
Joshua Schofield. What was the point? What was the
point of anything? Except that it would give him some
self-respect if he didn't have to live on his wife's
earnings.

Matthew put the pie in the oven at a quarter to six, as
he'd done many a time in the past two months, though
to be sure Martha was sometimes late these days; she
never so much as hinted at where she'd been. At ten
past there was a knock on the door instead of a lifting
of the latch. Jessie Lane stood outside, her shawl white
with snow, her basket topped with it. She eyed Matthew
warily. 'I just called to see if Martha's all right, with her
not bein' in this afternoon, an' no message or anythin'.'

He stared at her blankly. 'Not in? But she bain't here,
either. The house is as I left it at dinner time.'

Jessie scuffled her clogs in the snow. 'I thought she were poorly,' she said uneasily, 'what with her losin' weight an' that.'

He looked away hurriedly. Losing weight? Martha? All he'd noticed was the flattening of her breasts as they became empty of milk. There was a horrible hollow feeling under his ribs. 'Have 'ee any idea where she might be?'

'Well, she spends her dinner hours at the graveyard, doesn't she? Leaves herself no time to eat a bite, most days. I have to save her a mug of me tea or she wouldn't even have a drink, let alone a bite.'

He was conscious that his mouth was open, and however much he tried he couldn't seem to shut it. When he spoke his teeth clicked repeatedly, like a man with the shivers. 'She – she be always at the grave? I didn' know that, Jessie.'

The shrewd dark eyes surveyed him with compassion. 'No? Happen she didn't want to worry you. I have to get home to me family, Matthew, or I'd go and look for her meself.'

'No!' Shame that she should have to suggest such a thing sent him leaping for his coat. 'I'll go now an' look for her. Do 'ee think she'll still be there?'

Jessie shook her head. 'I don't know where else to suggest. She's very low, Matthew. She doesn't say much, but I know she's worried sick about you.'

He didn't reply to that. He couldn't. He grabbed his hat and closed the door. 'Thank'ee, Jessie.'

Snow was swirling in the light of the street lamps as he trod the roads they'd taken with the funeral cart. She was losing weight? She was worried sick about him? She spent hours at the grave? She was his wife, yet he knew none of it. But she was always so calm, speaking to him only when necessary, showing no sign of distress. Wait a minute – he hadn't noticed much, but he had seen that her eyes were constantly puffed up.

For the hundredth time he recalled the bitter words

they'd exchanged that night, quarrelling while the baby breathed his last on the hard table among the clutter of a meal. He hurried on, wondering if he should aim for the market or Holden Street rather than the graveyard, but he decided to try there first of all.

The sinking sensation under his ribs grew worse. Perhaps she'd left him? That was it – she'd left him, found herself a room or something because she couldn't bear the sight of him! He broke into a run, guilt and panic and shame churning his innards, and grief for his son tearing his heart. And the snow continued to fall, quiet as a benediction.

Joshua swung away from the parapet of the bridge, nodding at the respectful murmurs and lifting of hats from those who were gathered there. Back in the carriage he scribbled in his notebook. 'Straight to Jericho, Zacky, and then take this note to Mr Fairbrother.'

He sat on the edge of his seat as they went, pulling at his whiskers. It was starting to snow, and when they rounded the last bend in the road he thought his great twin mills had never looked better than at that moment: every window ablaze, and on the tower the trumpet and the rose, illuminated by his newly installed lamps.

His beautiful Jericho, his well-cared-for people, his model community . . . or so he'd thought. He had believed his foremen and overlookers to be well-chosen, to be in tune with his own beliefs; yet a bag of bones like old Lingard had abused his position for years – *years*, mind – and he'd known nothing of it. That was what really cut at him: dozens of workers, possibly hundreds, had known what was going on and yet not one had faced him and told him of it, not even Joe Whitehead, or lower down the scale, Bessie Lomas. Were there other cases like it? Abuse of power, humiliation of women, ill-treatment of youngsters? He didn't know, but he'd damn soon find out!

Once through the gates he leapt from the carriage

and strode across the yard. 'Send for Mr Sam to come
to my office immediately,' he said to the lodge-keeper.
Thank goodness it was one of Sam's days at Jericho –
he wanted him at his side when he dealt with an issue
such as this.

He marched through the outer office. 'Get me four
runners at once,' he said to the staff. They exchanged
looks, but lost no time in obeying him. When Mr
Schofield spoke like that they all knew they must
jump to it.

A minute later Sam hurried in. 'What's wrong,
Father?'

'Plenty,' said Joshua. 'Listen to this. . . .' He closed his
eyes for a moment before telling his son. All his teachings
and preachings about how to treat the workers, and he
had to admit to this sort of thing going on.

Sam heard him out in silence, and crushed the impulse
to put a comforting arm around him. He simply said:
'You'll check on it before you take action?'

Joshua relaxed a little. They thought alike, him and
Sam, they did that. There was a tap at the door. 'Runners
here, Mr Schofield.'

Four young boys came in and stood bashfully by the
door. Joshua spoke to them in turn. 'Go to Mr Bennet,
the head overlooker in the weaving shed, and tell him to
send me – let's see, Lily Bracewell, Jessie Lane and Maggie Simister, as soon as he's put minders on their looms.
And tell him to come and see me himself when they get
back. Next, you two – one of you to East Side and one
to West, and tell all six floor managers from each side to
see me here at five-thirty prompt. Got that? Off you go,
then.' And to the next one, 'Take my compliments to Mr
Whitehead in East Side spinning room, and will he kindly
call to see me when he finishes at six o'clock. Then come
back here and wait until I need you again.'

Sam watched all this in silent approval. When his
father moved, he *moved*.

*   *   *

Only the snow and a distant lamp gave light to the graveyard. Matthew's heart lurched as he made for the grave. She couldn't have been here since noon. She *couldn't.*

She wasn't. He blundered around, calling her name, but the wind moaned through the snow-dusted trees, mocking his cries. He didn't know whether to be glad or sorry that she was nowhere to be seen; then he thought of the nearby canal. No, she wouldn't. . . . A mocking little voice in his head said: 'Why wouldn't she? You've given her no comfort since it happened, only blame.'

He ran out through the gate, thinking he should go back to Ledden Street in case he'd missed her, and almost bumped into a small, snow-covered figure still clutching a basket, stumbling along in the direction of home. She must have left the graveyard while he was rushing about, looking for her. Sick with relief, he leapt in front of her and grabbed her arms. 'Where be 'ee to?' he demanded, his voice breaking.

'Matthew,' she said faintly. 'I – I didn't know the time. I'll be late seein' to the tea.'

'Never mind the tea! Have 'ee been here all afternoon?'

'I don't know. P'raps I have. I'll lose half a day's pay. I'm not cold, you know, just sleepy.' To his horror she buckled at the knees, and as at their first meeting, he bent over her small prostrate form. But this time he lifted her up in his arms, basket and all. It registered, even through his fear, that there was nothing of her. Self-obsessed clod that he was, he hadn't seen that under her iron control his wife was fading away in front of his eyes.

'Martha,' he muttered, bending his head and planting breathless little kisses on her cold cheeks. 'Martha, don't leave me. I beg of 'ee – don't leave me.'

She made no response. He hoped she was asleep, but feared she was unconscious from the cold and lack of food. He stumbled on, and the snow whirled and danced, and at street corners the wind blew her shawl to the side of him like a banner.

At the house he tossed it aside and laid her on the wicker chair, removing her clogs and woollen stockings, and her striped skirt and apron. Her small feet were blue-white, but he kept them away from the fire and looked for something to wrap them in. All he could see was the blanket on Luke's cradle, so he grabbed that. Then he stared into her face. It was pinched and very white, with melted snow glistening on the wet cotton fluff that still clung to her hair.

To his deep relief she opened her eyes, and they widened when she saw his face only inches away. She didn't speak. 'Don't leave me, Martha,' he begged. 'My liddle love, I need 'ee.'

He saw the soft mouth quiver, her teeth catching at the lower lip, and of a sudden his heart seemed to leap inside his chest. He loved his liddle wife; he loved her, but he had never once admitted it, even to himself. He had never told her so, because until this minute he hadn't even known it. He cupped her small face in his hands, and in Saltley talk, rather than that of Devon, said clearly, 'Martha, I love you.'

Two great tears welled in her eyes and slid down her cheeks. Then she smiled, and it came to him that it was her first smile since the day she went back to work and left Luke with the minder. 'I love you an' all,' she whispered, 'I've loved you since the day you picked me up when the wind blew me away. . . .'

He leaned forward and kissed her very gently on her pretty mouth, then remembering she was half-frozen, began to rub her stiff little hands. She looked down and saw the blanket round her feet, 'Oh, Luke's blanket!' she said, and bent to remove it.

'He bain't be needin' blankets no more,' said Matthew gently. 'We've lost our liddle lad, Martha, so let's make sure we don't lose each other.'

'We'll talk about him, though?' she asked, tears threatening again.

'Every day,' he vowed. 'We'll mourn him, an' we'll grieve for him – together.'

There was a knock on the door. ''Tis Jessie, I expect,' he said. ''Twas her put me on to where I might find 'ee.'

But it wasn't Jessie on the doorstep. It was Joshua Schofield. Matthew gaped at him. 'Mr Schofield! Do 'ee come in! My wife be sufferin' from the cold. . . .'

Martha stared at her employer in amazement. She tried to rise from the chair but Matthew's hands on her shoulders prevented her. She saw Mr Schofield glance at the empty cradle and at once look away. 'I won't keep you more than a minute,' he said, 'but I wanted to call on you in person. I've sacked Lingard, and three of his superiors as well, for knowing of what he did and keeping silent. A dozen more have been given warnings, and I haven't finished yet, by a long way.'

Once again Matthew felt the force of the older man's personality, and knew a rush of joy that he'd read him correctly from the start, which after all wasn't so very surprising. The man who had been a father to him had taught him how to judge his fellows; for a moment Matthew imagined the old sailor to be there in the room with the three of them. But the visitor was still standing on their doormat, his caped coat dusted with snow. 'A cup o' tea, Mr Schofield?' he offered hastily. 'A bite to eat?'

Martha blushed that her husband had made the offer, rather than her, but the mill-owner shook his head. 'Thank you, no. I have the carriage waiting to take me back to Jericho to pick up my son, and then we'll go home for our tea. My real reason for coming is to tell you I can't give you your job back. You had the utmost provocation, I know, but if I reemploy you I go against one of my strictest rules, and I can't do that.

'What I can do is offer you the job of assistant gardener

at my house, with the prospect of taking over the bowling
green and grounds of my new Workers' Institute. Are
you interested?'

Matthew stared at him. 'I be interested,' he said, 'oh,
yes!' Interested? In getting out of the mill and back
to the soil – the black, peaty, fertile earth of Saltley?
Maybe to use his own ideas, create his own schemes?
'Thank 'ee, Mr Schofield,' he said hoarsely, 'thank 'ee
most kindly.'

'You'll start at thirty shillings a week, then, and we'll
talk about an increase if and when you take over as
groundsman. Come and see me at seven o'clock on
Monday morning at my house. Goodnight to you both.'
Waving aside their thanks he lifted the latch and let
himself out.

Matthew picked up Martha from the chair and swung
her round in the air, and they laughed together for joy.
His foot caught Luke's cradle and set it rocking, and at
that they both fell silent. She leaned away from him and
saw the glint of his tears. 'The next one might be a girl,
Matthew,' she ventured.

'You'd get your liddle Rose, then,' he agreed gently.

One day she would explain why she chose that name;
remind him of the day he came home from the park,
sun-tanned and smelling of flowers, with a stolen rose
for her under his hat. Deep red and fragrant it had
been, and warm from his hair, then for the first time
he had kissed her. . . .

They held hands in front of the fire before starting
their meal. A little girl called Rose was still somewhere
in the future. They would think about her very soon,
but not until they had mourned their first-born son.

When Joshua got back to Jericho the lodge-keeper was
looking out for him. 'Mr Sam says he'll be down in a
minute, Mr Schofield.'

'Down? Why, where is he?'

The man pointed. 'Up yonder. The flag were comin'

undone, so he went up to see to it. I did warn him
it weren't weather for bein' up on the tower, Mr
Schofield.'

Joshua went back in the mill and headed for the stairs.
This was another example of the linking of their minds.
After the upheaval of the last few hours he'd been longing
to go up there, snow or no snow. The flag had become
a symbol of what he believed in, and it did him good
to be near it, to touch it. Now, Sam was preventing it
from breaking loose. Weary after a demanding day he
climbed the stairs, and found himself slowing by the time
he reached the last flight. Then, stepping out on the roof,
his weariness was banished by the exhilaration of being
high above Jericho with his trumpet and his rose.

Sam was there, hatless, his blond head dusted with
snow, re-knotting the ropes of the flagstaff. 'Hello there,'
he said cheerfully. 'I won't be a minute. I knew you
wouldn't like to see it unfastened in the morning, or
maybe blown away. There, that'll do it.'

The wind was dropping, the snow had ceased, and a
few reluctant stars studded the heavens. Down below
they could see the lighted windows of Meadowbank
House and the street lamps of Saltley, strung like
jewels beneath the quilted white roofs of the town.
And yes, there were the lights of the railway leading to
Manchester. For an instant, Sam fancied he could make
out Tizzie's pawnshop, and felt ridiculously thwarted not
to be able to see the three brass balls.

Joshua put a hand on his son's shoulder. 'In the
last hour or two you've seen that it isn't all sweetness
and light running a place like Jericho,' he said quietly.
'When it's your turn you'll keep the flag flying, won't
you, on the standard up here, and in the standards you set as an employer, both at Jericho and at
the mine?'

The big new lamps illuminated Sam's eyes and mouth
as he said simply. 'You can trust me on it, Father.
And while we're quiet up here, I want to tell you I'm

proud of the way you've dealt with things since Uncle Charlie died.'

Joshua made no reply but looked up to his flag. Newly anchored, it streamed out on the last gusts of wind, and it warmed him to the heart to see it. 'There's some happenings, some people, that we never forget, Sam, no matter how long we might live. But we mustn't look back. We've got the first of a new generation of Schofields on the way, and so we look to the future!'